G000271719

30th March 2018

Once We Were There

A NOVEL

Dear Hanan,

With every book I read, there's always a story behind it. I hope when you look back at this book you'll think of your uni days :)
I hope you enjoy this book as much as I did, get ready for a roller coaster of emotions!!

BERNICE CHAULY

Love,
Dhania

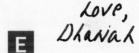

EPIGRAM BOOKS
SINGAPORE · LONDON

Epigram Books UK
First published in 2017 by Epigram Books Singapore
This Edition published in Great Britain in March 2018
by Epigram Books UK

Copyright © 2017 by Bernice Chauly
Cover Illustration by Priscilla Wong

A CIP CATALOGUE RECORD FOR THIS BOOK IS AVAILABLE FROM THE BRITISH LIBRARY.

ISBN	978-1-91-209861-3
PRINTED AND BOUND IN	Great Britain by Clays Ltd, St Ives plc
	Epigram Books UK
	55 Baker Street
	London, W1U 7EU

10 9 8 7 6 5 4 3 2 1

www.epigrambooks.uk

For Tasnem and Leia

PROLOGUE

MY NAME IS Delonix Regia. I am named after the most flamboyant of all tropical trees, the flame of the forest. My father, a well-known lawyer and an avid naturalist, had a particular passion for tropical flora and their Latin names.

On the day I was born, he planted a seedling in our garden. Today, it stands taller than our house, where the end of the garden meets Gasing Hill, and where the red flowers fall onto the grass like a magical cloak. As a child, I once saw a black cobra weave in and out of the flowers, this glittery black slash easing the crimson cover left and right. I was struck with fright and watched it slither into the leafy green undergrowth and disappear into the jungle.

I have long memories of rain. Soft tropical showers, majestic, thunderous storms, and itinerant drizzles, which would come and go for hours, days. The Malaysian monsoon is a vehement creature, powerful and glorious, yet tender enough to soothe one into the most delicious of sleeps. This is how I remember the rains. My childhood came with the rains.

And this, my father's garden.

ONE

Kuala Lumpur. KL. *Kala Lumpa* or *Kala Lampur* to the white man, the Mat Sallehs. City of sinners and sex. Sodom and Gomorrah. It was 1998, and the city was the "party central" of Asia. Of the world. Drugs had opened up the minds of this one-time placid society and bayed in a new revolution, in a time when people hungered for freedom from authoritarian politicians, from the police, from their mindless jobs, from themselves.

Ecstasy had hit the town, in a way that could only be described as monumental. There were feng tau clubs in Bukit Bintang, Cheras, and Jinjang that catered to the Chinese riffraff, the ah bengs and ah lians who felt ill at ease in the posh, uppity bars like Museum and the Backroom Club.

There were clubs for Indian gangsters in Sentul and Selayang; there were dodgy dangdut clubs on Jalan Ipoh and Brickfields, where the girls would dance with you, get high with you, and then go down on you; there were underground clubs that opened up after the other ones closed, then stayed open till people had come down from their highs.

Dealers were raking it in. MDMA was on everyone's lips and tongues. There was pussy and dick everywhere. Pink. Brown. Yellow. Black.

Everybody was high.

DJs flew in from all over the world to play to hundreds—no, thousands of people who swallowed pink, blue, white pills. Everybody wanted E. Nobody drank alcohol, water was the salve for the days and nights on sweaty dance floors.

Ecstasy was prayer. Ecstasy was the new god.

The great Asian financial crisis was crawling out. Billions were lost, millions gained. The ringgit had been pegged at RM3.80 against the US dollar. It saved us. Our ASEAN neighbours didn't fare so well.

The Petronas Twin Towers were finally complete. The towering phallic monstrosities had transformed the city. And there were stories that bled upon storeys for fodder. It was the topic of conversation at every dinner table, every mamak stall, every kopitiam between Bangsar and Cheras, how ugly it looked. How sterile, how un-KL, how Western.

Aiyoh, so sci-fi.

Like Gotham City.

So ugly lah.

Celaka betul.

Celaka. Cursed.

Cursed to never be built.

Before the Towers, the site was the Turf Club. Built by the British because they knew the land was unsafe for any structure taller than a coconut tree. Underneath the turf was a network of limestone caves. To build the world's tallest twin structures above hollow caves was an act of folly, of utter stupidity.

It was a disaster in the making. Mahathir's "twin pricks", that's what they were. A sign that Malaysia had come into its own. That "we" had arrived. That our quest to have the world's tallest flagpole, its longest beef murtabak, and the biggest mall in Asia had succeeded—and that Malaysians had something, finally, something, to be proud of.

These towers, designed by a New Yorker of Argentinean descent and built by rival Japanese and Korean engineering companies who had to pump millions upon millions of tonnes of concrete into miles of limestone caves, had validated our feeling that Malaysia had arrived. Never mind that it was built by thousands of Bangladeshi and Indonesian workers slaving away on meagre wages, some of whom had been crushed to death in hushed-up accidents. That they'd died senselessly like frogs, *mati-katak,* for another notch in our country's race to become a First-World nation by *looking* like a First-World nation.

The towers loomed over KL, a new symbol for the city, like the Sears Tower, like the Empire State Building. We had come to be defined by two eighty-eight-storey shards of concrete, aluminium, glass, and steel. Two towering octagons inspired by sacred Islamic geometry. From distant suburbs to the Golden Triangle, the Twin Towers rose above everything else, flanked by the KL Tower, now dwarfed and comical with its pink shaft. This was engineering at its best, this was the strongest steel in the world, capable of withstanding tremors, because its steel beams could bend under pressure.

It was haunted, like every other building in KL. Yet the ghosts of the fallen would never be venerated here.

Instead, people would flock to Gucci, Bally, Prada, British India, Chanel, Dior and Aseana to proselytise the gods of haute couture.

The newly built Bukit Jalil Sports Complex was sprawled out and ready for the Commonwealth Games. Malaysians were gearing up for the world stage, our time had come to show the world that we were capable, that Malaysia Boleh! *Yes, we can!* That we had arrived.

In September, everything changed.

On 2 September, Malaysia's Deputy Prime Minister Anwar Ibrahim was sacked by Mahathir Mohamad, the dictatorial, authoritarian Prime Minister who had ruled for 17 years.

On 11 September, the Commonwealth Games opened with no-expense-spared fireworks, pomp, and circumstance. Ella, the pint-sized Malaysian songstress, performed the theme song of the games, "Standing in the Eyes of the World", with smouldering black eyeliner and poor diction.

I hope you enjois!—to screaming multitudes.

On 20 September, Anwar Ibrahim was arrested.

On 29 September, he appeared in court with a black eye.

Malaysia, the beloved country of my birth, would never be the same again.

Run!
The gas is coming again!
The mosque!
Get into the mosque!
We ran, like thousands of crazed rats. Our clothes were

drenched and I realised immediately that it was impossible to run with soggy shoes. My hand instinctively covered my camera lens. *A wet lens is a dead lens.* My feet slipped and slid inside my drenched sneakers. I did not need or want a sprain or a broken limb. Sumi grabbed my hand, her eyes wild.

Are you okay?

I nodded. Our slippery hands held fast. I heard screams as some tried to rub the tear gas from their eyes, giving in to instinct. There is nothing like tear gas to make you angry. Politicise you. Our politicians had no idea what they were doing. Revolutionaries were created on the street, that very day.

The protest took place a few hours before Anwar's arrest that night. We had gathered outside the National Mosque, getting handphone messages that he was going to be there. I picked Sumi up from her apartment in Sri Petaling and we drove into the city. The traffic jam was bumper to bumper all the way from Jalan Parlimen, cars inching up against each other, as we snaked along the road, all the way to Dataran Merdeka, Independence Square. A detour towards Central Market enabled us to find a spot in the parking lot. There were thousands of people already walking towards the mosque. You could sense the excitement, the anger. It was brittle, electrifying.

Anwar was sacked for supposed sexual misconduct—specifically, adultery and sodomy. In a country where draconian laws still harked back to the time of the British, giving someone a blowjob or having anal sex was a heinous crime.

The daily papers barked out offensive headline after headline, demonising Anwar.

Sodomite! Adulterer! The Rise and Fall of Anwar Ibrahim.

These words unleashed a national fury and Malaysians of all ages took to the streets. It was Reformasi. The Malaysian Reformation had begun.

Mahathir's regime had created a generation of Malaysians who were complicit and afraid. The Internal Security Act ensured that. Detention without trial. Guilty until proven innocent. You were always guilty. And even if you weren't, you'd still be.

Sumi was angry. We all were. She had studied law in the UK and we'd both been writers at *The Review*—"The smartest men's magazine in town"—for two years. We liked each other from the start, we understood each other. We liked to drink and talk. We knew that what was happening was historic. And that it would change us forever.

By the time we got to the mosque, we could barely see Anwar, who was perched on a makeshift podium. We could only hear him through the loudhailer. All around me, I saw faces twisted in anger. I started taking pictures.

Let them do their job! The media is showing us who they really are! Dogs! Anjing! Liars! Penipu! They supported me and now they want to see me guilty. Guilty! Do you think I am guilty?

The crowd roared. Some fifty thousand voices, all shouting in unison.

No! HE is guilty!

Allahu Akhbar! Allahu Akhbar!

Together our fists rose in solidarity.

We who are gathered here in Kuala Lumpur pledge to defend the freedom and sanctity of the nation to the last drop of our blood... We resolve to revive the spirit of freedom... We will not suffer injustice and oppression in the land... We will not suffer the replacement of foreign oppressors with those raised from among ourselves... We oppose all cruel and oppressive laws which deny the people their fundamental rights and freedoms... We denounce those who corrupt our system of justice... We denounce corruption, abuse of power and the conspiracy devised by a greedy elite to blind the people to the truth in order to maintain their grip on power and wealth!

The crowd roared.

Reformasi! Reformasi!

Anwar, voice hoarse and fist raised, continued.

We raise the spirit of freedom! We are united against oppression! We are united in our resolve to establish justice! Long live the people! Give victory to Reform! We demand the resignation of Mahathir Mohamad!

Sumi and I looked at each other. We grinned widely. The revolution had begun.

Behind us, the Federal Reserve Unit trucks rolled up and the clanging started.

As if out of politeness, the bell rang three times. And then jets of water hit us like a torrent of stones. A merciless pounding. Water bullets. We were getting a beating.

We screamed. I fell against a man behind me. He fell against someone else and together we tumbled to the ground like tiddlywinks. Arms, legs, hair, everywhere. All flailing. We got up and we started running. Or tried to. There was panic, confusion. We ran into each other, smacking into arms, chests, elbows. No escape. There was water in my mouth, in my ears. My camera was under my shirt. Sumi had vanished.

The crowd moved like a school of fish; it swayed to the

right to repel a predator, then to the left to consolidate with greater strength. Right. Left. Right. Then another gust of water came and the configuration broke. I was in a sea of wet beasts, sweaty and angry in a swirling, hot sea.

I heard the hailer again.

Undur! Undur!

Retreat! Retreat now!

The crowd moaned. It was low, gurgly, like fish out of water, drowning in air. The water ceased. Bodies were exposed, stunned. Brown. Yellow. Black. Soggy eyes stared ahead at the figure on the podium. He was still there. Anwar stood strong and resolute.

We will fight this. We will overcome this. Malaysians will rise, now! This is the time to rise!

A tide of drenched people. We could smell one another's unravelling scents: salty, raw, ripe.

Reformasi!

Reformasi!

Reformasi!

Tens of thousands of voices, screaming in unison.

With our lungs, our hearts, our faces. Our bellies, our tongues.

Then Sumi was there, by my side. She had blood on the side of her face.

What happened?

It's okay. Run. It's coming. Now!

And then we saw it. A canister flying above us, a metal bird, wingless. Then another. We swirled again to avoid it, but the configuration was broken, the moment was gone. Too late. As it fell, slivers of gas escaped streaming out like thin white fingers.

Then, it started.

Your breath stops. Your eyes sting, like they're being gouged out by an interning dentist. The nerves in your nose begin to explode. Panic. Panic sets in.

I grabbed Sumi.

I can't see!

I got you. Just hang on!

Run!

Lari!

Run!

To the mosque!

Shit! The gas is in the mosque!

We ran up the stairs. My slimy sneakers slipped and I crashed onto the steps. My knee hit the white marble floor. My camera fell, heavy; my zoom lens thudded, then bounced with a splintering sound. Then, darkness.

My cheek was shoved onto coarse carpet. I opened my eyes, lungs heaving. I tasted gas in my mouth and I raised my nose upward to breathe. Above me, the cloud of gas still hung like a grey shroud. Others were on the ground, retching.

Loud weeping. Strangers vomiting. A large woman in a scarf sprawled on the floor, sobbing.

Ya Allah, Ya Tuhanku, tolonglah kami.

God, help us all.

The bastards had tear-gassed the National Mosque. A sacred sanctuary.

Fucking assholes! Fuckers!

Sumi hissed through a dirty towel. Her eyes were wild.

Here, breathe! It's still damp.

She took it off and gave it to me.

Take it! You're okay. You're going to get a motherfucking bruise, but you'll live.

She managed a muffled laugh.

I grabbed the towel and shoved it against my nose. Took deep breaths. It was pungent, sweaty, sharp, I almost gagged. Bile was threatening its way up my gut; I forced it back down.

I looked up to the domed ceiling, and its stark, lean curvature gave me a shiver of comfort. I turned around. The floor was covered with men and women, some prostrate, some lying down, some curled up in the foetal position. There was a dull ringing in my ears and the heavy sounds of my laboured breath.

You're fine. You're safe… Sumi muttered.

I nodded. Everything hurt. The insides of my head felt scorched. Fried.

Slowly we got up. Some rubbed their eyes in wonder, some were still in shock. Shouts of acute pain.

The cloud had dissipated; the air was clear again. As the air conditioning kicked in, vents sucked out the angry gas. Many had started praying, prostrate on the ground. Soft murmurs surrounded me.

I pulled myself up. Shivered. Everything was still wet and my knee hurt like hell. I turned and retched; out came clear yellow bile. I wanted a cold beer.

Sumi nodded. She felt the same. We stumbled out, Sumi supporting my arm. All along the street, hundreds huddled up against each other. Hugs were shared, some brave smiles. I clicked again and again, my lens still intact, images of solidarity after tear gas. Weak shouts of *Reformasi!*

The rallying cry had to continue. I set the camera to autofocus and let it capture continuous frames of people stealthily disappearing into the folds of the city.

It was dusk. Then, sudden music. A relief, a comfort. The *azan*, blaring out of the minaret above us. The mosque still had its voice.

Allahu Akhbar, Allahu Akhbar...

We grabbed each other and walked slowly, shoes still squelching, as silently as we could into the damp twilight.

Two hours later, at exactly 9pm, masked policemen armed with sub-machine guns stormed into Anwar's house in Damansara Heights, frightening his wealthy neighbours, startling well-dressed diners sipping Chianti in nearby restaurants, as they arrested him under the Internal Security Act in plain sight of his four terrified children and his wife.

Nine days later, he appeared in public again. He stood there, in front of the High Court, waving his hand while cameras of the press from all over the world captured him. That image.

Our Deputy Prime Minister, right there, brutalised, beaten. His black eye was printed on every major newspaper in the world. Kuala Lumpur, city of mud, city of sin, of tear gas and riot police, would erupt again and again.

And again.

* * *

Take a city, imagine it encased in a snow globe and shake it upside down.

Like KL. There would be no snow, of course.

But there would be monitor lizards, tigers, giraffes, refugees, domestic workers, Bangladeshis, girls in pigtails and navy blue school uniforms, nasi kandar with all the condiments, chopped green chillies, beef in dark soya sauce, crab curry, cabbage with turmeric, mustard seed and dried red chillies, guns, machetes and parangs, BMWs, Protons, Kancils, Ferraris, Porches, BMW bikes, strawberry-flavoured condoms, pink Ecstasy tabs, politicians, policemen, taxi drivers, footballers, red plastic furniture, dogs, cats, parakeets, rabbits, snakes, ducks, the occasional slow loris, and some of most morally reprehensible people on the planet.

We had come face to face with a reckoning, as if we had to pay for all our sins in one go and yet find redemption at the same time. KL had unearthed a side that no one had ever seen before; it was new, exhilarating, but entirely unpredictable. Thousands had woken up, but no, this wasn't like Indonesia where Suharto had resigned. *Resigned*. He was shamed, by his own people, students who took to the streets, by the tens upon tens of thousands. Indonesia had witnessed genocides, millions had died in seas of blood, but we didn't share the same script. We had a bloodless transition from colonial rule to independence, we had only one major incident of racial riots in 1969. But what we did have was an endless simmering. Of something, and everything.

But, this. This. With Anwar, we had something to fight for, something to write about. We needed to document it, we had to write it, record it.

Fight it.
We had to fight it, we had to fight back.
And we did.

The Review was a monthly magazine, funded and edited by Lan, short for Roslan. His mother was Malay, his father English and Iban, the largest indigenous group in the state of Sarawak.

Call me Fairman, he'd say if you just met him, shaking your hand vigorously.

Roslan Fairman was born in Kuching, Sarawak, in Malaysian Borneo, raised in KL, sent off to Harrow at ten and then went on to read law at Oxford. He had inherited his father's law firm but had decided that a career in journalism suited his dress sense and temperament better.

No, he'd insist, *I always wrote; did law just because the parents wanted it.*

He was tall, wore a battered bespoke waistcoat and kept imported copies of *The Guardian* on his desk in a neat pile. He had a shock of hair that kept falling over his face, which he'd swing to the right, much like a singer in a 90s boy-band, except for the expensive tortoise-shell glasses and the worn, handmade Church's shoes. We all decided to call him Fairman; it seemed the most apt as he was the editor of a magazine, after all.

The Review consisted of four full-time writers, one advertising exec, one secretary and one tea lady. There was Jin, short for Eu Jin, who was sullen and smelt of whisky in the morning. He wrote all the features on finance—business, investment, property. The boring stuff, except he was a whiz at it. Harvard Business School. Dropped out in his final year. Reasons unknown. He pissed off his mum and dad who practically disowned him; he was forced to live in a room in his uncle's mansion in Damansara Heights. Drove a beat-up white Proton Saga. Had terrible dress sense, but I'd heard that he was a great fuck from the girl who sometimes helped with the audits. He could go all night and was apparently hung like a horse.

Then there was Imran, who'd left a job with Barclays in London to come back to KL because of his father's dementia. He wore a battered Savile Row blazer—wool and silk combo— to work, every day without fail. How he survived the tropical heat in that thing was nothing short of miraculous. He persisted, as it was part of his desired image of being Malay-born but British-educated.

Fuck off, wankers! A shout followed by a loud thump on the desk. That happened at least once a day. We'd look at each other and roll our eyes. Imran was a stickler for details, and if or when anything, or anyone, contradicted his research, he would fly off the handle. Or he'd just swear, for no reason at all.

Imran and Fairman were drinking buddies, and would often disappear at 5pm on the dot to go to the Bulldog round the corner from the office. They'd start with a dry ale and end the night raucously with Guinness.

Imran was stocky and a little wide in the hips, with pert buttocks which sometimes looked odd at certain angles, but he had a smile that could slay you. Every time he talked to you, he'd lean in and you'd get a whiff of his cologne and you'd melt. Penhaligon's. Found only at Harrods and other exclusive shops. Sandalwood and orange. He rolled it off his tongue once when he was drunk. *Pen-ha-li-gons*. Four syllables. Very posh.

One night, as I was coming out of the ladies in the pub, he threw his arm around me and crushed me against his chest. *I'm drunk, Del, take me home. I'm yours.*

He kissed me. Hard. Then it was urgent, probing. Too much tongue, too wet. He slathered my mouth with beer. I pushed him away. He stumbled back, laughing, wiping his full lips with his right hand. *Prissy, that's what you are,* he slurred and stumbled into the men's toilet.

I had a soft spot for Imran. He intrigued me. I was flattered that he had kissed me, but I didn't know if it was because he was drunk or if he liked me. The next day, I went into the office, half nervous, expecting an apologetic Imran, reticent maybe, would he ask me on a date? But nothing happened. He was at his desk, thumping the keyboard for all it was worth. I shrugged. Nothing lost, nothing gained.

Rose, our tea lady, looked like she was 90. She had been Fairman's housekeeper for almost ten years and he couldn't bear to have her leave for the Philippines once her contract ended, so he paid for her to stay on. She couldn't make decent coffee or tea, and could barely dust, sweep or vacuum, so Sumi and I took turns to clean the office from time to time. The toilets were everyone's responsibility, so in fact, Rose was there as a reminder of Fairman's childhood—or lack of it—and that all was well in his world. There was a story going around that she had drowned Fairman's pet kitten in the toilet bowl when he was a kid, and when she stood there unmoving, every day, staring out the office window, I often wondered about the horrors she had seen. I remember Fairman saying once—*her father was in the army, Marcos got to him*—as he drew his hand across his throat in a flourish.

Sumi read law in Leicester, England and specialised in human rights. By the time we met, she had already worked in Hong Kong, Iran and Indonesia. She was also back in KL to look after her ailing mother. *Nothing terminal, thank goodness, but god, can she be a nag!* Filial piety. Didn't matter how long you'd been away. If your parents needed you, and if you were born and raised Asian, you just had to be there.

The office's secretary Jackie doubled as Fairman's personal assistant, bill payer, salary dispenser, agony aunt, nurse, occasional moneylender and chauffeur. She got us home when we were too drunk to hail a cab or stumble to our cars. She was the office saviour, our veritable Good Samaritan. We all loved Jackie; she was the heart and soul of the office and she mothered us all in her no-nonsense manner, with her ample derriere, painted eye-brows, frosted lipstick and her ancient blue Mercedes which smelled of Salem menthol cigarettes.

Our advertising executive Ridzwan Muhammad Nordin, or Riz, barely spoke to any of us. Nobody knew why. Maybe he hated the fact that he was working for a bunch of drunken Anglophiles. His sat, back straight, headphones perpetually stuck in both ears, twirling a pen in his hands with expert dexterity, brows twisted in a constant frown. He did his job well enough despite his poor social skills: ironic, as he had to sell ad space to keep the magazine going. He never once joined us at the pub, or partook in any office excursions. He was just there to sell ads. He came to work, stepped out for lunch, had three cups of coffee a day, went to the mosque to pray on Fridays—which neither Fairman nor Imran ever did—and went home at exactly 5.30pm every day.

The Review's office was located on the ground floor of a shop lot at Phileo Damansara, just off Jalan Damansara. Sumi and I took turns to carpool to get to work, so we could save on petrol. Our salaries weren't much: we made minimum wage and slightly more, but we knew that the writing was what mattered. And Fairman gave us that freedom.

The magazine kept pushing the boundaries of journalism; it was risky in many areas by Malaysian standards, but we didn't care. As long as our Fairman stood by us, we would keep writing until someone saw it fit to shut us down. Our covers were sometimes controversial—we had lawyers, architects, a once-exiled student activist, a comedian, a popular musician, someone who was gay and HIV positive and, the month before, Anwar Ibrahim. Imran had written the cover story and he was mad, infuriated that Anwar was now behind bars.

He knew it was coming, you know. He fucking knew. Bastard wanted him out!

There was a brittle tension in the office. We were operating on adrenaline, gumption and a compulsion to flirt with risk. After Anwar's arrest, we were on the streets again and again. We took to wearing sneakers to work every day, just in case there was another protest, and there always was. Every day. As the trial progressed the stories became more and more lurid: semen-stained mattresses, a how-to on sodomy, a self-inflicted black eye. It was vile. Whatever dignity we had as a country was gone; the spectacle was the fodder of international

headlines. Such was the malaise of Malaysians. Our judiciary
had become a mockery of justice and we were sickened to
the core.

We had written stories on the new sex drug Viagra, the
Clinton affair, Matthew Shepard's death and the demise of
Suharto, but none matched the ferocity of the Anwar story.
As expected, other players were dragged onto the murky
stage: Sukma Dermawan, Anwar's supposed step-brother,
who was alleged to have been sodomised 15 times; Azizan,
one of Anwar's aides, who had denied being sodomised, but
later retracted his story; Dr Munawar Anees, scholar and
speech-writer, and around them a motley crew of rogues
and villains, all in powerful circles, with the Prime Minister
on top.

It became our main story. We dug and we wrote, getting
angrier by the day, getting drunk and having heated
conversations at the Bulldog, waking up with blistering
hangovers, but pushing, constantly and consistently, the
boundaries of whatever little press freedom we had.

On 13 November, the last day of the trial, foreign press
packed the High Court. The UN Special Rapporteur for
Malaysia, Param Cumarasamy, was not allowed in. Furious,
he vented at the press. *This is an obvious and blatant miscarriage
of justice!* He had sat in courts for trials on Cambodia,
El Salvador, Haiti and Rwanda, and here he was, denied entry
to the delivery of the verdict of the most watched trial in
the world.

By 8am we were all there at the courthouse, waiting for
the verdict, along with the foreign press. It was humid from
the rain earlier, the sky a stark, cloudless blue. And then it

came, first like a hushed whisper between illicit lovers, then a barbaric yawp. A tearful press secretary came out and softly mouthed the verdict. Anwar was sentenced to six years in prison. Screams of dismay.

What? No! No! NO!

Fairman, Imran, Sumi and I were all there. Wan Azizah, Anwar's wife, came out of the courthouse in tears, surrounded by her two elder daughters, weeping openly. Then an angry horde.

Reformasi!

Reformasi!

Anwar emerged, face drawn, herded into a Black Maria like a common criminal. The crowd surged forward. It was a farce, a mockery of justice.

Six fucking years! For what? Six fucking years! Six fucking years!

Imran repeated it again and again like a bad mantra in the Range Rover until Fairman told him to shut up. We sat in silence as we drove past the police cars, past the frenzy of the screaming, weeping supporters, past miles and miles of traffic, cars honking, drivers white with shock. We got to the Bulldog and started drinking. We drank shots. After one bottle, Fairman ordered another. *More vodka! Drink up guys, tomorrow we start again.* Imran wept openly, Fairman took his glasses off and buried his face in his hands. Sumi and I smoked cigarette after cigarette, staring at two guys playing pool, until it was time to leave. We had drunk two bottles of vodka. I got home and threw up, passing out on the toilet floor.

The next day, with heads pounding, we sat numb at our computers, staring into black screens, not knowing what to write. We were devastated, gutted.

Two days later, *The Review* was shut down, for reasons that were undisclosed. I remember Fairman coming out of his office, his eyes wild. *Guys, we've been shut down.*

Fucking wankers! Imran threw his coffee mug at the wall. *Always wanted to do that!* He smiled, then started throwing papers into a box.

We got to work. We grabbed files from the cabinets and shoved them into black garbage bags. I ran into the photo archives and pulled out negatives and prints, trying to arrange them with some semblance of order into boxes. I grabbed leftover stocks of film in the fridge and shoved them into plastic bags. Fairman shouted, *Save all your floppy disks, make sure they're marked and give them to me before you go.* Imran took charge and stood by the door, marking handmade lists. *The Review* had been around for only five years, precious noteworthy years, and our archives were worth saving. Riz and Jin packed up their desks silently and efficiently; in spite of what was going on, they still remained emotionless. Rose kept sighing and shaking her head. She packed up the kitchen things, muttering in Tagalog, stacking up mugs and old plates. *What you want me to do, Sir? Keep or throw away?* We threw out a mountain of paperwork. Jackie drove her car to the front and we stuffed bags of rubbish in the front, back and boot. She made ten trips to the dump that day. Fairman was on the phone making calls. He got no answers that day. His beloved stack of backdated *Guardian* newspapers had to be thrown out. *Only take what's necessary! We have to get out by today or we're fucked!*

The Review's license had been revoked and for the first time in my life, I felt angry enough to draw blood. It was the end of a short era, our spirits were crushed, and when Riz walked out the office door for the last time, I swore I saw him wipe away a tear.

You can't do that!
What? An assassination? I'd be doing us all a favour.
How? How would you do it?
There are ways.
But he's guarded by a small army, armed to the teeth!
Yeah. You know that they call him now?
Mahafiraun.
The great pharaoh?
Bastard. Kiss my ass. Mahafiraun.
Hmmph!
I wish he would just drop dead.
Black magic.
Sure, let's find a bomoh in Kampung Baru who can whip up a really devious spell. Something that will make his penis fall off or something like that.
Yeah, if you can get a bomoh to stop rain and thunder, damn, why not an evil politician?
Except his bomoh is probably more powerful than any other in KL.
So how?
Shit, man.
Bugger! Fucking bastard!
Fuck!

We had been drinking and were probably on our fourth

gin and tonics. An empty can doubled as an ashtray on the arm of my chair. Sumi's apartment was sparse, but there were two comfy armchairs with Afghan throws and large, fluffy cushions on the floor. A pair of wooden candlesticks from Istanbul. An Iranian saddlebag with colourful wool tassels—gorgeous but too prickly to lie on. Boho-chic. Cool.

The almost empty bottle of gin sat between us and there was already a line of empty bottles in her kitchen from our drinking sessions over the past few weeks. We'd lost our jobs so we had been reduced to drinking at home.

One more gin pahit coming up! Gin, served up with a sliver of lime, colonial style.

Goddammit, Sumi, you need a planter's chair. I am a sweaty Englishman, waiting for his houseboy to bring his noontime gin.

A planter's chair? Where the hell am I supposed to find one? Do they even still make them?

Antique shops. My dad found one in Malacca. Kutty's.

Drive down there one of these days?

Sure. Why not?

We clinked glasses and sighed simultaneously.

I feel so helpless.

Tell me about it.

I was chain-smoking Sempoernas: skinny, sweet Indonesian clove cigarettes. Sumi didn't smoke as much as I did, but that day she did. She took one from me, lit it up and inhaled deeply.

This is going straight to my head.

We'd been talking about options. There was a protest that day and we were exhausted from running the streets. The number of protests was growing and KL had seen nothing like it. Malaysians were angry, and people were coming out in droves to show their support. Fear had left us. Years of indoctrination were rendered futile. People had woken up to an anger that had to be released. And for many, the only option was to just show up on the street, to be seen and to be heard.

I felt a measure of pride, and to be running next to strangers felt more meaningful than anything I had known until then. It was full-throttle adrenaline; it was heady and rich, it made us bolder and more reckless, as if history had conspired and collided into one moment, where all could be free.

There were coiffured ladies linking hands with women from the kampungs, men, women and children from the suburbs of KL. There was no issue of being Indian, Chinese, Malay or Other, we were one, we were all the same opposed against injustice. We had never been so bold.

It was inspiring; I felt proud. Proud that people were coming out of their houses to stand on the street with us. It was historic, we would rewrite the history books or at least try to.

The day before we'd read that a 15-year-old girl had been arrested as she'd pelted a policeman with an empty gas canister. She was hauled away kicking and screaming, and one newspaper showed a close-up of her face twisted in rage. The headline screamed, "RENEGADE TEEN".

The papers are so shit right now, it's so bloody biased.

Well, what do you expect, they're all scared and they have to toe the line, otherwise they'd lose their licenses. Look what happened to us.

Nobody reads the papers anyway, it's all lies.

So what do we read then—apart from the threads and Sang Kancil?

Sang Kancil was an independent online journal that was the cumulative observations of our very own veteran journo MGG Pillai. Apart from Sabri Zain's online *Reformasi Diary*, which was a brilliant documentation of the day-to-day street protests, there was no other alternative. The real news was out there on the streets, and we were being fed lies by the mainstream papers.

Sumi stood up, then sat down again, quickly.

Oh god, too much gin.

It's the Sempoerna. Goes straight to your head.

She sat down again and inhaled deeply.

What if? What if?

What?

If we started something!

Like…?

An alternative newspaper, something that we can all write for.

What do you mean?

Citizen journalism.

I sat up, lit another Sempoerna and sloshed more gin into my empty glass.

You think Fairman would approve?

Heck, he'd fund it, no?

It could be like an underground newspaper, something that we can send out to everybody.

Alternative news—on the Internet, on a website…

From the street!

Opinions, columns, photos—document it all! We can do this.

I was drunk, but it made sense. Why not? Take it into our own hands.

Call him now!

We did. And that's how it started. After half a bottle of gin and many more Sempoernas, *Saksi* was born.

Saksi. Witness.

We were going to bear witness to the Reformasi movement. We were going to do it our way. And we were going to do it right.

The People Accuse

Saksi *is a site for independent journalism. Our first issue focuses on 20 September 1998, when a massive demonstration took place in Kuala Lumpur. Features, opinions, photography and other stories analyse and document the events of the day and subsequent developments.* Saksi *is a weekly magazine that is constantly updated.* Saksi *will present news that is real. News from the streets. News from our reporters who are not afraid of telling the truth.*

"Blue Boy, please."

Marina had said "please" almost like "peh-lis", which sounded like "polis" to the taxi driver who picked her up. She didn't know why she was so nervous, she just was. Maybe she should have just said, "BB, please."

KL's first gay bar, opened in the 80s, was located on the corner of a slip road off Jalan Bukit Bintang, right beside the five-star Regent Hotel. Open till late on weekends, it had become an institution, where men went to meet other men to be entertained. Where drag queens donned wigs and powder, fake eyelashes and heels, padded bras and gowns, and sang gay anthems like "YMCA" and "I Will Survive" with heartfelt gusto.

The taxi driver had been listening to a religious channel on the radio. He cleared his throat and turned it up even louder. Unperturbed, Marina settled back in the seat and observed the traffic. Cars choked the road she was on. Motorbikes weaved in and out, families thronged the Batu Road night market on her left. She saw a woman struggling with plastic bags, dragging a screaming child behind her. High above, invisible wires held up a glowing tapestry of crisscrossed lights. Even the trees had lights that streamed downwards, and then upwards, like shimmery magic wands.

"So pretty," she whispered.

Two days earlier, Marina had arrived in KL from Lahad Datu, Sabah, with nothing more than a small gym bag of her best clothes and a piece of paper scrawled with three items:

1. Blue Boy—behind Regent Hotel.
2. Chow Kit Drop-in Centre—ask for Tini.
3. Kak Min—for cheap room.

She had emerged from the cheap flight into a futuristic-looking airport. The bus ride into the city—45 kilometres, so she'd been told—cost nine ringgit and took two hours. The seats were comfortable and she immediately fell into a deep sleep, later waking up with a sore neck. She got off at a bus station and asked around for a bus that would take her to Chow Kit.

She had 400 ringgit to her name and paid a 200 ringgit deposit for a room next to Kak Min's place. It was in the heart of Chow Kit, on Lorong Haji Taib, where transsexual sex workers like herself found work. Young men from Sabah, in Malaysian Borneo, who had no choice but to come to the Peninsula or Semenanjung as they called it, to work.

The first thing she needed was a pair of shoes, and that was what she bought from the shoe shop from Sungei Wang, the shopping mall Kak Min took her to. She was not used to wearing heels, not ones with a stiletto. These had a high arch and had cost fifty ringgit, the most she'd ever paid for a pair of shoes. But they were from that shop that all the drag queens went to for their shoes and she had paid in cash. It felt good.

The taxi came to a stop and Marina straightened her feet and stretched her calves as she got out of the car. The driver kept his eyes down as he took the ten-ringgit bill from her and straightened the white kopiah on his greying head. Quietly, he uttered a Bismillah. "More of them now than ever," he muttered to himself, then sighed and eased his car into the busy street.

She started walking down the dimly lit alleyway. She was told to follow the street "until you see them". "Mainly older white men and young Malay boys," so she was told. Marina didn't want a sugar-daddy, she wanted to make her own way in life. But, she was "open to options", as she'd told others from time to time. Life presented itself in ways that she had to embrace. And if a man presented himself to her in more ways than just wanting to fuck her in the mouth or her ass, she would be open. Open to his condo, his chequebook, his car, his leathery, hairy balls and his eager cock. The greedy looks came soon after. Like the looks from those men on the street, stuck against each other, eyes raking her up and down as she smiled at them and sashayed in.

"Is there a cover tonight?" Marina asked shyly, her voice barely audible above the blasting techno music. It was dark, but a mirror ball was throwing specks of light on the walls. The boy behind the counter arched a plucked eyebrow and nodded. He had dusky pink lips and wore a skimpy yellow top.

"Yes, Friday night, with show and one drink. Twenty ringgit only."

Marina took out her purse, ruffled her hair with her slightly sweaty palms and carefully peeled out two ten-ringgit notes. She noticed a scratch on one newly painted crimson nail and grimaced. She clicked her tongue in annoyance.

The boy gestured for her wrist and he pressed a stamp onto her skin. His hands felt cold and clammy. A yellow fluorescent skull glowed back at her.

"Enjoy!" he said in a sing-song voice.

Marina turned and saw an older man standing a few feet away and smiled at him. He eyed her from top to toe, taking in her teased hair, her high-waisted red skirt, her silver heels. He was balding, but his startling blue eyes were clear and focused.

His black T-shirt was slightly bunched over his taut belly.

"Hi, I'm Marina. And you are?"

The music was loud, so she had to repeat herself.

"I am Hans, new in KL, first time here."

She smiled at him and he responded with a toothy grin.

Marina took Hans by the elbow and together they manoeuvred their way into the narrow space filled with sweaty bodies around the dance floor. She stood taller than him. Her hips met his rotund belly, and they both giggled. The music was the latest techno and house, the stuff of all clubs. *Cantaloop*, the jazzy, hip-hop number, loosened hips, mouths, tongues.

Hans had his hands on her thighs, and he grabbed her waist.

"I want to fuck you, now."

Marina was taken by surprise. She wanted to watch the drag show, but she needed the money, it would mean fifty ringgit for a blowjob in the alley at the very least.

"But Hans…" She looked toward the stage, bent down and spoke into his ear. "I want to see the show, can we fuck later?" A flicker of disappointment crossed his face.

"Sorry, but I have an early flight to catch, maybe we can meet again another time." He grabbed her hand awkwardly, kissed it and shrugged, then shoved a name card into her hand.

Marina took his card and blew him a kiss. She had to stay, she wasn't ready to leave just yet. "Okay, Hans, see you next time. Don't forget me, okay?"

Marina kept dancing on her own until the music stopped and a bald Caucasian man wearing heavy make-up, a white bustier and a long hooped skirt came on stage. The crowd clapped politely. A small Chinese man, his hands folded across his waist like a Mandarin, walked in behind him and sat at the piano on the stage. They nodded to each other and the performance began.

For an hour, Marina listened to the most exquisite music she'd ever heard. The bald man stood in the middle of the stage and sang hauntingly in a language unfamiliar to her. His crimson lips made large O's and made him look like a clown, and as she stood there in the middle of Blue Boy, amidst sweaty strangers and the strange music, she felt beauty. Her feet ached and her toes pinched against the new silver straps, but she felt a calmness wash over her, as if the city she had yearned to come to had just welcomed her into its fold.

IT WAS ALMOST midnight on a Friday and I was walking down Jalan P. Ramlee. I'd decided to take a cab and meet Karin at the club.

Every two weeks, I took Ecstasy. It had begun as a girly night out some months ago, but it had become regular. Sumi didn't like it, said it made her feel *like the world is coming to an end, too much emotion, can't handle it.* But Karin, well. Karin and I loved it.

I got off just behind the Shangri-la Hotel as I didn't want to get stuck in the tight squeeze of cars. The taxi driver appreciated it too and raised his eyebrows as I asked him to keep the change.

There was a crowd and the sharp click-clack of handmade heels. Expensive cars purring in a row, all inching towards the valet. Women in designer clothes, sequined tight-tight skirts, expensive glittery clutch bags, guys with slicked-back hair and straight backs.

Karin was my age, 26, and had recently married *Cleo Magazine*'s most eligible bachelor of the year. The wedding was a no-expense-spared glittery weekend affair at the Carcosa. A colonial-style extravaganza of white and gold; guests partied on the hotel greens, drinking from gold-embossed champagne flutes under tents that had twisty gold minarets, tulle from chandeliers, lilies everywhere. The cake was a five-tier frosted dream—*it was the most delicious vanilla butter*—and guests stayed on partying at the Long Bar till dawn.

I'd known Karin since we were kids at Methodist Kindergarten in Petaling Jaya. Her German father and Cantonese mother lived three doors down from our street in Section 5, and we had grown up together. Karin, beautiful, long-limbed and sleek like a gazelle, with bouncy copper curls and piercing blue-grey eyes. She was on the cover of every magazine in town, and one of the most sought-after models in Malaysia and Singapore. And she had married Kai, who was also of mixed blood—Malay-Irish—and they were KL's celebrity couple of the moment. *Ladies and gentlemen, please welcome Kai and Karin.*

Karin's father was a structural engineer and had travelled frequently around the region. One night he showed up with a skinny Thai woman at their door and asked Karin and her sister to call her "Big Sister".

Karin's mother, Aunty Kim, diminutive and ferocious in her humiliation, screamed at her husband and his "slut" so loudly that the entire street had heard her. What proceeded were the most filthy indignities in English, German and Cantonese I had heard in my twelve years.

I remember seeing Karin huddling next to her Indonesian maid by the metal gate, her face pale with fright. She wore pink pyjamas and clutched a teddy bear. I didn't see tears, but I imagined them streaming down her cheeks.

Karin's dad disappeared after that and Aunty Kim took to drinking until she met a nice Indian doctor at the Polo Club, and later married him. Karin had meanwhile become the most scandalous and envied girl at Assunta Convent; she was gorgeous, smart and the school's top athlete.

And we were friends. I was three inches shorter, rounder, flat-nosed and pimply, and three shades darker than her honey-alabaster skin. *But you have SO much character, Del. At least one of us has that.*

She was a pothead, most of us were—rebellion was part

and parcel of growing up privileged in PJ—and together we got up to mischief that made the girls at Malory Towers look like amateurs. We were never expelled—we came close to it— but as head of the debating team, I was too much of an asset, and she was in the sports field. As long as we kept bringing back medals, which were shown off during assembly, we were in the good books.

My handphone beeped.

Hi darling, running late. See you inside! Mwah.

From the outside, you'd never think that KL's most notorious club would be in the basement, but it was. The cramped corridor was already loud with chatter. It smelled musty and the familiar dark-red walls led to a door that would let in one person at a time. I could feel the music vibrating through my heels.

It was the beginning of a night with no end. I closed my eyes, said a quick prayer and walked in. The Backroom was a church for us to redeem ourselves with others who wanted to commune with the divine. Mass communion. Tab on the tongue. *The body of Christ. Amen.*

Fifty bucks got you a pill. Most times it was good, really good. Sometimes it wasn't. The bouncer smiled, gave me a thumbs-up, a wide smile and a wink. *This one good. Don't worry.* It was a pink one. Karin was the expert, so I put it in my purse for later. We'd pop it at the same time and then wait.

The podiums were already full of swaying, gyrating, topless men. Three, four to a pole. Oiled torsos, skin-tight jeans, some slightly unbuttoned. These were the beautiful gay men of KL. Muscle-Marys. Pumping iron non-stop just to show off their buff bodies. Gay culture was starting to take off, and this was a sign of liberation. They could be themselves, and it was a bold "fuck you" to the establishment.

The dance floor heaved and throbbed. I stood by a railing and hoped that Karin would see me.

It was the time of the night when many were already high. I knew what it was like. An orgiastic release—especially when the rhythm would crescendo and the pounding would satiate us—until the next one came along.

Karin was late and I was getting impatient. I went to the bar. *One vodka lime, please. The real stuff please.* The petite Chinese bartender gave me a smirk, as if to say—*Bitch, we don't sell fake booze here!*

It was packed. Really packed. Soon enough, I'd run into people I knew. But Karin knew *everyone*—she would, of course. Models knew other models. And models knew all kinds of people. On weekends like this, you'd have people from all over—Jakarta, Bangkok, London, Berlin, Amsterdam. People flew in to drop E, dance their tits and asses off, get laid and fly back. DJs were paid big bucks to spin and we had the best flown in from all over the world. We had no press freedom, we had police brutality, we had an authoritarian government, and we had MDMA.

And when we got high, we would just forget. Forget about our shitty jobs, bosses who were pricks, the 2.5 kids at home, the mortgage, the credit card bill, the cops who would beat up sex workers whom they hauled from Chow Kit, the lies our politicians told, the bad adverts on TV, the lack of intellectual scholarship in our universities, Malay rights, the refugees who were being beaten up at detention camps that very moment. If only everyone could take E—there would be peace, joy and happiness.

It was naïve idealism, I realised, but then, all I wanted to do was fry my brains and get completely off my head. The club was really filling up. There was a steady stream of people coming in now, and there she was.

In a tight red dress. Prada bag and high heels. Curls and lip gloss. Walking towards me. *Babes, so sorry. Traffic was insane. Mum was talking to me non-stop about this condo that she wants to buy in Mont Kiara for investment. I told her KL is going through a real-estate bubble and that she should wait. Then Kai calls from Jakarta and I have to talk to him, cos I haven't seen him in two weeks. Then one of the heels of my Prada broke and I was so trauma, for like five mins. Anyhow, I'm here. So let's party!!!*

Karin had two tabs. *The blue ones are better, babes. We can have the pink ones for later.*

A bottle of water each. We put the tabs on each other's tongues. *To tonight, darls. Let's live forever!*

The E normally took about twenty minutes to kick in. Normal being subjective. It depended on your mood, what you'd eaten that day. The time of the month. And then the endless "live forever" toasts. I bet that's what everyone felt like. I looked around. There was a blonde who looked like the ex of an ex. She was tottering on heels, in an ultra mini. Model. Giggling her head off. Dirty dancing with a dark guy who had his arms and hands all over her. She glanced in my direction and her eyes were glazed. She was as high as a hawk.

E made you feel invincible, in a different way than coke. This high came on slowly, easing like delicious champagne into your veins. I looked around and smiled. And nodded my head to the music. Damn, it felt good. We were all in communion with the great god of E. We were all one with each other, one with ourselves. No malice, no greed, no hunger, no thirst. We were complete.

The tingling would start in the stomach, then move upwards like a golden trail, until it spread all over your arms, chest, neck and, like a crown, settled on your head. Your body was all light, sensitive to every touch, every motion, every stimulus. Your skin felt alive, longing for love, light, glory. *Glory to all. Hail the Almighty.* It just felt holy, it felt like you should give thanks.

Then, you'd start to jump a little, sway, move in unison with the tide of music, feet on the ground, touching the earth's core. You'd feel it inching up your heels, thighs; the earth was alive, and you with it. You'd feel like rejoicing in the power of life. Your stomach would lurch, empty of all remorse, vengeance, anger.

Only joy. Oh. Joy.

Karin grabbed my hand. Hers felt cold. Our hands clutched each others' hungrily. Her eyes turned steel grey, like twin bullets. We swayed into each other, hips moving in unison.

E made you speak the truth. Apparently that's why shrinks used it as couples' therapy at exclusive ashrams in India and New York. Couples who had not been intimate or connected took it to fall in love again. Or to speak the unadulterated truth. It saved marriages, lives. It put people in touch with themselves again. It allowed people to *feel* again.

At a certain point during the night, as if by clockwork, everything would climax. It was a moment when there was synchronicity. The music was perfect. The mass of people on the dance floor would heave like some kind of amorphous creature, a cloud of bees or birds. A flocking. A gathering. Of souls. We were all high, riding the wave, all peaking together. It was fabulous.

Karin turned to me. *Oh my god, this is so good. I feel so good.*

I closed my eyes. She sounded like she was slurring and everything was slow motion, but it wasn't. I felt like I was floating off the ground. I felt light, airless. No more pain. No more anything. Just bliss.

My mother was killed in a car crash. She slammed her BMW into a pole and was killed in an instant. She was drunk, and probably didn't feel a thing. I was 14.

Mother was an only child, as was Papa. Both sets of grandparents could only manufacture one child each, and my parents had gravitated to each other, like lost puppies. I too was an only child, my parents capable of copulating only so much. Or perhaps Mother never wanted any more children, or even me to begin with.

They met when Mother was acting in a theatre production of a local play where she played a prostitute, and she looked *luminous, like Natalie Wood.* Papa fell for her at first sight. Every time he told this story, he would grasp her hand and Mother would throw her head back, and they would kiss quickly on the lips, as if to seal their love again.

Mother came from Ipoh, Perak, the tin-rich town of limestone caves, kway teow noodles with chicken slivers, chubby bean sprouts and beautiful women, where Chinese millionaires made and lost their fortunes and whose children went to English boarding schools and came back with thick accents and pasty spouses. Born to working-class parents, she went to the Convent of the Holy Infant Jesus on Brewster Road and became a rebel. At 14 she became part of an all-girls gang called The Heartbreakers, and was once almost suspended from school after being caught smoking with a group of boys from Sam Tet—in the graveyard beside St Michael's Church during school hours. It was scandalous. The nuns were horrified and she became the undisputed "rebel chick" of the school.

Mother was a restless soul from the very beginning; she couldn't wait to get out of Ipoh; and when she did, she couldn't wait to get out of KL. Papa was her ticket to a better life and she stayed with him, only because he loved her. Perhaps that was a little harsh. I am sure she loved him too, but I know he loved her more.

She was never happy, even when she said she was. Even when he gave a new necklace, or a new watch.

Oh darling, how beautiful. You've made me the happiest woman in the world.

Darling, darling. My darling husband. How I love you.

She said it all the time, perhaps to convince herself that she was lucky, that she was happy.

Papa gave her everything. A beautiful house, a car, all the designer clothes, shoes and handbags she desired. And his heart. He was the consummate husband, with eyes for no one else. Yet my mother was never part of the living; she flitted in and out of rooms, corridors, conversations. She barely raised me, she fussed over a cup of tea more than my feverish skin, and let the maid bathe, feed and nurture me. I don't think I ever felt the hard crush of a mother's love: the endless kisses, the coddling, the sniffing in between the cracks of the neck and shoulder, the shrill wail of dismay when a dummy dropped from a mouth, the touching gazes with unconditional love. I don't think my mother ever loved me. I don't think she was ever capable of loving anything, or anyone.

She took to drinking, and I don't ever remember her without a crystal tumbler of whisky. Or vodka, or gin. Mother with a cigarette in her mouth. Mother only waking up after I got home from school. Looking dishevelled at three in the afternoon. Mother sitting by herself in the garden, by the pool covered with leaves. Her wavy hair piled high on her head, her black eyeliner smudged, in her sarong, the one that she had worn in the hospital the day she gave birth to me.

Mother. My mother.

My beautiful, terrifying, threatening mother.

Papa never recovered from the shock of her death. For years, he sat at his desk in his study, surrounded by his leather-bound law books in ornate, antique Dutch bookcases. His work suffered, his reputation for being one of the top human rights lawyers in the country diminished, and the phone just stopped ringing. No more invitations to parties, dinners, open houses. He aged overnight, his thick hair turning grey, and he retreated into a cave. We stopped having conversations, we stopped going to Raju's for thosai and tea, we stopped our weekend walks in Gasing Hill. My father was also dead in a way, becoming a mask of a man, retreating into the shadows like me.

Two shadows, flitting in and out of darkness and light, in between the crevasses of each other and the walls of our home.

Saksi took off.

Sumi knew how to work the website; she had a knack for new technologies, and we ran it off the few computers that weren't confiscated from the office. They took everything else. The Ministry of Home Affairs now had our back issues, invoices, receipts, POs, files and files of faxes, all manner of paperwork and of course, Fairman's beloved copies of *The Guardian*.

The Review wasn't the only magazine that had been shut down. We heard of others; another men's mag that had written a piece about the corruption that went on during the Commonwealth Games and an art magazine that had pictures of the Jakarta student street protests. It seemed that anything that had anti-government sentiment had been silenced.

We ran *Saksi* out of Fairman's apartment in Damansara Heights and the four of us stayed on as stringers. *Look, I don't know how long I can afford to do this, but let's hope we get some hits, and then maybe we can get some ad money to keep us going.*

But Imran suggested that we get our pieces syndicated. *Can you imagine if we were picked up?*

Fairman laughed. *What? By the mighty* Guardian?

And why the hell not? We have to try! And who the hell is

going to give us ad money? To write this? What, you think we can still rely on the banks? The property market? Fucking Ralph Lauren ads? Get real, Fairman!

Imran was right. No one was going to risk investing in an independent news journal. It was too dangerous, and everyone was being watched. A sniff by the Home Ministry could put you out of business. We were on our own.

Riz, Jin and Jackie had to go, but Rose was there to make us endless cups of tea and coffee. I taught her how to properly brew coffee and tea—*the water has to be boiling hot, Rose*. We lived on sardine and egg sandwiches.

The New Straits Times and *The Star* were spouting overt government propaganda so the public was being fed lies. Fairman paid us thirty cents a word, it was the best he could do. We knew he was dipping into his trust fund, and we were grateful.

We wrote features, opinion pieces and posted black-and-white photos. Reportage style. Good ol' Fairman. He was such a decent bloke with us all—we ate and slept in the living room, surrounded by his mum's quirky bric-a-brac. She was a real royalist, so the walls featured gold-rimmed Charles and Diana plates, ornamental spoons, brass horseshoes, watercolours of the English countryside and Laura Ashley-style calico curtains.

KL was crawling with journos from all corners of the world. After Jakarta, KL was the next big story, so many just stayed on in the region. AFP, AWSJ, FEER, Reuters, AP, the *Post* from Jakarta, Bangkok, Hong Kong, Washington and the Beeb.

We'd meet them on the streets, you could spot a foreign journo in two seconds—there was that air of fatigue around them, of blood and bombs—exchange cards, and then invite them over for drinks.

The apartment became quite the hub for late night after-protest, after-court sessions. There was a lot of talk and some pretty serious drinking. I discovered then that most journalists were alcoholics—*It just comes with the territory*—some of the conversations were harrowing and comical. Old "war" stories would come out—these were after all real journos—and Sumi and I would sit awestruck and listen to their stories, whilst we all got drunker and drunker.

There was Josh who prided himself in *banging pussy* all the way from Rwanda, the West Bank to Bosnia; Will who had dodged live bullets in Dili and was imprisoned for a day in the most filthy cell ever described; Ken the lanky Canadian rookie who had spent a week in Bangkok before KL; and Langton from Chicago, the veteran, who chain-smoked Marlboro Reds and drank himself into a stupor and growled from time to time, *You gotta know when to get in, and when to get out.*

There were few female "war" reporters, so to speak, Langton would say that *the chicks in the field were only good before they had kids, once they did, they got soft.* Lost their edge. *Nobody wanted a chick hanging around, they were an easy target.* We were the only chicks in the room, so sometimes we got the feeling that we were just meant to be seen and not heard. These guys had been through the mill, had been in the frontlines, had dodged real bullets, seen dead bodies. They were heroes to us. Will had met Xanana Gusmao, the ultimate poster boy for human rights, as I dreamed of a day that I would meet him in person.

Langton had been in South Africa in '94 and had been friends with Ken Oosterbroek, Greg Marinovich, Joao Silva and Ken Carter; the four photographers known as the Bang-Bang Club. *I was there in Thokoza that day. Oosterbroek was hit. Fuck. Never forget that. All those bodies. Hell. Still get nightmares.*

After a while, it was just a party every night, we never knew who was going to show up. KL was crawling with Special Branch officers so we had to make sure that we knew who was coming through the door. My latest feature had generated a lot of interest and Fairman had started getting phone calls late at night. There would be calls, and then you'd hear clicking on the other side. They were spying on us, tapping our phones.

It was basic reportage, I didn't think that I was capable of presenting dialectic arguments—what was happening was complicated on so many levels of Malaysian society—all I felt I could do was write what I saw and heard.

In my heart, I knew that the seeds of change had started to take root, the country had woken up, and the fear that had gripped us since Mahathir came to power was slowly being questioned and eroded. There were, of course, many who rallied against Anwar, staunch Mahathirists who felt that it was better to have a devil they knew than one they didn't.

Could Anwar be trusted? Could anyone be trusted? All we knew was that the country was on the verge of a new beginning, and this is what we had hoped for.

It had arrived, finally on our doorsteps, like a bouquet of fresh flowers from an unknown admirer. And we were ready.

Sign of the times

Times, they are a-changing. Delonix Regia *ponders the signs.*

20 September 1998 is an important date in our post '69 political history. Malaysians walked, some of us covering a total of six miles, beginning a search for self-determination lost to a regime that has both coddled and cowed us into submission. The steps I retrace here are part of a landscape of political and cultural signs that we are discovering anew, and in which I am both eyewitness and participant.

The events around the incidents at Sri Perdana and Masjid Negara can no longer be told in a naïve fashion. Too much is at stake for those who oppose the Reformasi movement, as well as those who support it. As this nation is polarised by the current crisis the ability to speak with reasonable objectivity diminishes, as do forums in which to negotiate our differences, whether they be political or cultural.

Old Sites, New Signs

It's important to remember that the day began with the relocation of the Reformasi rally from Dataran Merdeka to the Masjid Negara. Yet, with his undeniable charisma and oratory skills, Anwar, through both the tone and substance of his speech, went beyond the symbolic confines of the site to establish that the Reformasi movement intended to speak to all Malaysians regardless of political and religious convictions, and beyond ethnic group affiliations. For sceptics as well as supporters, the atmosphere was electrifying. More so when Anwar declared that we—the rakyat —should reclaim Dataran; but he did so by first demanding the crowd agree to be peaceful.

We poured into Dataran—estimates run from a low of

fifteen thousand to a high of a hundred thousand. No head count, though, can detract from the significance of the moment. Here was a broad spectrum of Malaysians demonstrating their feelings; maybe against the increasingly debased political style of the Mahathir administration, maybe against the management of the economic crisis; certainly, for many, in support of their displaced leader.

Under the shadow of Bukit Aman, the Ministry of the Interior, which looms over Dataran Merdeka, Anwar addressed the crowd through a less than adequate sound system. Shouts of "Reformasi" were occasionally overtaken by demands for people to sit so that we all could enjoy the spectacle equally. After a speech that was hardly audible to me, Anwar was carried on the shoulders of his supporters, and no indication was given as to what would come next. But it felt like the crowd made its desires known as we found ourselves moving down Jalan Raja Laut chanting—some "Reformasi", some "Allahu Akbar", others "Hidup Anwar"—waving at onlookers and making a loud but friendly racket. Nothing in my experience was as exhilarating as this, spontaneously reclaiming the streets.

Twenty days later, on 10 October, thousands staged a noisy drive-past on Jalan Tuanku Abdul Rahman. The police did not intervene as people cheered and chanted; and then walked to Masjid Negara; finally returning to Dataran. The standoff lasted half an hour. This time when the crowds dispersed we walked towards the FRU line and shook hands with them. One or two officers refused my hand, but most obliged. More signs.

So. The signs were these.

I was coming down from E. Karin was nowhere to be seen. I felt hollowed out. Needed to get horizontal. Get home.

E makes you head to the bathroom and you empty your bowels. Sign number one. My stomach felt like it had been pumped out, like there was a long icy slug moving up and down my throat and whirling around my insides. I was hot and cold, hot and cold. My hands were clammy and I would have been grinding my teeth for hours. My jaw would ache for days. My eyelids were sluggish and I was completely talked out. I felt like shit, my brain felt like slime and all I wanted in the world was my bed.

You start talking nonstop and you allude to certain attributes to persons known and unknown and you say things like, *God...I love...you...man. This is so...fucking...beautiful. Time for change. This country...has...to...change. You're... important. Your work...is so...important. This...is...the...time. It is NOW.*

You transform into a gushy, lovey-dovey mess and become one Big Love Machine.

Sign number two.

At around 5am, the club was slowing down. People were huddled in corners, some still dancing and chattering, inhaling cigarettes like their lives depended on it and swigging back gulps of water. You could always tell the ones who just kept popping pills all night, they looked like overcharged Energizer bunnies. Hundreds of empty plastic bottles everywhere. Clubs like this sold water for ten ringgit a pop on weekends. It was criminal, but there's where the money was.

Where the fuck is Karin?

I saw Malique, whom we were dirty dancing with earlier, Karin sandwiched in between. He was her favourite make-up artist, and a real party animal. He was stretched out on a couch in the corner and in the dark I could see his eyes and trademark smoky-eye make-up.

Hey, have you seen Karin?

Del…fuck man…still tripping…can't stand any more… penat sial. He grinned sloppily.

Have you seen Karin?

I think…I saw her leave…

What? Who with?

Dunno, he shrugged, started giggling and lit a cigarette, *Hey…chill out lah…Karin can look after herself.*

I suddenly felt anxious. This was the horror about coming down. The anxiety. The imagined panic. The fear. I ground my teeth and immediately popped some gum.

Hey man, got any valium?

Malique was talking to someone else, a girl with thick eyebrows and a skirt hiked up her thighs. Her eyes were glazed and she was slumped in a corner. She mumbled and struggled to get up then staggered back onto the couch. Malique started giggling even more.

I sat on a chair for a while, thinking, trying to think of what to do. Everything was a blur. I didn't recognise faces, they all became shadow-blobs, moving, dancing shadows.

The music started rising again and Malique couldn't hear me. My throat was clammed up and the slinky waves of panic jiggled harder inside me. I started shivering.

Sign number three.

I had to figure out what to do. I didn't want to stay in

the club. Not anymore. Only the hardcore druggies would be left—they'd have the club all to themselves and keep going for another 24 hours. I'd heard stories of orgies and heroin and overdosing. The club stank of stale air. I stank too.

I took a quick look around and went into the toilet. Someone was throwing up. There was a girl sitting against the wall, head lolling to the side. Karin was not answering her phone. The air smelled of dank sweat and vomit. I ran.

I rushed out of the front door and gasped. I realised that I had been holding my breath after I ran out of the toilet. The light hit me, my eyes hurt. I blinked them open. I took a final gulp of water and threw away the bottle. Swallowed. Took a deep breath. Above, the sky was pretty, like pink and orange cotton candy.

The road was deserted, silent. I walked up the road, my heels click-clacking on the road.

Fuck Karin. Fuck. Fuck. This is the last time I'm doing this with you.

I was mad as hell. Karin had a terrible habit of disappearing with people, especially ones she'd just met. If they had drugs, she was gone in a heartbeat. She had the constitution of an elephant, which I could only attribute to her genes. Once she told me she had popped five E's in one night.

You're going to OD one of these *days.*

She laughed, of course. *Not a chance in hell.*

I walked on, furious at her, at myself, my heart flapping in my chest. I just needed to get home, shower and sleep.

Miss, are you all right?

I kept walking.

Miss!

I turned and I saw him.

Miss, your skirt is torn, are you all right?

I looked down and grimaced. My skirt was ripped on the side, exposing my thigh. *Shit. Fuck. How the…?*

I was quite a sight, apparently. This he told me later, over and over again.

You, standing there in the morning light. Torn skirt, red shirt unbuttoned, standing like a five-year-old tottering in her mother's heels for the first time. Your hair glowing around your shoulders. You were shivering, your eyes wild. And I, like a fool, fell in love.

That's how I met him. The man who would one day become my husband and transform my life forever.

TWO

HE WAS UP.

Jet lag permeated his body and he had tossed and turned around for hours. He'd taken a pill on the thirteen-hour flight and still, he could not sleep. He leaned over to the side table, reached for the tall glass, drank all the water in it and stretched his stiff body.

"Damn these flights," he muttered.

The air conditioning in his room hummed. It was too cold. He got out of bed and pulled the curtains open. Light flooded into the room and he covered his eyes. He'd told his parents over and over again that the only good thing about the apartment was that it was in the heart of the city, but it offered no views. Only the tops of other buildings, endless traffic and the relentless party-goers who straggled in and out of the clubs on weekends.

His stomach growled. He thought of a hot, flaky roti canai with lashings of chicken curry, dhall and a hot cup of tea. He wondered if the old Indian lady with the stall down the road would be open. A quick shower eased his nerves and he picked a fresh T-shirt and shorts from his open suitcase. Fifteen hours ago, he had been in freezing London and now he was home. The last conversation he'd had with Jessica had been unpleasant.

"You fucking bastard, leave again, like you do. Fuck you!"

He'd hung up and deleted her number.

It was over, and she no longer had a hold on his life. It was time for new beginnings, newer and better things.

He had taken the lift down, waved at the Security Guard as the thick glass doors slid open.

"Hello, Sir, nice to see you again. Have a good day, Sir," the guard said in a Nepali accent.

The heat hit him in the face. Immediate beads of sweat converged on his nose and forehead. The morning air held the promise it would be cool later, with some rain.

Then he saw her, a young woman stumbling down the street. Her long hair and clothes were dishevelled. She walked past him, her hands reaching out to keep herself from falling.

He walked quietly behind her and kept his gaze down. There was no need for unnecessary conversation this early in the morning. But her gait was uncertain, her feet unsteady.

A simple question would do, he thought.

"Miss?"

She turned and glared at him and he felt a quick shiver on his neck. Her eyes were bright and slightly glazed. A line of mascara smudged on one side of her nose. Cheeks slightly flushed.

"Miss, your skirt is torn, are you all right?"

She reached up to brush her long hair back from her face and then looked down to smooth her skirt. She looked up and smiled.

I REMEMBER THE first time an incubus came to me in my sleep. I was 12 and that morning, Sister Martha had given me a telling off in Catechism class.

Girls! The road to hell is paved with stones, sharp thorns and demons. Waiting for you by the side of the road, she tittered, her spindly arms waving about. *But the road to heaven is paved with roses and angels singing in a chorus, welcoming you to join Our Lord Jesus.* She smiled and crossed herself, her eyes gazing upwards.

Our Standard Six Catechism class of twenty girls clad in navy-blue pinafores suddenly grew hushed. Susan Tan, who was seated next to me, looked like she was going to cry. Undeterred, I stuck my hand up and stood up to ask.

Sister Martha, how do you know that the road to hell is paved with stones and demons?

There was a loud giggle from the back, and someone went *Shhhh!* Sister Martha glared out of her thick, black spectacles and her beady eyes squinting in anger.

Well, Delonix, it says in the Bible that when you die, you will be presented with a choice. If you have been good, then you will go to heaven, but if you have been bad…

I interrupted her. All eyes were on me now.

What do you mean by bad?

Sister Martha now stood in front of me. I could see tufts of nostril hairs and the cheap plastic from her badly-fitted dentures.

Dear girl, if you lie and cheat and steal, then you know where you are going!

Susan Tan was in tears now and looked at me in terror. She grabbed my hand and shook her head.

But, what if you're just a little bad?

More giggles. Another loud *Shhhh!*

Sister Martha smoothed down her starched cream habit, glared at me and screeched, much like a witch, I thought. She even had a hooked nose.

Even if you are just a little bad, you will still go to hell!

The entire class turned to look at me and they all started giggling. Even Susan Tan was trying to smile, but not smile at the same time.

That night, I dreamt of demons and angels, and a paved road with thick, gnarled thorns, strewn with blood-red roses that led into an eternal fire. I heard mortal screams, and the raucous shrieks and snarls of lurking demons.

An incubus then came to me, sliding into my bed from the right. I felt his cold fingers creep over my shoulder and onto my budding breasts, and my body tingled with pleasure and paralysis. My limbs, mouth, frozen. Eyes glued shut. Heart thumping, I forced myself to pray—*Hail Mary, Full of Grace, the Lord is with thee, Blessed art Thou amongst women and blessed is the fruit of thy womb Jesus, Holy Mary, Mother of God, pray for us sinners now and at the hour of our death, Amen.*

I could still feel it, a weight upon me, clutching my hands, gripping them like a vice. It was on me. I could not breathe.

Help, help me, Jesus.

With all the strength I could muster, I forced it off, bucking my knees and almost kicking the blanket off.

Hail Mary, Full of Grace, the Lord is with thee, Hail Mary, Full of Grace, the Lord is with thee, Hail Mary, Full of Grace, the Lord is with thee.

It was gone, and my bedroom smelled foul.

Mummy! Mummy! I screamed. She never came.

I was a sinner, I had sinned and I had paid for it. I had questioned Sister Martha and I had paid for it. A demon had visited me in the night and I felt the pleasure of his visit. It would be the first of many. I turned over and the clock displayed a gleaming 3.03am. I had sinned, and I had eternal damnation to pay.

He walked me to his car, guiding me gently by the elbow, and he opened the car door for me. The seat felt cool, the insides smelt of pine. KL was rousing to life. Traffic was sparse, and the air outside was balmy. He played U2 on the stereo.

We spoke a little, but my tongue felt knotted, dry. My jaw ached from the hours of needless chatter at the club. I was spent, dried out, my voice hoarse.

His name was Omar. Half Malay, half English. He was back from London where he worked and lived. His family had an apartment in the Pan Global building, which overlooked the club, and he had been walking to get breakfast when he saw me.

I was afraid to look at him. His nearness was disconcerting. I was coming down and I felt vulnerable, like the insides of a young coconut being scraped slowly by a child with a broken spoon, but it didn't stop me from stealing glances at him when his eyes were on the road.

Sharp jaw, curly dark brown hair. Light eyes with flecks, skin that was darker than Fairman's. A distinct mole on the left cheek. Black glasses. Expensive. An old Rolex on the left wrist. Golden hairs on his arm. Scholarly. Lean. Either the well-read type or the financial type. I leaned my head against the window and closed my eyes, letting the low purring of his car lull my mind into quietude.

Traffic was building up. It was a long way to PJ, but we drove in silence. I dozed off and he shook my arm gently as we passed the yellow arch separating KL from Petaling Jaya.

I directed him to my apartment, a rented floor of a 70s semi-detached house close to my childhood home, but in the poorer part of Section 5. When I walked up the stairs, I felt self-conscious and as I pulled my torn skirt around, I felt his eyes on me.

As I opened the front door, the words tumbled out of my mouth.

Don't leave, please stay. I don't want to be alone right now.

I felt foolish, like a damsel in distress, something I never ever thought of becoming.

He smiled and shrugged. *Sure.*

I had no valium and it felt like the world was colliding into me. He picked up a chair, sat down by the balcony and stared out. I offered him a glass of cold water from the fridge, which he accepted gracefully. The balcony overlooked a playground, empty this time of the morning, but he seemed happy to sit and stare, content in his thoughts.

I like your balcony, he said when I came out wrapped in a towel. *It reminds me of my grandmother's house on the east coast.*

He got up and walked towards me. I held my breath. He grabbed both my shoulders and turned me towards the bedroom.

You need to sleep, he said firmly and pushed me towards my bed. I felt embarrassed, my bed unmade, my flat a mess. He seemed so cultured, sophisticated. I turned to say something, but I decided not to.

I lowered myself slowly onto the bed, needing to be horizontal. I didn't expect him to, but he sat down next to me.

There, there. Sleep now, little lost girl.

His hand fluttered over my hair, and with the first stroke I suppressed a moan. He stroked my hair, my face, my arm. It was exquisite. Gentle. When I woke up, the windows streamed with a humid, yellow light. My body was sticky with sweat. He was gone. I got into a panic.

Who is this man?

And why had I asked a stranger to take me home? Invite him in? Have him sit on my bed? The universe had aligned its forces for our paths to cross in the most unholy of ways.

I gulped down a glass of cold water greedily. It was still Saturday morning. The weekend loomed. I opened the fridge and a dried-up apple stared back at me. I sat numbly on my bed. I drank more water. I curled up on the sofa and turned on the TV. I needed chatter in the room. I surfed the few channels I had, and decided to check my handphone for messages. The boxy black words peered out of the square screen.

Sorry sorry sorry I felt so out of it that stuff was so strong. You were sitting with some guy so I left. You okay?

Babes, are you OK??

Can you PLEASE answer

Freaking out now

Babes please CALL ME

I was never doing it again. Never doing E again. Never going out with Karin again. Ever.

I walked around the apartment, pacing up and down.

Omar. Omar. Who the hell are you?

Then I saw a pink post-it on my door.

Call me: 012 323 0929

I dialled the number. Each button a nervous, loud bleep. Three rings.

Hi, it's me. From this morning.

His voice, soft, a slight pleasing pause.

Hello…how you feeling? Sleep well?

I took a deep breath and tried to speak unhurriedly, but.

I'd like to see you, if that's okay. Sorry, I don't mean to be pushy or anything, I just don't really want to be alone right now.

A slow breath.

Yes, I understand.

An hour later, he was downstairs. I got into his car, and as I sank into the cool leather seat, I felt like weeping—I don't know why. We went to Raju's and found a quiet spot under a tree. He had a roti, I had teh tarik and thosai. He ate hungrily, with his fingers. Our eyes met and parted several times. I was overcome by shyness, but each time he caught me looking at him, he smiled as if he understood. In the light, his eyes were almost green.

The waiters hovered around with buckets of white rice and stainless steel containers of curries. Entire families seated around us. Children refusing to eat, sullen fathers slurping tea and shoving huge morsels of vegetables, mutton, fish into cavernous mouths. Mothers in saris, silent, brooding. Bursts of loud chatter.

He asked for the bill in Malay, paid and thanked the waiter. When we got into the car he turned to me and said, *I don't know what's going on, but this seems like the most natural thing in the world to me. Right now.* He put his hand gently on mine.

All I could do was nod. There was nothing to say.

We went back to my place. We undressed hurriedly and flung ourselves on my springy bed. In moments, he was inside me. He felt like home. It felt careless, devilish but so, so good. We made love three times and by the time we were done, we were hungry again.

I felt like a truck had hit me and burrowed itself into my belly. It sat there, like a stone, unmoving. Him, lying there, like that.

Omar. Omar.

It was reckless, unbridled.

It was an instantaneous love.

So. Omar Tunku Malik.

This was unlike anything I had known. It felt dangerous.

The only man I had ever truly loved was my father, but that was the love of a child for her father. This was different. This was a woman's love, for a man. Grief had consumed my father, killed whatever life he had left. My mother's death had devastated him. I wondered if this man would consume me the same way. I wondered if I too would become a shell of a person. I wondered if this kind of love would destroy me.

He was two years older than me. Studied engineering at Cambridge—the kind of privilege only boys like him had. The kind that was a birthright. His mother, English, from Norfolk, and apparently descended from the earliest Normans who plundered and conquered those lands. His father, Dutch,

Javanese, with some claim to Malay royalty. The embittered fucked each other to get ahead—but in actual fact, it was to make sure that bloodlines never ended.

Jangan Melayu hilang di dunia.

The Malays felt that their land had been taken from them, and that they now had every right to reclaim it. *May the Malay race never cease from the earth*. A union of paradoxes.

I had never been with a Malay man before. I was throwing myself into treacherous territory. I think I was afraid of the fact that he was Malay, that my preconceptions of who and what he was would spell a difficult and uncertain future. Something I wasn't entirely sure I even wanted.

But one night, after the lovemaking and the wine, I told him about the tear gas, about running the streets, *Saksi*, my friends, writing and recording the Reformasi, my anger at Mahathir, at the police, the courts, the injustice of it all, my sympathies for Wan Azizah and Anwar's young children, I poured out my heart and mind, I ranted and raved, I wept from frustration and more anger, and Omar, he listened and said nothing until I was done.

So…do you think I'm mad?

No. Why would I think that?

You're really quiet.

I was listening.

Oh. And…

I think it's time, this is the time. Let's do this.

This?

Fight. We need to fight back.

Yes, we do. We must!

Yes?

Together?

A firm nod, a kiss sealed it.

And there it was. This was the man I would fight with, for a country that we both loved. For justice. For freedom. For Malaysia.

JESSICA HAD CALLED him again. He had finally managed to recover from the jetlag, but her habit of calling in the early hours before dawn to hurl expletives at him was becoming too predictable and intrusive. Getting involved with Jess was a mistake, one he hoped he was not making with Del.

He had vowed to not get involved for a while but he found women a necessary distraction. He wanted to come back to Malaysia to feel the fervor of Reformasi. Reading about the street protests ignited latent fires in his heart. He had been away for too long, transplanted in a land that he had no desire to grow up in. England was home, but Malaysia was where he belonged.

The young woman he met had a passion, the kind that he himself lacked. He never had to fight for anything. Privilege and wealth had made him soft; he was ambivalent about the world. But now, the country was at a crossroads, and he wanted to be part of the new wave of change. He felt that he had become too English, his Malay rusty, sad. His grandmother had taught him songs, graceful Malay pantuns that he had so loved as a child.

"More, Tok, the one about the cempedak and the banana!"

His grandmother would laugh, pinch his cheeks and sit him on her thigh and together they would sing the *Rasa Sayang*, the folk song all Malaysian children grew up singing:

> *Buah cempedak di luar pagar,*
> *Ambil galah tolong jolokkan,*
> *Saya budak baru belajar,*
> *Kalau salah tolong tunjukkan.*

Rasa sayang, hey!
Rasa sayang sayang hey,
Hey lihat nona jauh,
Rasa sayang sayang hey!

Pisang emas dibawa berlayar,
Masak sebiji di atas peti,
Hutang emas boleh dibayar,
Hutang budi dibawa mati.

Omar had not felt inspired about anything for years. He had put up little resistance in his life. His father had dictated everything by remote, somehow. From him being sent to boarding school, to the subjects he took for his O- and A-Levels, getting into Cambridge, to a quick succession of spritely, blonde English girlfriends whom he bedded in university and then in London.

It was all rather predictable. Even Jessica was somehow scripted into his life. Everything just *happened* to him, especially when he didn't want anything to happen in particular. When he met her out on the town with his mates one night in a pub in Farringdon, she had seemed shy about the fact that he was, to all appearances, from the east.

"Malaysia, that's where you've got those lovely white beaches yeah."

"Yes, we do have quite…a few of them."

"Have you been? Must be oh…so gorgeous."

"Yes, well…"

He didn't mention that his father owned a small island off the east coast, and that his fondest childhood memories were of summer holidays swimming in clear, deep emerald waters, frolicking with green turtles and clown fish, tossing a line into the sea from the battered sampan with his father, gutting the fish and cooking it over a fire on the beach. Moments like that stayed with him. Like the smell of fresh innards being ripped from fish bellies, and the taste of grouper and barracuda sizzling from the marinade of onion, garlic, lime and chillies over a charcoal fire. Licking the last flakes of fish from his fingers and nodding when his mother asked if he wanted more rice. Or more coconut water. "Yes," it was always yes.

Within an hour, after five vodka shots, Jessica was riding him in the ladies' bathroom, head back, shrieking like a banshee. A week later, she was unpacking a pink suitcase with wide-eyed glee in his studio apartment in Shoreditch, and he wondered how on earth he had gotten her there. He didn't even want her there, but she had found her way into his life, his apartment and his bed.

A month later, after the news of Anwar's arrest, he had decided to leave London for good and so he ended his brief, high-sexed relationship with Jess. No doubt, she was great in bed, but she also wanted to be his wife. He knew that she was in love with him—they all fell madly for him somehow. He had no idea why. Perhaps it was his nonchalance, the kind of easy parley that certain women longed for. Perhaps the less one gave them, the more they yearned for.

With Del, it was different. He hated to admit it, but yes, it was love.

WE WERE VISCOUS, we slid into each other like two halves from the two-headed four-legged mythic creatures that Zeus created. We finished each other's sentences, we thought the same things, despaired over the same things, we read the same books, loved the same music.

I would spend my days at the *Saksi* office, write, edit, get the pieces out, upload them onto the website. And then he would come pick me up. We'd rush back to my place, tear our clothes off and make love till we screamed. The sorry state of politics incensed us. We made love with our tongues, fingers and teeth. There was blood. It turned us into animals; we fucked to stay sane, fucked to go insane.

Then, we'd lie on my bed and smoke cigarettes. He never liked the covers, so he'd be there naked, and I would put my head to his chest and hear his heart pounding. I loved him so much I wanted to punch him, claw his face, bite morsels, tear flesh off. I felt possessed, like one of the women from *The Bacchae*, inspired by a beastly, primal longing that made me ache for forests and trees. I saw shadows lurking in the dark and heard low guttural moans. I knew that this man could be the beginning and the end of me.

Hey you, come here.

I slid up towards him, on all fours, naked. His eyes were slits and the flecks in his eyes glowed like fiery seeds. He touched me lightly with his mouth. His tongue played on my lips, then moved inside my mouth, teasing, and then he sniffed my neck deeply.

Cium sayang.

Sayang. My love, my love.

Sayang. Darling.

He eased inside me, and pulled me up in one swoop. I was over him, my hair covering his face, chest, shoulders.

You're so beautiful, Del.

His eyes burned into mine and when I mounted him, a frenzy seized me. Sweat drenched us, glorious and golden. And before I came, I saw visions of myself on a horse, thundering through a forest, mist rising from the ground and when the explosion came, I was on the pinnacle of a rock, arms outstretched, looking at a black sky.

Omar said he wanted to change Malaysia. We talked about reform, of needing to get rid of the status quo, of ridding the Malays of subsidies. He believed the National Economic Policy had crippled them, made them dependent on government handouts—instead of making them resilient—and the Malays had become greedy, only wanting more and more, but without doing it the hard way. Without having to work for things.

Embrace the land. We need to let our feet kiss the ground again. He kept saying it again and again. *Tanah air—this is our homeland. Our. Homeland.*

The sons had to return to the soil; the tar and concrete had corrupted the very nature of what it meant to be Malay. Perhaps, the only option was to return to the past, to embrace the colonial construct of the "lazy native"—an ideology which undermined native labour with a certain consequence and ease, yet which allowed Malay culture and tradition to flourish. To acknowledge the fact that they were once Hindu, live off the land, follow the harvests, bathe in clear, clean waters of the rivers made alluring by nubile virgins in batik sarongs, who laughed and sang in clear voices—and then govern a people who were gentle with a firm hand.

We were this, the Malay rulers were this. They knew who they were. The fact of the matter is we have become who we are not meant to be. So what if they sat around with their courtiers and drank tea and smoked all day? There was jealousy and treason, there was bloodshed when it was needed, but the very nature of who we were was simplicity. We only wanted a life that we knew we always had. Change was a detriment, we did not know how to manage it. We became victims of ourselves. We have become rotten to the core.

Omar spoke with such passion, such clarity. It was dangerous rhetoric, but I knew there was a truth to it and I began to understand his infernal struggle of what it meant to be Malay.

But for now, the battle lines had been drawn. We hated Mahathir. We hated what he had spawned. We had to end the regime, we had to do what thousands of others were doing on the streets. Omar got tear-gassed for the first time, we stood and shouted in solidarity with the others. Many were getting arrested and hauled into Black Marias, thrown into smelly lock-ups. And we bailed them out.

We wrote articles, we took pictures, we attended rallies, we stood and sang the Negaraku with Anwar's supporters, we supported Keadilan, the new Justice Party founded by Wan Azizah, Anwar's wife. We stood on street corners with hand-made slogans and placards, we drove activists in Omar's car to and from the courthouse, we drank endless cups of tea, talked of more reform, of plots, conspiracy theories, we were reckless, we did not care.

We were in love, we were fighting for what we believed in and that was all that mattered.

Anwar's trial had once again attracted the world's media to our shores. His black eye became emblematic of our dissent. It was representative of all that was wrong and all that had to be righted. The Inspector General of Police Rahim Noor had later confessed that he had personally delivered the black eye. Not his finest hour. People rioted.

Saksi kept getting more recognition and our stories kept getting angrier, edgier. Fairman had been questioned once by Special Branch—three officers showed up at the apartment one morning and took him away. Sumi, who had started seeing him—*We just have sex, lots of it really*—had to bail him out.

Imran had started writing a daily column called Face Off. He had lost twenty pounds from running the streets and looked leaner and browner by the day. *Saksi* had close to fifty thousand hits a day and Imran's popular pieces were visceral and pointed. His commentary on the trial became iconic and the foreign journos used the site as a reliable source as to what was really happening on the ground.

The local newspapers kept getting boycotted by KL-ites. It was shit news, and many refused to read it. Any of it. So, we kept the site going, we knew that we had to be the voice of reason, the only voice that was free in a country that was imploding within itself.

KL had woken up to a fury. Something that lay latent for so long had unleashed itself. The streets became fluid; it beckoned the multitudes of people who ran across the asphalt, it broke our falls, it carried our blood and sweat into the drains and rivers that birthed the city. We knew that there was no turning back. And that many took risks—the long row of shops on Jalan Tunku Abdul Rahman had paid a price too. Jalan TAR was the backbone of the protests; it was the trunk that fed the leaves, branches and roots of our anger. That road had also swallowed the racial riots of '69. The shop lots then and now had owners who were sympathetic to us. Some had been fined and threatened by the cops. Most just barricaded their doors when we ran, some let us in where we waited until the tear gas and water cannons all stopped.

KL seemed to be a maze of unruly streets when I was a child and there were only a few places that I could remember as landmarks. Once a year my mother would take me to a shop called Pei Ping Lace on Jalan TAR. It was at the end of a row of shophouses which sold all kinds of fabrics, and above it was a carpet house run by an old blue-eyed man from Kashmir with the longest silver beard I'd ever seen. Owned by a Chinese family with small children, the lace shop sold the most exquisite hand-embroidered fabrics and lace from China. In glass cases and encased in shiny plastic envelopes, there were rows and rows of tablecloths, runners, napkins and bedclothes. Starched, thick, white cotton sheets, with delicate flowers hand-sewn into the edges of scalloped pillow-cases. It came in sets. Matching duvet covers, bedspreads, and long dutch-wife cases. My mother loved those sheets, she said that they made her feel like the Queen of England when she slept. She would trail her fingers across each piece, caress it lovingly, saying, *Imagine the work, Del, all that work, sitting there for days, just for one piece.*

She would spend hours deciding on what to buy, and I'd sit there bored, staring out onto the street, watching the cars ease in and out of traffic. I'd see the toddlers waltzing around in their walkers, pink and red dummies sticking out of their mouths and sometimes I would stick my tongue out at them. When she was done, we would emerge onto the street and make our way to the famous nasi kandar place on the corner, *Where all the famous stars from the fifties and sixties used to eat,* she said. She would order a mee mamak pedas, and I'd have the rojak and cendol. We'd sit and eat in silence and then drive home.

It was the only time my mother ever took me out to town. Once when I ran past the shop house, dodging tear gas with Omar pulling my hand, I saw that Pei Ping Lace had closed down. The doors were boarded up, and the blinds were drawn. I closed my eyes and when I opened them, I felt hot tears running down my face.

MARINA DECIDED TO go shopping. She needed to give herself a day off from work and get herself some new clothes and perhaps some new make-up, or some perfume. One of the girls had told her about Masjid India or the Indian Mosque market, which was a half-hour walk from Chow Kit.

KL's red light districts were many and scattered across the city, but Chow Kit was where men came to have sex with transsexuals. She was sharing an apartment with two other transsexuals and she had a room, a clean bed with a recently purchased mattress along with pink, flowery sheets. There was a narrow kitchen with blue tiled floors and the stove was next to a window, which overlooked an alley where the children of sex workers kicked around an old football, and where she made instant noodles from time to time. In the living room, there was a couch, two chairs and a stuffed teddy bear propped up next to the television. Marina enjoyed watching the Malay soaps during the daytime and late at night after work.

There was a bond among all the sex workers in Chow Kit; they looked out for each other. If a client was abusive, they would all avoid him. Word got around about clients who refused to wear condoms, and those who had weird fetishes. Marina had been lucky so far, she had not had any issues or problems with her clients. Most of the men she had sex with were married to women they had no desire for. Marina had a theory that most Malay men were bisexual, many closeted due to religious and cultural values, and many desperately unhappy. So for fifty ringgit an hour, Marina made their lives liveable again and gave them the pleasures that only she could and left them with smiles and promises of more.

The rows of shops along Lorong Haji Taib were fronts for brothels, but many were genuine businesses as well, some having been there since the end of WWII. There were coffee shops that sold rice, noodles, spicy soups and curries; there were car dealers, cloth and biscuit merchants, printing shops and wholesale shops for jewellery, clothes and plastics. Many clients sat quietly waiting their turn at the many coffee shops, before climbing up staircases to simple rooms that had a mattress, a window, a cheap table fan and rolls of toilet paper on a side table.

Marina was content. She had enough money to send to her mother and she had enough for herself. The purple hormone pills were expensive, but she had to keep taking them. A sex change operation in Thailand was going to cost almost 8,000 ringgit and by her estimates she would be able to save that amount in five years. She would finally become a woman.

As she walked towards Jalan Tunku Abdul Rahman, with a smile on her face, she suddenly realised that she was surrounded by hundreds of people, all walking in the same direction. Some were carrying placards.

Reformasi! Keadilan! Undur Mahathir!

Reform! Justice! Mahathir Resign!

She had heard that there were street protests because the Deputy Prime Minister had been arrested for sodomy. She thought that if that was the case, then all her clients, including herself, should have been arrested as well.

There was a hum in the air, and the people around her were laughing, clapping, smiling. Soon, she was thrust into a crowd of thousands and as they crossed Campbell Street onto the Sogo supermarket, they could barely move. Cars were honking, thousands screamed in unison.

Re-for-ma-si! Re-for-ma-si!

Marina held on tight to her handbag. There were people of all ages, young, old, mothers, fathers carrying their children on their shoulders, youth of all races, singing and clapping together, old men in faded batik shirts, women in tudungs and colourful baju kurungs. Everyone was smiling.

Soon, the shouts became a roar, the voices sounded like a swarm of insects, and the crowd started moving.

"Where is everyone going?" Marina asked a young woman in a purple scarf. She looked like a student.

"Dataran!" the woman screamed excitedly. "This is amazing, kan! Aren't you proud to be Malaysian today?"

Marina smiled back. The crowd around her had become more frenetic. She had to do what she had planned for the day.

She eased her way out of the crowd. The sun was behind a cloud and she saw a cluster of balloons cutting through the air. She made her way onto Masjid India and saw hordes of shops selling colourful garments, saris, sets of salwar kameez, leather slippers, sticky sweets. A medicine man with bottles of oils and tinctures for health and sexual stamina, made from roots, leeches, sea cucumber. Farther down the road were shops selling open vials of musky perfumes, thick blades of black kohl from India, shops that sold holy books and white shrouds for the haj.

She bought two vials of perfume—sandalwood and jasmine—some black kohl, a green blouse with orange flowers, a pair of pink sandals, a long black shawl. Pleased, she sipped on a bag of iced coconut water as she walked home, swinging her bags from her left arm and ignoring the catcalls that followed her.

LIVING TOGETHER HAD become a habit, so when Omar decided that we should share a place, it seemed the right thing to do. We decided to rent a three-bedroom apartment in Bangsar. The rent was far more than what I could afford, but he simply said, *just look after yourself and I will take care of the rest.*

Papa had inadvertently turned my mother into a kept woman and I had no intentions of ever becoming like her. Financial dependency on a man was an area of particular dread for me. Omar was secretive about his money and there were times, admittedly, that I got suspicious of where it came from. Of how much of it he had. Of how it seemed limitless. Papa was a wealthy man, but when I went to university, I lived frugally. Papa only sent me what was needed, never more. So I lived like my friends, not like the wealthy Chinese or Hong Kong students, who had credit cards and who bought brand-new cars. I bought second-hand clothes, I rode a bicycle, I stayed in houses that were almost condemned.

Omar had expensive tastes—soft cheeses, Italian wines, tailored shirts and handmade English shoes—much like Papa—and I sometimes wondered if this was what drew me to him. I liked a man who dressed well and Omar's vintage BMW, which once belonged to his father, was impeccably maintained, the sleek blue veneer always polished and the leather spotless and scented.

Papa had been kept abreast of my love life and he seemed pleased with what I'd told him about Omar.

Yes, Papa, Cambridge. Engineering. Articulate enough. We're moving in together.

My father had become more of a recluse. He had turned down Anwar's request to be lead counsel in his trial, and had retreated even more within the walls of his study and into the pages of his books. Whenever I went home I'd smell the sweet vanilla smoke from his pipe and see piles of plates stacked neatly by the wall. He lived on whole-wheat bread sandwiches with processed cheese, sliced tomatoes and liver pate, milky sweet Milo and 12-year old whisky. And papaya. The trees in the garden had fruited ample bosoms of the fleshy orange fruit and if the birds didn't get to them they would all be eaten by my father.

The garden had become unruly with weeds. The rows of heliconia, crab's claw and bird of paradise were thinning, and the slender, once glossy leaves dry from lack of water. But there were no flowers, none of the deep red, pinkish yellow and orange flowers that used to grow in abundance. The white and purple lilies in the dragon pots had all wilted. The orchids, all of his prized expensive orchids—which my mother loved, and cut and put into vases all over the house—were dead. Rows of handmade terracotta pots hung like a macabre installation from their wooden gallows. And the pots on the two-tier benches that our gardener Raja built over one weekend were choked with tall dried stalks. Even the buds had fallen off.

The only thing that thrived and grew with wild abandon were the papaya trees, lush and pregnant with fruit. The birds were responsible for the baby trees, which grew around the three big ones. And then there was the bamboo, the cluster of skinny bamboo which grew like a fortress, and which I believed sheltered a family of snakes—king cobras to be precise. Raja had ceased to come every day as Papa had stopped paying him. But once a month, he would come to cut the grass by hand and I would leave him a fifty-ringgit note underneath a flower pot. I did not want the garden to be completely overgrown, but whenever I stood in the garden, I was at a loss as to what to do. Everything needed trimming. I would have to spend hours on my knees, digging up weeds. I would get bitten by mosquitoes and the grass would make my thighs itch.

I remember watching Papa in the garden, squatting in his sarong and singlet, floppy white hat, smoking his pipe. Papa humming a tune, digging up weeds, trimming the orchids. Mother sitting in a rattan chair under the shade of my tree, the flame of the forest, red flowers all around her. Them chatting about something, then laughing in agreement. My father nodding to what she was saying, the smoke swirling around his head. The scent of tobacco in the evening breeze, the bamboo leaves flitting like skittles . The water in the pool a deep blue from the mosaic tiles. The promise of a good dinner, television and conversation. Papa's mutton curry. Hot fluffy white rice. Music on the gramophone. Them dancing to Bing Crosby. Those were our weekends, until Mother died.

Now, the house filled me with sadness and I would feel the desire to leave after minutes. The curse of being the only child rendered me somewhat distant and uncommunicative. I could not reach out to my father. I didn't know how to. I had no words to articulate to him, no way to understand the void that had consumed him. I wanted to kiss his cheek like I did when I was a child, hanging on to him for dear life while he spun me around and around till I was dizzy.

The house had withered outside, a testament to the tropics, but inside, it felt abandoned and unloved. The paint on the walls had aged and the damp had settled in mouldy pockets. My mother's beloved Persian rugs smelt of cockroaches and the paintings that Papa had collected so lovingly—because Mother loved art—stared into empty rooms and hallways. Papa sat alone in his study. He slept alone and woke alone, his life a testament to self-imposed solitude and loneliness. He refused to see or talk to anyone. It terrified me. I did not want love to do this to me. I did not want to lose contact, touch, desire. My father did not love again. He chose not to. Not even me, his only child.

When I brought Omar to the house for the first time, Papa emerged from his study in his sarong and singlet, pipe in mouth, smelling of whisky, dishevelled hair unwashed.

My father, the once-great human rights lawyer.

Omar shook his hand and was led into the study. Papa smiled and said that he wanted to have a chat and closed the door silently behind Omar. I walked to my bedroom and sat on my bed for all of two unbearable minutes and then decided to go into my father's room, the room once reserved for guests. He had kept it sparse. A simple white Indian cotton bed sheet adorned his bed, smelling of vanilla and his aftershave. A worn white singlet with a huge hole was thrown over a chair. Slippers by the bed. A half-empty glass of water. A bar of smoothened Pears soap in the bathroom. The dragon pot full of ice-cold water.

I stepped quietly into my parents' bedroom. My mother's antique dressing table, with the oval mirror, her perfume bottles, Dior lipsticks and silver bangles. Her pearls, which she wore on special occasions. Their wedding picture still on the wall, my father in his dark suit and my mother's eyes gazing up from the white veil. Her clothes were still in the glass and teak cupboard, where I used to sneak into and find secret things. In the drawers, love letters, Valentine cards, a skinny black-strapped Art Deco watch still in its oblong case, a crystal necklace, an antique pocket watch with the inscriptions RC.

And in the corner on a Malacca chair, her Japanese silk caftan, which she wore throughout the day, sometimes from morning till night. Now faded into a dusky pink with streaks, the blossoms barely visible. A memory of my mother with her loose hair, striding though the house with a glass of vodka in her hand.

I sat on the bed and stared out the window into the garden. My tree. In spite of everything, it had grown and flourished. And the crimson flowers fell in anarchy onto the uncut grass and into the pool. The tears came furiously. How terrible and tragic life could be. How unfair. How ruthless and unkind.

That's where Papa found me, my face curled into my mother's caftan, asleep on their marital bed.

Wake up, Del. Time to go.

I saw Omar standing in the hallway, his face tight and drawn. I went into the bathroom. My tears had left dried rivulets of salt on my face, so I splashed myself with cold water and rubbed my cheeks and my eyes. Then I pulled my hair into a ponytail.

Goodbye, Papa, take care.

I will, Del. I will.

Omar drove home silent. He never spoke of what my father said to him that day. We went home and made quiet love.

On 13 April 1999, Anwar was sentenced by the nefarious judge Augustine Paul to six years for corruption. Two months later, he was sentenced to another nine years. Both sentences were to be served consecutively.

We were beyond anger. Men had turned into savages. The judiciary was in shambles. How could a court not uphold the rule of law? How could a judge make a mockery of justice? Was there ever going to be justice?

Omar and I took to the streets. The city once again was brutalised by tear gas, from hurt, from sadness. KL, which was mother, father, surrogate mother, sister, brother, lover, friend, was once again violated. We were unwitting witnesses to each other. KL could not protect us, and neither could we protect it. How could we love a city that brought nothing but sickness to our souls? And how could we hate it?

How could a mattress be made into a scapegoat? How could a lowly mattress be shown in court again and again with semen stains, as witness? The soiled mattress on which Anwar supposedly sodomised his half-brother and advisor was brought in and out of court like a shamed prostitute. That poor tainted mattress with splotches of dried semen. Out of thirteen stains, ten matched Anwar's DNA. Parents shielded their children's eyes from the newspapers on the stands.

The headlines were vile, lurid, completely obscene.

Imran was a man possessed. His opinion pieces got angrier and more brazen. He was the go-to fixer, writer, contact on the ground for the journos who had once again descended on KL. Many had become friends now, chums for the cause. The late nights, the drinking, and the conversations continued. Sumi and Fairman had started living together, so they sometimes barricaded themselves in the bedroom for fast, furious sex. Imran held court. Omar and I sat, held hands and listened to the endless tirades.

One night, I woke up to searing abdominal pains and a damp bed. I thought I had wet myself. Something was wrong. I did not know that we had conceived a child in the sullen erotic moisture of our bedroom, and now she—for I believe it was female—had decided that this life was not to be. The world was too difficult to live in, and when I was in the hospital, in between the cold gusts of anaesthesia, I felt a warm hand on my chest and thought of my mother.

Omar was silent for weeks after that.

Our lives now had sadness, which had meaning, I suppose. Meaning meant history. We had made a child, and lost it. *I had lost it.* My womb was incapable of making limbs, a skeleton, a brain, eyes, ears, perfect toes and fingers. Hair. Eyes—would they too be green like his? I couldn't keep it in my womb. There it had been, lying in layers of uterus, blood and muscle, I didn't even know.

How could I not have known? Was my body so foreign to me that I did not know that I was with child? Or was I just too worn out to feel the flood of life in my body? I blamed myself. I had to. I saw Omar differently after that.

As a father. That he and I could be a family.

I drank myself to sleep. Empty bottles of wine lined the kitchen wall until they were sealed into bin bags and dumped into rubbish bins. The clattering of empty bottles became familiar.

Drinking hollowed me out and I felt even more lost. Omar left me alone in my grief. Until one night, after a political rally. I stumbled downstairs for water, parched and drunk. I saw him sunken and slouched in a corner by the fridge. His head was in between his knees. He looked up, and I could see that he had been crying.

His head felt heavy and warm in my hands. There were no words. Just an empty womb between us.

But there was love, yes.

There was love.

This was a grief that was unfamiliar. It did not come with a sense of recompense or relief after tears; it felt ancestral, ancient. As if my ancestors had come back to reclaim something that they had left behind. Vengeance. It was primal, visceral, dark. I was hovering in a place of in-betweenness. I did not understand it at all.

I wasn't even sure why I grieved. A child would have thrown our lives into chaos. We would have been forced to marry, and I would have faced an inevitable conversion into Islam—an act which filled me with trepidation. And we were scarcely ready for anything apart from reacting to the headlines that filled us with more rage every day.

I would have been angry and pregnant, pounding the streets in frumpy skirts and sneakers, shouting slogans and getting shoved into the other hapless, sweaty activists. Getting tear-gassed. It would have been completely foolish.

I took to roaming the streets. The city was less hostile at night and I would take a taxi to Old Market Square and walk towards Dataran Merdeka, passing the confluence of the two rivers that gave the city its name—muddy estuary. Kuala Lumpur.

A hundred and fifty years ago, this area was filled with thieves, vigilantes, and opportunists. I imagined exhausted Chinese coolies lying comatose in opium dens, the noisy clacking of mahjong tiles in the hands of drunk gamblers, the swiftness of the rickshaws and the drone of snores from street dwellers. Yap Ah Loy, the Chinese-born Kapitan, had turned the tiny mining village into the most important town in the Malay Peninsula and was sheriff, businessman and visionary. He introduced public services and amenities, brought in thousands of mainland Chinese coolies to work in the mines and slowly, built the foundations of a city. Life revolved around the tin that was found upriver and the daily haggling and selling took place in the market square. There was meat and incense and spices. Women selling vegetables and fruits, steaming noodles with pork broth, Indian curries and pungent pickles. Brothels for sex. Malay traders selling fabrics, knives, potions for magic spells. Rhino horn, tiger testicles, bear claw, dried seahorses, elephant penis, golden, sinewy globules of dried birds' nest, bark, herb, roots for strength, vitality, insomnia. The endless spoils of the seas and the rainforest.

The graceful copper domes on the Sultan Abdul Samad building gleamed. The courts were silent at night, and all the fury of the day would sink into the curve of the walls. I was fond of many colonial structures, but this was by far my favourite. The elegance of AC Norman's design embraced the neo-Moorish, Mughal, Indo-Saracenic influences of the time. Across it lay Dataran Merdeka or Independence Square, where our founding father Tunku Abdul Rahman shouted with a raised fist, *Merdeka! Merdeka! Merdeka!* as the Union flag was lowered for the last time. He was a man of honour, a real gentleman, a politician who worked for the people of the new nation. That was then.

But now, there was no honour left in our politics. There was only rot from a gallery of rogues who were set on driving our country into ruin.

There were kids on skateboards, trying out new flips in the light of the street lamps. There were furtive lovers huddled in the shadows, tired labourers shuffling home, and as I wandered further down into Chow Kit, the ladies of the night emerged. Some of them beautiful, slim men with shaved calves, hiked up skirts tottering on stilettos, teased hair, crimson lips.

I had done a feature story on sex workers for *The Review* and I had spent time interviewing women and transsexuals who were in the trade. One woman had been raped at knife-point, then slit from her vagina to her anus and then sold into slavery to a Chinese towkay for five years. Another had to continue working whilst her dead child was putrefying in her womb. She eventually died of septicaemia, poisoned by the blood from her foetus. Then there was Ariff, or Michelle as he preferred to be known, disowned by a father who branded him a "syaitan", a devil, and cast him out of his home in a fishing village.

I recalled these stories as I walked on, guided only by instinct and the will to keep walking. My story paled in comparison to theirs—and yet I felt weak, haunted by a thing that had not yet become anything.

Hi, sayang. You okay tak?

Behind me, I heard a deep giggle and I smelt cigarette smoke. *You nampak macam sedih.*

I turned around. A statuesque transsexual towered over me. She was in a short denim skirt and a pink top with spaghetti straps. Had soft frosted pink lips and a large black mole over her right eyebrow. Her hair was straight and highlighted with streaks of blonde and brown. She sashayed like a supermodel while puffing on a slim clove cigarette. She was beautiful.

Huh? I wasn't sure if she was talking to me.

Hi honey, you look sad. Want some company?

I shrugged. *Yeah, sure. Do you want to walk? Where you going?*

Nowhere, just walking you know. I should be working, but I can walk.

And so we walked. The eyes of passers-by dug into us but she moved those hips to an invisible tune as if she were on a catwalk. In heels. I couldn't keep up. We found a 24-hour mamak place and ordered hot tea.

The waiter served us our frothed tea with a smile that struck me as over-familiar. But she nodded, lit another cigarette and cocked an eyebrow. I pictured the plump waiter's loins grinding into hers in a dark alley, squirting his

seed into her, and then wiping his forehead with his sweat-
and curry-stained towel.

Embarrassed, I took a sip of the tea and immediately spat
it out. It was scalding hot. A tissue appeared at my mouth
and I saw long, glittery nails.

Go slow, honey. You okay?

I sputtered and nodded, eyes brimming with pain.

*Good. My name's Marina and I think we're going to be
great friends.*

THE MISCARRIAGE AFFECTED Omar more than he'd expected. He had never thought of himself as a father. All of a sudden his life had an unfamiliar meaning. It felt like success, but a pain-filled form of success.

"Ah there it is. Pain," he blurted out loud one day.

It wasn't like buying his apartment in Shoreditch at a bank auction, neither was it like shagging three women in one week. Those were pure, unadulterated glories. That was coincidence, being at the right place at the right time. So how was this different? Was it—different?

The past months had made him feel alive. Getting tear-gassed, running the streets, seeing Malaysians come together in solidarity for a cause: it had given him a passion, a fervor that he had never quite felt before. And being with Del— moving in with her, living with her and then conceiving a child—it was as if he had come to be everything that he was not.

There were times when he felt out of his depth. Del knew so much about the country and felt so deeply for everything. Her drive and desires extended themselves to not just the need for change, but for a deep awareness of her self. She was the kind of woman that he had hoped for yet feared at the same time. She was instinctive, kind, fiercely protective and intelligent, but there was a kind of darkness to her that he could not fathom. The kind that was given shape on the day he met her father.

He was assailed by sadness as soon as he walked in. The house smelled of neglect and dust. He knew that Del was ashamed of the state of her childhood home: "Papa stopped living after Mother died and the house is a mess." But she had wanted him to meet her father. She walked through the heavy front door, closed it with a thud, took her shoes off, whispered, "He's in the study," and pointed to a door down the hallway.

Omar took his shoes off, looked up and saw cobwebs on the ceiling. The vast garden had crept in, creepers and vines entangled with the furniture and the curtains. Immediately he thought of snakes, and wondered if there was indeed the possibility of a family of cobras living in the house somewhere. He padded silently behind Del.

The house was in semi-darkness, and apart from the hallway, there was little light let in. It was airless and stale. Heavy drapes hung silently, as if they had been unmoved for years. They walked through the living room full of antique wooden furniture. He spied a Victorian-style cupboard with delicate triangles of glass. It reminded him of the one his mother had bought at an antique shop somewhere in Suffolk. The carpets felt moist under his feet. They came to a door and in a corner lay a neat pile of unwashed plates, mugs and silver cutlery. Del knocked on the door, cleared her throat and whispered, "Papa, Papa. We're here."

There was a low cough and shuffling footsteps approaching the door, which swung open.

Del's father was a tall man, with a shock of grey hair, metal-framed glasses and a full beard. He wore a white singlet and a sarong. His shoulders were hunched and his arms were fleshy; Omar could tell that those arms were once muscled and strong and that Del's father was once a handsome man.

He gave Del a long hug and then kissed her forehead. Father and child held each other close. He saw the resemblance.

Del had her father's eyes, his mouth.

"Papa, this is Omar."

Omar held out his hand and Del's father shook it.

"Come in," he said.

She smiled and walked away.

The study was big, lined with books in wooden bookshelves from floor to ceiling. Beautiful carpets were strewn across the floor and three large paintings of landscapes hung on a section of the wall. The room smelt of sweet tobacco, and there was a small ring of white smoke hovering over a large Dutch antique desk. An old air conditioner rattled, cooling the air. Del's father walked slowly towards the leather armchair behind his desk and gestured for Omar to sit. The desk was covered with papers, books, fountain pens. The room reminded Omar of a scholar's den, that of a quasi-madman who had retreated from the perils of the world and into the sanctuary of books.

Del's father picked up his pipe and started puffing.

"Sit, sit. You are back here for good?"

Omar sat down, the leather chair squeaked. Del's father continued puffing on his pipe.

"Yes, sir."

"You work?"

"For my father's company. We import parts for luxury cars. There's a KL office and that's where I work now."

"Ah, and your parents?"

"They live in London, sir. My mother prefers to be close to my grandmother. I have a younger sister in university."

"And she is reading…"

"Sociology sir."

Omar felt that he was back in boarding school, being

quizzed by his Headmaster. There was a sudden silence.

"I love my daughter very much, my wife…" He gestured to a picture behind him.

"I understand, sir."

Del's father took another puff of his pipe and the vanilla-flavoured smoke curled upward lightly into the air before it dissipated into nothing. Omar was perplexed. He wanted to say, "But you have a daughter who needs you, she is here, alive, in your life." But he didn't.

"You love my daughter, yes?"

Omar nodded.

"Then you must be good to her, for she deserves only kindness…your love."

"Yes, sir."

"So be it then. Know that I am grateful."

Omar nodded. Del's father spoke clearly, assuredly, as if he had rehearsed what he was going to say. It was succinct, concise. It felt like he was making a deal.

"Now if you'll excuse me, I will get back to my reading."

Omar stood up and, on an impulse, asked, "May I ask what you're reading, sir?"

Del's father looked up.

"Baudelaire, his essays. In the original French. You know his work?"

"No sir, I'm afraid I don't."

"Well then. Perhaps you will one day."

"Perhaps. Thank you, sir."

Del's father looked down at his book and Omar knew that he had been dismissed. He got up and glanced quickly at the picture on the wall behind the desk. It was a wedding portrait.

Del's mother was seated in a chair, her hair coiffed, her face in a fixed smile. Omar could see that she had been beautiful.

At the door, Omar turned to take one more look at the old man now hunched over a book, immersed in a world that only existed within the pages of a book, confined in the walls of that room. And in a moment of clarity, he understood that Del was utterly alone. She was an orphan. That her father was dead to her as he was to the world.

WE STARTED CAMPAIGNING for Keadilan while Anwar was in jail, serving his sentence. We'd heard that he was in solitary confinement and that he was made to sleep on the floor, without a mattress, aggravating his already bad back. Elections were coming up and we knew that we had to galvanise as much support as possible. Keadilan was a new political party and it had to be prepared to contest in the election. Public sympathy was ripe, and we needed to capitalise on it. Every day Omar and I arrived early at the campaign headquarters, packing large boxes of leaflets into the car and then distributing them in housing areas. This had to be done on foot—by lunchtime we would have canvassed an entire housing estate.

We focused on areas like Kepong, Jinjang and Segambut, which were opposition strongholds. This was the Chinese heartland, and many of these voters had voted for the Democratic Action Party for years, and were angered by Anwar's arrest. We met old ladies and old men who would give us the thumbs up when we handed out leaflets.

Itu manyak teruk la.

Kesian itu Anwar.

Macam mana boleh buat macam itu?

They spoke in broken Malay, but it all meant the same thing. *This is a terrible thing. Poor Anwar. How can they do this to him?*

One morning after we arrived at the party headquarters, we found Wan Azizah agitated and upset.

He's been poisoned.

Anwar had been taken ill and rushed to hospital. He had been vomiting and complaining of severe abdominal pains. Wan Azizah was denied visitation at the hospital and we staged a noisy protest outside the hospital gates. Hundreds of people showed up. Days later, the forensics report stated that it was arsenic.

Ten thousand people took to the streets again. We were tear-gassed. The water cannons were brought out in full force. The water was laced with something that made us itch uncontrollably. Omar hurled furious insults at one FRU officer and he was taken down with a baton. I rushed to help him, and I felt a hard thwack on my head and blacked out.

When I woke up, I was inside a lockup. My head throbbed and my right arm felt numb from the way I had been lying down. The floor was damp and smelled of urine.

Hey, you okay?

It was Sumi. I nodded.

Bastards are taking their time. They've set bail but they're making us wait. How's your head?

I tried to speak, but my mouth was parched and dry. I managed a croak. Slumped against the wall, I felt an odd sense of calm. There were women I recognised. The youngest looked like she was still in secondary school. We all smiled at each other. There was nothing really to say. We sat quietly and retreated into silence.

There was a long, narrow window with bars just below the ceiling. Outside, I could hear the noise of the traffic. I imagined people bustling to and from work, having tea, fried bananas, coffee. I was hungry; my stomach churned loudly. I imagined a mound of steaming rice on a banana leaf. Minced spinach with spiced coconut, fried bitter gourd, a dollop of fiery chicken varuval, crispy popadums and a pool of chicken curry in the middle of the rice.

Fuck, I am starving.

Me too.

We both laughed. Sumi and I sat and held hands. Food. The only other thing that bound us together as Malaysians. Anger and food.

Two hours later, we were let out. I saw Omar sitting on a kerb, talking to someone and smoking a cigarette. There were about fifty of us who had been arrested and locked up overnight. There were hugs, high-fives and chatter. I ran to Omar and kissed him.

You okay? I asked.

I am now. A bit bruised. You?

Head hurts like hell, but I'll live.

The Dang Wangi police station was right in the heart of the city, and from a distance I heard the call to prayer.

Sayang, let's eat.

Fairman had come for Sumi in his car. We all got in and headed to the best curry house on Jalan Gasing, and there we ate our fill.

Marina introduced me to her world. And had a story that moved me to the core. I learned about pre-pubescent street urchins from the backwaters of Sabah and its derelict sea town shanties, headed to KL to find the only source of work they could. As sex workers. She had come from a village flanking the small town Lahad Datu, the eldest son of a fisherman and his wife, and the eldest of four siblings. Cross-dressing was not frowned upon in her family as generations of men who felt like women had existed in seafaring communities in that area. Religion and social norms were tied to a hybridity of Islam, Christianity, and Dayak and Bajau beliefs steeped in magic that came from the mountains, the rivers and the seas. For fishermen especially, the worship of the sea and its gods and goddesses was paramount. The sea brought fortune, but also great hardship and danger. Marina's mother knew that her son had female inclinations and never stopped him from tying his sarong the way women did.

When Marina—or Rashid then—was 14, the neighbour's son kicked down the flimsy zinc door of their house and sodomised her repeatedly until she passed out. Marina's father hacked the boy up with a parang and threw the pieces in the sea as a sacrifice to the gods. Fearing retribution, Marina had had no choice but to flee the village. It was the last time she saw her family. She hitchhiked to Kota Kinabalu where she begged on the streets and started sniffing glue with other runaway kids.

By night, they sold roses wrapped in cheap plastic to young lovers and tourists at the city's many waterfront cafés. When the chill of morning arrived they huddled against each other for warmth on thin mattresses in a derelict house belonging to the begging syndicate they found themselves indebted to. They scrounged for scraps from local restaurants, occasionally getting full meals from a portly Pakistani who owned a tandoori place and demanded payment in sexual favours.

Marina, who had then grown into a sleek, beautiful boy of 18, got on her knees three times a week to suck the man's fat penis in the restaurant's dank toilet, almost gagging, not from the bloated penis that threatened to suffocate her, but from the odour of rotting food that clogged the drains behind Restoran Al-Tandoor.

When Marina turned 20, she had saved enough money to buy a plane ticket to KL and headed for Chow Kit. She had been told by a *friend-of-a-friend-of-a-friend* that it was the best option for someone like herself—*you could start work at 10am and be done by 2pm if you were lucky*. Marina met many others from Sabah, young, lanky boys who were Bugis, Bajau, Suluk, Bisaya and Rungus, or a little bit of everything. The mixing of tribal bloods in Borneo had become more fluid than ever. And then there were boys who felt like girls and boys who had no other option than to end up on a street in KL selling themselves for cheap.

Marina spoke simple English—she had learnt it from reading newspapers and on the streets in KK when she tried to converse with tourists—but mostly Sabah Malay, peppered with "bah" instead of "lah", the colloquial equivalent to the peninsula slang.

Kau ni kawan baik bah.

Yes, we had become good friends.

You need to stop worrying about me, Del. My life is hard, but it's good. I can pay my bills, send some money to my mother, I have nice clothes, shoes, make-up, its okay. My life is okay.

I felt like I had to save her. From what, I wasn't sure. But in spite of all her tragedies, Marina still smiled, opened her mouth, and spread her cheeks to allow men to penetrate her in all manner of ways, to ram their sorrows away into her body.

* * *

The miscarriage made me realise the certainty of motherhood and the mystery of pregnancy. To have something grow inside of you until it becomes a person is a miracle. But in time the despondency lifted and work became once again the focus. The elections were weeks away and the campaign for Keadilan's first foray at the ballot box was going to be the beginning of a new era in Malaysian politics. There was so much work to be done, and although it was difficult not to be radical, that fervor was still something we had to capitalise on.

We met activists who were musicians and poets. We met intellectuals who were riding on idealism and political will. We met people who were just plain angry, and the flag we all carried with us was the hope that one day, justice would arrive at our doorstep like Santa Claus, bearing gifts of repentance and goodwill. Many disaffected youth were coming to volunteer for the party. At the end of each day, when they returned to the sanctuary of their underground clubs where punk music ruled loud and hard, they took with them their anger and their rhetoric.

Fairman and Sumi were busy with *The Review* and Imran was basking in his celebrity-type status, attracting scores of young female fans whenever he went out. Sumi kept me abreast of all his conquests. *Yeah, students. He's got a type now.* The Canadian journalist Murray Hiebert had been jailed for a month and the conviction drew foreign journos to the city once again. Imran was writing and entertaining non-stop.

There were times when I thought about my mother, in her smallness and her growing belly. Did she suffer from morning sickness? Was I an active foetus? Did I make her heave and groan with discomfort?

I found myself in bookstores, sliding my fingers through pregnancy books. Countless images of robust bellies, cross-section diagrams of mother and child, black and white babies in slumber. Upside-down babies. I wondered if I would ever know. I wondered if I would ever be able to push a child into the world. I wondered if Omar really and truly knew what I felt like, still.

There were times when I felt like all I wanted to do was to look after him. Be there when he woke up, serve him coffee and breakfast, say *goodbye honey, have a good day!* Buy the groceries, pay bills, clean the house and be there to welcome him when he got home from work. I wanted to be the all-Asian wife, consummate in her mediocrity and in her mind. No worries, except for what to cook and what to wear. If only life were that simple. Perhaps it really could be that simple. Perhaps. Living together was agreeing with me. With us.

I tried to make our apartment as comfortable as possible. On weekends, we scoured Malacca for antique furniture; marble-top coffee shop tables, teak dressing tables with oblong mirrors, Peranakan dressers with ornate lion's feet, pre-war medicine bottles, heavy black Dutch lamps, green glass baubles once used by fishermen on the east coast, blue and white ceramics, silver cutlery, old lace.

I wanted to make our home, yes *our home*, as comfortable as possible. Prints of old Malaysiana. Fabrics, photos, paintings. Omar filled his study with books. We had a guest room. It seemed so adult, civilised. I became a little housewife of sorts, and Omar didn't mind. In fact, I think he liked it. He cooked too from time to time, and talked about frequenting farmers' markets on weekends in London to concoct and cook his own recipes.

I had never been in love like this, and I wondered if it would have the same kind of pitfalls I experienced with the man who took my virginity one chilly winter's night in Montreal. It was after the Cowboy Junkies had played at Les Foufounes Électriques and the DJ had started playing a remixed version of Kate Bush's "The Jig of Life". Already intoxicated from wine and the sonorous, sexy voice of the lead singer Margo Timmins, I'd danced, twirling my long black skirt on the dance floor and I felt dizzy. Wild. We smoked a joint on the stairwell and everything felt loose. I wanted a man that night, and the music, the cheap wine and the sharp breeze on the walk home, had added a spring to my step.

We hummed "Sweet Jane" as we stumbled into my apartment and peeled our clothes off. José and I were in the same Philosophy class and he had asked me out that evening, on a whim. He was from Guatemala and was articulate, bold and effusive. His dark curls and black eyes were radiant that night and I took him into my bed—and into my heart—for three whole years.

Our nights were spent getting stoned, eating falafel with day-old bagels from the Jewish café downstairs, drinking copious bottles of cheap Bulgarian wine and sleeping curled in each other's arms on my futon after lusty lovemaking.

But I knew it wouldn't last and I didn't see him coming to Malaysia, so things got bitter. He became cruel and hurtful and one night slammed me against the wall, screamed *puta puta puta* and left. I saw him only once again after that, and he apologised for saying what he did and that he really did see us as professors with babies—him in Philosophy and I, English—living a suburban life with holidays in the Canadian Rockies and South America. He did love me and I suppose I loved him too. But it would never have worked, and that same sense of practicality was what made me fearful to invest in Omar.

In the lead-up to the election, we spent days putting up flags, banners and posters all over KL. No tree, lamppost or wall was spared. Swarms of banners engulfed entire neighbourhoods, some being torn down like an unwanted pestilence. Wan Azizah was running for Anwar's constituency up north in Penang, but we had to make the party as visible as we could.

One Friday night Sumi and I stood right outside Echo, a bar and club owned by a friend. After a few shots of tequila, we started shouting *Reformasi!* while waving the Keadilan flag with wide grins on our faces. Some cars starting honking in support and one driver started shouting back at us. His thick, swarthy face was red with drink.

Sodomy lah, beb.

He continued: *Anwar likes ass.*

Sumi screamed back. *Yeah, stick it up your ass too! Asshole!*

Not everyone agreed with us. There were too many old alliances at stake and many who thronged these bars and clubs were not only privileged, they were also corrupt. Not everyone wanted change.

Bangsar had become upmarket almost overnight. Establishments tried to outdo each other and KL's glitterati poured onto the streets in stilettos and high slits. Three rows of shoplots that used to teem with cat-sized rats which had been exterminated to make way for sleek convertibles driven by rich kids from Damansara Heights who waved their bling-ed hands to shrieking friends.

On a Friday night, Bangsar was the place to be seen in. It set the stage for upward mobility, for the rich kids of politicians and technocrats and social wannabes. Those who stood with the right crowd, and did the in-thing. Drugs were cut and sniffed on toilet seats, pills were passed around from fingers to tongues. It was a good time to be young, beautiful and rich. Catwalk models towered over young captains of industry, beauty queens mingled with DJs, men with skinny girls, men with boys, women with older men, women with boys. All dressed to party. All dressed for sex. Music spilled onto the streets. Techno, hip-hop. A veritable carnival. The endless clinking of glasses, the swish of hair, tight asses and perfume. This was the generation whose parents survived the war and the Japanese occupation—the foundation of the new federation, who were half this and half that, who had trussed up trousseaux and trust-funds, international school educations and western degrees.

And yet there we were waving the flag for our hero in prison, with a black eye, a bad back, his spirit still unbroken.

Perhaps we were foolish to believe that politicians could change things. That "things" could be somehow righted with gumption and sheer will, political or otherwise. That there was a right and wrong, that the notion of a certain afterlife that had been preached to us in school bore weight. That somehow, we could navigate through life with a semblance of what we needed to right the wrongs of our society—with optimism, bravado and what we believed to be truth.

Truth—that word had always beguiled me. What was the nature of truth? Was it the duty of ordinary folk to define it, was it the duty of artists to speak and write the "truth". Was everything ever that absolute? Could it ever be? Could politicians ever speak the truth? Or was it intrinsic for humans to lie?

I remember Sumi recounting the recent breakup of a volatile two-year relationship and when in a fit of despair she had said, *You can't handle the truth,* he had dragged her by her hair and gave her not only a black eye, but the most hideous purple, yellow, blue bruise all over her right arm. An archipelago of anger. So, the desire to speak of the truth itself was dangerous. Perhaps if she had kept silent, she would not have had to admit herself in the emergency ward in the dead of night, another statistic to the sad and sorry story of domestic violence.

I think that truth is possible. Still. In spite of what I knew then, and what I know now.

On 29 November, Election Day arrived. Frayed nerves and adrenaline pumped us up for days before that. We had campaigned non-stop in our constituency. Tens of thousands of leaflets distributed, endless bottles of water shared along with buttons, T-shirts, posters and flags. We were exhausted, but the most important act had yet to be done.

That morning, I drove Papa to the La Salle school where

our polling station was. He was neatly dressed for the occasion and as I stood with him in the long line of people in the queue, he observed.

Here we all are, voting for change, but can we deal with the change that we want? This country has been so corrupt for so long, how do we know that Anwar himself is not corrupt? Do you believe that Anwar is the answer to this country? What if he isn't?

I sighed.

Papa, anything is better than Mahathir.

Yes, but don't you think he has done much for Malaysia?

He needs to go.

But he won't, Del, not for a long, long time.

My father's statement depressed me. I saw a man in a wheelchair being pushed by a girl who was about ten. A young man in a white kopiah and a neatly tucked-in shirt. A lady with a rattan basket full of groceries from the market. I spied a fish wrapped in newspaper, cabbage, and a huge head of broccoli. The lady was fanning herself with a newspaper. I hoped the fish would not spoil. We were standing in the hot sun, the line snaking through the car park and into the school compound. Here we all were, ordinary Malaysians exercising our right to vote. Were we all voting for change? Did people believe in the power that we could change our futures?

Millions voted but many didn't; it was still easier to deal with ambivalence in the face of adversity, and better to stick with the status quo. Malaysians could be the worst fence-sitters. Better the devil you know than the one you don't. The new party had yet to show its ability to govern. Anwar was in jail and all some of us could do, really, was continue to fight the fight that he had started. Or really, just vote. Every single vote mattered. This much we knew.

In the end, the same thing happened, as it had for the last five elections. Justice was served like a sandbag in the trenches of WW1. Useless and unjustifiable. Mahathir was victorious, and smiled smugly from the television screen in Fairman's apartment. We had brought only alcohol and cigarettes to calm our nerves.

The newscaster on TV3 looked insipid in her headscarf and her male counterpart kept fidgeting with his sheets. The ruling coalition of the Barisan National had won two thirds of the vote. We were devastated. Then Mahathir came on and gloated like a sow in heat. His vitriol was as potent as if he were in the room.

It was over. I threw my glass at the TV screen. It shattered. *I hate him. Hate him. Hate him!*

I crumpled onto Omar's shoulder. He was wordless. Fairman and Sumi clutched each other, defeated, exhausted. A montage of clapping, cheering, camera flashes. Mahathir paraded like a hero surrounded by cronies, rogues, gutless thugs. Fairman's cat was snoring on the rug. I was moved to tears.

We carried on with a certain measure of sadness and futility. Omar was reflective and thoughtful and talked of going into a business partnership with Fairman. Their Englishness was a commonality they thrived on and it became a salve of sorts, both of them reverting to its peculiar brand of humour and intellectual tropes. And when Imran found time to join them both at the Bulldog from time to time, they were happy. Three pseudo-English lads, bonding over football, pints of beer and endless banter.

Fairman and Sumi were in a relationship too and they seemed happy. We had to find ways to be happy. There was so much uncertainty around us and we gravitated towards things and people that made us feel safe, secure. It was that simple, really.

In retrospect, I guess there was always sexual tension between those two, the sly comments, and snarky remarks they sometimes shared were some measure of affection. We felt like comrades fighting a battle that we were surely losing, but we had to keep trying.

There were nights when the four of us sat and drank whisky till dawn, speaking only of politics and change. We weren't aligned as Marxists or Socialists, and although we had all dabbled with some kind of activism as students, this was no time for armchair theorising. We had to *put your money where your mouth is,* Fairman said. We wanted a country that had checks and balances, where the judiciary functioned independently, where politicians were not imprisoned on trumped-up charges, where democracy worked and thrived. Where people were not bullied and coerced by fear. Where freedom of speech was available to all. Where the government was loved by its people.

My relationship with Omar was the cornerstone of my life. I felt understood, appreciated, loved. But, there were times when I felt that I could lose it all. After all, my father had lost my mother, just like that.

I sometimes thought of asking Omar what my father had

said to him that day. I didn't want Omar's pity, though I sometimes saw it in his eyes. My father had made the choices he did. His decision to not really feature in my life was yes, perhaps a little selfish. But that was Papa. And I had resigned myself to the fact. And ever since Omar entered my life, I was not alone any more. We had become intertwined with each other. Our rhythms merged, days and nights were seamless. It was the most important thing in my life— nothing else mattered.

By now he was running his father's company. He wasn't fulfilled by the work, but felt obliged to, since his father had given him the best education and worldly experience money could buy, and this was his way of repaying it.

Give me some time, Del, I will figure it out, what I really want to do.

He was not as secretive about finances as before, but I knew that he sometimes felt over-privileged and unworthy of his family's wealth. He was generous and made sure that all our bills were paid, he bought groceries, took me out to dinner from time to time. I felt for the first time in my life that I really and truly had a man who was capable, someone who had my back, someone I could trust with my life.

I suppose I'd always felt guilt about José. I knew that I had treated him unfairly and discarded him when my time in Montreal was up. It was as I'd said, "I don't love you anymore, can you go away now?" I didn't think that I was inadvertently cruel. Perhaps I *had* used him for companionship and sex. Yes, I did love him, but that love felt like a pond. This, with Omar, was as vast and unknowable like the deepest of ocean trenches. I imagined this was the kind of love my father had for my mother. The kind of love that came only once in a lifetime.

I thought of Omar day and night, and the scent of him filled my pores, infiltrating the hours I spent away from him. I had never wanted the nearness of another human being as much as I wanted his. If I closed my eyes I could hear his sighs when I took him in my mouth, I could hear the way he moaned when he was inside me, his quick cry of release; I could see the iridescence of his eyes when he was aroused, the way he pushed his hair back with his fingers; I could see the way his hands grasped the steering wheel and how the hairs lay, the way his lips bent to the right when he smiled, his laugh when we joked together, the way he trailed his fingers on my skin. I suppose this was the kind of love that could really and truly exist. A great love.

Sumi and Fairman were also in the process of defining their relationship. From the frivolous, *we're just fucking* to *we're living together, kinda*, to *we're going on holiday to Bali*, theirs was also a pairing that had simply become stronger.

I love him, Del, I really do, I mean he's nerdy sometimes and drinks way too much tea, but he's a really good man, and he's kind and sensitive and considerate. He turns me on in a sexy, weird way. We're good for each other, we really are. He makes me laugh, Del, like an idiot. I laugh till I'm silly. That's never happened before. I think this is it, this is the man I am going to be with for the rest of my life.

Rest of my life. The finality of it all. The possibilities that now loomed between a man and a woman. Marriage. Children. A house. Happily ever after. *The end.*

So in the midst of the same draconian mandate by a

Prime Minister still hated by many, the four of us shared an awareness that we were on the threshold of new lives, lives that we would share with someone other than ourselves. The path to adulthood was more impending and palpable than ever, and it seemed to be paved with roses.

When I was a child we had a maid called Bernadette. She had lived with us from the time I was born, and was indispensible to our household. I imagine my mother had practically handed me over to Bernadette as soon as her confinement was over because all I remember of my early childhood was this matronly Indian woman who perpetually smelled of turmeric and coconut oil. She had a room next to the kitchen with an altar that had a picture of Mother Mary and that of a handsome man in robes with a bleeding heart that glowed. Yes, I used to think that Jesus was very handsome. When she was not cooking or sweeping or ironing, Bernadette sat in front of the altar, rosary in hand, praying. As a little girl, whenever Mother and Papa were out, I would go to her room, lie on the bed sucking my milk bottle in cotton knickers and a singlet, then reading or playing with toys. I remember the ceiling with water marks, a cloud of spidery mould in one corner, Bernadette's thin pile of clothes on the shelf, a red plastic alarm clock, old copies of "the Catholic newspapers" on her desk along with an orange Cuticura can of talcum powder, a brown glass bottle of coconut oil and a blue plastic comb.

Bernadette was an orphan and had worked with one

other family before ours. She never finished secondary school and could only read and write basic English. She was very devout and went to church as often as she could, sometimes dragging me along when there was no one else at home. She came to us when she was in her mid 20s and stayed with us until Mother died. She made creamy curries with fish and crab, mutton varuval, perfect round chappatis, chai with cow's milk. She took the bus from Jalan Gasing to the market and back every day for almost 14 years. One day as she was getting off the bus, a motorcycle hit her and broke her leg in three places, and she had to be hospitalised for a month at Assunta Hospital.

I was six years old at the time and we found another maid from the same orphanage. Her name was Girly. She was 19 and had boyish hair. One night, when Mother and Papa went out, Girly took me into her room. First she took off my pyjamas, then she asked me to lie down with her on the bed. Then she guided my fingers to her breasts, and asked me to kiss the dark brown nipples. I did as I was told and Girly moaned and groaned beside me, rubbing her body against mine. Suddenly, we heard the car drive into the porch and Girly panicked. I heard Papa's voice as he walked down the stairs into the kitchen.

Del, Del, we're home. Where are you?

Girly squeezed me under the bed, her hand around my mouth. I remember the cold floor. The door opened and I saw Papa's feet from under the bed.

Del, Del. Where are you?

I sensed the worry in his voice but I could not make a sound. He turned, walked out and closed the door. I scrambled out from under the bed, and then realised that my panties were wet. Girly put my pyjamas back on and carried me up the stairs.

Sir, sorry sir. I took Del for a walk in the garden. We were sitting near the pool. Sorry, sir. Very sorry, sir.

Don't sit outside at night, Girly. There are snakes in the garden, you know. Mosquitoes too. Don't do it again.

Yes sir, very sorry, sir.

Papa carried me to my bed and read me a bedtime story. I looked up at my wall and saw the painting of Humpty Dumpty and thought of how all the king's horses and all the king's men who were trying to put him together again.

I think what mattered more than anything seemed to be what was right in front of me. It was so obvious now, the anticipation of being in the relationship gave me a sense of security that I had not felt since my mother died.

I had also started going to the drop-in centre in Chow Kit, the one which Marina and other sex workers frequented. Once a week, I taught nine women and transsexuals whose ages ranged from 15 to 55, who hailed from all parts of the country. All had come from extreme poverty and had fled their small towns and villages and, in most cases, systemic and prolonged sexual abuse. It was grim work but I felt that by empowering these women with the rudiments of basic English, they could at least be more pro-active with their clients.

Please use a condom.

I want safe sex.

Please do not hit me.

Please be gentle with me.

Many clients came from the working class—labourers from Bangladesh and Indonesia, to the occasional backpacker—so these women and men were basically spreading their legs for just tens of ringgit. A blowjob was cheaper, of course, and many clients refused to wear condoms, rendering the workers extremely vulnerable to sexually transmitted diseases and HIV. The centre had started distributing free condoms after a government initiative to prevent the spread of HIV among sex workers, but in reality it had little effect.

Most days I had all nine students. They would show up chattering and settling at the desks that were set in a semicircle. I would ask them to tell me about their week and many would chirp in unison.

Sama aje.

The same.

Kerja, cari makan.

Work. Put food on the table.

And they would giggle and laugh, in the most polite of ways. Even the big burly transwoman, Honey, who towered over all of us in the heels that she always wore, even at ten in the morning.

They all had families to support, and some had children. Minah had a son, aged 10, who always glared at me with disdain. He was a scrawny little thing, with scabies all over his arms and face, who refused to learn to read or write, but who was an expert when it came to pimping for his mother. He was the one who approached potential clients, making eye contact with them and then deftly negotiating a price. There were times when I really thought that he saw me as a threat.

Then there was Jaya, who had fled from an oil-palm estate in the heart of Perak whilst she was six months pregnant with her father's child. Nini was the centre's darling—she was born with cerebral palsy, but she was happy and content in her crib surrounded by toys.

One day I showed up to class and found Jaya in tears with a black eye and bruises on the right side of her face.

What happened?

He slap me.

Why?

Because I ask him wear condom. He don't want. Then he pull my hair and kick my stomach.

I just sat and hugged her, while she sobbed loudly. Nini sat and smiled in her crib.

Then I go back and wash with Clorox because he don't want to wear the condom.

What? You wash what with Clorox?

She looked at me with eyes that told of only pain and heartbreak and they pointed downwards. So it was true. I had heard of stories of bleach and vaginas and how the girls used it to clean their insides. I could only imagine the horror of what it did to the sensitive folds of flesh, of how it tore up the mucous membranes. And then they had to continue working, with or without condoms. That night, as I lay with Omar, I thought of a pink, bloodied vagina and dreamt of a giant river of pestilence and pus.

MARINA DECIDED TO go across the road to get some food. It was a Saturday night and the streets were surprisingly quiet. Marina put on a pair of shorts and a faded pink T-shirt, and slipped on a pair of plastic sandals.

The night air was cool. The weather lately had been hot, dry. Many of the girls were ill with the flu and cough. Many smoked too much but the arid heat swallowed them up in the stifling streets, creating a cocoon of confined illness. Many were also addicted to heroin. Some nights, you'd see a two or three of them shooting up in the alleyways, squatting in the dark, their presence betrayed only by the intermittent flares of cigarette lighters. Marina had never tried heroin and didn't intend to.

The coffee shop below her apartment was empty, except for a table of men drinking beer and smoking. One of them leered at her when she walked past.

She could see the glow of light from the pasar malam, the night bazaar selling clothes in five-ringgit bundles, fake designer watches, shoes, leather jackets and the herbal preparations popular with men who believed in their power to make erections last. Leech oil, sea cucumber potions, and tinctures made from anything else in nature that resembled a penis. She had a client who was insistent on rubbing on such oils during sex. It was a hindrance to putting on a condom as the experience often resulted in an oily, sticky black mess. But the erection always lasted, and the client would eventually have to pay for two extra hours.

She loved nights like this. The quiet streets gave her time to contemplate, think about things. She passed an alleyway and saw her friend Nita decked out in an all-black number.

"*Cantiknya baju.*"

Nita smiled and blew a kiss, pushing out her new breasts.

"Tapi so slow tonight lah."

Marina waved back and walked on. Her long hair blew across her face as she stood on the traffic intersection. The shop across the road served the best nasi kandar in town—rice with a selection of meat curries, a speciality from northern Malaysia. Marina had to watch her weight, as did all the others. She often had fruit for dinner, two cups of instant coffee mix for breakfast, and takeaway noodles or a roti with some dhal and curry for lunch. So she felt that she deserved a full meal that night, a whole plate of rice with hearty beef in thick brown sauce, curried crab, dollops of cabbage in turmeric and mustard seed and a crunchy green chilli.

Nasi Kandar Muhammad Yasin had been around for decades and was open 24 hours. People came from all over the city to eat there and people who sat at the tables were from all classes of KL society.

There were three others in front of her. A lady with two children, one fussing while the other, a pudgy boy with round spectacles, kept adding dishes to his already heaped plate. The boy then carried the precious plate with two hands to the table where his sullen mother and fretting sister sat. As Marina took her plate into the air-conditioned section of the restaurant, she spotted two policemen seated in a corner. She didn't like cops and she avoided their gaze. They were sipping tea and the one whose back faced her turned around and looked at her. Marina headed towards an empty table close to the washroom. She sat facing the wall and started tucking in.

The beef was slightly chewy but tasty and she licked the

dark sauce from her fingers. She picked up half a crab, put it in her mouth and lightly squeezed the shell and its contents with her teeth. The crab flesh spewed out. It was fresh, sweet and the spices were in perfect combination. She swallowed, almost wriggling with delight. With her hand she mixed rice with vegetables and curry into a little ball and scooped it into her mouth. She then cracked the crab legs with her teeth and slowly sucked the flesh out. Every bite was savoured and relished. When she had finally scooped up every grain of rice with the curry, the plate was spotless, save for the pile of crab shells. Marina got up and went to the sink to wash her hands and mouth. In the mirror, she could see that her mouth was stained red from the curry and she looked like she had just been kissed.

Marina paid and left. It was a hefty RM22.90 for the meal. Half an hour's work, she told herself, but it was worth every morsel. She decided to go for a walk to help digest her dinner.

Round the corner, she saw a homeless woman stake her space in front of the Honda showroom. She knew that the elderly Chinese woman barely spoke and only grunted. She sat propped up by a pillow on layers of brown cardboard, and was buried in her dinner, a free meal handed out by charities every Saturday night. She looked up and smiled at Marina and nodded, her teeth covered in rice. Marina smiled and nodded back.

Before her rose the Twin Towers, glittering in the night, looking to her like twin rockets about to take off. Marina leaned against a chain-link fence next to an empty parking lot, taking in the awesome view. Then she heard footsteps and in the next instant, felt the breath on the back of her neck. It reeked of tea and cigarettes. She turned abruptly. It was one of the policemen she had seen in the restaurant, so close to her that his thick polyester trousers rubbed against her thighs. From the corner of her eye, she spotted the other one, hanging back at a small distance.

"*Buat apa sini?*" he snarled softly. "*Pelacur pondan.*"

He grabbed her hand and pinned it against her back as his other hand slammed into her mouth. Then, pulling her by the hair, he dragged her to the car parked by a tree. There, he grabbed her breasts and squeezed them, hard. She winced in agony. The hormone pills had made her breasts sore and tender. She looked wildly round for the other policeman, caught his eye, and knew he would do nothing to stop his mate. A momentary relief as her assailant let go of her breasts to pull his pants down, but in the next instant, she found her face in front of his groin, her head caught in his vice-like grip. Resistance was impossible. She took his penis in her mouth and sucked him off, gagging when his come spurted into her throat.

They left her there, vomiting out the nasi kandar that had given her so much pleasure just a few minutes ago. Marina stood up, wiped her mouth with her hand and leaned against the tree to steady herself. Only then did she become aware of the furious tears that salted her mouth.

THE NEW MILLENNIUM was approaching. As the Y2K bug sparked a global panic, we were told to "party like it's 1999" because the digital repercussions could spell the end of civilisation as we knew it. Banks would collapse, personal accounts would fade into oblivion, airports, airplanes, hospitals would simply stop functioning, all because computers would not be able to distinguish 2000 from 1900. People on life support would die. Planes would crash into each other. Refrigerators would stop working. Digital watches would stop. Purchases of upgrades went into overdrive, everyone was backing everything up and overnight computer techs were born. You had to have records for proof of everything. Proof of your bank balance, your dental records, your car loan. Your existence. Documents were printed and kept in safes. Supermarkets started running out of food, water, batteries; cars queued up for extra gallons of petrol, collected in containers and then stored in the corners of living rooms, kitchens.

The seat of the Malaysian government had moved to Putrajaya—or "prince-city-success"—named after our first Prime Minister, Tunku Abdul Rahman Putra. A city erected on the swamps south of KL in Sepang and the tracts of land owned by the indigenous people called the Temuan. Mahathir had a vision of creating a Multimedia Super Corridor, or the MSC, linking Putrajaya, Cyberjaya and the gleaming new KLIA airport into a superhighway of information, high-speed Internet and a glowing version of a futuristic era.

New companies scrambled for tax breaks. Getting MSC status meant that you had access to billions of ringgit of government funds; you could start a music studio, a production house, a film company, a radio station, a telecommunications network, a TV station. Punters were raking it in, there was money to be made, there were infinite possibilities. If it had to do with technology, anything was possible. The braver and bolder you were, the better. New universities sprouted on vast, tree-less campuses. There were degrees in gaming, special effects, morphing, animation, CGI. Overseas expertise was lured in to teach. There was talk of Hollywood sound stages. There was talk of George Lucas, Steven Spielberg, the Weinstein brothers. We were leap-frogging into the future.

Putrajaya was built around an artificial lake, gargantuan buildings lined wide boulevards. Tens of thousands of civil servants and their multiple children poured into new apartment blocks. Government offices were divided into "presints" of brazen high-rises. The Ministry of this and that. At 5.15pm sharp, there would be a flood of veiled, chattering women and sullen-looking men going home in brand new Protons and Peroduas, settling after dinner in front of Astro, watching CNN or HBO. It was fabricated, glittering, garish. The Prime Minister's office faced a boulevard, with gilded Mughal-inspired domes. We wanted to look classy, we wanted to create new architecture, each building had a different design. It ended up looking schizophrenic. Two hippos were shipped in from Africa for the brand new wetlands, along with other animals. There were flamingos, herons, otters, exotic ducks. There were artificial lakes for boats, wakeboarding. There were magnificent steel bridges, curly lamp posts studded the pavements every ten metres, there were parks, schools, hospitals. There were parts that looked sleek, others looked bleak. There were highways that curved over flowers and concrete, there was a souq, there was a mosque of pink Italian marble. It was the new capital.

Fairman had decided to throw a New Year's Eve party at his parents' house, a 70s style bungalow at the foot of Kenny Hills. It had verandas designed for languid afternoons, white walls, high ceilings, antique fans and old "Made in England" bathroom fixtures. Almost a hundred people had been invited, and cars wound gracefully all the way down the bottom of the hill. Tall meranti trees towered at the back, like guardians of a suburban forest. A symphony of cicadas conspired against the four-piece jazz quartet. Fairman's parents stood at the entrance, greeting the guests as they arrived. It was a fairly mixed crowd, with a smattering of artists and activist types, high society folk who graced the pages on the Malaysian Tatler, and dozens of screaming children running away from long-suffering maids.

I suddenly felt very shy, Omar and I had made an effort to dress up. After all it was the millennium, the dawning of a new age, a new century, a new time. I was wearing the only designer dress I had, a green silk halterneck from Donna Karan, which I had bought for Karin's wedding.

You look gorgeous, darling, very fuckable.

I looked at him, feigning shock. He simply raised his eyebrow.

You know you are.

We headed towards Sumi, who looked foxy in a scarlet dress with a high slit, and Fairman, very formal in a crisp white shirt and dinner jacket.

Quite a party here, Fairman!

Let's just hope the electricity doesn't go out.

We have another generator, just in case, my dad you know, doesn't want to leave things to chance.

And as if on cue, Mr Fairman walked over to us and said,

Well, well, if it isn't the fabulous four! Eat, drink. The night is ours!

The fabulous four, indeed. We looked at each other and grinned. Omar grabbed my waist.

Darling, I have never been this happy. I want you to know that. Here, now like this. I want you to know.

I did know. How could I not? I looked at him, there, like that. His hair curling slightly in the humid night, his eyes brimming with love. I kissed him gently on the lips.

Delonix Regia, will you marry me?

I choked. Then gave my answer with a flurry of kisses on his face, and my cries of joy were drowned out by the clapping from the small crowd who had gathered around us.

A toast! A toast!

Yes, Omar. Yes!

He twirled me around on the grass, then, the most tender of kisses. We laughed like silly children, delighting in newfound secrets. Everybody raised their glasses, and as I looked up to the sky, I saw a crescent moon with a sprinkling of stars. Midnight came and went and the world did not end.

The night Marina told me she had been raped, we were in the mamak coffee shop, the one we first came to not so long ago. We had tried to make it a point to meet there from time to time as we not only enjoyed each other's company, but I had begun to trust her more and more. It was an unusual friendship. I felt I could be so open with her, that she would not judge me and that she too would not be judged.

Her long hair had been straightened and dyed a honey blonde with highlights. Her make-up was simple and elegant, and she wore a blue blouse with buttons and a short denim skirt. The waiters in the coffee shop straightened their backs a little when she sauntered in. A wolf whistle from one corner. Marina ordered a ginger tea and lit up a cigarette; she sat down with the cigarette poised in one hand. She looked absolutely gorgeous.

I love your hair. It's beautiful.

Kan? I love it too. My new style. Simple and chic!

Her hands were expressive, her nails sharp and manicured. She sucked hard on the cigarette.

How are you? Work okay? I asked.

Same regulars. Cukup. And you?

I sighed and said, *Omar is thinking of starting another business, and by the way…*

Marina nodded and lowered her head.

I stopped mid-sentence, sensing that Marina had something to say.

I must tell you something. That's why I wanted to see you.

Is something wrong? Are you sick? Hurt? What?

A loud clang made us jump. One of the cooks had dropped a big pot and a loud stream of expletives in Tamil ensued. The coffee shop owner was livid but calmed down soon after. The guilty cook slunk into the back and disappeared. Marina took a deep breath and lit up another cigarette.

So the other night I went out for dinner. After that I went for a walk, you know, down that nasi kandar place and I just walked for about five minutes. Then these two policemen came and started bothering me. One of them was asking me questions like buat apa sini? Called me names. The other one was quiet. Actually they were in the same restaurant and they followed me.

She paused to take a sip of tea. I had a bad feeling about what she was about to say.

So the one who was bothering me, you can imagine what happened next.

Did he rape you? I whispered.

She nodded.

You know these fucking assholes, they do it all the time. Last week, someone else kena... And they arrest us and put us in jail! I am so tired of these bloody police. So tired of what they do to us! They treat us like animals. They think we're stupid? That we're not going to do anything?

She stabbed her cigarette violently into the ashtray, and then looked straight into my eyes.

My whole life I am dealing with men who rape me. I am fed up. Enough. Del, I want a lawyer. Can you help me? Do you know anyone?

That night I wrote a letter to my dead child and burnt it. I watched the paper turn into black flakes which then fluttered and disappeared into the night.

To my unborn child—
from the golden light
that you came
to which you must now
return

until you and i
seed of your seed
fruit of my womb
energy-egg into flesh
our love union

until then
child of light
you are free to roam
the realms of nameless souls
and child spirits

until we meet again
and part no more.

THREE

CROUCHING TIGER, HIDDEN DRAGON

OMAR RANG THE doorbell again. He glanced at his watch. It had been ten minutes since the first ring and he'd told himself he would wait fifteen minutes at the most. He had rung the doorbell at three-minute intervals and so, this was going to be the last effort. His neck was starting to itch and he was desperate for the bathroom. Seconds later he heard a shuffling and the door slowly opened. Del's father emerged. His face brightened when he saw Omar.

"Good morning, sir," Omar said.

"Ah, sorry, I was in the shower."

Del's father unlocked the door. Omar slid his shoes off and stepped into the house. A whiff of aftershave lingered in the doorway like a second guest. It was Old Spice, the same aftershave his father used. Del's father closed the door and turned the lock. Omar offered him the cardboard box in his hand.

"Ah, and what's this?"

Omar cleared his throat quietly. "Del said you like egg custard tarts."

"I do indeed. The one near Tong Woh?"

Omar nodded.

"I shall enjoy this very much." Del's father chuckled in delight as he walked down the hallway. Omar followed him, inhaling the scent of the familiar aftershave, and was suddenly assailed by the image of his father, freshly showered and shaved, in a singlet and sarong too.

The morning light streamed into the hallway from the open ventilation slats in the wall. Del's father strode through the light and the dust particles. He started humming.

The door to the study was slightly open and the sound of classical music greeted them. Violins, then the gentle seduction of a tinkling piano. The room was filled with sunlight from the open windows. It felt alive. The music came from a gramophone, on a small side table beside a pile of books. Del's father bent over it and lifted the gramophone arm. The music stopped, the needle startled into a scratch and the room sank into silence.

"Do sit, please."

"Thank you, sir."

Del's father walked to the table, placed the box of egg tarts on the top of some books, settled into his chair and picked up his pipe.

Omar sat down. He felt nervous, unsure of what exactly to say. He had rehearsed possibilities in his mind and on the drive over, had thought—"Keep it simple. Just keep it simple." But now that he was facing Del's father, the words he had so precisely rehearsed fled from him.

Omar felt that he needed to focus on something, and so he stared at the now-familiar wedding portrait. He found a spot—Del's father's necktie—and fixed his eyes on the small black triangle. Del's father had started puffing on his pipe and a cloud of vanilla-scented smoke descended slowly upon them. A soft breeze blew in through the windows. Outside, there was a rustle of leaves, and a bird chirped loudly.

It would be the black bird, the one with the yellow beak. Like the ones that used to wake him up in the mornings. Omar remembered the tall palm tree that stood outside his bedroom window of his childhood home. When the tree had ripe red fruit, there would be scores of those birds pecking at the fruit. Chattering, yes. Endless chattering. The memory of the birds reassured him somehow.

"Sir, I've asked Del to marry me," he started, then slowed down to say, "and she has agreed."

Del's father took another puff of his pipe and turned to look at the window.

"Beautiful day. The rain helped."

"Yes, it's not so humid…" Omar replied quickly.

"How will you live?"

"Sir?" The question rattled him.

"How will you live?" Del's father asked slowly. His voice was gentle but firm.

"I plan to start a business, to go into partnership with Roslan Fairman. I believe you know his father, sir?" Omar asked.

"Bill Fairman?" Del's father asked, cocking an eyebrow.

"Yes, sir," Omar replied.

"Bill's a shark. You should know that. Not to say that his son is the same." Del's father leaned back into his leather chair. It squeaked.

A sudden gust of wind slammed a wooden shutter in the study against the window frame. Omar jumped slightly in his seat. He became conscious again of his bladder, now uncomfortably full.

Del's father let out a little laugh.

"I apologise for that. It's not for me to judge. Bill was a good lawyer—once."

Omar nodded. "Fairman, or Roslan, rather, and Del are close associates as you know, and I have come to think that he and I could go into business together. You see, I intend to use our skills, combined, to form a company that specialises in the construction of roads, expressways, in Malaysia and beyond. There's a lot of possibilities in Africa—Sudan for example." Omar paused and continued, "I love your daughter, sir, and I want to be able to provide for her in the best way possible."

"And you think this kind of business would be the way to go?" Del's father shot back.

Omar felt a sudden surge of anger. He was being questioned by a man who had ceased to be anything. A man who had stopped being a father. A man who had given up his right to ask him how he was going to live—and provide—for himself and his future wife.

"Sir, I will do whatever it takes to make this marriage work."

Another gust of wind surged into the room. Papers flew off the desk and Omar stood up to retrieve them but Del's father sat unperturbed and raised his hand to stop Omar.

"This country is rotten to the core. You must know this."

Omar sat down and nodded.

"Right and wrong sometimes look like the same thing. And you might only realise which is which when it is too late."

Del's father fixed his eyes on Omar. He continued. "I have to trust you. Del loves you. I can see that."

Omar repeated, "I love her deeply, sir."

Del's father smiled and said, "Then that's all, really. That is all there is to it. Just love her."

That was all Omar needed to hear. He had to leave that instant. He stood up and said brusquely.

"Thank you for your time, sir. We will keep you informed about dates…for the wedding,"

Del's father nodded and continued puffing on his pipe. He had swivelled the chair to face the window and seemed lost in thought.

"I will let myself out, sir, please don't get up."

Del's father said quietly, "She's all yours now. She is."

"Thank you, sir."

Omar walked, then ran down the hallway, closed the front door, bolted the squeaky gate, got into the car, slammed the accelerator and drove like a fiend to the nearest petrol station where in a urinal that stank of pink mothballs and ammonia, he released his bladder with a shudder and a loud sigh.

"Right, glad that's done," he muttered.

Outside, ominous-looking clouds had started to gather, and soon it began to drizzle.

So, I HAD to convert. To Islam. I dreaded it.

The inevitable fact was that I had to convert into Islam and if I didn't, we couldn't get married. Omar was not religious, neither were his parents. But in order for the marriage to be legal, I had to do it.

Imran volunteered to accompany me to the Islamic Department of Kuala Lumpur as a male witness, or "wali". There, he had to state that *yes, I am a Muslim*. But when he was asked to recite the Shahadah he shook his head, shrugged and was glared at fiercely by the lady in the bright yellow tudung at the counter.

Kenapa tak tahu? Betul ke dia ni orang Islam? She was merciless.

Yes, he is Muslim, but he has lived abroad for a long time. His Arabic is rusty, I replied.

She raised her eyebrows and looked as if she was ready to flay him. She scrutinised his glasses, his worn tweed jacket, his shoes and his pale skin. She shrieked loudly: *Maybe he should recite the Shahadah again so that Allah will once again be reminded of who this man is.*

Imran had turned a bright red and his forehead started to glisten with sweat, so I quickly read the Shahadah, which was on a piece of paper she pushed into my hand. I adjusted my headscarf, feeling self-conscious; it wasn't a tudung like hers, but a light silk shawl I'd simply wrapped around my head. I read it silently a few times and when I was ready, took a deep breath.

Ashadu Allah Ilaha Illalah, Muhammad Ar Rasullullah.

I said it twice. It sounded slightly better the second time.

There is no God but Allah and Muhammad is his Prophet.

There it was. My fate had changed. I was no longer

a heathen, I was cleansed of all my sins and I would go to heaven when I die.

There was a stack of forms that had to be filled in. I needed dates, specifics of the wedding, or nikah. Omar and I had decided on a Muslim name, Leila, which meant "night". I started filling out the forms. The lady in the tudung gave me a laminated card, which stated "Islam, Nur Leila binti Abdullah @ Delonix Regia". She smiled as if to say, *You're one of us now.*

The forms needed Omar's signature so I said that I would bring them all back in a few days. I could see that Imran was becoming more and more agitated and the lady in the tudung was simply not letting up. She kept glaring at him and poor Imran looked like he just wanted to disappear into the flowery upholstery that covered the chair he was sitting on.

We left and as we walked out towards the parking lot, Imran finally burst.

Fucking cunt. Did you see the way she looked at me? Like I was some kind of idiot. Bloody hell, who the fuck does she think she is? Some low-life clerk in some fucked up government institution. This is it, Del! I am never getting married in this country. So what if I can't pronounce a bunch of words in Arabic, there is no need to make me feel like an infidel! Cunt... Fucking cunt! I hope her husband gives her the clap. I wouldn't fuck her if she was the last woman on this fucking planet... Fuck off!

He stormed around the parking lot, smoked two cigarettes, swore some more until he was calm. We drove in silence until another outburst.

I'm sorry, Del, I just think this is bloody ridiculous. I don't understand why they make it so hard for two people to get married. It's fucked up! It's downright intimidation. What kind of country is this? It's barbaric! Fucked up!

I kept silent. The kind of dread I felt was not unreasonable. I was now a Muslim. Forced to convert, like so many others. Forced to embrace a religion I did not want.

Hey, you okay? I'm sorry, Del. Sorry for this. Omar's a good guy but I am just sorry you have to go through this shit.

It was far from over. I had to take a one-month class on the tenets of Islam, learn how to pray, learn how to say the Al Fatihah and then sit for a test. And if I passed, we had to attend marriage camp over two weekends.

I felt like crying. This was the last thing I ever thought I would do. I didn't want a new name, I didn't want to become a Muslim. Imran leaned over and grabbed my hand. *Hey, just do it, you know. Just do what they ask you to do. Don't question anything, okay? It'll be over soon enough...* I nodded and looked out the window. I told myself that it was worth it. That Omar was worth it. That it was the only way we could be together, exist as husband and wife in the eyes of the law.

Traffic was thick. We inched our way past the National Museum and then all the way down Jalan Bangsar. It was almost lunchtime on a Friday and people were making their way to the mosques for prayers. It was a humid, sticky afternoon. Imran pulled hard on his cigarette. *Damn, I should have taken the shortcut...now we're stuck in traffic.* I took a drag of my cigarette and felt a small wave of nausea come over me.

WHAT DO YOU mean, it's pointless? What kind of legal advice is that?

Sumi, Marina and I were seated in the office of the drop-in centre in Chow Kit. Marina pulled herself off the couch next to me, stood tall in her heels and lit a cigarette. Kak Su—or Big Sister Su—was seated at a table piled with files. She lit up a cigarette too.

Sumi sighed and repeated what she had said earlier. *Making a police report when it was a cop who raped you is not going to work. You didn't struggle, there was no force. You basically did what he wanted you to do.*

Marina was livid. *But he raped me! Forced me to suck his cock! What could I do?* She wrung her hands in frustration.

Sumi nodded. *Yes, I understand, but I am also trying to make you realise that...*

That what? Isn't oral sex a crime here? Look at what happened to Anwar! He is in jail supposedly for this, right?

Sumi said, *Sodomy, it's for sodomy.*

Same thing isn't it? Marina shot back. *Rape is rape!*

I was trying very hard to understand both points of view and completely empathised with Marina, but the fact of the matter was that she did not have the name of her rapist. Both cops had taken off their badges, they were off-duty and could have been from any of the police stations in KL. There was no case. Sumi was right. Marina had no case.

If you go to report this, you are going to be marked. Cops will mark you, and because you work on the streets, because you are a trans sex worker, they can arrest you under Section 28 for dressing as a woman. However, if this happened, then you would have a case.

What? Marina looked utterly confused. *What do you mean?*

Kak Su was shaking her head and took a long drag of her cigarette. *So many cases dah macam ni. The trans community has no rights, we have no rights at all. We are not human beings to them.*

Marina continued and waved her right hand. *Wait! So you mean, if I am arrested as a man for dressing as a woman, I can fight?*

Sumi reiterated: *Only if they rape you again. In the lock-up, or whatever. Then you can make a case against the police. Police brutality.*

Kak Su continued. *Some more, because we are Muslim, Section 28 is under Syariah Law, not Civil Law, and that is even more complicated.*

I kept quiet. I could almost see the wheels turning in Marina's mind. She had started pacing quickly, almost tripping on a plastic bag of more files on the floor.

So now you're saying that I shouldn't make a police report. But if I am arrested for cross-dressing, then at least I am on record and if I am in the lock-up and if I am raped again… then I can do something?

Sumi said quietly. *Yup.*

Okay, then. Okay. Marina picked up her handbag, bent down and stubbed out her cigarette in the pink metal ashtray, which was already full of butts. *Have to work, bye! And thanks for the info.* She looked at Sumi and me, forced a smile and walked out of the office.

Sumi and I looked at each other. Kak Su shook her head and said, *Ala, give her time. She will realise after a while that there is no point. As long as she can work, she will realise that it's better than being in the lock-up. It's the most horrible place. Full of bed bugs, the floor is always wet, you sleep on cardboard.* Kak Su shuddered. *No food. No water. Been in and out so many times. Like that lah. What to do?*

His name was Pete.

I had been in Montreal for just over three months and was starting to feel more settled. I was staying at the houses of residence in a room, cramped and narrow. I shared it with a girl with big blonde hair and close-set blue eyes who weighed everything she ate on a food scale. She was a Physical Education major and was obsessed with everything that went into her mouth. Lynn, short for Marcheline, wore frosted lipstick, only pink and blue tracksuits, and listened to the Canadian rock band Rush. She was from a village in northern Quebec and spoke French and fluent English, which was apparently unusual for some Quebecois.

My parents made sure that all of us spoke English because we're against any kind of referendum. We want to be part of Canada, she said with pride.

Her breakfast was peanut butter on a rice cracker. Lunch was salad with chicken breast. She snacked on bran muffins and lite cola and had pasta for dinner, alternating between cream and tomato sauces. *I love cheese, but it has soo much fat!* She never varied her meals and never changed the way she dressed.

Pete was in my Philosophy class. He was from Manitoba, with the lightest eyelashes I'd ever seen. I think he found me intriguing. My name, where I came from, the way I dressed—all fascinated him. I felt his eyes on me all the way from the back of the class right from the first day and it took him a week before he talked to me.

Delonix. What kinda name is that?

It's Latin.

Delonix. Delonix. Put ma pants in a twist. Twist it. Come on, come on, twist it.

I walked away. He ran after me.

Hey, I was just teasing, you know. Sorry.

It's not funny.

Yeah, I know. Let's hang out sometime, okay?

Whatever.

I shrugged and walked away. I could feel his eyes on the small of my back. I didn't like him, but I was a little flattered that he had talked to me. Books were my main preoccupation and hours were spent in the library or the many bookshops around the city. Sitting in cafés, reading and drinking coffee, nibbling on fresh buttery croissants, daydreaming, writing, studying. That was what I did most days after classes. And then I'd collapse on the narrow bed and sleep hugging my pillow hoping to squeeze out my homesickness, dreaming of rainforests and snakes, longing for rain.

One weekend we had a frat party in the halls. Pete lived in the halls of residence on the other side of the campus and it was our turn to host the boys. Lynn had gone back to her village for the weekend. It was my first hall party and I had no idea what to expect. The posters said that it was a toga party so most people showed up draped in their bedsheets. There were kegs of beer, bottles of vodka, tequila and gin, and stacks of

Old Dutch potato chips in all flavours. Hip-hop was blaring from someone's CD player. The common room was full of people in various states of undress, making out.

Drinking was serious business in college, so when things got going, the guys got to it like soldiers on a dawn raid. A hose would be shoved into a willing mouth and then the whoops and cheers started. I sipped some white wine and stared at the mayhem unfolding in front of me. One by one, the guys started projectile-vomiting beer and half-digested chips. It was disgusting. I decided that I'd seen enough and turned to go back to my room down the hall.

Hey Del, where ya goin?

Pete's toga had come undone. He had tucked the fabric into his pants and he struck a comical pose. I giggled. He took a gulp of beer and came right up to me.

His eyes were a light blue, and I could see yellow flecks.

Wanna make out?

I could smell the beer on his breath. He didn't seem that drunk. I felt awkward.

Come on, Del, Del. It'd be swell.

He took my hand, kissed it gently and led me with a flourish to the end of the hallway. I opened my room door and thought in a panic. Were we going to have sex? I did not have condoms. Did he? What would we do if it came to that?

He kissed me gently, probing my mouth with his tongue. He tasted sweet. His chest was pressed into mine, it felt warm. I felt a strange thrill in my groin as his hands went up and down my back and then slowly into my bra. He tickled my nipples with his fingers, then guided me to the bed and pressed himself on top of me. His mouth was everywhere, my nose, eyes, ears, neck. Everything was wet. He lifted up my T-shirt and eased my bra off. His mouth was on my right nipple, then my left, then his hands went for my jeans. I turned my head and said, no. *No, Pete. No.*

Okay, Del. Sure.

His mouth was on mine again, and I felt him move over me. I could feel his erection, hard against my thigh. Then, it was on my chest. He swooped over me and it was in my mouth. His penis in my mouth. His thighs pinned my face down. I could not move. Couldn't breathe. Two. Three. Four. On the fifth thrust, he filled my mouth with his come. In shock I swallowed it all, turning my head to one side, some of the bitter saltiness dribbling out.

He slowly slid next to me and hugged me, kissed me on the cheek, muttered something inaudible, stood up, picked up his bed sheet and left, closing the door softly. Outside, I heard more screams and whoops. I ran to the bathroom, stuck three fingers down my throat and threw it all up. I drank a whole bottle of white wine, sitting in bed, blanket around me, body shaking. I could not cry. I felt nothing. We avoided each other after that. He dropped out after two semesters and I never saw him again. I never told a soul. Not José, not even Sumi. Omar? No fucking way. I would take this to my grave.

It was my personal shame. I was stupid, stupid, stupid. And I got what I deserved.

So Omar and Fairman decided to go into business. Running *Saksi* had depleted Fairman's trust fund somewhat by *give take two hundred K*, so the most logical option for both was to go into a business partnership. Omar's degree in civil engineering would finally be put to use and Fairman's father's law firm would oversee that contracts were signed and sealed. I suppose I was relieved that Omar had exhibited some sign of ambition—or practicality—we were going to be married after all, he had spoken to my father like a gentleman, and now he was going to make sure that we had a financially stable future. Both young men had to prove to their fathers that they were capable of building and creating their own paths in life, and I knew that Omar felt it especially. He did not speak of his father much, but his mother and his sister Lulu whom he spoke to every week were very precious to him.

Fairman decided to pass on the *Saksi* mantle to Imran—the poster boy incarnate for alternative journalism—who had found investors to make it work as an independent online daily with *ads and all, like proper! Saksi* already had the reputation of having the most edgy online reportage, it had a following of more than one hundred thousand subscribers, so it was a step forward in a direction that would challenge the role of the online media even more.

Thirty ringgit a month, times a hundred thousand, that's three million in the bank, every month! Fuck!

Imran was right. There was money to be made, and people were willing to pay for news that they could trust. He had decided to rename *Saksi* to *MalaysiaTimes* and that's what it became.

Ladies and gentlemen, we are now live! Go to MalaysiaTimes. com *to subscribe, and I am Imran Kadir, your Editor-in-Chief.*

We were at Fairman's late one night, and Imran tried to do a Michael Jackson-style moonwalk but almost tripped on the carpet, recovered, composed himself and took a bow. He took a swig of whisky from a bottle and raised it.

To Tunku Malik & Fairman. TMF Sdn. Bhd.

Two motherfuckers, he started.

Fuck you too, wanker! Fairman retorted.

We were all drunk, but there we were. *The Review* had become *Saksi* and now it was *MalaysiaTimes*. I looked around and saw Riz and Jin who raised their glasses—*To* MalaysiaTimes *and TMF! Cheers!*

Imran had asked Riz and Jin to work with him. After *The Review* closed, they had gotten jobs elsewhere, but Imran managed to convince them to be part of his team. It felt like a reunion of sorts, but it also marked the beginnings of new things. Of good things. We had to evolve. We just had to.

Sumi and Fairman were definitely a couple and it was a matter of time before he, too, popped the question. Imran was on his way to charting new ground in Malaysian journalism, and Omar and I were going to be married.

Omar had his arm around me. I was protected, I was safe. He loved me. He was doing everything right. Fairman and Sumi were locked in an embrace, their foreheads touching, their eyes full of love. She was all smiles. Imran swaggered and swore, his belly full of red wine and single malt. Riz and Jin were flushed with drink.

I had every reason to be happy, deliriously happy, even. But in that moment, in that living room where so much had happened, where so much had been said and done, where gallons of alcohol had been consumed and stories told by some of the best journos in the world, I felt the cold hands of melancholy on my neck.

The next evening, Imran decided to hold another party for his investors and his new staff at a newly opened Spanish tapas bar in Bangsar. We were all there, still hung over from the night before, there was a sense of revelry—we had to imbibe, eat, be happy, get drunk. The outward expression of happiness was necessary.

The bar was full of boisterous chatter but once again, I felt afraid. Apart. From everyone there. Things were too good. I didn't trust it. At the end of the night, I was huddled in a corner, my worry like a shroud. I sat and drank quietly watching the crowd.

Sumi had to drag Fairman home. He was loud and drunk. Imran was still holding court with a nubile Chinese intern in a black dress who had attached herself to him, taking in his every word. She had just graduated from NYU and was apparently "a writing wunderkind", as Imran put it. When Omar came to get me, I had had five glasses of wine and was ready to pass out. *Darling, let's go.* He held his hand towards me, and pulled me up from the cubicle. We walked out into the street. The night was just beginning for many, and I felt those cold hands on my neck once again. I put my head on Omar's shoulder and whispered, *I love you, I love only you.*

The next day on 29 April, the High Court upheld the corruption charges against Anwar Ibrahim. The appeal had gone to waste.

I knew it. Our celebrations had been premature. Foolish. We had been partying for two nights in a row and to wake up to this on the third day was a slap in the face. It was a top story and of course, it made the news internationally. Which boded well for Imran and his staff who went to work hungover the next day.

And what was I to do? I was no longer needed as a journalist. I had no need to rush after deadlines anymore, no need to run around KL chasing interviews with my camera and my recorder. Imran had far better writers now. I needed to have a sense of purpose, my work at the drop-in centre was important, but was it real work? What was I contributing to the struggle? There were days when idealism trumped and the simple act of doing laundry seemed delinquent and a complete waste of time. There were days when I struggled to find meaning in anything. There were days when all I had beside me was despair. That was one of those days.

Omar and Fairman were looking at potential office spaces. Sumi was at the Legal Aid Centre volunteering. I read the news on Yahoo and I felt a surge of anger. I felt alone in our apartment, I felt reckless. And I did a terrible thing. I called Karin.

MARINA WAS READY for work. She was planning to walk down Bukit Bintang and maybe head towards Bukit Ceylon. *Star Hill and Ceylon Hill.* What odd names, she thought. There were no visible hills, and she suddenly groaned. *My heels! Damn, what if there really are hills, will I have to take my shoes off and walk barefoot?*

"Aduh," she sighed.

She made an effort to dress well, she didn't want to look like a drag queen, so she made sure to play down her make-up, keep it subtle and *au naturel.* She used nude, warm colours, no blazing lips or eyes. Her hair was washed, blow-dried and curled. She wore a tight sleeveless black top with sequined tassels and a short denim skirt. She looked like a woman; the only giveaway was her Adam's apple. The hormone pills were already pushing her breasts out and making her voice higher. Her legs and armpits were freshly shaved, her legs and calves gleaming with body oil. She was almost a woman. Almost.

She knew she was taking a risk. Transsexuals didn't really work so visibly in those parts, so she was a little worried, but she needed to know. Know if she would get arrested, and if she did, how things would unravel. The night was full of endless possibilities. That was one thing Marina knew she always had—balls. She had learnt to deal with fear a long time ago. She had thought long and hard about what Sumi had said.

"There is no case. If you make a police report you will be marked. They will make your life hell…"

She started getting catcalls. It was a Friday night and in the few Middle Eastern restaurants on the strip, there were only men sitting at the tables. Lecherous eyes followed her. Someone called out.

"Eh pondan, where are you going?"

Pondan—she laughed at the word. It's supposed to mean "effeminate man", but "pon" and "dan"—what did they stand for? Nothing! Mak Nyah—that's another word they used. "Mak" for mother and "Nyah" for transition. Probably the most accurate. "Bapok", another word, old school. Was it meant for the ones out of work, with saggy breasts and rotting teeth? Or the ones who put on too much make-up? Who knows? She had been called all of the above. So many Malay words for someone like me, she thought. Must be confusing for some.

"*Pergi jalan-jalan, nak ikut?*" she replied cheekily, flashing a smile. Then remembering they were probably foreigners, she said, in English, "Am going for a walk, wanna follow?"

She kept walking and almost bumped into a woman in full hijab, gripping two small children with both hands. The woman's husband had stopped to look at a menu on a stand and as Marina walked past them, she saw the woman's kohled eyes look her up and down. Marina thought, *what a life*. She was better off being a pondan than having to cover herself up completely.

She walked on, crossed Jalan Sultan Ismail and took a short cut to Ceylon Hill. She was headed for a gay club that only opened on Friday nights. She wasn't sure where it was but she was certain she would know it when she saw it. There were only a few establishments on the main road, the Cuban bar on the corner and a couple of French and Italian restaurants. Couples walked on the pavement holding hands, anticipating romantic dinners by candlelight, fine wines and quiet conversation. So romantic, she thought.

There weren't many cars on the road, so when the red sports car pulled up right beside her, she knew that she was being solicited. The window whirred down and she saw an older man in a red T-shirt with grey hair beaming at her.

"How much?" he asked. His voice was warm, his eyes twinkly.

"A hundred—just for you."

Marina opened the door and got in. She was immediately assailed by a musky cologne and the chill of the efficient air-conditioning. The man wore sharp-angled glasses and had a slight moustache. The car purred like a metal beast and she felt as if she were floating on the road.

"You like it?" the man asked, gesturing to the steering wheel, "It's a Ferrari."

"Wow," exclaimed Marina, putting her hand to her mouth. They both laughed. Marina turned to him.

"So, you nak apa? Blowjob? Hand job? You want to fuck?"

The man turned to Marina, shrugged and smiled. "Anything," he said.

By this time they had driven up Ceylon Hill and they could see KL Tower in the distance. He had parked the car under a tree, next to a massive water tower, which looked like a giant mushroom. There were a few stately bungalows around them, flanked by tall trees. The night was still.

"Blowjob is fine," he finally decided.

He has kind eyes, Marina thought as she leaned over. The man leaned back and sighed as he lowered his seat and wriggled to help Marina unbutton his trousers and slide off his pants.

He had a portly tummy—obviously rich and well-fed— and as his limp penis slipped out from under the zipper,

Marina got to work.

She licked her tongue up and down the shaft and then sucked it into her mouth. The penis sprang to life and Marina started playing with it, using her tongue. The man started moaning, grabbing Marina's hair and pulling her head towards his groin.

"Don't pull," Marina whispered. "It hurts."

"Oh, sorry," the man replied, a look of concern flitting over his eyes.

Marina took the penis, now fully erect, into her mouth and down her throat. The man groaned. Marina could take deep thrusts and as she slowly pulled the penis out, she tickled it lightly with her tongue. Her hands grasped its base, filling the penis with blood, and she continued licking.

"Yes, ohhh," he moaned.

She then let go of it and she continued thrusting her mouth in and out, up and down, she licked his balls and his anus, she continued pleasuring him until she knew he was about to come. She thrust her mouth into it and as she drew out, his sperm spewed out over her lips. She used her hand to jerk him off completely. He lay there, silent, mouth wide open, until his orgasm came to an end with a deep shudder. Marina took a small packet of tissues from her handbag and slowly wiped up the rest of it, dabbed her mouth and then smiled at him.

"Good?" she asked.

"Yes, very good." The man was lying down, his body still limp. Marina scrunched up the tissues and put them into her handbag. The man smiled at her and slowly put the seat up. He pulled his trousers over the tops of his thighs and Marina helped him with the zip. She started applying lipstick whilst looking at the rear-view mirror. The man reached into his wallet and pulled out two hundred ringgit notes.

"Here," he smiled. "Plus a tip."

"Oh, thank you!"

"Can I see you again?" he asked quietly.

"Hmmm, I guess," Marina said coyly.

They drove slowly down the hill, passing several 50s style apartments on the left. In one of them a party looked like it was in full swing. People drinking, smoking and talking on a large balcony. The man dropped her off at the bottom of the hill, and before he drove off, Marina shoved her card into the pocket of his trousers.

"Make sure your wife doesn't find that," she whispered.

The man didn't answer but grinned widely and as he drove off into the night, Marina thought of her mother and what she used to ask after a good home-cooked meal.

Puas tak?

"Ya, puas."

Yes, she was content.

SOME OF US are cursed. It's a thought that has never quite left me.

Poor little rich girl.

Everything comes at a price I suppose. I mean, everybody has problems but mine just seemed to be compounded by a kind of lethargy that had become familiar. I never really talked about my mother, I never talked about the rape in college, I never even told my father that I had a miscarriage. And I never told anyone about being molested by Girly. What would be the point?

Some of us are cursed. We just are.

Doomed to live lives of desperation, never to be fulfilled, simply because we are incapable of it. To have happiness be that elusive thing, unreachable, unattainable. Impossible.

I had everything I needed to make me happy. Yet. Anwar Ibrahim was in jail, his broken body forced to lie on concrete floors. His soul was unwavering, his spirit on guard. His was a battle, a war that was going to continue for a while. His enemy was clear. But who was my enemy? Who was I fighting? Was I going to be strong enough? Was I capable of being a wife? A mother? What was I really capable of? Was I good for anything at all?

Karin picked up.

Hey, babes… She sounded sleepy. I heard a yawn.

How are you? Late night?

Not really. Just a friend's birthday. Too much blow, though. Karin's voice sounded scrunched up, as if she was settling into a pillow. I got straight to the point.

Got any E?

I heard Karin take a deep breath. She sounded cold.

Thought you weren't gonna do it anymore.

Yeah, well, you know what it's like sometimes.

You wanna hang out or go somewhere? I heard a lighter clicking in the background, a clearing of the throat, the swift intake of a cigarette. Karin was up. The prospect of another drug-fuelled evening had charged her. She was up.

I don't care, really.

Okay, babes. Come over in an hour.

I hung up and looked at my watch. It was almost four o'clock. I walked to the new indie bookstore in Bangsar and browsed for almost an hour. Picked up books and looked at them. The young boy at the cashier had long hair and a goatee. He smiled at me and asked if I was looking for anything in particular. I shook my head.

I sat in a corner with Lawrence Durrell's *The Alexandria Quartet*. It had been one of my favourite books in college. I opened a section on Justine and started reading. It brought back memories of cold winter nights, huddling for warmth in bed, staying up to finish a book. I kept glancing at my watch. I could feel the trepidation in the tips of my toes. My hands felt clammy.

What the fuck am I doing? I hissed through my teeth.

Omar would be furious. I had promised him that my days of doing drugs were over. Sure, we smoked pot from time to time, but Class A drugs were definitely off the list. I wondered if this was what my mother felt. The only sense of purpose being to wield a crystal snifter of vodka every day. Mother had her vodka. Del and her drugs. There it was. Cursed to end up like my mother. I didn't care. Maybe it was because I cared too much.

At 5pm, I hailed a taxi and got in. I didn't want to get stuck in rush hour traffic. I was in a daze, with the singular aim of getting high. The kind of daze addicts get into when they know that the next high is minutes away. That lull, the blood in the veins slowing down, as if to anticipate the next jolt. The heart sinking into a short stupor; a cat napping, before the starving dog is unleashed. The nostrils flaring, the tongue licking the lips in anticipation, the stretching of the gums, cheeks, the mouth going *aaaah, aaaah, aaaah*. There was no logic to it, there was no sense in thinking it through. In mentally going through the motions of what the next few hours would bring.

I got to Karin's flat and she let me in. She had just showered and the apartment was full of light from the open windows. Her hair was longer than ever and she looked skinny. She kissed me lightly on the cheeks.

Long time no see, huh.

Shit, you lost a ton of weight. I blurted. She had. Cheekbones tight, her shoulder blades sharper than ever.

Kai left. She pursed her lips and plopped herself on the blue leather couch. Her apartment was done up in blues and whites. A little too minimalist for me, but it was very soothing.

Jesus. When? I sat next to her.

On the table were stacks of women's magazines. The *Cleo* mag on top had Karin on the cover. The make-up was vivid, the eyebrows arched. The eyeshadow a shimmery turquoise. The lips, glossy pink.

Nice pic. I said.

It's work, babes. Work. Pays for everything you know. She lit a cigarette.

So, what happened?

You know Kai's bi—right? She took a puff and looked at me.

No…?

Well, he left me for some guy in Jakarta. Some other model.

Fuck!

Yeah, fuck them both.

She got up and walked towards the kitchen. It was a studio apartment and the kitchen was right next to the living room. I eased myself onto the blue leather, propped a pillow between my thighs and looked out the windows, wide open, overlooking the tops of houses, trees.

White wine? Or champagne? She asked, opening the fridge.

Whatever, I don't care.

What's up with you?

Nothing.

Hmmph. Yeah right.

She brought over a bottle of white wine and two glasses.

Wanna talk about it? She asked as she twisted the corkscrew until it popped.

No.

She handed me a glass of wine. The sight of the clear yellow liquid invigorated me. We clinked our glasses.

What shall we toast to? Karin took another puff and her eyes lit up.

And at that moment a thought came to me—a terrible thing really.

What if my mother had taken her life? What if she had crashed her car deliberately?

To be honest, I didn't really know the intricate details of the crash. Papa always said, "The car hit a lamp pole and it killed her instantly." But was it because she swerved to avoid something? Did she run a red light? Did she do it intentionally?

I downed the glass of wine and as I poured myself some more, I asked.

So, what drugs you got?

MARINA HAD JUST walked past the Cuban bar when she saw a group of well-muscled men dressed in tight T-shirts and jeans. *We must all be going to the same place*, she thought.

The road was bustling, there were people milling about on the streets, stylish men and women who were out to party. She looked up and saw a group of men sitting on two adjacent balconies, sipping cocktails, smoking, laughing. One man started kissing another passionately on the lips, oblivious to the others.

She followed the group of men into the white colonial-style bungalow, which had a blossoming frangipani tree by the entrance. The sweet scent of the white flowers hovered over the entrance as the door was opened by a man in a black suit.

As soon as she entered, the sound of thumping music swirled down the circular staircase. There was a cover charge of twenty ringgit and as Marina opened her purse to pay, one of the guys in front of her turned and said, "It's okay, she's with me."

Marina smiled to thank him, then took his hand as they walked up the stairs. A large painting of a bald girl against a blue background loomed above them. They had to slow down as they reached the top of the stairs, the guys in front of them pushing their way in.

It was all men. Men of all races, size and shape. In T-shirts, some topless, in suits, in yellow and pink neon. She squeezed her way through men caressing and hugging each other, smoking, laughing, drinking. She wondered if this is what Disneyland felt like. To have all your dreams come true in one place. She got many smiles and she smiled back. She felt like one of them.

The thumping got inside her head, the music was frenetic. The bar was a long, oblong island featuring a wall of bottles in the centre. The dance floor was on the other side of the room, and she saw a blur of moving bodies.

"What would you like to drink?" her new friend shouted.

"Anything," Marina shouted back.

The others from his group had disappeared into the crowd, and she stood alone, her back against a wall. She opened her purse, fished out a cigarette and her lighter. A man in a white T-shirt turned to her.

"Can I have one, please?" he asked.

"Sure," she replied and offered him the pack.

With clean, manicured fingers, he eased one out of the pack and smiled widely at her.

He had cropped hair, dyed blonde, his eyes accentuated with black liner with a shade of glittery eye shadow. His eyebrows were beautifully plucked and arched. A quick laugh betrayed bleached, even teeth.

"Thanks, you're a gorgeous gal." He took the lighter from her hand and lit the cigarette. "You a working girl?" he asked cheekily.

Marina raised an eyebrow and winked at him.

"Cool!" he said and winked back. He wriggled his shoulders and his bum to the music and turned to join his friends.

Marina continued puffing on her cigarette, watching the bartenders pour wine into glasses and shake pink cocktails into martini glasses. This was the kind of club she had only imagined existed in places like Bangkok or Las Vegas. This was a classy club; there were people with money and talent in this place. She imagined film directors, bankers, artists, architects, engineers, hairdressers. There was conversation, there was culture, a vibrancy she had not felt anywhere else before. There were people from all over the world. There was power in the room. Gay power. Trans power. Pondan power. Mak Nyah power. Yes, even Bapok power.

Her new friend had braved the crowd, two drinks held high above his head. Long flutes of something bubbly. They clinked glasses and as Marina took her first sip, she realised that it was her first taste of champagne.

I GOT REALLY, really high.

I was unsure of how much I'd taken but it must have been more than anything I'd ever done before. The fact that we were in Karin's apartment must have made us feel safer. But that was also foolish, as we could easily have gone over our limits. Karin's dealer had delivered the stuff personally as he was in the neighbourhood. We bought Ecstasy, coke and Valium.

Hey, this is good stuff, the best. He gave us a swift salute before he left. *Enjoy!*

After a bottle of white wine, we took the E. When it kicked in, we started dancing. Karin turned the volume on her stereo right up and we just let it rip. Let it loose. Let it fly. She was friends with the top DJs in town, so she had party mixes to last hours. A little bit of drum and bass, some happy house and a lot of techno with all the right flourishes.

Then we did coke.

It's snowing, babes! Look! Karin laughed and she pounded the little white mound with two credit cards, like a Chinese chef with two meat cleavers.

We did lines and lines of it off Karin's glass table. And later when it was gone, we licked fingers to pick up the remnants and rub it into our gums. It was delicious. My body tingled with delight. We were so high.

It was a night of psycho-babble. Our tongues were loose. We wept, we laughed, we professed love, we begged for forgiveness, we danced and jumped like the schoolgirls we once were. We drank some more, smoked some more, talked until there was no sense of time or space, only a great big drug-addled void of timelessness. We were light beings, flitting in and out of breaths, of universes. We were fragments of our selves. We were fairies. We were specks of nothing.

There was no more pain, no more worry, no more anger.

Just bliss. Joy. Wild abandon. Recklessness.

Hours went by and when we were done, when all the drugs were done, Karin and I fell asleep like contented kittens, curled around each other on the fluffy white carpet.

When we were awakened by the front door crashing open and a barrage of harsh voices, I opened my eyes to see Omar staring down at me, his eyes a combination of fury and concern, and then, disappointment.

"IT'S A RAID!"

The music ground to a halt, people stopped dancing, stopped moving. Everything stopped. A gritty silence.

Marina stood there, in shock. Someone whispered: "Fucking cops are here."

There was a sudden flurry of movement.

"Tepi, tepi," a loud voice shouted.

A line of five policemen strode in and the crowd parted like schoolboys shamed by prefects at assembly. Four policemen stood facing the crowd, while the fifth barked loudly: "Foreigners can go! Those with Malaysian IC please stay back."

There were loud groans and sighs of relief. Loud twitters of protest.

"But you must show us your ID before you go. You must have ID or passport. If you don't have, you cannot go. Understand!"

His eyes were bulging from having to shout. Suddenly the walkie-talkie in his hand blared out and he jumped. He turned the volume button down and glared at the crowd.

"Okay, please form two lines. Foreigners here and Malaysians here." Using his right hand to indicate two lines, he continued. "We will also do a urine test, so please be ready. Okay? Gerak! Move!"

The crowd started to whisper, there were nervous giggles, sobs. The man with the arched eyebrows looked at Marina and drew his hand across his throat. "I'm fucked," he whispered.

Marina was afraid. The man who had bought her champagne was nowhere to be seen, she had lost sight of him. Slowly, two lines emerged. The foreigners were herded down the stairs, and the Malaysians were made to form a line heading towards the bathrooms.

More cops came up and from the street. The sound of sirens grew louder and a sudden wave of fury flooded her.

Marina hissed under her breath. "Arrest me, you fuckers, arrest me now and see what I will do to you."

Omar was silent. His mouth a grim line, his eyes cold.

My mouth was dry. I rested my head against the car window and stared blankly out. It was early morning, and rush hour traffic was peaking. I had already come down, and I felt deflated, my palms clammy and cold. All I wanted was a bottle of ice water, a shower and my bed. Our bed.

I didn't feel tired. I knew that if Omar wanted to talk, I would. I would tell him exactly how I felt. I would be honest with him. I would tell him that I no longer wanted to marry him. I would tell him that I felt that he could do better. I would tell him that I felt like a failure. I would…

His handphone rang.

It was in his trouser pocket and he gestured for me to get it.

I slid my hand into it and I felt his thigh stiffen. He was angry, more angry than I had ever seen him before.

I licked my dry lips and clicked the green button.

Hello. My voice croaked.

Del, is that you? It was Sumi. She was curt. *Jesus, Del, I have been trying to call you for hours! Where are you? Where's Omar?*

He's driving.

Omar looked over at me, mouthing silently. *Who is it?*

Am at the police station in Jalan Hang Tuah. Come now! Marina's been arrested.

Shit! Okay. I'll tell him. We'll be there soon.

What now? Omar muttered.

It's Marina, she's been arrested. I sighed and looked out the window. I straightened my seat and sat up. My heart started beating faster and that familiar thrill of adrenaline-charged anger willed me to sit up straight and grit my teeth.

I turned to Omar and said: *I will talk to you about what happened, but right now, now I need coffee. My friend has been arrested and I need to help her.*

By THE TIME they got to the police station, Fairman was already there, standing beside Sumi, who glared openly at Del.

Omar took stock of the situation and asked, "What happened?"

"There was a raid at a gay bar along Changkat Bukit Bintang last night and Marina was picked up," Sumi said.

"What for?" Omar asked.

"Section 28?" Del replied.

"That's right."

"And how do you know this?" Omar snapped at Del.

"It's okay," Sumi interjected quickly, soothingly. "There's nothing we can do now anyway. She's in the lock-up till Monday."

"Seriously?" Del moaned.

"It's a Saturday, nothing gets processed till Monday," Omar cut in curtly.

"We should know this, right? From the good ol' days..." Fairman quipped with a laugh, trying to break the tension.

Omar turned sharply on his heels and started walking. "Right, let's go!" he said over his shoulder.

The morning heat had turned sultry. Sweat had accumulated at the base of his throat, the back of his shirt already drenched. There were days when he longed for the cool London air, the ability to walk out of a building and not immediately feel like getting under an ice-cold shower. He was not in the mood for pleasantries and all he wanted was to get back into the air-conditioning of his car, go home and try not to wring Del's neck.

He was reminded of the time his mother accused his father of having an affair and of the shouting that went on in their house for days. He was averse to shouting now. His mother's fury had left him scornful of confrontations, and he was tired of tears, emotional blackmail, drama. He liked to end things quickly, with little or no provocation.

He braced himself for what Del was going to say to him. And of what he would say to her.

THE WALL TILES were green. The brown slime on them seemed recent, it wasn't caked. Her mouth felt awful and her make-up was probably smudged. The azan told her it was dawn.

Marina remembered running down the beach with her dad. They had just come back from a fishing trip and they had caught huge prawns, which her mother would later cook with onions, garlic, curry leaves and fresh chillies from the garden. The dawn had just broken and the first sliver of the sun broke through the purple sky and the sea turned azure. Then, piercing though the winds in the coconut trees, the crackling sound of the mike came on. The imam was at the mosque ready to sing the call to prayer.

Allahu Akhbar, Allahu Akhbar, Allahu Akhbar, Allahu Akhbar.

That dawn prayer in the morning. That morning so perfect, she realised that a god that could create such beauty was a god of compassion, of mercy and love. She realised that god loved her for who she was—a girl trapped in the body of a boy. But now, she was trapped in the filthy belly of a police station. It stank of rotten food in clogged drains, and she remembered the owner of Al-Tandoor back home. Of having to suck him off in return for food. Of the filthy toilet she had to kneel in. Of the scent of curry on his fingers. She sighed and looked up. The call to prayer was over and the weekend loomed.

The loud cop had singled her out at the club.

Male or female? The one question she had never been able to answer.

"Tengok IC."

Marina handed over her identification card.

The loud cop took one look. "Rashid bin Husin. Dari Lahad Datu, Sabah. You are a man and yet you are dressed like a woman. You know this is a crime, yes?"

Marina kept quiet. So many eyes were on her. She took a deep breath and walked calmly towards the stairs. "Sure, arrest me."

A loud cheer broke out. People started clapping.

"You go girl!"

"Whoo hoo!"

"Be yourself!"

The loud cop turned and shouted. "Quiet! Diam!"

Marina walked down the stairs and out onto the street where the open doors of the Black Maria greeted her.

WE DROVE HOME in silence.

After Omar parked the car, I got out first and walked up the flight of stairs to our apartment. I unlocked the front door and immediately started peeling my clothes off. I felt dirty, sweaty, like there was a week's worth of grime on my face, my armpits, in between my toes.

I ran naked into the shower and when the ice-cold water from the shower spattered on the top of my head, I sighed loudly and let the water wash all over me. I wanted to weep but I couldn't. I wanted to scream but I couldn't. I felt spent.

Then, the door to the shower stall opened and Omar came in.

I felt his arms around me, his warm body hugging me with strength, then tenderness.

A guilty sob escaped my lips, and then the tears came mingling with the cold water. He just held me like that, kissed the back of my head, my neck, until I felt his desire on the small of my back.

I turned and kissed him. I held his face and looked into his eyes.

I want to wring your bloody neck, he said.

I know.

Know what? That you did E? Got wasted? With Karin?

There was water in my eyes, and they smarted. He brushed my eyelids with gentle fingers and kissed them.

Why? Del. I want to know why.

I just wanted to. Get wasted. Just forget about—shit.

And you didn't think to tell me? He took a deep breath. *I didn't know where you were, I was worried.*

Yeah...I'm...sorry.

He kissed my eyelids again.

I don't know if I can do this, Omar. I kissed his mouth, wanting to shut him up.

He kissed me back. His gentle tongue probing me. I stopped and said.

This, getting married. Kids, maybe. I don't know.

He sighed.

I kissed him. More urgency, this time. I just wanted to make him happy, I didn't want to talk about it all, not all in one go. *I feel lost. So fucked up.*

He pushed me against the corner of the shower and entered me from behind. I gasped, my hands pressed against the wet tiles. He grabbed my fingers and went even deeper into me. His body against mine, again and again.

I love you Del. Just be who you are.

He pushed into me, our bodies so familiar in the taking and giving of pleasure.

Just be. Be my wife. Start there.

His voice broke. He was inside me, all of him. My face slid against the wet tiles. He sought my mouth, our tongues licking, sucking. The water like a balm, washing us clean, washing me of my worries, washing away all his anger.

Oh my god, Del. I love you.

And as he moaned his release, I felt better, knowing that I had a man who loved me, a man who loved me more than I loved myself.

ON MONDAY MORNING, Marina was let out of her cell. For two nights she had slept on cardboard and she had a terrible crick in her neck. There were two cellmates, two guys from the raid who were thrown in a few hours later. They had tested positive for drugs and were also going to be charged that day.

She was starving, thirsty. She needed to empty her bowels, she needed a bath. Her cellmates were young gay guys, Amin and Fred, both from Johor Bahru. They were terrified and they slept huddled against each other, crying softly before the snores came.

Food was meagre. They were given stale buns, white rice with the smallest portions of fish imaginable and packets of sweet iced drinks that had to be shared.

The cell stank worse at night and they heard cries from other cells that held the women. The hours bled into each other, there was little conversation, there was no desire to talk, share their lives, bond. There was humiliation. Marina was made to feel shame.

In the Black Maria, she had been handcuffed. She sat in the back on her own, dazed as the vehicle drove through the streets of KL. And when she arrived at the police station, the cop at the counter wrote out the charge. He leered at her and said.

"You ni...prostitute?"

"I want to call my lawyer."

He laughed at her. "You? Lawyer?" He turned to his colleagues and shouted, "Eh, this pondan wants to call her lawyer. Betul ke ni?" He then stood up and said, "You are being charged under Section 28, where you can be fined one thousand ringgit or be jailed for one year or both. Do you understand the charge? Faham tak?"

Marina nodded. Then they took her into a room and a female cop asked her to take off her clothes. Marina looked up at the fan, which was covered in black dust. The window had bars, and she heard crickets outside. Goose bumps covered her flesh and her nipples hardened. She was cold.

"Panties okay," the cop said picking up Marina's clothes. Marina was clad in a red g-string, she tried to cover her breasts.

"Bend over," the cop ordered. "Cough."

Marina asked for the toilet. It was a squat toilet with no door. The female cop stood nearby facing her. Then she was handed a gown, which looked like a hospital garment. It was dirty and smelled of sweat. The female cop's eyes showed concern, but she was silent. Marina was taken to her cell at the opposite end of the hallway from the toilet. Her bare feet felt sand, slime, things she dared not imagine. The cell was a room with a bare floor. There was a stack of cardboard in one corner. Marina found a corner, unfolded a piece of cardboard and sat on it. The female cop locked the heavy metal doors and walked away. Marina was alone in the cell, in the dark.

SUMI PICKED ME up that morning to go to court.

Omar had to work, there was an important meeting with a client for a large contract and he had to go in. We had spent the weekend talking and making love. We were seized with a renewed passion, spending hours in bed, making love once, twice, then again and again. Omar was insatiable. He said, *I just want to be inside you, all day.*

It was carnal, but it was love. We drank wine, ate soft cheese and crackers, fed each other with our fingers, read, slept and made love. It was glorious, the sharing of our bodies. We whispered, moaned, shrieked under the sheets, in between breaths, our bodies sticky with pleasure and sweat. We lusted after each other. I felt safe from the world outside, and Omar was my protector, the one person I could turn to, the one man I trusted with my life.

He had forgiven me. *But why? Why did you do it? Get so wasted like that,* he said, his head on my breast.

I don't know what to do with my life. You all seem to…and I don't…

Know what? A sense of purpose?

It's not just that Omar, I feel useless.

Useless? That's harsh. Why are you so hard on yourself?

I'm sorry, I won't do it again, I promise. I am going to be the best wife to you. Just let me start with that.

You want to?

Yes, this marriage is going to be the most important thing in my life.

It was a solemn promise. His eyes searched mine, seeking confirmation. I was going to make it right, I was going to do things right.

At the Syariah Court, Sumi and I found Marina standing next to a potted plant, smoking. She was dressed in long black pants, a long-sleeved blue shirt and her hair was tied back in a ponytail. I had never seen Marina without make-up before and I was startled.

She shrugged and smiled when we walked up to her and we both hugged her long and hard.

Hansem tak? Marina laughed.

Did they do anything to you in there? I asked.

Marina shook her head. *No. But it was horrible, just horrible…*

Sumi interjected. *I am not a Syariah lawyer, so I don't know how this is going to work.*

It's okay. There is someone here from Legal Aid.

She stubbed the cigarette out with a pair of men's sandals. Her crimson toenails stuck out.

Let's go in. You have your tudung?

Sumi and I nodded. We were on sacred ground, and our heads had to be covered.

The courtroom was smaller than I'd imagined, and it was already packed. There were at least fifty people seated and more were coming in. The large ceiling fan whirred, but it was still stuffy. I wished I had something to fan myself with.

Marina grabbed my hand and walked towards the front of the courtroom where she was met by a young lady wearing a pink tudung. We saw some empty seats and sat down.

Sumi whispered.

That must be her lawyer, she looks really young.

What's the worst that can happen?

She gets charged, but it will be a while before the hearing. Hopefully she gets out on bail.

A side door opened and the magistrate walked in.

Bangun! A court official announced.

We stood up. The magistrate was a middle-aged woman in a black jacket and a white tudung. She nodded sternly and sat down.

Sumi whispered again. *There's a lot of cases here, this might take a while.*

I had never been in a courtroom before and although this was just a hearing in the Syariah Court, I wondered how the law worked differently for Muslims. I knew that the penalties were harsher, and that there were different laws for marriage, divorce, inheritance, custody of children and crime. My conversion to Islam meant that I too would be subject to Syariah law.

One by one, the cases were tried. The magistrate was brief in her remarks.

There were cases of petty theft; two young boys caught stealing from the mosque. The sentence was two years in juvenile detention. I looked at the scrawny boys who could not have been more than 12. One was scratching his head non-stop. I wondered if he had scabies. These were poor kids from the kampung who probably stole money to buy food. When they were led away a woman in the front burst into tears, and begged the judge for leniency.

Tolonglah, tolong. Itu anak saya.

She was led away sobbing.

Then a teenage girl who was visibly pregnant and a boy of about 18 stepped forward.

Oh my god. This is the worst, Sumi whispered. *Unmarried couple. They'll be sent away and the baby will be born in prison.*

Poor kids. Those poor, poor kids. There would be no

possibility of bail for this kind of crime. Sure enough, the magistrate glared at them both and spoke harshly.

You will both be sentenced to two years each in jail. Your baby will be born in jail. This is what you have done to yourselves and you only have yourselves to blame.

Bloody hell, I whispered.

That's Syariah for you. No mercy.

What about the kid?

The kid will be fine. Two years in jail, then they come out and get married. Sorted.

The two teenagers were led off separately, she to serve her time in a female prison and he, in a male one. Who knew of the kinds of horrors they would encounter in those two years? Would their love survive? There were no tears for this young couple, no family who pleaded mercy for them. They had probably been disowned by their families, shunned by their villages, cast out like lepers.

Sumi and I looked at each other, wordless.

Then Marina was called.

Rashid bin Husin. Kesalahan Section 28 dalam undang-undang Wilayah Persekutuan, Kuala Lumpur.

Marina stood tall. Her lawyer, diminutive, beside her.

The magistrate softened when she spoke. She must have seen multiple cases like this. *I will let you out on bail this time. But see this as a warning. If you are arrested again, you will not get off. Faham?*

Then she sighed and shook her head. And took one last glance at Marina before she turned back to the stack of files in front of her. *Next!*

We were elated. Marina was going to be let out on bail.

Wait, no second hearing? I asked.

Let's ask her lawyer, Sumi replied. *Like I said, I am not sure how this works.*

We both rushed out the courtroom and almost bumped into Marina's lawyer.

We both thanked her profusely and took turns hugging a much-relieved Marina.

Aren't you happy? I asked.

This happens over and over again, you know. It's not like the law is going to change. We need to challenge it. It's not just about me, you know. There are so many of us. And how many more times does this need to happen?

Marina stood there, impassioned, eloquent, her hands expressive.

Her lawyer spoke quietly. *You need a lawyer who will fight this for you. I can't do this pro-bono. This was a one-off Marina, I can't. Sorry.*

It's okay, I will figure this out. Marina smiled widely and said, *Thank you, darls, you are both angels for being here!*

Marina was tired that day, but she woke up early and called for a taxi to Damansara Heights. It was the day of the wedding and she was to be the Mak Andam, responsible for the hair and make-up for the bride. She was no expert but her skills were good enough, and Del had insisted.

She packed a bag with all her brushes, an extra change of clothes, and a toolbox full of make-up. One of her friends, Honey, had recently left the country to go live with her boyfriend in England. Honey, who was a full-time sex worker and part-time make-up artist, had bequeathed her kit to Marina, after giving her a few sessions in professional make-up application.

Marina had never seen so many kinds of brushes in her life, nor had she seen such a range of blusher, foundation and concealer. It was such fun, learning how to contour the human face, play with colour, highlighter, blush and brush.

She got into the taxi and a few minutes later, they were stuck in a massive traffic jam.

"Apa ni?" the taxi driver muttered.

The taxi was on Jalan Tun Perak, heading towards Dataran Merdeka and there was a slight drizzle. She saw a group of teenage boys emerge from behind the taxi, they were carrying placards. Marina strained her head to see what the placards said.

Mahathir Undur! Mahathir Resign!

A large caricature of Mahathir had been cut out. It made the prime minister look like a rogue, with a misshapen nose and dark-rimmed eyes. The taxi inched forward and they heard a roar of voices, shouting in unison.

"*Reformasi! Reformasi! Reformasi!*"

"*Protes lagi,*" the taxi driver complained.

"Protests are important," Marina said emphatically. "We have the right, don't you know. This is a democracy."

The taxi driver snorted. "Hmmph. Not until this man goes to jail." He gestured at the placard.

When the traffic light turned green, the taxi finally moved and they stared in silence at the sea of people who had turned up.

"So many," Marina muttered.

The roar became a hum, people were straining to listen to a speaker with a loudhailer. Marina rolled the window down. She felt the energy from the crowd, the anger, the surge of hope, the air of optimism.

"Reformasi!" she shouted.

The taxi driver was startled. And he too shouted, "Reformasi!"

They smiled and chatted, barriers broken. The sky had cleared and the sun was starting to peek out.

When she arrived at the house, there were a few cars parked along the road. The security guard waved her in, smiling. Tents had already been set up for the reception, chairs and tables covered in cream-coloured fabric. Bouquets of white roses and tuberoses on tables. Fake chandeliers dangled precariously from the tent tops.

Omar's mother greeted her, and ushered her into a large bedroom. Del was seated and already dressed in silk sarong and a kebaya top of fine French lace.

Del ran to her. "I feel sick."

"*Aduh, kenapa sayang?*"

"Too many people, I can't do this."

"It's just you and Omar, okay? This is your wedding day."

"Yeah, yeah. I just feel sick. Want to throw up."

"Throw up then. You'll feel better."

Marina walked Del to the bathroom. Del quickly doubled over, heaving. Yellow bile spilled out into the toilet bowl.

"I can't do this Marina, I can't do this."

Marina took some toilet tissue, folded it into two and wiped Del's mouth gently.

"Come on sayang, let's make you beautiful."

I LOOKED LIKE my mother.

My hair was wound tightly into a French twist, covered by a light veil, which fell softly onto my shoulders. The lace kebaya, the white silk sarong with hand-drawn flowers, the beaded satin shoes. Creamy pearl studs and a single pearl pendant. My eyes, smoky. Nude lips. I had never looked like this.

This was a woman who was going to get married. I was that woman.

I was seized with a sudden gust of trepidation. I started hyperventilating. I did not know what to do.

I sat down and looked at my hands. Twirls of red henna wound themselves intricately into a flowery pattern that covered both hands. It had taken hours and hours to draw on and hours more to dry.

Del, are you okay?

I nodded and looked out the window. The day was perfect. It had rained the night before and I had slept deeply, lulled into a cavernous universe. I had dreamt well and woke rested and fresh. The air was cool, lush, green. The leaves had been bathed and were glossy with hope.

Marina sat in the corner and lit a cigarette. Omar's sister Lulu poured herself more white wine.

Lulu had arrived from London the night before. She was jetlagged, had barely slept and was already on the way to being completely drunk.

Eh, jangan minum sampai mabuk, okay. The party hasn't started yet!

But Lulu didn't care. Then there was a knock at the door and Omar's mother walked in.

It's time.

Lulu swigged the last of the wine, pressed some lipstick onto her already crimson lips and said, *This is it!* She giggled excitedly.

I started walking out the door, Marina and Lulu following me. Marina towering in heels and a sequined pink kebaya. Lulu in a white baju kurung.

I entered the living room and was gestured to a chair. Beautiful Persian carpets had been brought out and spread on the floor, where people I didn't know sat, men on one side, women on the other. I felt as if all their eyes were on me. In the centre sat Omar and the Kadi, facing each other. The air was thick with expectation, incense and the sweet scent of white lilies. I sat down, my stomach in knots. Omar's head was bowed, his eyes closed. He was wearing a cream-coloured baju melayu and a songkok. We had matching outfits. He looked so handsome. Our eyes met and he smiled. I felt better. He got up and walked towards me. All heads turned. I wanted to run back into the room. All those eyes staring.

Omar kissed me on the forehead. I took his hand and kissed it. That was it, the gesture had sealed us as man and wife. He led me to the centre of the room and the Kadi recited a blessing. I heard cameras clicking.

Bismillah-ir-rahman-ir Rahim. Allahu Akhbar, Allahu Akhbar, Allahu Akhbar.

It was done.

Then, a blur. Food. Plenty of it. Lamb kurma, beef rendang, pickled little pink onions that looked like baby mice. Us seated at the head of the tent, glass chandeliers above. Omar feeding me with his right hand. Me feeding him back. Papa looking lost. Fairman, Sumi and Imran waving like mad and blowing kisses. I took a sip of the sickly sweet pink drink and felt my stomach lurch. I got up, excused myself.

Omar looked concerned. *You okay, sayang?*

Marina grabbed my hand. *Kenapa? What's the matter?*

I smiled weakly and said that I had to go the bathroom.

I ran into the living room, past the guests, little children in bright outfits, almost tripping on the carpet, dragging Marina after me. The Indonesian maids staring blankly. Clutching the banister up the stairs. Into the bedroom. The bathroom. And face over the toilet bowl. I retched violently, the remnants of the pink drink and then streaming yellow bile. My face was drenched with sweat, and I imagined streaks of Mac powder and mascara running down my face.

Ya Allah, Del, what is going on with you?

I stumbled to my feet, and saw my face in the mirror. Lipstick smeared, eyes watery. I looked pale. My mouth still dribbling with saliva.

Del, do you think you're…

The bathroom door opened and Omar uttered the word.

Pregnant?

I threw up once again.

I rinsed my mouth. Our faces together in the bathroom mirror. Husband and wife.

Gently, he took my hand and sat me down on the bed.

Marina smiled, her manicured hand covering her mouth.

Oh darling, darling Del. He kissed me on the forehead, then gently on my cheeks. And we fell onto the white, embroidered pillows and started laughing.

* * *

I threw up every day for 39 weeks.

The doctor said, *It's severe morning sickness, one in every ten women gets it.*

Every morning it was the same. Bright yellow bile, doubled over, head in the toilet bowl, then the sink, then the toilet bowl again. Omar couldn't take it anymore. In the first weeks, he would stand behind me, holding my waist with both hands, while the violent retching pulled at my back and neck muscles. When I got bigger, he couldn't reach around me and I couldn't bear to have him near me. My body felt like it was being torn apart and the sounds that came out of my mouth were that of a wild animal. The deep guttural moans would range in registers from reptilian to feline.

He said he felt guilty. *Sorry, my god. Jesus fucking Christ. Del, I am so sorry.*

Sorry for what? Getting me pregnant?

For months I only ate crackers, dried sesame-flavoured seaweed and soupy noodles with tofu. Nothing else would stay down. If it was bland, it was good. The scent of laundry detergent made me nauseous. Traffic made me nauseous. Music made me nauseous. My body had become an unknown creature. I yearned for soft pillows and lemon scented candles, new-age music and long stretchy black skirts, snow, maple syrup on thick buttermilk pancakes, sticky fudge on vanilla ice-cream, bread soaked in balsamic vinegar. I was in danger of becoming anaemic. Apart from the folic acid and multi-vitamins, I had to take iron, zinc, magnesium. More pills. I could not eat meat; I could not face a lamb cutlet, pink, dead chicken thighs, fish with glassy eyes. I stared at animal parts in supermarkets, trying not to gag. Instead, I caressed apples,

peaches, grapes, avocados. I could not watch any violence on
TV, no machine-gun wielding heroes creating carnage. No
wars, no alien invasions, no winged creatures with supersonic
eyes. No haunted houses, or dead girls with long, wet hair. No
ghosts or exorcisms, no demonic possession.

The baby grew and grew. The little black sac on the
ultrasound became a heartbeat. Then a spine, floating in
amniotic fluid. Then fingers, toes, bones, eyes, teeth. I
went for long walks, did yoga, tried to listen to Mozart and
Shostakovich. Sat cross-legged, meditated. Swam. My black
maternity swimsuit stretched until the seams were visible. I
rubbed my growing belly and thickening thighs with lavender
and olive oil. Omar stroked my back at night. We made love
sideways. We slept like spoons. I wanted him sometimes to be
rough. But he was afraid of hurting the baby.

It isn't going to make a difference you know.

*It just feels weird. I don't want to hurt it. The movement…
won't it jiggle it too much?*

*The baby is in the womb, sayang. She is safer in there than she
will ever be.*

Safe. Yes, she was safe in there. Safe, from the big bad world.

I had managed to make a baby this time. My body worked.
It did what it was supposed to do. A miracle. It was going to
be a girl, I just knew.

One day as I was reading, I felt a lurch and I saw an
impression of a foot. A little foot with toes. My baby's toes.
My baby in there.

I thought of Mother and her pregnancy and remembered
that photo of her pregnant with me. It was taken on a beach
on the east coast, in Kelantan. Papa sitting next to her. She

was wearing a flowery dress and her hair in a short bob. They both wore sunglasses and his hand was on her belly. They looked radiant.

I wondered where it was, that faded photo. I thought of my father and I decided to call him. The thought of his brooding face made me stop after the second ring tone. I needed to be happy. I was going to be a mother and I had to let my sad father go.

It was going to be a girl.

I had met a midwife, Lisa, and together we planned the birth. I had wanted it to be at home, in the bath tub surrounded by music, incense and candles but Lisa, originally from East London, had said that it would be risky, and if there were problems with the birth, there could be serious consequences.

What if the baby is breach? What if you lose too much blood? What if the cord is around the neck? You can't imagine anticipating certain scenarios, especially since it's your first baby. If you and Omar were living right next to a hospital, a home birth could be an option, but you're not, and you know how long ambulances take to get anywhere in KL. If it's rush-hour traffic, or in the middle of the night, you'll be in serious trouble. Don't want you to bleed to death now, do we? We can have a birth plan with no drugs, but you need to be in a medical facility. Let's think of a home birth for your second child, okay? Del! Listen. Look, women still die in childbirth, it's not as simple as you think. An unexpected complication could be fatal. Let's not take the risk, shall we?

Apart from the morning sickness, the pregnancy had been progressing well. I was putting on the right amount of weight, I was healthier than I'd ever been in my life. My face, eyes, teeth, skin. There was a sheen to everything. Like how some film directors used to put Vaseline on the camera lens to soften the image. It felt like that. Omar kept saying that I looked luminous.

I was constantly active; the nesting instinct had kicked in and one night I managed to put together the cot entirely on my own, to Omar's dismay.

Why didn't you let me help you?

Because I wanted to do it. I couldn't sleep and I needed to do something.

I couldn't help myself. I folded and refolded baby clothes. I rearranged things in the dead of night. Baby wipes here, nappy cream there. Diapers in the corner. I sat in that nursery for hours, imagining the baby in my arms. I had bought a stack of CDs: music that resembled the human heartbeat, music with the gentlest of drums and flutes, whales' song, Andean pipes, new age Celtic harp, Gregorian chants. I bought them all.

A girl. A baby girl.

We had not thought of a name. She was due in three weeks, and every day my belly grew and grew. The books always said that the last weeks were the worst, and that one had to "rest, stay free from stress, enjoy the last moments of your pregnancy." I could no longer see my toes. My belly protruded outwards and upwards like a melon, hard and ripe. The baby was now pressing down on my bladder and I would sometimes have preferred to simply stay in the bathroom instead of waddling in and out every fifteen minutes.

One night I used an entire roll of toilet paper.

Women stopped me on the street, in the malls. Asians have a morbid fascination with pregnant women, unabashed in giving thoughts or opinions.

Wah, your stomach so high, must be a boy. Got name ah?

So low, must be due soon, huh? Must be girl lah.

Twins ah? So big!

I waddled. I could no longer walk straight. The extra weight had added pressure on my lower spine and I had to resort to acupuncture to ease the pain. I stopped spending time in front of the computer, I stopped using the microwave, I rarely used my handphone. I wanted the baby to be clear of all kinds of rays and radio waves. I read all kinds of do's and don'ts. I wanted the perfect birth. I wanted the perfect baby.

Miraculously, Papa had started to come around. He started calling me once a week, then once every two days, then once a day. For months, I refused to go to see him, simply because I couldn't deal with the state of the house. The maid still came to clean and do his laundry but during the rest of the week, piles of plates accumulated on the hallway outside his study, glasses with Milo stains and rings of mould piled up in the sink, unwashed laundry stood almost stiffly to attention, the grass was uncut, the water in the swimming pool resembled tepid tea with loose leaves. I was sure there were frogs spawning in the pool, along with thousands of sacs of squirming mosquito larvae. It depressed me. I had no idea what he did in his room all day, all week, all month. He just read and read. Pored over books on history, religion, theory. Then one day he said this.

Del, I am going to write a book.

Really? Oh Papa, I think that's a great idea. What's it about?

History.

Of…?

Well, it's early days yet…but we shall see.

My father was going to become a writer. I thought it was wonderful. He was energised about the thought that he was going to be a grandfather. He started by taking the car out more, going to the club, hanging out with his old law buddies, talking late into the night over whisky. He started dressing properly again, in tailored shirts and leather brogues; he made an effort, more than he had made in years. His eyes sparkled again and once after I was ready to leave, he reached out for me and gave me a gentle hug.

Your mother, she would have been so happy…so, so happy, Del.

I hugged him back tightly, my belly pressing into him, my heart leaping for joy. How the eminent birth of my child had transformed my father. How the years of sadness had fallen away, and given us the possibility of new life again.

I should not have driven that night but I did.

Sumi needed to talk about the state of her relationship with Fairman and we decided to meet at a café in Bangsar. I was two weeks away from my due date but I wanted to see her, wanted to carry on the way I had been throughout the pregnancy. Being active was part of the plan, right until the baby was on her way out.

The café was crowded and full of boisterous teenagers eating cake and drinking sparkling wine. It was a trendy-looking

French-fusion bistro which specialised in desserts, with comfy leather seats, chrome and marble furniture and Art Nouveau prints on the walls. The teens looked like they were back from summer holidays. Rich kids with fancy handphones, coloured hair and new accents.

We found a quiet table in a corner and as I tried to sit down, Sumi remarked, *Jesus, you're huge!*

Tell me about it. I feel like a beached whale.

I had peppermint tea. She had white wine. After one sip she blurted out that they were at a point in their relationship where it was either going to lead to marriage or a prolonged cohabitation with no end in sight.

So how?

He hasn't mentioned it, but I have a feeling that it will come up soon.

Why don't you mention it?

I don't know. I guess I still believe in courtship.

Are you happy?

Yeah. I think we're really meant for this. Never thought I'd love again. I think I want kids…

Does he?

Yeah… He talks to Omar a lot. You know, about the future.

Really?

Yeah, it's good that they can talk.

It's important.

So Del, what do I do? I need to know where I stand!

You don't want to seem desperate, so just wait a bit more.

For how long? Maybe he's not sure.

I really doubt that. You guys are good. Just give it some time. Trust him.

That's just it. Trust. Can I really? Is this guy for real? After what I've been through?

Shit, Sumi. Look at me. I am going to be a mum! I'm fucking scared. This is for real!

And there it was. It all came out. How I did not want to end up like my mother, distant and afraid. How I wanted to love my child, to be everything a mother should be and more. How petrified I was. How everything was so unknown.

Lisa kept saying, *The birth is a few hours but you will have to parent your child for the rest of your life.* All my focus had been on the birth and the pregnancy, being well and healthy. What if I became a shitty mother? What if I didn't bond with my child? What if I developed post-natal depression? What if my milk didn't come through? What if I tore badly during the birth? Would I still be able to have sex? Would it hurt?

Sumi heard me out. She sat and listened and held my hand all the way through dinner and dessert and walked me to the car and made sure I put my seatbelt on.

Get Omar to call as soon as you go into labour, okay? Go home and get some sleep. Rest. Stop worrying. You have to take this one step at a time.

I nodded.

Hey, Fairman will ask you to marry him. I know it.

Sumi nodded and blew a kiss.

SMS me when you get home?

I drove out of the parking lot and eased the car onto the street, thinking of what we'd said to each other. Omar was working late so the thought of a hot bubble bath and another cup of tea was comforting as I drove past young couples, clutching each other, readying for the night of partying ahead. I drove slowly, deliberately. Home was minutes away.

I waited for the lights to turn green, and as I turned onto the road, I heard a crash and a hard jolt on my right. The force pulled my body to the left, something hit my head then I blacked out.

I woke up and heard shouting. The windscreen was spiderwebbed and through it I saw a couple screaming at each other. A hard knock on the driver's side window. Slowly, I wound it down.

Are you all right? Can you open the door?

An old Chinese face looked kindly down at me.

My arm hurt, but I got the door open, unclicked the seatbelt and tried to get out of the car.

His eyes flicked with concern when he saw my belly and he started dialling his handphone.

I am going to call an ambulance. Are you feeling okay? Is there anyone I can call? Your husband?

The young woman was now hitting the man she was with. I could not make out anything they were saying. There was a small crowd gathering and we were blocking traffic. Cars started honking impatiently. I nodded at the man, who had taken my hand and was guiding me out of the crowd. A police siren edged closer, scaring the couple. The girl went hysterical when she saw me.

You fucking piece of shit! Look what you did! She's pregnant, you fucking idiot!

Then she ran towards me. Her eyes were completely glazed. She was obviously high.

Are you okay? So sorry…are you all right?

I sat down on the pavement. My elbow throbbed. I could not turn my head to the left. My neck felt sprained. There were police, faces peering at me. An ambulance. Then Omar. His crazed eyes. Being lifted onto a stretcher, oxygen. Hospital doors. Lights. Darkness.

When I woke up again, I saw Papa and Omar on either side of the bed. Sumi almost tripped coming through the door.

She's awake! Then a furtive kiss from Omar. Papa grabbed my hand. Sumi squeezed my other hand until it hurt.

The baby's fine, she's fine. Not a scratch, no distress at all.

Papa shrank into his chair. He hated hospitals. His face was pale with fright. Another car crash. Sumi took him home after the doctor came and said that I could leave the next day. Then it was just me and Omar. I didn't know what he was going to say. His back was to me and when he turned, his face was contorted with pain.

Del, when I got that call, I punched a wall. I know it wasn't your fault, but why? Why, for god's sake, did you go out? The baby is two weeks away, what were you thinking?

He was a mess. I sighed. I didn't feel like saying anything because there was nothing to say. It was a senseless accident. The car was hit by a teenage boy, off his head, high as an elephant on ketamine. It was not my fault. But Omar needed to rant.

I want to wring his fucking neck! I could kill that little shit! Omar, calm down.

Del, I can't lose you. This accident made me realise that you, this baby, you're everything to me. My life. All that I live for. I mean, I know, but the thought of losing you now, like this. I can't. I can't.

Strangely, I felt calm. I had to be the strong one then. He climbed up onto my bed and I held him, he clung to me, like a terrified child. The baby started kicking, and Omar placed his hands over my belly.

I felt them both, my husband and my baby, needing me. Finding strength in me, in my body. Our hands intertwined, holding each other's bodies, giving what we needed. I felt more courage that day then I ever felt in my life.

Later that night there was panic on the floor. Nurses were running around, visibly upset. Then Omar got a call on his handphone. It was Fairman, his voice so loud Omar pulled it away from his ear.

Turn on the TV, now!

In that hospital room, from a television high up in the corner, we saw the planes fly into the twin towers in New York City, we heard the screams of patients from the other rooms, we saw the collapsing steel and concrete, the inferno. We saw multiple dots falling to the ground, people falling or jumping to their deaths. I felt hot tears on Omar's cheek. I could not cry. The horror. The absolute, inexpressible horror of it all.

Two weeks later, I was back in the hospital, this time with a dilated cervix, fast pulsating contractions in a tornado of pain.

The contractions were a surprise, at first bearable, but then they bore deeper and deeper into my body, like a drill that charted a course through bone, blood, sinew. It was a primal pain, visceral, profound. She was moving through me, pushing through me. I felt like I was going to break, like the splitting limbs of a doll being torn apart. I had not known that the human body was capable of delivering such pain. I sat up, I sat down, I kneeled, I squatted, I growled like an animal, crawling around on all fours. I breathed in and out and groaned. Deep guttural moans. There was music in the room, and incense, and Omar and Lisa.

I didn't want any drugs, so the pain was excruciating. I lost track of time, but it had been hours. By the time I was fully dilated, I was on the verge of exhaustion. And then I had to push. Pushing a baby out of your vagina is a wonder, a feat only possible when you're in the thick of it. When Lisa said *Push, Del, push,* I did.

Omar was behind me, his arms wrapped around mine. His lips on my neck, whispering. *Baby, you can do this. Love you, love you. Come on, baby. Push.* My thighs pressed against my chest, my neck arched in pain. I felt a contraction coming, and pushed with all my might. Every bit of strength, with every ounce of the possible, I pushed. I saw the bright flicker of light, the lotus flower of serpent energy, coiling up and up and down and down, the oily scent of blood and birth, and my slippery baby easing into the world.

There she was. She opened her eyes, and I felt a powerful slap from the universe, a surge of love, pleasure and pain. She was out of me.

Omar cut the cord, and my baby girl was taken away to be weighed and cleaned.

Push out the placenta, Del, just a soft push now.

I felt it slip out, like a large sponge; it looked like a round lung, bubbly and bloody.

She's losing blood, it won't stop. There was panic in Lisa's voice. *She needs a shot. Now!*

I felt light, weak. The room was folding in. I heard the baby cry.

Del, Del! Omar grabbed my arm.

It kept flowing out of me, this blood. I could smell the salt and metal of it, I felt nauseous, my head fell backwards, I slumped into the warm pool.

Del! Lisa, do something!

I sensed Omar's fear. Then felt a sharp prick in my thigh. A cold patch spreading.

It's stopped. The bleeding has stopped.

Thank god!

Lisa pulled me up gently towards a pillow. They turned me, pulled away the plastic sheet with my blood. Omar came towards me, with our daughter.

Her face, still spotted with traces of afterbirth, was scrunched into a frown; she uttered a sharp cry and her eyes flickered open. Wide and green, like her father's.

I saw the universe and the greatest of loves.

I guided her to my breast and she opened her mouth to suckle. There she was.

Omar and I looked at each other, and we saw only love. And then, kisses of joy.

FOUR

ALBA

"ALBA. ALBA."

Omar breathed in her name again. *Alba.*

"My daughter," he said.

She was fast asleep, her eyes shut, her tiny fists in tight little balls. They had just come home to their apartment, and in the sanctity of their home, he could finally breathe, and reflect on the single most profound moment of his life. His mother filled the fridge with food before she left and the sickly sweet smell of flowers overpowered the apartment. He sat on the couch and gazed at her, asleep in his arms.

She was so small. He cradled her gently in the crook of his left arm, not wanting to wake her, and he let his eyes rest on the miracle that was his daughter. Her head of dark brown hair, her fair skin still flushed from the birth. The midwife had exclaimed at how much hair she had when she crowned.

Alba, swaddled tightly in a light cream blanket, her rosebud lips, her eyelashes long and curled upward, her cheeks pink. How beautiful and perfect she was. Ten fingers and toes, all there.

Omar was stunned, wordless. Nothing had prepared him

for this moment. No one had told him that this love would be like a kick in the balls, in the gut. He had never imagined a moment like this was even possible. This was the kind of love that drove men to fists, to blood, to bitter court battles, to the ends of the earth and back.

She yawned suddenly, her tiny mouth opening and closing in minute perfection. His heart leaped with joy, then pain. He felt confusion, then wonder. How could she yawn and then go straight back to sleep? He then remembered the pain that he had felt when Del had the miscarriage. He remembered the despair, the loss of hope.

This was a gift from the gods. His prayers had been answered. He wanted Del to be happy again, but he had underestimated his own emotions. Everything he had done in his life had led him to this moment. All the achievements, all the mistakes, his fuckups, his misanthropic moments, his personal battles, his doubts, all the women he'd fucked and not fucked—everything had led him to this. All roads had led him to Alba. This glorious, magical moment where he held his daughter in his hands.

He wanted to weep, but instead made a silent vow. He would love and protect her and be the best father to her, he would raise her to be a good and righteous person in society. And then he remembered what his father had said to him: "Whisper the Shahadah in her ear when she is born." Omar leaned over and whispered:

Ashadu allah illa ha illalah
Muhammad ar Rasul lullah
Baby girl, come to god
Baby girl, my baby girl

* * *

WE NAMED HER Strelitzia Alba, the Latin name for the white bird of paradise. Alba meant dawn, as she was born at 6.59am on the 25th of September, after 15 hours of labour. Papa had managed to find the seeds of this rare species from a heliconia grower, and planted a row of strelitzia right beside my tree in his garden, burying the placenta in the dark soil as he did.

Mercifully, I had not torn, thanks to Lisa, who asked me to push only when the contractions came. Within 24 hours I was discharged with Alba—as we decided to call her—and an entourage that included Omar's parents and their female relatives, thousands of ringgit worth of flowers, greeting cards and my small overnight bag. I could walk.

In the bathroom for my first pee after the birth, I winced in pain as the urine coursed over my battered and stretched vagina. My belly flopped like a fleshy balloon. My breasts were swollen and sore and my face was still flushed from the exertion of pushing. But I felt drugged from happiness. Sheer elation. Giving birth was a thrill, and I was a mother. I felt high. I looked at my daughter, bundled up like a slug in her tiny car seat, and felt such a surge of love that I knew I would kill to protect her. Draw blood, slice off a man's face or arm, if I had to. I finally understood what motherhood could do to a woman.

My milk came in three days later and she drank like a fiend, constantly hungry. I slept in spurts, had frantic dreams, then woke to feed her again. Omar stayed home for two weeks until we had a consistent schedule. He bathed and changed her, sang to her and carried her in and out of rooms. I saw how he loved her, this creature that resembled him more than she did me. They had the same eyes, dark brown hair. She was of my blood and his but she was more of his. Her cries were soothed by his lullabies, nursery rhymes, and her eyes blinked in emerald countenance. Omar was in love with his beautiful Alba.

How exquisite she was. Her tiny mouth which opened and closed when she yawned, her little fingers with white half moon nails, her arms which flailed in the air, the scent of her cheeks and neck, of milk from my bosom and the creaminess of the bath bubbles, the soft folds of flesh on her thighs, the thick tufts of hair on her head, the soft fontanel, beneath that, her brain, the soft pulse of her heart when I lay my ears next to her. How exquisite she was.

Months passed and she grew beautifully. I got into a rhythm for bath-time, feeding, playtime, nap, feeding, nap, walk, bath, bed. She learnt to turn, squirm and cry to get her way. Papa, too, was besotted with her. Evening walks with Alba up and down the roads from his house. How she laughed and smiled to the neighbours. Her hair bouncing in the wind, her chubby thighs so warm and smooth.

My father was alive again, he sat in the garden, reading to her, pointing at pages in books, he carried her when she fretted, sang to her. Omar and Papa, completely consumed by this child.

But I was exhausted from lack of sleep and the constant breastfeeding. She refused formula and I was reduced to feeling like an animal bred for its milk. On some nights, I slept with her in the guest room, napping in between.

She would wake up and drink from me noisily, clutching at my breast with her little hands, sometimes biting my nipple with her gums, waking me up. At dawn she would try to sit up, chattering in her own language while I stared at the languid swish of the curtains until my eyes closed and Omar came to take her downstairs. I would sleep again, then stumble downstairs to see them both, locked in a circle that sometimes made me feel like an outsider.

How she laughed when she saw her father, how he kissed her toes and watched her squirm in glee, how his face lit up when she curled her hands around his face. How she sat obediently nodding her head when he showed her how to stack wooden blocks, how she screamed *kah kah kah* when he tickled her tummy, how she shrieked with joy when he picked her up and threw her into the air. How alike they were: Like father, like daughter. Was I ever like my father?

She would cry when he had to go to work, she would wail and stretch her hands, refusing to let him go. How he would stand there talking to her saying that he would be back to play with her at the end of the day. How he would kiss her, untangle her arms and legs around him, hand her to me and then reach to kiss me quickly before gazing lovingly at her.

Did he still love me? Or did he love her more?

I was tired and still fat; I had not lost the extra weight. I avoided mirrors and tight-fitting clothes. I wore loose, flowing shirts and skirts, sometimes contemplating my pregnancy clothes. Every day was a fat day and there was never enough time. The glow I had from the pregnancy had long abandoned me. My hair was listless and dry; my face dull, pimply. I had no desire to put on make-up, a dress, heels, make myself look good for him. Sex was infrequent.

But one night, during a storm, he came to me. Alba was asleep, snuggled under her favourite blanket and her Winnie the Pooh pillow. He kissed me on the neck and led me to our bedroom, and then he took off my pyjama shorts and T-shirt, lifting it over my ripe, milk-laden breasts. Kissing and sucking my nipples gently, then forcefully. I threw my head back and let him take me. I had missed him and I showed him how much. In the height of the storm, the curtains lashing against the open window, he pounded into me again and again. My hands grasped the window railings and I was reminded again that he loved me, *I love you, I love you*—our passionate cries drowned in the spattering rain.

Moments like that didn't come very often. I was still adamant about not wanting a maid, so I cooked, cleaned, fed, nursed and tried to run the household as best I could. Omar and Fairman were getting larger contracts and their office of five staff had to double. He never told me much about the work they did, just that it involved the construction of expressways in and around the Klang Valley. He seemed happier, finally working with people in his area of expertise. Fairman took on the legal aspects of their contracts and Omar designed the structural aspects of the work, often coming home with rolls of blueprints. TMF Sdn Bhd was working out and the partnership flourished.

On some days, I struggled. I often wondered about the work and life I once had. The tear gas, the writing, the brittle anger we all shared: I missed it. Motherhood had robbed me of a life that I could never have again. My options were forever limited. There were times when I looked in the mirror and I did not like what I saw. My body had changed, my face weary and lined, my eyes sometimes sad. I did not know why. I was a wife and mother, and I was in a good place. I felt grateful, but there were times when I felt that cold, familiar emptiness. The world was a far more dangerous place. A child had transformed my existence, and I was afraid. Fear had crept in like an unwanted ghost, haunting the shell of tired existence, taunting me.

I loved Alba with such ferocity, I sometimes kissed her until her eyes puckered with pain. She ruled us with her smiles, her chatter, her endless sing-song gibberish, and her wonder at everything. Teaching her words, feelings, colours, animals, it was all a joy. *What a joy she is. Such joy.* But she got bored quickly, had a tempestuous scream, and when she did not get what she wanted, she was like a fury, a creature with eyes that spat fire. Perhaps I was afraid of who she would become, that her strength would outstrip mine. I feared that she was draining the life out of me, that I would become insignificant. That she would be all that Omar wanted and needed.

I was racked with confusion. Sleep deprivation was becoming a form of torture; I craved sleep more than anything else. A good night's sleep seemed so impossible. Surely not all mothers suffered this?

One night, I dreamt of a pontianak, the vampiric ghost of a woman who had died in childbirth. Malaysians have a profound belief in the spirit world and in the spaces that inhabit the visible and invisible worlds. There are many names for many kinds of ghosts but the pontianak was the most feared of all. I had never seen one, but I sometimes felt the presence of entities in my father's house. Gasing Hill was rumoured to harbour ghosts, and some nights, I would feel a presence in the hallway between my room and my parents' room, as if I was being watched.

Omar was away on a business trip, his first to Sudan, and I was alone with Alba in the apartment. She had been testy from teething pains and I had soothed her sore gums with ointment until she stopped crying. I fell into a troubled sleep.

She came to my door, this long-haired creature with blood-red eyes. There she was, a figure in white, floating above the ground, face contorted with evil. I heard a screech, and then a gust of wind as she tried to come in through the front door. I slammed the door on her arm as her fingers reached for me, greying with mottled flesh and talons, I pressed against it with all my might, but the door burst open again and again. She wanted my child, and I fought this creature like a wild thing, clawing at her with my arms and legs. I could see into her eyes, the blackness of her soul, and the whisper of a profound sadness. Then I sat bolt upright in bed, choking with terror. Alba was in her cot, fast asleep, but the window, which I had closed and locked, was wide open.

CEYLON HILL WAS the last green haven in the centre of Kuala Lumpur, dotted with a cluster of graceful colonial-style apartments. Their curved balconies of cantilevered concrete hung over thick, lush jungles, with verdant wild banana plants and local foxes or musang. These were enviable spaces. Inside, large, airy sitting rooms with clear glass window panes beckoned in cool evening breezes, delightful on cloyingly hot days. On the top of the hill, a water tower overlooked a handful of cream-coloured bungalows built in the 50s, still lived in by some of KL's oldest families. The apartments below, in contrast, had become popular with burgeoning artists and musicians who had begun populating them, finding the cheap rent affordable in the final vestiges of colonial glory.

On weekends, there were parties with live music, performance poetry, cheap wine and marijuana. There was talk of reform, angry, wild, avant garde gestures. Fiery speeches from activists, musicians, filmmakers. There was hunger that had to be fed, a need for expression, a need for dissent. A movement had sprung up in the arts community. Their logo—a black question mark against a yellow background with the slogan, Artis Pro Activ—APA. Apa—What? What was going on? A question for those in power. A question that demanded answers.

Across the road, the KL Tower glimmered at night, music thumping from its base, where wild raves fed music and Ecstasy to techno-addled youth. There was always a time to party.

In the four years since Reformasi, KL had thrived. There were more expats than ever, many who had come for the drugs, stayed for the girls. DJs fell in love with locals and procreated, and so the culture of mixed bloods carried on.

Down the road from Ceylon Hill, a row of refurbished shop houses had become the centre of KL's nightlife. Bangsar was old news. There were tapas bars, Irish pubs, German gastro-bars and one gay bar. Frangipani, the white colonial bungalow which had been transformed into a French-fusion restaurant with an upstairs members-only club, continued its Friday gay nights despite numerous raids, and hundreds came out to "cuci mata" or feast their eyes on young, nubile boys. Women and men packed the floors, champagne and cocktails shimmied off bar tops, mixologists twirled bottles with ease. There was chatter, kissing, extravagance. The women were beautiful, the men even more so.

There was always talk of money. KL was becoming more cosmopolitan. Foreign investment was higher than it had been and the KL skyline was proof. New buildings competed for thinner and leaner shards of sky. Investor confidence was strong, despite the shocking announcement from Mahathir that he was going to resign.

On 25 January 2002, as if straight out of a Malay daytime soap opera, he had stood in front of thousands at his party's general assembly—the United Malays National Organisation, or UMNO—and said with tearful hubris, "It's time for me to go, yes, it's time for me to go."

"No, no, you can't!" shrieked the Minister of Trade and Industry, her red tudung falling over her face. More ministers rushed to the stage, unabashed in their grief. Mahathir was bathed in uncommon hugs. Their beloved leader, their visionary, the authoritarian tyrant who had fashioned a mandate for Malaysia was finally going to leave after 22 years in power as Prime Minister.

Thousands celebrated. In bars, in restaurants, in mamak stalls, in homes and in the privacy of bedrooms, ordinary Malaysians thanked their gods for the unthinkable. Some were saddened, most were stunned. A Malaysia without Mahathir. It was unimaginable, it was uncertain. It was utter folly.

Anwar was still in jail, inching through his sentence. His back had deteriorated; his spine would suffer lifelong consequences from having to sleep on concrete. The world condemned the Malaysian government for its draconian actions. Mahathir retaliated by blaming George Soros and the Western media for twisting truths.

"You are jealous of our success, our fundamentals are strong," he infamously retorted.

Yet, KL continued to thrive, the city was alive with intangible possibility. It was this that armed Marina that night when she stepped into Frangipani, her hand on a man who had booked her for the night. She was no longer the same person who had left the same club in a Black Maria a year ago. No longer a streetwalker, but now a high-class escort, she lived in a different world. When she walked up the stairs into the doorway, the crowd of boys and men parted to let her through, and the music and the flaming lights swept her away.

OMAR WAS WORKING late the day it happened. He had just returned from Sudan and he was jetlagged and tired, but there were documents, plans that needed to be finalised. The television was on in his office and the news came on. A teary Mahathir came on the screen and said that he was going to resign as Chairperson of the Barisan National, the ruling coalition that had governed the country since Independence, and as Prime Minister of Malaysia. It was also the final day of the UMNO General Assembly and traffic would be bad near the Putra World Trade Centre, so he decided to finish the paperwork and head home after 8pm.

As if on cue, his handphone rang.

"You see the news? Bloody hell!" Fairman was shouting into his ear.

"Yeah. This is absolutely insane," Omar said and paused. "Are we going to be all right?"

They were about to sign million-dollar contracts and Mahathir leaving could pose problems. It could cause jitters with their foreign partners, and as a Bumiputera company, they had the ease of contracts, not just because they were Malay, but because both their fathers had made sure that their sons got a fair share of the spoils.

"I'll get those contracts signed as soon as possible."

"Yes please, or we're fucked."

Fairman hung up and Omar stared at his reflection on the glass that divided him and the KL sky. His tie had come loose, his hair ruffled and disarrayed, his eyes riveted to the Petronas Twin Towers in the distance. It was inconceivable. The man who had created the Malaysian Reformasi was retreating, the man who had brought Anwar to his knees would no longer be the most powerful man in Malaysia. The man who had given certain meaning to his life was bowing out, to be immortalised in the pages of history.

Omar opened the top right drawer on his desk, pulled out the bottle and the crystal snifter beside it, unscrewed it, poured out the amber liquid, and lifted the hand-cut glass to his lips.

He suddenly remembered the scent of tear gas, the volleying screams of people pounded by water cannons, Del with her wild eyes and snarling mouth screaming, "Mahathir Undur! Reformasi!" It was over, but instead of feeling any measure of joy or relief, he felt nothing.

As the whisky swirled around his tongue and slid its fiery tail down his throat, he picked up the picture frame. Del cradling Alba, taken moments after her birth.

It was all for them now. Everything that had meaning was contained within the four corners of that gilded frame. He finished the whisky and thought of cradling Alba in his arms. All he wanted was her.

I KNEW HE was at the door. A struggling Alba squirmed her way out of my arms into Omar's.

I got her, he said. *I got her.*

Her cries stopped almost immediately upon seeing her father. I was on the verge of collapse.

Oh god. I whispered as I stumbled to the couch and fell onto the pillows. *So tired, so tired,* I murmured, my voice trembling, threatening tears. Alba started crying again, her high-pitched screams slightly muted and hoarse from the hours of being unsettled the night before. She was teething and had been impossible to put down. I had tried everything humanly possible to soothe her. My head felt leaden on the pillow. I could not move, my calves ached from pacing up and down and my arms felt like I'd been carrying weights non-stop for 12 hours. Omar started talking and singing to her, she settled for a while until a shrill wail escaped her.

Maybe she has colic? Omar suggested softly, leaning into my ear.

I don't know, I don't know, I whispered back.

Maybe a bath will help. Omar said, while swooping her down towards me. Alba gurgled and smiled, her chubby arms trying to grab me. It was so typical of him. All he wanted to do was play with Alba when he came home. And all I wanted to do was curl up into a ball and sleep for days.

Say mama, mama.

Go away, I need to sleep, I said.

She is four months old today, darling, Omar whispered

So she is. I tried to sit up but immediately felt dizzy. *Sorry, it's been hellish.*

Omar sat down next to me, Alba snuggled contently in his

arms, sucking on her fingers. I leaned my head on his shoulder and kissed his cheek gently. *Look at us, our little family. And one very tired mummy.*

We love you, tired mummy. Omar leaned to kiss me. Alba struggled in his arms, her legs kicking in the air. She was unhappy again. He stood up.

Right, bath time it is.

Let me nap, please, just for half an hour. I stretched my arms over my head, let out a big yawn, put my leg over a cushion and fell into a deep sleep.

When I woke up, Omar was in front of his computer on the dining table. He looked showered and refreshed.

Hey there, gorgeous, how you feeling? he asked. *Want something to eat?*

Where's Alba? I stifled a new yawn.

In bed, listening to the heartbeat music and she's happy. Omar gestured to the baby monitor on the table. We both heard her gurgling to the sounds that were coming out of a CD player we'd installed close to her cot. It was an ambient track that combined a human heartbeat—which supposedly helped babies sleep—whale song and guitar.

I should go check, I said.

No, leave her. She's fine. Just let her be.

I sighed and sat down next to him. He continued typing then shut the laptop a few seconds later.

Want a salad? Or a sandwich? he asked as he opened the fridge.

Doesn't matter, I grunted.

Sandwich it is then. He smiled.

I'm sorry, I feel like a friggin' zombie.

I know.

He brought out tomatoes, cheese, mayonnaise, lettuce, smoked salmon wrapped in paper and put it on the counter top. He reached into the bread bin and brought out a loaf of sourdough bread I had bought the day before. I watched him slice the bread and then pop it into the toaster. He'd started humming as he sliced a large red onion into thin slices. He knew I liked onions with salmon. Then he assembled the sandwich, layering the onions, lettuce, salmon and thinly sliced tomatoes, putting another dollop of mayonnaise on top and then a generous sprinkling of freshly ground pepper.

It was meditative, watching him like that. My husband preparing me a simple meal was an act of love, and my tired eyes felt energised, knowing that we would have a few moments alone together, eating a meal like we always had.

Here you go, my darling. Omar handed me the plate. *Eat!*

It sounded like a demand and I bit into the sandwich obediently. The crunch of the bread gave way to a textured filling of smoked fish, fresh vegetables and a creamy mayonnaise. I was ravenous. He smiled and nodded, reached into the fridge and brought out a bottle of white wine, uncorked it and poured me a glass. It felt so normal, just like old times.

The baby monitor crackled and we heard Alba fuss, the put-putting in the throat before a perfectly formed wail flowed across the dinner table to my ears. I gulped a swig of wine and swallowed the last of the sandwich.

Let me feed her and come back, okay? Give me a few minutes.

I kissed Omar quickly on the lips and hurried towards the nursery. The room was bathed in a warm light with butterfly shadows from the night-light dancing on turquoise walls, and the scent of lavender coming from a burner in the corner. There were stars glowing on the ceiling and as I peered over the cot, I saw Alba staring fixedly at the stars, then at my face. Her mouth puckered up and a cry formed as I picked her up.

I sat down in the armchair and guided her to my breast. She suckled hard and drank noisily. I felt her fingers clutch at my breasts, and heard her swallow every few seconds, it was the most exhilarating feeling of all, knowing that I was the sole source of her nourishment. I remembered reading something about how the human baby was the most vulnerable of all to the elements. Newly-born calves could struggle to their feet, hatched turtles had to evade hungry birds and scramble into seas, but the human baby would not survive without shelter or nourishment. How vulnerable they were. How weak.

I was startled when I felt Alba being lifted gently out of my arms. I had fallen asleep again.

She's out. Omar whispered and as he lowered her into the cot she started fussing, but he went *shhh shhh shhh* and patted her gently. Within seconds she was asleep. We turned off the butterfly light and tiptoed out the room.

Once outside, Omar kissed me. He gripped my shoulders tightly, cupped by face in his hands and kissed me again. My exhaustion turned into passion and there we stood outside our daughter's room, kissing and moaning like lovesick teenagers.

* * *

Two hours later, I heard her cry again. Omar and I had made love, showered together and made love again. It was the most sexual we had felt in a long time, a reminder of what being a couple meant, what being a couple deeply in love meant. I hadn't had more than two hours of continuous sleep since Alba was born, and I felt that I was slowly but surely being stripped down. Being in Omar's arms, having him inside me, telling me over and over again that he loved me, made me feel safe, protected. He was the man in our family, he was Alba's father, and he loved her. But I still needed sleep, and we had sacrificed sex for much-needed sleep. I rubbed my eyes and stared at the dark ceiling. I felt defenceless, knowing that in spite of everything that Omar did, I was still her primary source of life.

I padded into her bedroom and turned off the baby monitor. Omar needed to sleep, and I needed to feed Alba again. I picked her up. Her head was beaded with sweat and her nappy, bulging. I took her to the nappy table, and unbuttoned her onesie. She waved her arms and legs in the air, fussing loudly and as I stuck the tape on her new nappy, I decided to change her onesie for a pyjama bottom. The digital clock on the side table glared 2.33am. I sighed. It was going to be another long night.

I decided to take her back to our bed, deciding against feeding her on the chair then leaving her in her cot. She would feed, then sleep, then wake and feed again. Omar was snoring slightly and I slid under the covers, with Alba on my right breast. Her mouth sought my breast greedily and in seconds, I could hear the familiar sound of her satisfied swallowing. She pulled at my breast more and I grimaced when her little nails scratched me.

I closed my eyes and felt the coolness of the air-conditioning on the back of my neck. Alba stopped sucking as if to take in her surroundings, her eyes darting around as she kicked her legs in contentment. I was filled with a sudden rage and wanted to squeeze those thighs. The exhaustion had come and gone, but this time there was anger.

MARINA SPOKE CLEARLY, enunciating every word.

"Presenting the President of the Mak Nyah Association of Malaysia," she said while staring at the mirror. "MNYAM. Meen-nyam, mee-ne-yam," she said again. She pursed her lips and continued patting the bronze liquid liner on her lips.

"What are you doing in there?" a male voice said from the bedroom.

Marina dabbed her lips with a tissue, smiled and twirled out the door.

"Morning, sayang," she began. "Presenting the President of Meen-nyam, M-N-Y-A-M, the Mak Nyah Association of Malaysia!" She twirled and raised her hands in the air with a final flourish. "What do you think?"

He sat up in bed, his portly tummy barely covered by the duvet, his hands scratching the salt and pepper hairs curling indignantly against his fleshy chest. He noisily slurped down a glass of water while swallowing two triangular blue pills. Marina sauntered towards his outstretched arm, giggling.

"Want some more?"

She leaned over and kissed him on his lips. He grunted and pulled Marina towards him. "Come here...to me." Marina loosened her bathrobe, gasped slightly as the cool air hardened the nipples on her newly rounded breasts, still warm from the shower, and he lowered the duvet where his thick, hard penis revealed itself. Marina swooped down and took it in her mouth, while he stared straight ahead. The smell of ripe lilies and the breakfast of animal protein and fruit sullied the air, and Marina was made to feel that she had to pay for her à la carte meal along with the crisp white sheets and shower head with torrential pin pricks of water which had massaged her shoulders and back with the dexterity of a blind masseur. He was now moaning softly and Marina took his penis and rubbed it in between her breasts.

"So much bigger now," she said, lightly kissing him all over the face.

"Yes, I can see that," he said, smiling.

"Tell me."

His eyes were glazed as his chest heaved. "You know what I always want."

Sunlight was streaming into the room, heating the air. She thought of closing the curtains but he shook his head. "I want to come in between those twin towers."

Marina knew that behind her, the two phallic structures stood, half-monoliths in the blue sky, cloudless, stark. She took his still-erect penis, emptied out a tube of lube and turned to face the sky. She gasped as he entered her and as she bounced up and down to his loud panting, she closed her eyes and thought of what it would be like to be a bird, singular and free.

HE'S RESIGNED? I shouted. *Why didn't you tell me this?*

I thought you knew.

How? I don't even have time to brush my teeth, let alone read newsgroups or emails.

Are you upset?

Yes! Fuck. You know how important this was.

Sorry. I was trying to figure it out myself.

Really? What happens now?

He leaves and Pak Lah takes over as PM.

What? He is just going to walk away?

The man resigned, he is allowed to do that. Walk away.

I sighed. *This changes everything. What do we fight for now? I mean, I know we fight for Anwar, but if this fucker walks free, we're still fucked.*

He's going. End of an era. It's over.

And what about Anwar? He's still in jail.

Well, somebody has to pay for it.

Wait. What? Aren't you worried?

About what?

Contracts? What else?

We're all right.

How? You think foreign companies won't doubt you because you have daddy's name in the fine print? That's okay?

Omar was silent.

Come on. Admit it! You're just like all of them. Cronies!

Del, please.

No. Omar. You can't do this.

Well, I don't have a fucking choice.

You do!

How?

Do your own thing!

My own thing? You joking? What? Like make things out of bits of wood? Sit on a rock and pontificate? This isn't about me anymore. It's about you and Alba. I have a family now.

So you work like a dog, I raise her and we see each other on weekends?

No! Why are you saying this?

Because you are becoming someone I never thought you would.

Your ideals make no sense! I am doing what is right, what is necessary for ALL of us.

I thought we believed in the same things.

We do! Del, I am running a company that builds bridges, we build roads. I am doing what I do best.

With government contracts and the right connections.

That is really not fair, Del.

Well, he's gone now. Great. Fucking great!

Calm down.

I need to get out of here.

Del—

I need to think, need to—

You don't have to like what I do, but you need to understand that this is a job, this is work, this is what I do now. I am taking care of you and Alba. Because nobody ever took care of you, Del. Not your father, not your mother.

I shook my head. *I can look after myself. I can look after Alba, but I don't know if I can look after you.*

Omar took a step towards me and took me in his arms. As his eyes probed mine, his voice was calm yet urgent.

Just be here, Del, just be here.

* * *

ALBA STRUGGLED TO walk, cruising along the sides of tables, clutching the edges wildly.

From the kitchen, Omar shouted in thunderous applause. *She's walking! Look! She's walking!*

Alba tottered towards me in her diapers and curls, holding a wooden toy clown that went *clack, clack, clack*. She walked straight into me and hugged my knees, then looked up and smiled, showing four teeth. Omar lifted her up and twirled her around and around, her laughter pealing like little bells, as if fairies were in the room. She was a wonder to us all. When she sometimes slept between us, we would gaze at her for hours, first inhaling her scent—talcum powder, lavender oil, breast milk and goodness—then lightly touching her dark curls, her high smooth forehead, her lashes, the almond curve of her sleeping eyes, her full cheeks, upturned mouth, the three folds of fat on her arms and thighs. Her chest rose up and down, ten fingers and toes all intact and untainted by the filth of the world. She was glorious.

I had come to terms with being exhausted, and focused on being the best mother I could. Once Alba started sleeping through the night, I had time to myself. Time to read, take long baths, and make special meals for Omar when he came back from trips abroad. Time to have a sense of normality.

A child disrupts everything, and time becomes a ventricle of loose possibilities. I had to learn to accept this. There were infinite possibilities in a day, from what Alba was going to learn, to the number of teeth that were sprouting in her mouth, to the expansion of her vocabulary. But time was also dictated by how long it took to buckle her into her car seat, which she did not like, to folding the pram and putting it into the boot, making sure the bag with diapers, change of clothes, juice, milk powder, milk bottle, snacks and toys was present, to getting into the car and turning on the engine with a sigh of relief, driving to intended destination and taking child, bag and pram out again.

It was numbing at times. My brain was used to more serious matters, and the game of motherhood was unwieldy. The world around me felt flaccid, there was a certain need to navigate through people, objects, doors, stairs, bodies of water. There was a heightened sense of calm, but underneath it all, a constant nagging and unrelenting worry. It dulled me, spontaneity was impossible. There had to be an order to things. How my universe had changed! I felt trapped. Motherhood was a curse that could only be lifted when a body is lowered into the earth. And there were times when I felt that tired, that only the earth could save me, only death could release me.

The day Sumi and Fairman got married was also the day that Alba turned one. The hotel on the Batu Ferringhi beach in Penang was transformed by the silky, white fabric dangling from the pine trees, twinkle lights and giant candles. Against the fiery sun on the horizon, a small group of family and friends presided over the non-denominational ceremony, officiated by a woman who was a known spiritualist and healer.

Rather new age, don't you think? Omar whispered.

I think it's cool. I smiled back as I straightened Alba's bow
on the back of her white dress. She was the ring-bearer and
already looked tired and bored. I whispered to Alba, *Just walk
slowly and hold the cushion in front of you.* As the sun dipped
into the sea, the lights came on, illuminating all of us, making
us look like druids. We numbered about fifty, including
family and the closest of friends. Imran was present with a
stunning Indian woman in a turquoise sari, his new girlfriend
presumably. Then there was Fairman's parents, his siblings and
their partners, Rose, most of the staff from the company and
their spouses.

Sumi looked radiant. Her hair was up and styled with
baby's breath, and she wore a white sari with a gold border.
Fairman was in a morning suit and looked absolutely dashing.

The spiritualist asked for the ring and Alba tottered over
from us to Fairman. Some in the audience whispered, *So
cute...ahhhh...* Fairman picked up the ring from the cushion,
gave her a kiss on the cheek and she ran back to us. Omar
picked her up and cuddled her, and I whispered, *Well done,
darling.* When they read the vows to each other, the waves
crashed louder onto the shore, the wind blew up and swirled
around our feet.

*I promise to love and protect you, for all the rest of my days,
whether healthy or sick, until the ground claims me... I do... I
do... You are now husband and wife.*

As Fairman leaned in to kiss Sumi, the cello player started
playing the marriage waltz and the newlyweds turned to
us, beaming with joy. We clapped and whooped and I saw
Fairman's mum wipe her eyes.

The reception was in the ballroom and as we made our way

there slowly on the grass, I said to Omar, *Let me take Alba up to the room, change her nappy before dinner.*

It seemed to be the right moment as Imran came up to Omar and said, *Let's hit the bar!* and thumped Omar on the shoulder. *Oh and by the way, this is Nim.*

The beautiful Indian woman smiled at us and in an American accent said, *What a gorgeous child! She did very well not dropping the ring.*

Yes, well, gorgeous child needs to have her nappy changed, I said. *See you all later.*

I made my way up the stairs, carrying Alba, who I knew was tired and ready for bed. I was ready to pass out too; the journey to Penang had been long and arduous. We had decided to drive from KL, instead of letting Alba experience her first plane journey, and it was a six-hour car ride. We thought it fitting to celebrate Alba's first birthday along with the wedding. The plan was to get the hotel to make a cake, which we would cut the following day at teatime.

Alba had been restless the entire journey and I had to resort to sitting with her in the back seat, playing with her and comforting her. I had a headache and got carsick, and felt nauseated for hours. We had arrived in Penang just before the rush-hour traffic and made it to the beach in good time.

We'll take her to the beach, Omar had said. *She can at least make a sand castle and you can get some sun.*

I don't want sun, I'd mumbled. *I want to sleep.*

Sure, you sleep and we will make sand castles, won't we, Alba? Omar peered into the car mirror to look at Alba. At that time I was sullen with tiredness, and the thought of having sand up my thighs was not appealing at all.

As I entered our hotel room, Alba let out a wail that meant that she was tired, hungry and ready for bed. I gave her a quick wash in the shower and peeled off the grey silk dress I wore for the wedding. I dried Alba next to the sink, put on her teddy-bear pyjamas and saw my reflection in the mirror. My eye shadow and mascara had smeared. I let loose my hair from its tight bun and saw a woman who was still beautiful, with slight flab in the arms and waist, but a woman who was a mother, and whose child was smiling and calling *mama, mama*. Alba reached for my breast and I unhooked the bra, my nipple spilling out. There we were in the mirror, the image of mother and child. I smiled and said, *It's beddy time sweetheart, beddy time.*

The hotel had put a small bed beside ours; we did not want a cot as she had outgrown that. I made her a bottle of milk , and as she lay down next to me, I sang to her and caressed her face. Her long eyelashes cast shadows on her cheek. She drank the bottle noisily and emptied it. My head felt heavy and I thought I would nap before joining the reception downstairs. I closed my eyes for a few seconds and when I opened them, Alba was already asleep.

OMAR KNEW THAT Nim was eyeing him. They were still at the bar, seated tightly around a small table waiting for Fairman and Sumi to change for the reception and then make an entrance in the ballroom. Imran had been updating Omar about *Malaysia Times*, which had over one million subscribers, making the business of journalism more lucrative than ever, and Imran a very wealthy man. Omar sipped his gin and tonic and moved his thigh away from Nim's sari, which had been slightly pressed against him. She was a stunning woman, he thought, noting her flawless skin, high forehead and dark brown eyes. Her lips were full and her neck, elegant.

"So, where did you two meet?" he asked politely, tired of hearing Imran prattle on and on.

Nim smiled, cocked her head to one side and asked, "Where do you think we met?"

Imran put his hand on Omar's thigh and said, "She works for the CIA, she's a spy," and clicked his tongue, winking at Nim.

Nim let out a laugh. "Oh please, stop it," she said, and looked intently at Omar. "Just because I'm American, live in DC and carry a gun doesn't mean I'm a spy."

"So what are you then?" Omar asked, intrigued.

Imran butted in: "Get this, she's a weapons expert, and we met at a conference in DC. You know that the Americans think Iraq has WMDs right?"

Nim shrugged and raised a thick eyebrow. "No comment," she said. "Yet."

Omar raised his glass and downed his gin and tonic. It was his second drink and he felt loose. He was in good company and the conversation was, for once, not about Alba or legal contracts.

"Another round?" he suggested, and raised his hand to attract the attention of the waiter at the next table.

"Sure." Nim smiled coyly at Omar.

A mobile phone rang and Imran reached into his pocket to answer it. "Sorry, need to take this," he said and edged his way around the table.

"The world's changed after 9/11, America is more vulnerable than ever," Nim continued. "We—"

"Are all terrorists," Omar interjected. "It's a witch hunt, isn't it? On a global scale."

Nim leaned over, her face inches away from Omar's. He could feel her breath, smell her sweet, flowery perfume. "I'd like to hunt you," she whispered.

Omar leaned back and said, "I-I'm married. As you know."

The waiter arrived with their drinks and while he placed them on the table, Imran arrived with a bowl of nuts.

"Bloody starving, dinner better be soon, or I'll start eating something else." He eyed Nim blatantly. Omar stared into his third gin and tonic, slightly shocked at Imran's open innuendo, but then told himself that it was a wedding party and silliness was allowed. Besides, if he had been single, he would have allowed Nim to seduce him, and he would have been a more than willing shag.

A voice called out to the bar: "Ladies and gentlemen, dinner is served. Please make your way to the ballroom."

"Right, let's eat." Imran stood up and downed the rest of his drink, then offered his arm to Nim. "Shall we?"

Omar downed the rest of his gin and tonic and said, "Let

me just check on Del and Alba. See you in a bit."

Nim gave him a lingering smile, and as she kissed Imran on the cheek, Omar ran quickly up the stairs.

WHEN WE WALKED in, everyone was standing, making a toast. It was Fairman on the microphone and we caught the tail end of it.

To my beautiful, brilliant wife. I am indeed a lucky man. Cheers!

A waiter offered us champagne and we saw Imran waving at us wildly. We were all at the same table, along with Riz, Jin and their girlfriends, who had a startling resemblance to one another. The first course arrived. It was a lobster bisque with a warm dinner roll on the side. I broke off a side of the roll and spread a generous helping of butter, dipping it into the soup. It was slightly lukewarm, but delicious.

Wine, darling? Omar asked.

I nodded. He poured out a glass for me and then offered the bottle to Nim, who was seated on his right. I noticed that she did not touch the bread and sipped the bisque slowly. She laughed as Omar said something to her and put her spoon down, dabbing her mouth lightly with a napkin. I took a swig of wine and leaned over to ask, *What is Nim short for?*

Nirmala.

Omar quipped: *Nirmala is a weapons expert.*

Hmm, interesting. I felt restless and wanted the food to arrive more quickly. I decided to take my glass of wine and go talk to Sumi, who was seated at the main table. I slid out from my chair and Omar asked, *Where you going?*

Going to talk to Sumi, I answered.

But, it's the middle of dinner. He looked at me, puzzled.

It's okay…just a quick chat.

I took another large swig of wine and walked towards Sumi who also had a glass in hand. She looked like she had not touched her food. Seated at the table were both sets of parents, Fairman's siblings and their spouses. His dad was pouring whisky and Fairman looked like he already had a few. I smiled at Sumi and whispered, *Want to step out?*

She nodded and whispered into Fairman's ear. He nodded, dug out a packet of cigarettes from his jacket pocket and handed them discreetly to Sumi under the table. Fairman's dad was on the verge of another toast and we excused ourselves and walked quickly towards the main doors.

We walked towards the beach, the wind had picked up and the waves were crashing onto the shore. The pine trees were swaying slightly and the hammocks tied in between some of the trees were swinging from side to side.

You okay? I asked.

Sumi had turned away from the wind, trying to light a cigarette. I put my hands around the flickering flame to help, and after a few attempts, it was lit. Sumi took a deep drag and exhaled, the wind blowing the smoke back into her face. It whipped our hair and Sumi's long dress wrapped itself around her ankles.

Yeah, just tired, she said. *Want dinner to be over so I can go to bed.*

It's been beautiful, you know. Really special.

Sumi nodded and her eyes filled with tears. I gave her a hug.

Hey, you're going to be fine. It's just nerves. Family can do that to you.

It's just that it's so final, you know? This is it. I'm married. Can't fuck up.

I kept quiet. It had been more than two years for me and I already felt that I had been put through a wringer. *Take your time having a kid, just enjoy being married first.*

Sumi took a final drag of the cigarette and flicked it away. *We're supposed to be dancing on the beach later. What if it rains?*

We'll see, let's go back in.

Sumi nodded, I took her hand and together we walked briskly back to the hotel, the wind whirling around us, like impatient fairies.

OMAR WOKE UP with a hangover. Alba was climbing over him and he got a kick in the chin, which made him grimace. "Papa…" She smiled, then started bouncing on his chest.

"All right, all right." He sat up and rubbed his temples. He would have to take a couple of paracetamol to get through the day. "I'm up, baby girl."

The sun was peeking through the thick curtains and the air conditioning was a little too cold, so he reached for the remote and turned it off. He padded to the window and pulled open the curtains. Sunlight streamed into the room and Alba ran to tug at his feet. She wanted to go out onto the balcony. He opened it and they stepped out. A soft breeze blew in as Omar picked Alba up and kissed her cheek. "Look, it's a beautiful day, perfect for your birthday party, Alba."

She clapped her hands and said, "Want susu."

Omar turned to go inside just as the door to the neighbouring balcony creaked open. Nim stepped out, clad in a fluffy bathrobe. She waved at him and mouthed good morning. Omar waved back and closed the door. He had gotten very drunk last night, Imran dictating the number of shots they drank. After the wine, it had been whisky, then tequila. Nim had drunk just as much, saying confidently, "I can drink you guys under the table; it's in my genes, you know."

Del was still asleep. She had talked mostly to Sumi the night before, had stayed clear of the spirits, but had drunk a lot of wine. Omar filled the plastic kettle with water and turned on the television. Alba sat on the bed and shook her head at every channel until it came to a cartoon that she knew. As the animated characters danced across the screen, he heard the kettle boiling and turned it off.

He rinsed Alba's bottle out in the bathroom sink and saw that his eyes were bloodshot. He found two round white pills and quickly downed them with mineral water. The tin of milk powder was on the counter along with all of Alba's things—biscuits, dried fruit, nappies, folded clothes, extra milk bottles and teats. He put in five scoops of milk powder and poured in the boiling water, then mineral water. He shook it until the milk was frothy at the top, tested the temperature of the milk on his hand then gave it to an eager Alba who grabbed the bottle and started sucking on it loudly. He put a pillow next to her so she could lie on it, sat back on his side of the bed and closed his eyes.

Minutes later, he felt Del stirring. He leaned over and kissed her lightly on the forehead. She was still asleep, and as she turned over, he reached for the remote and lowered the volume on the TV even more. He slid down the bed, closed his eyes again, and thought of the many times he had been in hotels, of the debauched nights he'd spent with women, of the endless fucking and lovemaking, of the endless bottles of wine and champagne, breakfasts-in-bed, showers, baths, endless pleasure he'd given and been given, of the days that turned into nights and bled into more days. He'd not had days like that with Del, and the thought of such wanton, reckless hedonism, whilst watching his daughter drink from a milk bottle, filled him with revulsion and terror.

He got up, went into the bathroom, locked it and stepped into the shower. As the cold water hit his face and body, he felt revived; he scrubbed his hair and body and rinsed out his mouth. As he towelled himself dry, he ran the bath and filled it with bubbles. He put on a bathrobe, brushed his teeth and felt his stomach rumble from hunger. A good breakfast would right everything, clear his hangover and fuel him for the long day ahead.

I WOKE UP to find a note on my pillow.

Gone for breakfast with Alba. Sleep in, darling. O x

I showered quickly, remembering the events of the night before, the raucous laughter and conversation that took place first after dinner, us dancing to 80s music and to the copious amounts of alcohol that we'd all consumed. Fairman, Imran, Nim and Omar doing shots by the bar while Sumi and I sat, drank wine and smoked, amused by their antics. I found Nim to be enigmatic, but I don't think she found me interesting enough. After all, she was a high-flyer, a woman of the world, and I think she perceived me only as a wife and mother and not much of anything else. She didn't smoke, but drank enough to just stay standing, and when Imran was almost legless, she kept drinking. She kept darting looks at Omar. I was certain she found him attractive; a woman knows these things, and I was not a fool. I found no reason to fault Omar, as he kept his distance and did nothing to cross the line.

Throughout the night I'd kept coming up to check on Alba, but thankfully she slept through the night, the long drive and the sea air probably tiring her out. It was such a treat to be able to be among adults, doing things adults did, and yes, I had missed it. Sumi and I had shared some quality time and nothing untoward happened. But I had Alba's birthday party to do, I had to check on the cake and decorations, and make sure that all was well.

I dressed and went downstairs, my hair still wet, wearing a pair of jeans and a black T-shirt. As I walked into the dining room, I heard laughter and saw everybody seated at the same table. Alba was in a highchair, eating fruit from a bowl. *Mama!* she cried and everyone turned to me. Omar stood up and beckoned me to sit next to him. He kissed me on the lips as I sat down.

Sleep well? he asked. I nodded.

How's everyone today? I looked around the table. A murmur went up, and the most audible word I could hear was *hungover*. I laughed lightly. *Well it's a wedding, people!*

Fairman and Imran looked hunched and pale and as the waiter brought a carafe of coffee to me, Imran asked for more fresh orange juice. Sumi smiled widely and said, *It's Alba's birthday today, how exciting!*

Speaking of which, I need to go check on the cake. Omar stood up and Alba started waving her hands and protesting. *All right, young lady, you can come with me...let's go see what your cake looks like, shall we?*

But I was going to do that, sayang— I protested.

It's okay, let him, Fairman insisted. Imran nodded and retorted, *The bastard's not as hungover as I thought he'd be.* We all laughed. Omar carried Alba out the dining room, bouncing her in his arms, her glee filling me with happiness. I sighed and for a moment, felt complete.

Nim stood up and said, *I'm going to get more fruit, anybody want anything else?* I shook my head and proceeded to drink my coffee. Sumi moved over and sat next to me. She looked well rested and gave me a hug.

You okay? I asked.

Uh huh... she said, and gestured to Fairman. *He's not so good though.*

Hey, you guys should get a massage or something. Unclog your pores. Sit in a sauna...

No, the key is to keep on drinking, Del, hair of the dog,

you know, Imran said. *We got one more night, so let's make the most of it, huh? Or*—he looked at Nim—*you could fuck my brains out...*

Nim rolled her eyes and sat down. She picked up a piece of pineapple and inserted it in her mouth rather suggestively and Imran groaned.

Jesus, you guys. Get a room. Sumi threw her napkin at Imran.

Right, we're off then. Come, Imran ordered. *Woman!*

Nim giggled and allowed Imran to lead her off. She turned and said. *See y'all later.*

What a bimbo, I said under my breath, but Fairman heard me.

Now now, be nice, Del.

I got up, grabbed my plate and headed to the breakfast bar. The coffee was making my stomach churn and I needed food. I heaped on scrambled eggs, bacon, baked beans and sautéed mushrooms. This was the kind of breakfast I liked but had no time to prepare any more. The kind that Omar and I had most weekends before Alba.

When I got back to the table, Sumi and Fairman had gone, leaving me alone to eat in peace and quiet. I looked around the dining room and saw an older Caucasian couple in a corner facing the sea, and a younger couple who had their legs entwined under the table. Probably on their honeymoon, I thought. The scrambled eggs were creamy and buttery and the bacon, crispy enough. I ate until the plate was almost empty and sighed in content. A quiet breakfast, a rare treat.

I looked at my watch, which showed 10.45am. I had about five hours before Alba's tea party, so I sent Omar an SMS. The short stubby antenna had bite marks and looked like Alba had been trying to chew through the rubber exterior. Time to get a new phone, I thought.

A few seconds later, he replied. *We r in the office. Come come. x*

I drank the last of my coffee, wiped my mouth and walked out the dining room. I was assailed by piercing sunlight as soon as I walked out. Overhead, fluffy clouds gathered, the sea seemed calm and the pine trees swayed. It was the perfect day for a party. I walked through the lobby, nodded at the staff who said, *Good morning, madam,* and found my way into the hotel office where I found Omar and Alba sitting opposite a friendly-looking lady who said, *Hi, I'm Fernie, madam.*

Omar spoke. *Just paying up for the party…and we are good to go!* He signed the receipt, folded it, took his credit card and put it in his wallet.

Have you seen the cake? I asked.

Yup, looks great! He winked at me.

Alba reached out her arms to me. *Oooh, baby girl…you want to go for a swim?*

Great idea, said Omar, *we can swim, have some lunch and then have a nap before the party. Perfect!*

Have a great party, Alba! Fernie waved at us as we left the office, and as we walked away, I felt my heart explode into bursts of joy. Yes. It was perfect, perfect. Perfect.

They say motherhood is a joy. They say motherhood is bliss. They say motherhood changes you for the better. You think less of yourself. More of others. Of the world. They say motherhood is a gift from the gods. They say motherhood is the ultimate sacrifice, that your children are here to teach you, and you learn from them. They say that motherhood is hard, but your love for your child will help you get through the difficult times. They say there is no greater love than a mother's love. They say unconditional love exists between a mother and her child. They say this too shall pass, this too shall pass. They say when she sleeps, you sleep too. They say she will sleep through the night, when they reach a certain weight, they will be more independent. They say you will get your life back, eventually. They say you will not sleep for years, that you will never sleep through the night again, maybe when they're five. They say breastfeeding will help you lose the weight.

They say a child is here to test you. They say a child will wreck a marriage that is not strong. They say a child will bring you closer. They say a child is a balm for the troubled soul. They say a child will ground you. They say that you will develop instincts. All mothers do. They say you will never recover. They say that your child comes first, above all else. They say sex will cease. They say your husband will love you more. They say your husband will love you less, and the child more. They say your body will never be the same again. They say female athletes are stronger after motherhood. They say it is like running a never-ending marathon. They say you will worry and worry for the rest of your life. They say the work as a mother never ends. They say that you will learn to let go.

They say that when your child says Mama, you will fall in love. They say your child's character is there from birth, you are only there to facilitate who they will become. They are who they are. They say motherhood is the mark of being a woman. They say women who do not have children have not really lived. They say women who do not have children are selfish. They say women who do not have children live with regret. They say motherhood means you will never be alone. They say your children will look after you in old age.

They say some women never recover from post-partum blues. They say if you eat your placenta you will never get post-partum blues. They say the hormones in the placenta will replace the hormones you lose after childbirth. They say you can fry it with onions and garlic. That it tastes like liver. They say if you bury the placenta under a banana tree, the child will be bound to that place for life.

They say reading to a child from birth is good. They say speaking in multiple languages is good. They say teaching the child to swim is good. They say leaving the child to cry is good. They say sleep training is hard, but it's good. They say you have to be cruel to be kind. They say that the child will learn to sleep, will learn to sleep. The child will learn to sleep, in time. They say you need to trust yourself. That a mother knows. That a mother knows.

That a mother knows best.

Sumi called sobbing and said, *I've had a miscarriage, the baby is gone.*

I was silent for a long while.

Are you there? she asked.

Yeah, I said. *I am so sorry, Sumi. How? What happened?*

Doctor said there was no heartbeat.

You'll get pregnant again. It happens a lot.
Yeah, she sniffled. *I guess.*
You want to come over? Want to talk about it?
No, I…just need to be alone right now.
Is Fairman around?
Yeah. We went to the doctor together.
Okay, babes. I'm here if you need me.
Bye.

I stared at the dead baby lizard on the floor. It had leapt at me when I opened the cabinet under the sink. I hated lizards and had recoiled in fright while dropping the pot I was carrying. The baby lizard didn't have a chance. I felt terrible. I stared at its unblinking eyes, its short stubby tail, its tiny pink torso. I picked it up with a kitchen towel and winced as I felt its softness. I flushed it down the toilet and saw it swirl away. It was gone. Forever. Just like Sumi's baby. A little black dot in her belly, never to see the world, never to be born, never to be loved, never to be named.

Alba padded into the kitchen.

Mama, look! she said and held up a piece of paper with some squiggles. *Look!*

What is that? I asked.

Friends, mama.

Really? But… I kept quiet. The piece of paper had lines and circles, layered on top of each other. It looked nothing like people, or friends. *Well done, darling.* I hugged her. Her curls had grown and a haircut was due, but I had been too tired to get around to it. She was eating well, more than ever and had put on a kilo in the last month. She smelled of milk and oranges. Her little face beamed with joy, and she hugged me back and planted a wet kiss on my cheek.

Go draw some more, okay?

Omar was back for dinner and I was in the mood to make a chicken curry. Alba hurried off, her mission confirmed. She was becoming quite the artist; going through art blocks and paints, pens and pencils. She could draw straight lines, curly lines, curved lines and many attempts at circles. And again. And again. She loved playing with blocks, placing them on top of one another, she loved her dolls—they would be in the bath with her—and she loved her books, made of fabric, which always ended up in her mouth.

There were playgroups that I went to from time to time, but were mostly frequented by expat wives who were pleasant and cordial, but I never felt close enough to confide anything. I knew that some of them were worse off than I was, had husbands whom they hardly saw, especially those who worked for big multi-nationals, and those who travelled all around the region. The diplomats had it best. Maids, drivers, cooks, security guards. The whole package.

And Papa. Well, Papa had good days and bad days. He loved Alba but I couldn't really depend on him as a babysitter. I didn't like taking Alba to the house as it felt sad, but also, it was a breeding ground for all manner of bacteria, vermin and snakes. Papa said that a king cobra had found itself into his study and was coiled comfortably underneath the gramophone until he decided to put a record on. The snake reared up in fright and slithered with some familiarity into a hole in the wall, which apparently led directly to the garden. I shuddered at the thought, and imagined entire families of snakes now living in my father's house. The garden had completely overgrown as I no longer had time to visit, and the jungle had moved in. My father, tapping away on his manuscript in the midst of all that was wild. I had no idea what he was writing. No idea how he still managed to live the way he did.

Omar was travelling more and more and we saw less of him. There were times when I thought to myself that this was the life I was doomed to have. To have a husband who was there but not there. To have a marriage that was there but not there. To have a husband but to feel utterly alone. But I wasn't alone in the physical sense. I had Alba. But I did feel those cold fingers of fear at the base of my throat and in the pit of my belly. The same pangs of doubt that emerged after coming down from a high. The cold saliva in the mouth, the clammy hands, the sweaty temple. The ringing in the ears.

I wondered if Omar was having an affair. I questioned his need to be away so constantly. Work could be done via email, handphone, faxes—communication was more efficient than ever. Did he need to be away from us? Or did he just want to?

There were days when I was despondent. Bored. Afraid. Angry. Depressed. I loved my child, but I also saw her as a chain. I was tied to this life now. And there was no turning back...

THE FLIGHT FROM Hanoi had been delayed. Omar, making himself comfortable in the lounge with a coffee and a croissant, had started working on his computer when he heard a voice behind him.

"Well, well, if it isn't Omar…"

Nim was standing across from him in a grey suit, perfectly made up and coiffed. He stood up and extended a hand.

"Nim, what a surprise." He gestured for her to join him. "What are you doing in Hanoi?"

"The usual, brokering a deal with the government," she replied and sat down, crossing one leg over the other.

"Would you like some coffee?"

Nim shook her head, tilted it to one side and asked, "How's your gorgeous daughter?"

Omar smiled. "It's her birthday today, and my flight is late, so Del is not going to be too happy…"

"So it was a year ago in Penang? Goodness, how time flies…" Nim smiled and stared fixedly at Omar.

Omar took a sip of his coffee and debated against biting into the croissant, not wanting to have crumbs all over his tie and shirt, and asked, "How's Imran? You still together?"

"Oh, goodness no. Imran is just Imran, you know. He's into the news, and into himself, that's it. No time for anything serious."

"Right, a shame…"

"Not really. He was a great shag and that was that," Nim replied, matter-of-fact.

There was a loud clatter and Omar jumped. Someone had dropped a cup and the broken ceramic scattered itself around the room. He wondered if anyone else had heard what Nim said. He felt slightly embarrassed and shocked at her candour.

And at that very moment the lounge manager came towards him and said, "Mr Omar, your flight is boarding soon."

"Thank you." He stood up and extended a hand again to Nim, who took his hand and held it for longer than she should have. "Time to go. Well, take care and…all the best."

"You too, and give your beautiful daughter a kiss from me." Nim smiled and for a moment Omar saw a hint of sadness in her eyes.

As he walked away from the lounge, he thought of what her lithe body would feel like under his, he thought of how she would kiss him, and how she would moan when he was deep inside her. His handphone beeped and he saw the boxy black words flash on the screen.

Alba sick. Am worried. When are you back?

His fingers worked quickly.

Will land in three hours. Don't worry. She will be fine. xoxox

Guilt suffused him and he felt a pang of shame. His wife and daughter were in distress and all he could think about was banging a woman he didn't even remotely like. This was a reminder of the man he used to be, when sex was frivolous, meaningless, and a stroke for the fragile ego. The fact that he was still desirable to certain women was flattering, but he was never going to be unfaithful to Del. He knew of the silent suffering she endured when he was away, and although Alba was not an unruly child, he knew that Del struggled with herself, her feelings of inadequacy refuting instinct, on occasion. Del needed constant reassurance, and his absence was undesired, but he had no choice. Meetings had to be held, contracts had to be negotiated, renegotiated and signed and then his work began. He was the architect of new beginnings in countries that did not have the expertise that he had. There was pride in his work, pride in the firm handshakes with the ministers and executives he met, and a promise to deliver. He was a man of his word, and he would not fail.

Omar got off the plane and checked his phone. The SMS read: *High fever. Taking her to emergency at Pantai Hospital. Meet me there. Hurry!*

He replied: *On the way. Kiss.*

As the taxi sped off, Omar leaned back on the cool seat and sighed. He knew the kind of panic Del would be in and hoped that the fever was not a sign of anything serious.

When he arrived at the hospital, he called Del, who picked up after the first ring.

"I'm in one of the wards, just ask the nurse at the counter." She sounded harassed.

Omar pulled his suitcase behind him, walked through the hospital to the Emergency ward and spoke to a young nurse behind the counter.

"My daughter Alba has just come in. Do you know which room she is in?" he asked curtly.

"The little girl?" she replied. "This way, sir."

Omar followed the nurse, who could not have been more than 22 years old. He followed her into a ward, walked towards a bed covered by a blue curtain and pulled it apart. Del, seated in a chair, got up and flung herself at Omar.

"Thank god you're here," she cried, hugging him tightly, visibly shaken.

Alba was asleep, her eyelids fluttering. He felt fearful, seeing his daughter lying there, like that.

"What did the doctor say?"

"It could be bacterial or viral. They don't know yet. But they've given her a suppository to bring the fever down."

Omar hated the stench of hospitals, ever since his Tok had died. Her medically induced coma meant daily visits, a terrified, yet distant father, crying relatives and hushed, sometimes heated discussions with doctors and nurses. The smell had never left him.

"Can I speak to the doctor?" he asked the nurse who was standing by the other side of the bed.

"He is doing his rounds now," she replied looking at her watch. "But he will be here again in half an hour."

Omar leaned over and kissed Alba on the forehead. She felt warm. He pressed his hand on her cheek, which felt cool. Her eyelids fluttered and opened.

"Papa..." she whispered and started crying.

Omar sat on the chair, pulled it closer to the bed, pressed his lips on her cheek and said, "Papa's here, baby girl, papa's here."

IT WASN'T MUCH of a birthday.

Alba had to be on antibiotics for a week, and how she hated that bitter yellow liquid! How she wailed and cried and screamed. How she lost weight, and colour from her face. How weak she became, how fragile and helpless she seemed. How listless and fretful she was. Nothing pleased her. Nothing made her happy. Not the cartoons she loved, not the music, not the pens nor colour pencils, nor the books, nor the bubble baths. She cried endlessly, she would not sleep, she would not give us any rest.

When Omar said he had to leave again, I screamed at him. I lunged at him and said that I had not slept in days, that I was tired. *So, so tired. Please, Omar, don't leave. Can't you tell them that your daughter is sick? That I can't cope? Please, Omar, I am begging you. Please, Omar… Please.*

But he would not listen, he left anyway, saying that the job had to be done, that people depended on him, that promises had to be kept, that Alba was well enough, that she was eating again, and sleeping more. That I had to be strong, that children get sick, and that they are stronger than we think. That it will be fine. *It will be fine, Del, it will be fine.*

And so he left. And I was alone again with Alba.

And in my tiredness, and in my fatigue and in my day-old pyjamas, unwashed, oily hair and face, furry teeth and seething anger, I screamed at my sick child crying in her cot, at her standing there crying, in unchanged nappy and streaming snot, I screamed at her and said things that I should not have, I wailed and cried and tore at my hair and pyjamas and curled up on the floor I wept like her, my child staring at me wailing, and I like a crazed creature, spouting curses and venom, squirming in rage, my toes curling, my fingers reaching to grasp, pick, throw, shatter, all things in my way, I crawled on all fours until I reached the fridge and uncorking the bottle, drinking all that was in there, all the liquid that was clear and cold and refreshing and I drank it all until I was sated, the liquid fire silencing me, silencing all that pain, silencing it all, until my head felt light, and the stillness washed over me like a fog, and gave me sleep.

On 31 October 2003, Mahathir Mohamad ceased to be Prime Minister of Malaysia. He was replaced by his deputy, Abdullah Badawi, the soft-spoken, well-liked politician who hailed from Penang. Malaysians were joyous, exhilarated, relieved. The demagogue that was Mahathir was gone, it was the end of an era, the end of darkness and finally, there would be light.

All across the city, people celebrated. It was Halloween, after all, and there were parties from Bangsar to Cheras, Bukit Bintang to Damansara Heights. Mahathir masks were popular, caricatures of his fleshy eyes and jowls were paraded on faces, and Anwar's transposed black eye was met with howls of laughter, jibes and jubilation. There were parties on rooftops and bars, terrace gardens and bedrooms.

Omar and Fairman were in the office, having sealed another contract. They had just ended a conference call with their partners in Lagos and had gotten the go-ahead for another project that would start in 2004. Fairman thumped the table. Omar smiled and nodded his head.

"Wow, I was a little worried about that one, to be honest. Especially now." Omar loosened his tie and sat down at his desk, putting his feet up.

"I told you, I would sort it out, and I did," Fairman replied. "Come on, let's have a drink."

Omar slid open the drawer on his right and pulled out a new bottle of single malt. He rolled his chair over to the left to pull two crystal snifters from a bookcase. Fairman ruffled his hair, took out a handkerchief from his pocket and started cleaning his glasses. Omar peeled the thin metal covering off the top of the bottle and pulled out the cork slowly.

"Aaah," he sighed as he inhaled deeply. He poured generously into the two glasses and passed one to Fairman.

Both men looked at each other and chuckled.

"To us! And to Pak Lah. May we live long and prosper!"

"Indeed," replied Omar with a laugh. "Jesus, I'm fucking knackered." He put his feet back up on the desk and looked intently at the glass before downing the rest of the whisky.

"Whoa, slow down there," Fairman said.

"Listen, Del's had a really hard time since Alba got sick…"

"That, I do know," Fairman replied, "Take some time off, go on…"

Omar cut him off. "No, actually, I need Sumi to convince Del to get a maid." Omar's frustration took over. "She… she can't manage… Look, the work is what keeps us going, our wives know that and they need to figure it out…we're making real money now, and Del needs to get a bloody maid."

"Del's stubborn that way, she wants to do it all—on her own." Fairman agreed.

"Alba's two now and soon she'll be at playschool. Del can get her life back, go back to work," Omar continued, pouring himself another drink.

"Doing what?" Fairman leaned over and poured himself more whisky.

"She could work for Imran, go back to journalism…" Omar took a sip.

"Hmmph, that guy's gotten too big for his boots." Fairman started waving his hand. "He's become some kind of celebrity journo…he's on all these talk shows, on CNN and the Beeb, it's bloody weird."

"He has become a bit of an expert on the country, hasn't he?" Omar said. "He's more than qualified."

"Yes I suppose, but he's a changed man. That woman who tagged along with him to our wedding...well...anyhow. He's in the big league now." Fairman clicked his tongue.

Omar felt it on the tip of his tongue to say something about Nim, but he changed his mind. Nothing had happened, so there was in reality nothing to talk about. They finished their drinks in silence, as if pondering all the possibilities that Imran had in his grasp now.

"Are we good?" Fairman stood up. "Time to hit the road."

"Yup, I'll leave in a minute, you go ahead." Omar poured himself another drink. "Last one, promise."

"Good night. Say hi to the missus, and yes... I'll have a word with Sumi."

Fairman strode out and shut the door quietly. As his footsteps faded away, Omar swivelled his chair round to take in the view. He particularly liked it at night. From where they were, the skyline gleamed and glittered and the promise of a new country beckoned. But for Omar, it also spelt uncertainty. Malaysia had been governed by a ruthless and powerful man for 22 years. Things had a pattern, a place. Order had been created and carefully, albeit ruthlessly applied. People only knew fear, and fear had worked well. Too well. A new Prime Minister spoke of things unknown, but there was a glimmer of hope, a glimmer of a more effective democracy, and a chance of possible freedom.

"Freedom," Omar muttered under his breath. "Whatever the fuck that means."

He poured himself another whisky and as it swirled around in his mouth, he thought of the millions that they stood to gain from the Nigerians, the ongoing contracts in Vietnam and Kenya and he suddenly felt invincible. A hunger appeared like a simmering ball in the pit of his belly and that surge of promise beckoned, the world beckoned, the knowledge of profit beckoned. He, Omar Tunku Malik, was on a path that he never ever thought he would be on, and *that*, was the promise of freedom.

MARINA CALLED HIM Mr Ferrari; he was undoubtedly unhappily married and very, very rich. He was her most regular client and had almost single-handedly sponsored her new breast enlargements, and she knew that he cared for her. It was almost like love, she thought. *He cares for me, he looks after me, he SMS-es me to make sure I eat every day, he wants to know who I fuck and how much I make, and he is okay with all of that.*

Marina had come to taste the good life. She had a credit card, she had seen the insides of five-star hotels, she had come to like the taste of champagne, she had come to like fucking him and she had come to care for him. He was not the man of her dreams, by any means, but he was kind, considerate and generous to a fault. He had once offered to pay for an apartment, but Marina had said "No, I want to be able to afford my own place." She had registered the Mak Nyah Association of Malaysia at the Registrar of Societies—"Leave it to me," he said, and assured her that it would come to be.

He had been vague about who he was; she knew that he was in some position of power in the government, he was secretive about his personal belongings, his whereabouts, his work, his wife and his three children, and he travelled a great deal. *Where to?* she would ask. He would answer by giving her gifts. Chocolates from Switzerland. A wool shawl from Russia. A rug from Afghanistan. Jewellery from Morocco and Istanbul. *He has taste,* she thought. Apart from the rather dubious fire-red Ferrari he drove whenever he came to meet her.

A man of mystery. A man of some taste. A man of interminable lust.

Whenever Marina met him, she would be summoned via SMS to a hotel and be greeted by a butler at the entrance of the hotel and taken to a room that smelled like a boudoir. There were always fresh flowers, lilies and orchids, and champagne in a bucket. If he was running late, Marina would surf through the channels on the television, drink, order room service and prepare herself for him. Her legs smooth, nipples darkened with rouge, her privates waxed completely, and her desire growing by the minute. And when he appeared, he would come to her, kiss her all over, tell her how beautiful she was. And his penis was always hard, always, timing those blue pills perfectly, so they would fuck again and again, eat, drink, and fuck again, until the sun rose and he would rise to leave after breakfast—a full English breakfast with real bacon—and she would lie in bed, have yet another shower, drink until the bottle was empty, nap under those Egyptian cotton sheets, order lunch, eat, watch silly sitcoms, and then finally, leave.

And Mr Ferrari would SMS her or call, and say—*Thanks for a lovely evening, I look forward to seeing you again, soon. X*

Always the same message. Such a creature of habit, she thought. But she liked it, she had come to treasure it. She needed consistency in her life, and now she had it. From a man who was greying, portly and squinty-eyed, but a man who obviously felt for her, and maybe even loved her, a man whose name she did not even know.

It was this that kept Marina going, and when she was back in the back alleys of Chow Kit, giving a blow job to an Indonesian construction worker who smelled of concrete, cigarettes and sweat, she knew that Mr Ferrari would be there again next week, and the week after next, waiting for her.

* * *

MARINA HAD BEEN ill so I went to see her in Chow Kit. I brought her herbal chicken soup from a Chinese restaurant in PJ. It came in a clear plastic bag inside a larger pink plastic bag. Alba insisted on carrying it as we walked back to the car.

I want carry, she said. *I want.*

We had not seen each other in months and she whooped with joy when she saw Alba.

Aduh, so besar. She's growing up too fast!

Alba started singing *twinkle twinkle little star, how I wonder what you are, up above the sky to high, like a ... like a...*

Diamond!

...diamond...

In the sky...twinkle twinkle little star, how I wonder what you are.

We clapped along with her, her chubby arms and fingers waving in glee. She was dressed in a flowery dress from Bali, with alternate layers of blue and white, the kind that all parents bought from the street-side shops in Ubud or Kuta or Seminyak. It was a gift from Sumi and Fairman, who'd gone there for their honeymoon. Three sets in different colours and motifs. One formal, one for playing and another for a day out. This was the day-out dress, with multiple dolphins, frolicking in a cottony blue sea.

I'd only been to Marina's flat once before. It was a floor up in a shophouse, in between a brothel on the third floor and her friend Kak Min's flat. She still shared it with her two trans housemates from Sabah, who were also from seaside villages. I spotted new curtains: they weren't the same faded batik sarongs. The kitchen table was also new, with a pink table cloth and a vase of plastic flowers in the middle. The couch was the same, with the pronounced dip in the middle, but the television was a larger version of the previous one.

Marina walked to the kitchen and I followed her. She unpacked the soup and slowly poured it into a bowl. She was sniffling and blew her nose loudly on a tissue. She turned to look at me. Her eyes were watery and her nose pink.

I feel so teruk, she said. *This flu is terrible.*

Yeah, sorry but I won't stay long then, don't want Alba to get sick.

Thanks for the soup, darls... yummy!

Marina took another sip from the bowl and cleared her throat. *I need to get back to work, can't take another day off.* She held the bowl with both hands and drank all the soup in one long gulp. *Aaah, I needed that. Thanks so much, darls.*

We heard Alba laughing from the living room. She imagined herself in a playground, finding joy in random objects—an open magazine, a make-up brush, a tube of pink lipstick. *Look mama,* she waved the brush around and brushed her cheek with it.

Look at her, so cute! Marina exclaimed.

I missed Marina. She said she was working non-stop. *I found a sugar daddy who really, really likes me, and I think I have saved enough to afford the operation, I think it's time to snip it off, what you think?*

Who is this guy? I asked. *Is this the guy with the Ferrari?*

Yeah, she answered shyly. *He's really nice. He's not really a sugar daddy because I don't really want his money. He pays, but that's it, I don't want anything more from him.*

I was wary of course, a rich man professing undying love for a trans sex worker from Sabah seemed too good to be true, but perhaps it really *was* true love and Marina had finally struck gold. I was happy for her, but I told her: G*o slow, don't rush into anything and give it more time.*

More time? But it's been more than a year! Come on, Del, be happy!

I am! Really, I am, but can you trust this guy?

Trust? Can you ever trust anyone one hundred per cent? Ala, don't be like this…

She started coughing furiously and I rushed to get her a glass of water.

I am sorry, but I just don't want him to hurt you. You know, I'm worried, as your friend.

Del, I don't want your worry, okay, you just worry about your daughter and husband, dah cukup, no need to worry about me!

Then I knew that she was angry, I had said all the wrong things, I should have been happy for her, I should have celebrated the fact that Marina was going to finally be the woman she had only dreamed off. Loved, snipped and titted.

I think you should go, let me rest, sayang, just let me rest okay?

I sat in silence, twisting my hands, racking my head of what to say to make it all better. She was visibly upset and I chided myself again for being insensitive. I said that she of all people deserved love, that she had suffered enough and that if this man really loved her then she should accept all that he was willing to give her.

She kept coughing and asked me to go. *I don't want Alba to get sick. I will call soon okay.*

I got up and said, *I'm sorry, I didn't mean it like that... really. I'm happy for you.*

Then I grabbed Alba who screamed *Mama, Mama, no, no!* and ran down the stairs carrying her, almost tripping in my haste.

Perhaps I was too tired to even realise that I didn't need to go to the supermarket to get groceries. Or perhaps I did. I was in a daze, and drove the car as if on autopilot through the city, down the harangue of Jalan Tun Razak, past the roundabout, onto Jalan Semantan and up the hill into the parking lot of the shopping center in Bangsar. The guard waved at me familiarly and Alba waved back from her baby seat, chuckling while sucking on her thumb. I had managed to calm her down after Marina's and we sang more nursery rhymes in the car.

I kept telling myself that things would be better, that when Alba got older, when she started daycare or play school, I would have more time to myself. That I could drop her off, sleep and then feel more normal. I then thought that I would speak to Omar that night about looking at options for schools. Perhaps getting Alba out of the house for a few hours a day was the antidote to everything.

I walked into a café, ordered a vanilla latte and let Alba run around. I got her a chocolate chip muffin and together we sat and ate it. I felt brittle, fragmented. Had I been too insensitive to Marina? And why did I doubt her lover? Was I secretly happy that Sumi had lost her child? Or was I relieved?

I startled myself when I thought that. I had become a

monster. Was this what happened to women when they were sleep deprived? The mind becomes full of trickery. The mind unravelling, halved, quartered. I did not like who I had become, and at that very moment, I was filled with revulsion at everything. A husband, a child.

I looked at Alba and I saw a creature who had usurped my life, who now had control over everything. I had a life that was no longer mine. She took and only took from me. My sleep. My sanity. My youth. She, who drank from me like an endless ocean of milk. She, who rendered me like stone in a corner, watching her run towards the ornamental fountain, laughing to herself, speaking in her gibberish and the occasional word. In that moment, I wished I were a different person, somewhere else. In Barcelona, Paris, back in Montreal. I did not want to be in KL. I did not want anything. I just wanted to be alone. On a park bench somewhere.

I wondered how days turned into nights, and how time was dictated by naps, the changing of diapers, snacks, meal times, sleep, and then it starting all over again. Two years had passed, how many diapers had I used? How much poo had I cleaned? How much milk had she drunk from me? How many times had she been bathed? How many nights had I not slept right through?

I was being illogical, ridiculous, selfish, I had a child that I had given birth to, one who was healthy, perfect, I was perfectly able to care for her, I had a husband who loved us both, so why was I feeling the way I was? A fear washed over me, I suddenly felt incapable—that I had to see it all through—primary and secondary school, parent-teacher conferences, homework, swimming and piano classes, braces, pimples, crushes, teenage rebellion, tattoos, college, adulthood. Being a parent never stopped, there would be no breath in between, no time to recover, no time to salvage anything except sleep.

Then Alba came running to me, she came up to my knee and she saw that I was upset.

Mama. Mama. Mama!

I'm sorry, darling, Mama's very tired.

I picked her up and hugged her tightly. The scent of her hair, her skin, it washed over me like a balm. This was motherhood. It rose and fell, leaving you empty, half empty and then full. I kissed her nose, forehead, cheeks, her chubby, chubby hands. I told myself, it will get better. It will all get better. And together we walked into the supermarket.

I put her on the grocery cart, sitting upright facing me. She was used to it. I gave her a toy to chew on. I thought of baked salmon and asparagus for dinner, perhaps a sweet potato mash.

Yes, Alba, baby girl, salmon and sweet potato mash for dinner? You think daddy would like that? Yes, baby girl...

She smiled and said *Papa, Papa... potato...*

Then I remembered that we needed ground coffee and milk. And diapers, wine. Eggs, onions, garlic. Olive oil. Balsamic vinegar. Whipping cream. Lemons. *Those thin biscuits that he likes.* I walked towards the biscuit aisle, looking for those slim chocolate mint slivers. *They were out of stock the last time.* I saw them and grabbed three packets. Then I saw that they had oatcakes as well. *That would go nice with cheese.* So I took one packet and then realised that the grocery cart was three aisles back. I walked towards it, feeling better with each step. I would feel better after a nap, yes. We would go home and curl into bed together. The world would be a better place after more sleep.

I saw the grocery cart, I saw the things I had put in earlier. My handbag in the corner. But Alba, where was she? Could she have climbed down on her own? No, it was impossible.

I put the things into the cart and started pushing it.

Alba! Alba! Alba!

I walked up to the nearest cashier.

Have you seen my child? *Little girl. Blue dress. Two years old.*

No.

No.

No.

Concerned faces. The cashiers talking amongst themselves.

Have you seen a little girl in a blue dress?

Was she hiding in between aisles? I ran past row after row of canned food, noodles, flour, jams.

Alba!

Alba!

Where are you?

The security guards came.

Alba! Alba!

Madam, something wrong?

Madam, all okay?

Alba, where are you? Alba!!!

Madam, what does your child look like?

Madam, can you describe your daughter?

The announcement over the loudspeaker. All over the shopping center.

A two-year-old child is lost. She is wearing a blue and white dress. She has dark brown hair and her name is Alba. If anybody sees this child, please bring her to the information counter immediately.

Then, a crowd. Women with their own children, hugging them tightly. Men in suits. All peering at me.

Strangers. I wanted to throw up. A lady holding my shoulders, a glass of water pressed into my hand. The announcement again and again. The security guards on walkie-talkies.

Madam, we have closed off all the entrances and exits. We will check everything. Don't worry.

Fifteen minutes. They say that if a child goes missing in public for more than that, it is too late.

Was it too late? How long had it been?

Where is she? Where is my baby?

I started shaking. My voice, a blood curdling scream.

Alba was gone. My child was gone.

FIVE

After 48 hours, there was no message for a ransom. No phone call, no letter, no fax, no email, no SMS. Nothing.

Omar went through all the names on his handphone. He pored over their client lists, sat with the company accountant to figure if there were rogue debtors, people who had tried to undercut quotes, anyone who seemed doubtful or suspicious. Competitors? Yes, there were many. But they had heavy subsidies and he was used to playing the game on both sides. They received government concessions not just because the Minister of Transport was an old friend of his father's, but between him and Fairman, there was more than enough to go around, more than enough favours to pull and more than enough resources to run an office of twenty staff.

Over the past two years, TMF Sdn Bhd had done well. Over ten million in profit, continuing contracts in Vietnam, Nigeria and Sudan and the possibility of a new highway that would connect KL better than ever, a penthouse office at The Luxe in the heart of KL, a business partner he trusted. He had an apartment in Bangsar, a wife and child he loved dearly, more satiety than he'd ever experienced in his life.

And then, a nightmare. Del was falling apart at the seams, she was unravelling by the hour. She had done nothing for two days, and stopped eating. She became a creature on the couch, unmoving.

"Darling, please. You cannot be like this. Stay strong, Del. Please," he had pleaded with her that morning. Next to her limp body, an empty vodka bottle on the carpet, an overturned glass. She had drunk herself into oblivion.

"Darling, let's get you to the shower…come on."

She was a dead weight, she would not move. Her body fought him, her hands pushed against his gentle touch. Then she struck out at him and screamed, her face contorted into a grotesque mask of pain.

"Leave me alone! Go away! Leave me alone!"

He left her like that and drove the car out onto the street. The primary school down the road was in session. There were little boys on the field, kicking a football. At the traffic lights, in the corner of his rear mirror, he saw Alba's car seat strapped in the back seat, and imagined her waving a toy, laughing, singing *Papa… Papa*. He gritted his teeth and felt a muscle pinch in his cheek. He slammed his foot on the accelerator and whispered.

"I am going to find you. My baby girl. I am going to find you, no matter the cost, no matter what. That's Papa's promise."

And as he drove into the city, the tears that he had willed to be pent-up for the past two days, surged out of his chest, scorched his eyes and spilled onto his cheeks, while his hands gripped the steering wheel like a vice.

* * *

Inspector Awang put down the phone and stood by his desk, deliberating what he was going to say. It was a hot day and the air-conditioning inside the office was humming loudly. Omar noticed that small droplets of water were dripping onto the floor.

Omar asked again, impatiently, "Sorry, could you explain that again?"

Inspector Awang cleared his throat and spoke, firmly and quietly and pointed to a map behind him. "Encik Malik, the shopping centre is forty-five minutes away from Port Klang." Inspector Awang traced his finger on the map and then stopped, "Another forty-five minutes and you're in international waters. I am sorry, sir, but your child could be anywhere by now."

Omar stared at the Inspector in disbelief. Del sobbed loudly.

"And, there's nothing you can do?"

Inspector Awang sat down and beckoned Omar to sit. Omar shook his head, raked his fingers through his hair. Del stood by a corner window, staring numbly into the street.

Inspector Awang continued. "We are doing our best, but as you can see there are all kinds of possible scenarios."

"Scenarios? What do you mean?" Del choked.

Inspector Awang warned, "This could be a kidnapping, madam. We have to wait to see if the kidnappers ask for a ransom. But if you say you have not heard anything in the past forty-eight hours, then we have to assume that she has been taken."

Omar was quiet now, his voice stilted with anger. "Taken?"

"This would mean, what…?" Del pleaded.

"I am sorry, madam, but it's to early to speculate. Anything can happen."

"What? What? Are you saying?" Del shrieked.

Omar walked towards Del and hugged her. "Calm down, darling," he pleaded.

"I am sorry, madam, but we are doing everything we can. We shut down the shopping centre, we checked all exits and entrances, my officers checked every shop, asking people what they saw, we have interviewed more than fifty people…nobody saw anything…please understand, we are doing our best."

"She's not there! Can't you see! She's gone!" Del screamed.

Omar steadied himself. Del pulled away from Omar and paced up and down the small, airless office. The small Pondok Polis was more like a hut, compact enough to fit the Inspector's office, a holding room, one toilet and a front office for reports.

Inspector Awang felt sorry for the couple in front of him. His instincts told him that after twenty years of being in the police force this was not a kidnapping. This was a child who had been taken.

"Here is my card. Please call me if you need to… and thank you for meeting me here, the renovations at HQ will be done soon," he continued, hoping to dismiss them.

Del burst out, "But surely, you can do something? Send the coast guard out, check the boats…?" She was shouting by now. "Do something! Please. I am begging you!" She lunged at him, grabbing him by the lapels of his uniform, her eyes filling with tears, her voice hoarse. She then let go and fell to the floor, her knees prostrate, her head on the ground.

Taken aback, Inspector Awang knelt down. Del was banging her head on the floor repeating "Please, please... please...help us." Omar reached for her shoulders and tried to help her up but she pulled away.

Inspector Awang straightened up, smoothed out his uniform, looked squarely at Omar and said, "At any given day there are at least a hundred and fifty vessels, big and small, in those waters...just about six nautical miles off Port Klang. Once you're further out in the Straits of Malacca, there are hundreds of vessels, cargo ships, fishing trawlers, sampans, speedboats, luxury yachts, everything! And...you need a warrant to search international vessels, which we will need to get from the International Maritime Law Institute in Panama. You would have to go through Wisma Putra and the Ministry of Foreign Affairs. It would take days, weeks...! The paperwork alone will be a nightmare...! It is simply impossible, simply impossible!" He shook his head and glared at Omar. He then turned around and strode back to his desk.

Omar remained quiet, stunned by the new revelations. Del slowly pulled herself up to standing position, her eyes puffy, her mouth quivering with silent sobs. She squeezed her eyes shut, and forced her fist into her mouth, summoning herself into silence.

"Del, let's go, there's nothing more here." Omar threw a look of scorn at Inspector Awang, grabbed Del's hand and walked towards the door pulling her forward. She followed reluctantly and let out a wail, which came deep from the recesses of a grief, so primal, so visceral, Inspector Awang was forced to light a cigarette after he shut the door. He felt sorry for the couple and knew from the familiar feeling in the pit in his belly, now hardened by years and the evil in men's hearts, that their child would never be found.

THERE WERE NO words to describe this. This pain. What I thought I once knew, I knew no longer. There was a darkness and despair that plagued only people who had lost children. It was an unspeakable, unknowable thing. There was a void that could never be filled unless your child was returned. Until then, the desire to die was stronger than the desire to stay alive, and this was the terrible place I found myself in. After Alba was taken, a frenzy fed the media. It was a maniacal clown juggling a sick circus. The glare of the media, on us, like a 24-hour spotlight.

"Grandchild of famed human rights lawyer goes missing."
"Child taken from exclusive mall in Bangsar."
"Toddler taken from supermarket."
"KL is no longer safe."
"Activist parents lose child."

Our apartment became an instant operations centre for Alba. A day after the abduction, policemen and policewomen showed up, and we had to rearrange the furniture in the living room, move the couch, the coffee table, the TV consul, the book cases; we moved everything to fit tightly against the edge of one wall. They brought in foldable tables and chairs. We added extensions to power points, added phone lines, power lines, we set up a hotline with five different phones. We all sat and waited.

Thousands of posters were printed. Pictures of Alba were plastered on telephone poles, tollbooths, shop windows, ATM machines, the backs of lorries and taxis—from Kepong to Subang Jaya, Kinrara to Taman Tasik Permaisuri, Ampang to Taman Tun. It was on the radio, TV, chatrooms, the newspapers. Her face was everywhere. Imran had even created a special page for Alba on *Malaysia Times* and was coordinating all media releases and statements.

After 24 hours, there was nothing. No SMS, no email, no call, nothing. We waited for another six days, sitting at the phones, waiting, but there was nothing. Our days and nights had been put on hold, Inspector Awang came and went several times a day. The case was now being handled by D9, which was the Major Crimes unit of the Royal Malaysian Police, and we had to trust them, we had to let them do what they knew best.

On the seventh day DSP Wong, the head of D9 herself, came to see us, and she assured us that they were doing all they could, but the week was up. When the cops moved out with all the phones and wires and tables and chairs, the apartment felt like a tomb.

The shops in the shopping centre were checked again and again. Policemen and women ripped into every nook and corner, every cardboard box, every dumpster, air-con vent, every toilet cubicle, every conceivable space that could hide a child. Cars leaving the parking lot were stopped. Drivers had to step out, car boots opened, torches flashed into every cavity. Bags opened, seats unturned.

The CCTV cameras showed nothing. There was footage of Alba and me walking into the supermarket and then we walked into a blind spot. I felt cursed. The spot where I left her was undetectable. Footage of me running, walking, shouting, but nothing of her. She had simply vanished. When Omar arrived, I was already sedated by a paramedic. My eyes were glazed, fixated upon an invisible spot two feet tall above the ground. He hugged me tightly for all of three seconds then let me go, roughly.

What happened? Del, what happened?

I started shaking. Again, the same story. Recounting it for the tenth time. Then Sumi, Fairman, Papa, the police. All there. Standing together in an awkward line. More police. More statements. They wanted a picture of her. Omar gave them one. I had one in my purse, but he decided the one he had *was better, more recent*. I could not look at it. That was the beginning of the pain. All I wanted then was a cigarette, so I walked to get a pack from the supermarket. I was in shock. The lady at the counter averted her eyes, as if afraid. I strode out to the entrance and felt all eyes on me. The murky humid night hit. I lit it. As I inhaled deeply I felt my legs give way and I crumbled ungraciously to the floor.

A small child forms a physical attachment to her mother. And vice versa. Alba was like an appendage, a part of my body, like an invisible limb that was hand, leg, nose and mouth combined. She had become a part of me, the smallness of her fitting into the curve of my tummy and my chin when asleep, the weight of her on my chest when she suckled. My limbs felt limp from missing her, from not touching her, feeding her, bathing her, changing her diaper, combing her hair. Her body had occupied mine, and now I was lost.

My breasts leaked milk for days; I refused to pump them because I wanted to feel some measure of pain, until I woke one day and could not move my arm. My right breast had swollen to the size of a small melon, it was taut and hard and my nipple looked a giant prune, ready to explode. I latched on the pump and winced in pain as the milk spurted out into a milk bottle, which I then put in the freezer, next to the other frozen bottles of milk.

My days were empty. Omar was kind, he tried to be, but I was silent from shame, remorse. I waited for those words—*Why did you leave her?* But they were never said. The papers dug into us. The fact that we were activists once, that we campaigned for Anwar and Keadilan, the fact that I was a journalist for *The Review* and *Saksi*, had all come under scrutiny. I knew Omar was on the verge of bigger government contracts. So, he threw himself into work, as men do in time of crisis.

One day we sat and listened to each other, and I told him over and over again what happened, I told him of my exhaustion, the fact that I went to get "those biscuits", the fact that I was planning dinner in my head, the fact that that *goddamned supermarket was the safest in town!* The fact that I had left her for less than a minute, and *that she was there, right there, how could she have disappeared?*

He sat head in his hand, then stumbled into her room and started hurling things around. Her pillows, her toys, clothes. *Why? Why? Why?* The whys weren't a concern. Was she still alive? Who had her? Was she hungry? Was she safe? Was she afraid?

Those were the questions that drove me to the verge of a cliff so high, with winds so bitter and strong, and the abyss that loomed below got deeper and more sinister by the day.

I was sinking into a place that was inhabited by creatures of the id, so dark and impermeable that my waking hours were trolled by images of the most gory of demons to inhabit the human mind. I spoke to no one for days. Unanswered calls from Sumi, Marina, my father, all went to voice mail, my handphone beeping endlessly with its flashing eye and then going silent.

Until one day, the doorbell rang, and rang, and then came a series of furious knocks.

Hello! Puan Delonix, tolong jawab pintu. Ini Polis Diraja Malaysia! Tolong bukak pintu!

The cops were at my door. The day before, I had sat at the Deputy Superintendent's office, waiting for news. Watching them put out citywide alerts, then nation-wide alerts again. I watched them on walkie-talkies, handphones, go in and out of endless tea breaks. I had become a pest. I questioned and harangued them, a miasma of busybody-ness and persistence, an embarrassment perhaps. But I didn't care. My daughter was gone and it seemed that they were doing everything, but after one week, there were no leads. They had found nothing.

I opened the door and the first thing I heard was this— *We need you to come with us to the station, we just need to ask you some questions.* So they took me away in a police car, just like that with enough time to send an SMS to my father, *Papa they've come to take me, they think I am a suspect, help me.*

* * *

I remember the time when Alba had bronchitis. She was four months when it started with a terrible cough. I remember trying to give her medication, *She keeps spitting it out, Omar what do we do?* We tried antibiotics in a syringe, slipping it into her tiny mouth, in teaspoons, miniscule amount after amount, nothing worked, she kept spitting it out. Her little lungs kept getting more and more clogged up and we had no choice but to take her to emergency in a late-night panic.

At the hospital, they wrapped her up tightly into a cocoon and thumped her little chest with cupped fists— *thump thump* on her back, *thump thump* on the side and front in cycles, hoping to loosen the phlegm. And when it got really bad, they stuck a tube down her throat and sucked up the mucus that looked like old porridge, the oats yellow and thick from exposure. She had to be put on a nebuliser, her little face covered by the plastic mask, covering her nose and mouth, her breathing sounding like a clogged, gurgling sink. It was horrific. I stayed with her in the hospital for three days. My birthday was on the second day of the hospital stay and Omar showed up after work with some cheese, crackers and a bottle of wine.

We ate brie and drank the merlot quietly while she slept in quiet submission after screaming her lungs out when the tube went down her throat. *It's good, it's good, don't worry, it's loosening up the phlegm.* When the mucus was drained for the final time, she fell into a deep sleep and Omar and I snuck out, found the rooftop and shared a cigarette.

Happy birthday, darling, sorry it had to be like this!

I was woozy from the nicotine and the wine and swung

drunkenly into him. I had slept only hours so I was giggly and dazed. He kissed me back and then pushed me against the wall.

I want you now, Del, god I want you.

I wasn't ready for him, I couldn't even remember when we last made love, but there, I gave in. I had felt so helpless watching Alba, to see her like that, so small and vulnerable and us there on the roof I felt like a little revolt.

The night was clear, and the glare of the city comforted me, and in a gust of wind he took me from behind, groaning into me, and pressing me into a corner. I felt his hot breath, the taste of cheese and wine mingling into my neck and hair, my cheek being pushed into a concrete wall, his hands on my back, pushing and pulling my hips in and out of him. I thought of Alba in her little bed while Omar came, spilling his seed into me and onto the floor of that hospital roof.

For six hours, they interrogated me in a room with no windows.

State your name.

Age. Race. Religion.

Address?

Where were you educated?

What are your parents' names?

When and how did your mother die?

You have no other siblings?

Do you support the opposition party?

Are you a friend of Anwar Ibrahim's?

Is your father a friend of Anwar Ibrahim's?

What does your husband do?

What are his parents' names?

What was the last time you saw your daughter?

What dress was she wearing?

Are you a good mother?

Why don't you have a maid?

Have you been suffering from post-natal depression?

Have you ever been arrested?

What is your Muslim name?

Do you fast?

Are you and your husband practising Muslims?

Do you drink alcohol?

Have you ever done drugs?

State the names of all your previous employers.

What did you study in Canada?

How long were you there for?

Did you commit any crimes when you were in Canada?

We need the names and contact numbers of your closest friends.

Do you know that in most cases, parents are the ones who kidnap their own children?

Did you sell your child?

Are you and your husband on good terms?

Is there a reason why he would kidnap your child?

Have you or your husband any known or unknown enemies?

Why is your father not the lead counsel for Anwar Ibrahim?

Where is your mother buried?

Do you have friends in Israel?

Do you support the state of Palestine?

What is your political affiliation?

Have you ever read the Communist Manifesto?
Why did you not support the government of Mahathir Mohamad?
Please recite the NegaraKu.
Please recite the Shahadah.
Have you ever been to Cuba?
Do you know any political dissidents from Malaysia?
Are you aligned with any terrorist organisations?
When was the last time you went for a holiday?
How would you describe your relationship with your daughter?
How would you describe your relationship with your husband?

I answered everything. As best I could. And at the end, they let me go. I went home, drank a whole bottle of wine, took four Xanax and woke up two days later.

There is a very fine line between the world of the dead and the living. The notion of what is life and what sustains it can be debated, as it has been for centuries. By scientists, philosophers, artists, writers. All life embodies breath, form and matter. A building also encompasses that. It breathes, and it excretes waste in many forms. But some human beings don't do either. There is a young man in Nepal who has not eaten in years, he has only lived on the air that surrounded him, beneath the Bodhi tree that he has meditated under for years.

In life we are expected to be heroic, as buildings are, in the very desire to make ourselves be seen. A building has to extend itself into the sky, a monument of pride, exuberance. Human beings are expected to do the same.

The verticality of life has to sustain itself in all that we do—
to strive upward, to go forward, to not look back, to go
into an uncertain future with bravado and strength. With
restraint, so as to not offend or condemn, to be humble, to
do good. For the world, for humanity. To love all mankind
as your own. To contribute to society, to be heroic. Heroes,
heroines. The world needs them, otherwise there would be
no salve. Who would save us from ourselves?

The *übermensch*, the man that was more than human.
The hero's journey, where man has to go in order to grow,
to experience the "dark night of the soul", to face the abyss
and then climb upward to the light. Mythology colliding in
an age where it was impossible to be good in a bad world.
Why do good when only bad prevails? Why live when all
we face is death?

I grappled with these questions, vacillating in between
the desire to slash my wrists with every knife in the kitchen,
creating a splattered painting, and running screaming into
the streets, and checking myself into a psych ward. I did not
know what to do. I could not articulate anything without
lapsing into a crippling silence. I no longer knew how to
behave. I no longer understood the notion of humanity,
when the child I had birthed into the world had been taken
from me. Taken.

I woke up every morning as if I'd slept with my eyes
open. Omar and I no longer shared the same bed. He had
taken to sleeping on the couch in his study. We simply
avoided each other. Once we collided in the living room
hallway, and I saw a look so haunted in his eyes, rippled
with a kind of anguish I had only ever seen once before,

on my father.

He growled a *good morning* and shuffled quickly out the door into his car, as if I was a pestilence, a giant cockroach that had crept out of the crevices of the floor. I stood there in the emptiness of the house, the confounding silence thundering into my ears. I found half a bottle of vodka and drank it in three gulps. Then I emptied the drawer of knives, forks and spoons and started throwing them on the walls. Then I started throwing plates onto the floor. First just by dropping them from the top of my head, then a slight twist of the wrist sent it wobbling like a Frisbee a foot or more. Then I just started smashing them. First the everyday ones, the ones for simple meals, then the ones that we got for our wedding. Gold plated, embossed with flowers. Then the crystal wine glasses. Those were harder to break, the crystal shattering into miniscule screams.

Then the heaving came. I shook as the tears rampaged out of me, coming out of my nose and mouth like truncated gusts of water from a fire hose. I writhed on the floor until I was empty, until I fell onto the couch like a limp doll after being ravaged by a starving dog.

There was no news at all. After two weeks, my persistent calls to Inspector Awang could have been easily perceived as harassment. I called him the minute I woke up and almost hourly during the day. It was always the same.

I am sorry, madam, there is no news. I will call you as soon as I hear anything, anything at all.

I was deteriorating, marginally and minutely by sheer millimetres, but every day I got out of bed was a small victory. I had refused more interviews, and had blocked out all emails and phone calls from insistent reporters and bloggers. There had been so many false alarms and hoaxes, I thought it better to stay in the confines of limited Internet access.

Papa called me every day to make sure that I was okay, and that somehow became my lifeline. Now I understood his grief and could finally comprehend the extent of his sadness. But I told myself that he had lost a wife—I had lost a child and a husband. But the fact that my father was there comforted me, somewhat. How does one even begin to measure grief? My father's grief and mine were incomparable. There should be a way to denominate grief in the manner of physical pain. *On a scale of one to ten, what is the level of your pain?*

Mine was off the chart. The only thing that would have sedated me would probably have been an overdose of heroin, or enough alcohol to render me inchoate. I suppose it pained Omar to see me like that. I knew that he too was in an unspeakable hell and perhaps we should have gravitated to each other more, but the chasm that had appeared between us became a vast, unknown terrain. The new landscape, this new *terra firma* had begun to leave interminable scars and neither of us knew what to do.

When he was not at work or away, he would be at home, in the quiet of his study. We never went into Alba's room any more. It remained shut. It became an unknowable thing, a doorway into a black hole of pain. The pictures of garden fairies on the wall, her cot with the overhanging origami mobile that he had bought in Tokyo, the changing table with organic lotions and a Winnie the Pooh bag which held diapers, the night light that resembled a moon, the fluorescent stars on the ceiling, the fluffy pink carpet she learnt to crawl on, the stuffed toys, shelves of books, a pink and white cupboard with unworn clothes, rows and rows of soft leather shoes, all silent, unmoved.

Sometimes, I would walk past his closed door and wonder what he did in there. In his study. Was he working? Was he chatting online? Was he as lonely as I was? I did not know who my husband had become. Perhaps we had to start again, as strangers. I stood by the door many times, wanting to open it to say, *Omar I need to talk to you, need to hold you, need you to hold me back and tell me that it's going to be okay, they'll find her, they will. Help me, darling, help me. Please.* But I never did.

I had never felt more unwanted and unloved in my life. I had stopped putting on make-up, my extra weight had become familiar folds, my eyebrows stopped getting plucked and teased, my pre-pregnancy clothes all lined the wardrobe like a rack in a store. The green silk dress I had worn when Omar had proposed to me hung like a shroud, a pre-wedding relic of a life I could no longer have. I looked at myself in the mirror and started laughing hysterically, the ample woman with fleshy arms and a protruding belly was who I had become. The revulsion I had for myself filled me like hot lava, I tore my clothes off, and strutted like a deranged woman in the room, I pouted like a supermodel, then stuck out my belly and breasts, turned around and posed with my derriere pointed at the mirror. I tied a sarong around my chest and ruffled my hair. I picked up a glass half full with vodka and as I turned around I realised who I had become.

My mother.

FINDING A PRIVATE detective was not difficult, as Omar discovered. He'd heard that many were ex-police, specifically Special Branch officers who got tired of being on the corrupt, yet meagre gravy train. The upright ones who refused to take bribes were eventually shunned by the endemic racism that devoured many in the service. A quick scan in the yellow pages and one phone call later, PT Raja met Omar in the lobby of the Regent Hotel.

Omar had grown gaunt, his face thin from worry and lack of sleep. Work was the only thing that sustained him and he worried about the new contract, a controversial new road that would cut through the heart of the city. The Regent was on Jalan Bukit Bintang or Star Hill Road, KL's fashion boulevard, where malls like KL Plaza, Starhill Gallery, Lot 10, Sungei Wang and BB Plaza converged to give shoppers access to whatever their purse strings could afford. From diamond-encrusted watches in Starhill Gallery to fake Louis Vuitton bags in Sungei Wang, the street was a hub for locals and tourists, especially those from the Middle East who opened Persian and Arabic restaurants, introducing kebab, falafel and hummus to locals. Thousands of tourists from Dubai, Oman and the Arab states poured into KL in the summer: men with wives in full-black hijabs dotted the street with sweaty children in tow, mingling with street beggars and pungent smells that emanated from rat infested gutters.

A few hundred metres from the Regent, there were plans to build another mall on the site of the Bukit Bintang Girls School, one of the oldest all-girl institutions in KL. There were virulent protests and petitions from ex-students, but all fell on deaf ears. There was a price for progress, and Omar was beginning to know that more than anything else. He was seated on a leather sofa, in deep thought. He barely noticed the tall Indian man who strode confidently across the hotel lobby to stop two feet from him.

"Encik Malik?"

Omar sat unmoving, his shoulders hunched. PT Raja cleared his throat and spoke again. This time Omar heard and stood up quickly, almost dropping his handphone.

"PT Raja, good to meet you."

The private detective nodded, sensing a fatigue in Omar, and sat down on the far side of the sofa when gestured to sit.

"Call me Raj, please."

Omar handed him a sheet of paper and said, "The police report. She has been missing for three weeks now. We still know nothing."

The detective glanced at the document quickly and looked at Omar intently.

"Thank you, sir. I have also done some research, right after you told me about the case. I still have friends in Bukit Aman and I saw the case file. Inspector Awang is in charge, yes?"

Omar nodded, then sighed, "After all this time, do they have anything at all?"

The detective sat back in the couch and crossed his legs.

"No sir. This kind of case is extremely difficult to solve." He continued, "I won't lie to you."

Omar sank deeper into the leather sofa and heard it squeak under him, "But you will do your best to find my daughter."

"Yes, of course."

Omar tried to shrug off the image of Alba he'd had since he sat down. Alba on a swing in the park. Her hair bouncing. A pink dress with small flowers and yellow jelly sandals. Her tiny hand in his. The smell of her cheeks, her laugh. He cleared his throat and stood up.

"Shall we go for a drink?"

"Go ahead, sir."

They walked across the hotel lobby to the lift. They passed tourists as well as business types. As they waited for it to open, Omar felt a tap on his shoulder. He turned and saw Marina, who exclaimed, "Omar, how are you?"

Omar kissed Marina on both cheeks, and then turned to introduce Marina to the detective.

"PT Raja, this is Marina, friend of my wife's."

The detective smiled courteously at Marina. He did not like transsexuals; he knew that Marina's kind were often shunned and discriminated against and were forced to work in the sex trade, but he found no time to sympathise with them. They were an aberration of nature, and he found their deep voices and synthetic breasts distasteful . The lift dinged and opened. All three strode in. PT Raja pressed the button for the bar and then Marina said, "Top floor please."

Omar smiled at Marina and said, "You look nice." Marina was in a sleek black number, hair teased into a french twist. A classic pearl necklace adorned her neck. Marina chuckled and pouted her red lips and mouthed, "Thank you."

PT Raja stood stoically and fought to raise a solitary eyebrow. This was a high-class booty call and she was getting top dollar, more than what he made in a week. Marina glanced at him and immediately felt his displeasure.

"How's Del?" she asked quietly.

"Not good," Omar shook his head as the door shuddered

to a slight stop. The doors opened and the two men walked out. "Send her my love, please, she is not answering my calls," Marina pleaded as the lift doors closed with a muffled click.

There was a sudden uncomfortable shift between the two men. Omar cleared his throat and said, "My wife is in terrible shape, as you can imagine, and she...well, she always used to come around, but not recently. My wife does not want cheering up, as you can imagine. She just wants our daughter back."

Omar led the way to the bar. It was empty save for the bartender busy polishing wine glasses, who nodded and smiled at Omar, who then walked towards a corner cubicle and lowered himself onto the dark green couch. The light was low and he felt safe, unseen. The waiter asked for their order.

"Beer?" Omar asked. The detective nodded.

"Two Tigers please. Draft."

The beers arrived in tall frosted glasses. The bartender was a young Chinese boy, in his early 20s. "Will that be on your tab, sir?"

Omar nodded. They clinked their glasses and Omar let out a long sigh.

"Ah, nothing like a cold beer."

The detective agreed.

"So, am guessing that you don't get cases like this often?"

The detective took another sip of his beer and nodded, "It's mostly domestic cases. You know, wives checking up on their cheating husbands, or vice versa."

"Typical."

"But it can get very nasty, you know. At the end of the day, it's always about money—or children."

"Kidnappings?"

"Only once, sir, a boy was taken by his father. Custody issue. The kid ended up in Australia."

Omar drained the last of his beer and gestured to the bartender for another. "Can you help us? I know what you did before this."

The detective took another sip of his beer and cleared his throat. "In Special Branch—"

Omar interrupted, "Yes I know what you did in Special Branch, my wife and I were activists, so we know. Do you have inside leads? Who would do this? Why haven't we heard anything? Why?"

The detective sensed Omar's impatience and felt compelled to not say any more. Omar's second beer arrived and the detective felt that he was not going to escape the penetrating questions that Omar had probably lined up in his head. He was a careful man; being in the police force had taught him many things about human nature, and he had become more observant and instinctive over time. He felt Omar's quiet desperation, his confusion, his grief at not knowing where his child was. He wanted to help this man, but he knew that there were forces in the city that were not to be reckoned with, not by a common civilian.

But the beer had loosened him up. Omar was friends with a sex worker, his child had been taken, this was an unusual situation and he felt comfortable. They were in a classy bar, Omar had already finished his beer and was probably on a mission to get drunk. So PT Raja took a deep breath, and started.

"KL is divided into gangs, territories, numbers. For

instance here, Bukit Bintang, this is where all the action happens. Drugs, prostitution, your friend for example, she would not normally be in a hotel, she is a streetwalker, but things are changing. Now they can come into hotels, bars, not like before. The trannies can move, not like the others. You have some who are locked up, sex slaves, drugged, all kinds now. Girls, young girls as well."

Omar turned away. This was not what he wanted or needed to hear. "Go on."

"I was in vice before, so I know the issues. The problem now is because we have so many refugees, but because they are illegal many of the women are turning to sex work. So the demand is higher now. And sometimes, they sell their children to the pimps, because they cannot afford to raise them. These kids end up on the street, as beggars, or they're sold into the sex trade."

"And what are the police doing about this?"

The detective continued, resolutely. "It's very tricky, sir. The top guys, they're all involved, politicians, taikors, you know, the triad bosses, they are all working together. It's a business, big business, and everybody protects each other. It's like, you don't touch my turf, I don't touch yours. And you pay protection money. That's how you can do business here."

Omar shook his head and whispered, "Yes, I know all about that."

The detective took another swig of his beer and said, "You have no idea, sir. The corruption is very bad. This is also why I left the police. And young children, sorry to say...but they go missing all the time. So many, hundreds... every year."

Omar turned and stared at the detective pointedly, rattled

by what the detective had revealed. "So do you think you will find my daughter?"

"I..."

"Be honest, tell me the truth." Omar said quietly.

"Hard to say, sir. And I am so very sorry for you."

I HAD STOPPED sleeping. Stopped taking the pills, they made me feel paper-thin when I woke up. My mind wouldn't stop, it churned out images of Alba, morning into night and then into nightmares. A never-ending film reel of Alba. I was going crazy. My mind would not stop. I did not know how to make it stop. I made coffee, and sat a cup at the counter and waited for dawn to spill into the sky. I thought of the times I sat there with Alba waiting for the sun.

Alba, look darling, it's morning.

We would sit and watch television in the mornings; starting with the Teletubbies, *Tinky Winky, Dipsy, La La, Po, Teletubbies, Teletubbies, say hello!* then *Bananas in Pyjamas,* then *Barney the purple dinosaur,* then it would be nap time.

Morning, Del.

Omar strode into the kitchen. The TV was on, and he could see that I had been watching cartoons, like I did with Alba every morning. He came to kiss me, but I moved away, my eyes still glued to the prancing figures on the screen.

You need to talk to me, Del. I want to know what's going on with you. We need to try to get through this.

I kept silent.

I met a private detective last night.

I shrugged. *And. So?*

Look, Del, we can't give up.

Who says I'm giving up?

Pull yourself together… Can you try? Please?

I don't know how.

You have to try too. I am trying, Del, but why won't you?

The police can't find anything, what makes you think he can?

This guy is ex-Special Branch. He can help, he's well connected.

I giggled. *SB. God, how we used to hate them. Good luck,* I chirped.

He slammed his fist on the counter, then grimaced in pain.

Damn it, Del, damn you! Why do you have to make it worse?

I pressed the television remote, silencing it. Then I turned to him and in a voice that had been haunted by weeks of anguish, I said this.

I just want to die, Omar. I lost our child. I left her for thirty seconds and now she is gone. I feel worthless, I am in hell, because I put myself here. And all I feel is guilt, shame. Guilt. Shame. Every second, every fucking day. I blame myself. I cannot live with myself. I cannot do what you do. I cannot hope any more, because she will never be found. And you, you are making it worse, because you think she can be found. Alba is gone, we will never see her again. You know this, I know this. She is gone. And I have no hope left. So you can hope, but I cannot. So just let me rot in this hell.

The look that he gave me was one of remorse, then anger, then cruelty. Without a final glance, he walked out the door, and I knew that it was the end of our love. My marriage was over.

The Backroom had not changed in five years, but Karin had. She was gaunt, and her eyes were hollowed out. Her hair was teased with hairspray and mousse into an updo, and she wore an inch of make-up. She still looked good though, with a heroin-chic kind of elegance. I had been clean for five years, and it showed. Karin looked me up and down in my ill-fitting black dress, which curved over my tummy and stretched tightly over my thighs.

Babes, you put on weight lah.

No Karin, I haven't lost it all. Shut up.

Sorry babes, just saying, you know. Haven't seen you in so long… And you know I don't know what to say about Alba. I am sure the cops will find her, but you gotta stay positive, okay?

Her eyes flashed with concern, and I knew she meant it.

Yeah, listen, I don't want to talk, can we just party tonight?

Sure. How many you want? I got everything you need here.

Give me three.

You sure? That's a lot, babes…for you.

I opened my mouth and she placed three tabs on my tongue. I felt them, those three little round pills, ready for the taking. I swallowed a gulp of water, closed my eyes and felt that all familiar thrill. I was ready for the night.

I looked around me. There were some familiar faces, people I'd seen in TV ads and in Bangsar, types who ran in the circles that fucked film directors to get jobs, skinny things who took ice to stay even skinnier, make-up artists, models, the odd creative director here and there, and some really young Malay boys whom you knew were with fat, balding sugar daddies, veritable paedophiles. The music was good, even better than I remembered. Karin had disappeared and my guess was that she was probably on a mission to find more drugs, preferably of the powdered variety. The club was half-full, which was pretty good for a Thursday night.

I decided to sit down until it kicked in. I had never done

three at one go but I was certain that if the worst happened, I would just lie on a couch and stay still until it was over. I just wanted to get out of myself, to numb everything I was feeling. I found a couch, sat down, then got up again, feeling restless. There was nothing worse than waiting for it to kick in, so I walked around the club, trying to get a feel of the people there. I looked at my watch. 10pm. I had no husband, no child. Nothing. I had nothing in my life, nothing to care for anymore. No one. I looked up at the ceiling and saw a giant disco ball. Strange, I had never noticed that before. There were some people on the dance floor, and the music was starting to pick up. New tunes I'd not heard before, thumping rhythms, snazzy, sexy beats. Low rhythms. *Drum and bass. Love it.* I started moving my hips, when suddenly I felt it in the pit of my stomach. It swirled for a few seconds and then the surge leapt into the base of my neck. I was flying.

For hours I danced. I lost myself on that dance floor. I felt my spirits lift, I smiled and laughed to myself, I smiled at everyone who danced with me, I let them hold me, tease me, it was as if they collectively understood my grief, that they gave me space to just—be. This was the community that E created, we saw the truth, we saw what each of us needed, we knew how to take sorrows away, soothe pains, create salves, in the middle of the dance floor, we were all equals in pain, in joy, in suffering. There was no judgment, no morality call, I was not worthless, I was not ugly, I felt beautiful, wanted, appreciated, loved. It was all love and joy and translucence. I felt one with everyone on that dance floor. I felt Alba in my heart and I knew there and then that my little girl would stay with me forever. That she was in me, and that I would never, ever lose her. That I would see her again, one day, and all I had to do was get there.

It was going to be fine.

Then Karin showed up. Her finger gestured.

I followed her, past the gyrating couples, past the young people who smiled and danced with me earlier, past the white teenage kids who were giggling themselves silly, past the bar and the couches, up the stairs into a smoky room filled with people. I saw three men seated on plush chairs against a wall. All around us people smoking and drinking and sitting haphazardly on chairs and couches. It was the VIP room. Karin sauntered up to a guy and I followed her. I was tripping like crazy but I could walk, I felt like I was floating off the ground. I was grinding my teeth hard and my hands felt clammy, suddenly I felt cold.

This is her. This is Del.

He wore a white shirt with a jacket that looked like it was two sizes smaller. His girth stretched over matching pants and I saw gleaming black leather shoes. One leg crossed over the other. Brown ankle socks. He held a lit cigar in his right hand and I saw a gold signet ring on his fourth finger—the nail on his pinky was longer, manicured to a sharp point, customary of many Chinese men who believed that a long pinky nail would bring luck. His hair was teased into a bouffant, which made his head look unnaturally big. His face was puffy and his lips thick and red.

Nice to meet you.

His voice sounded sonorous and low, like a bulldog's. His eyes searched me up and down. I felt self-conscious.

I know your husband.

I stared at him blankly. *What?*

I looked at Karin and she gestured to her lips.

Your husband is a bad businessman. He make a lot of bad deals. Ask him to be careful.

What do you mean?

Tell him, if he does not listen, there will be trouble.

What kind of trouble?

I was starting to panic, my words coming out like squeaks.

More trouble.

He took another swig of his drink and turned away. The conversation was over. Karin came over and took my elbow. I almost stumbled on the carpet as she led me to a glass table in a corner. It was lined with coke, neatly cut, horizontal.

Who the fuck is that guy?

He's a taikor. Big boss.

Triad boss?

Uh huh. Trying to tell you something.

Karin took a rolled-up note and snorted a line. She rolled her head back and let out a soft gasp.

Fuck! Best shit in town. Now, do the same.

I don't want coke. I am tripping my ass off right now.

You don't have a choice. He's watching, you have to do one line, at least.

Paranoia hit me and I felt goose bumps on my arm.

I'm fucking freezing.

Just do a line, you'll feel better.

I took a quick look around me. A couple of women had appeared and started gyrating towards that man. They were tall. Russians, all blonde. All tits and ass, glittery triangles of clothing covering bits of flesh.

I took the rolled-up note that Karin handed me. I counted eight lines. I did one line with my right nostril, took a deep breath and then did a second line with my left. It went straight in between my eyes, like a flash, I felt a prickly bitter aftertaste spiral up my nose. The insides cackled and burnt slightly. I rubbed my nostrils and swallowed. Karin chuckled.

Told you. Good shit right.

I nodded. The colours in the room seemed brighter, more saturated. My eyes watered a little, then felt tingly. I felt wide awake. I didn't care what that man had said to me. All I wanted to do that night was to have a good time and forget, lose my mind. Karin got up and sashayed into a dark corner, blending in with upholstery. The party in the VIP room got more and more rowdy, the lines of coke were endless. The music got louder. I felt loose, sexy, bold. I started dancing on my own, the movement giving me warmth. Then I felt someone watching me. This guy who was slumped in a chair, in a white shirt which was partially undone. He looked young. I sidled up to him and started gyrating my hips in front of him, he smiled and nodded to the music. We both laughed. He was cute. He gestured.

Come here.

I sat down at his feet and he kissed me. His face felt smooth, his jaw lean, his neck fragrant with citrus and a light musk. His hands flitted over my body lightly, then more firmly. We kissed again.

You wanna get out of here?

I shrugged. We kept kissing, and I wanted him all over me. My insides felt smooth, like liquid glass, moving in a uniform grace, I felt like a well-oiled machine. I was perfect, my body was perfect. My lips, eyes, mouth. Wet, silky. He got up and pulled me to him. His eyes pierced into me, glinting with danger.

Let's go.

As we walked out, I saw Karin's bent head in a corner, over some guy's lap. She smiled and stuck her tongue out and mouthed something like, "Have fun, babes." The room was completely packed with people. All moving, all swaying. All high.

You driving? You sure?

I do it all the time. Love driving when I'm high.

It was a humid, sticky night. My skin felt clammy. We got into his car, a silver Porsche. It was stupid, but there I was, in a stranger's car. He held my hand and smiled. He was young, confident, bold. Then it was all a blur. The lights on the street flashed by, the music in his car, riding the lift to his apartment, kissing and undressing in the living room, our entwined figures reflected on the tempered glass windows, the lights, champagne, more champagne, more lines, more kissing until we were completely naked.

God, you're beautiful. So fucking beautiful.

His hands and mouth were all over me, fingers splaying expertly, making me moan and grit my teeth in pleasure. Tendrils of light and cold zig-zagging across my body. It was delicious. Then he put himself inside me, and I looked at his eyes and face and was filled with revulsion and pain and horror and all I wanted to say was *No, No, No, get off me, this is wrong,* but I didn't. I thought of Omar and my lost baby girl and I turned my head away so the tears would be unseen and fall silently.

When I woke up, sunlight streamed through the thick glass panes into the living room. Two bottles of Dom, smudged lines on the table, clothes, shoes strewn around. The Twin Towers bounced light from the morning sun. I had never seen them this high up. This was a view from a million-dollar penthouse.

I padded to the fridge to get water. More bottles of Dom lined the fridge.

I heard him moan softly from the couch. *You're not leaving, are you?*

Just getting water, want some?

I felt like I was walking on shards of glass, the soles of my feet hurt, my calves ached. My fingers were trembling.

Umm, any chance you got some Valium… or Xanax?

He chuckled. *Getting the shakes, huh?*

He stood up. I saw what I already knew. That he was lithe and supple, his body sculpted and lean. His skin taut like new leather. I turned away and remembered that I had licked him all over. He walked towards the bedroom and came out with two pink pills.

Here, take this, or we can do more lines. Your choice. He smiled.

I'm Del, by the way. Wasn't sure if I got that across…last night.

He grabbed me and licked my lips. *Hmmm. I know. I'm Shah.*

Shah. With the penthouse, Porsche, designer apartment and sexy tongue.

Stay here, relax. We can do as much coke as you like and fuck as much as you like.

I looked into his eyes and saw that he was kind, warm. There was gentleness there.

Or you can go. No pressure.

He eased me back onto the couch, and kissed me deeply. I stayed.

Three days later I walked into my apartment. When I opened the door, I knew that Omar had left. There was just an air about it, and when I walked into the bedroom, I saw that his clothes were gone. The bathroom, empty of his toiletries, his shoes, bedside papers all gone. His study was stripped bare, as if it had never even been populated with books, antiques. Nothing was broken or out of place, it was as if he had packed everything with kid gloves. I ran to the bathroom and turned on the shower, hot. Full blast. I washed and scrubbed myself till my skin bled.

Three days of cocaine, Ecstasy, champagne and sex had rendered me naked and exposed. I felt dirty, contaminated by the world, by grief, the swollen plague of pain. I felt worthless, shamed, like a deviant of the worst kind. I couldn't understand why two people who loved each other could not talk, communicate at the most basic level, speak of their grief. Perhaps some kinds of grief are more devastating than others, perhaps losing a child is the worst grief of all, so much so that in the end, not talking about it was the only thing to do. The world does not prepare you for many things, but losing a child is a certain kind of hell that is perhaps reserved for people who need to be punished. For being a murderer in a past life or a cruel leader who massacred millions, a heinous charlatan, a paedophile, a cannibal who ate little babies, a mother who killed her own children, someone who committed suicide. *I wanna die. I wanna die. I wanna die.* I said it over and over again as I stood in the shower, the hot water pelting me like sharp stones.

I loved Omar. Still, of course. But I meant every word I screamed at him. I was a bad mother, I left my child for thirty seconds in a shopping cart and she got taken. I deserved it, I deserved what happened to me. Or did I? Nobody deserves to have a child taken, least of all someone who was good. I was a good person, I led a good life, I was moral and upright and fought for what I believed in, and I was married to someone who felt the same. We were equals, we shared the same ideals, we fell in love, got married and had a beautiful child.

Alba, Alba, my darling, sweet, precious Alba.

Where are you?

Why? Why? Why?

I stumbled out of the shower and collapsed on the floor. The screams that came out of me were primal, vociferous, blood curdling. I was a woman let loose in hell, in a biblical malevolence, in a banal horror unlike any other. I was cursed, cursed to have a child taken, cursed to have a husband who would not speak, cursed to be motherless, cursed to have a father who was also silent. I was cursed, and all I wanted to do right there and then was die.

Friends. Karin. Sumi. Marina. Imran. Fairman. Friends who were supposedly there to help you. Be there. Be present. Friends before Omar. Life before Alba. Life with Omar. Life with Alba. Life after Alba.

There were days when I wish I had not met Omar. Things had meaning then. Working for *The Review* and *Saksi* channelled my anger, my frustrations, my fervent desire to tell stories. I had a purpose, I had stories that needed to be told. I, no—we, tried to be the best versions of ourselves. The country demanded that of us, and we demanded it of ourselves.

Malaysians had always been fearful but the Reformasi had transformed us, it made us brave, it made us feel that we could fight, we believed that change was possible. There was solidarity between us, friendships that could ride out tear gas, arrest, heartbreak, one-night-stands, occasional fumblings in dark corners. Perhaps the antidote to the human condition was stasis, to live with what you could, to not venture into the unknown, to just accept the fact that life was meant to be what it was, there and then. Right there, right then.

Life before Omar. Life before Alba.

I knew they cared. I knew that Sumi had called me at least once a day leaving heartfelt messages, but I had never returned a single one. Marina had called too, but she was in and out of KL with her lover and she seemed concerned, but there were times when I couldn't tell with her. Tragedy changes people, distorts friendships, destroys marriages. People sent emails, messages of support, yes, but did they really, truly understand? What could Sumi have said to make me feel better? I didn't want sympathy, I didn't want concern. My heart had been carved out of my chest, and it lay like a piece of meat on a chopping block. I felt grubby, truncated, masticated. Nothing anyone said could put me together.

There was still no word from the police. Nothing. My sense of helplessness was distorting me, the only thing that took away the pain, however momentary was the drugs. I just wanted to get high. I just wanted to forget everything. I went back to the club again and again. Shah and I became lovers: I needed to be felt by a man, by his hands, to be picked up and put down. Almost every night, I'd meet Karin at the club, pop E, dance and then head back to Shah's where we would do coke, listen to music and talk. Shah was young, but savvy and smart. He had been educated in Australia and his father owned the building he lived in. Karin knew better than to judge me, she knew that Shah was good to me, so she said nothing.

Shah was kind, he loved coke and he loved to fuck me when he was high. I had started losing weight, the drugs had killed whatever little appetite I had for food and soon, I started feeling better about my body than I had in years. I knew he had other lovers, that didn't bother me, I knew that he liked threesomes as well. Once he fucked me along with a beautiful Ukranian girl with a huge mouth that he paid thousands for that night. We did so much coke, I had a nosebleed for days. Nothing meant anything anymore. My body was just a piece of flesh. Which would die and fester and rot.

He knew that I was in pain, and he just gave me what I needed. His body, and endless lines of cocaine. We would talk about music, film, art, travel—he had driven across Australia one summer—and books. He was extremely well read and talked about writing a book *when the story is ready to bleed itself out of me.* His voice soothed me and his soft Australian drawl became a salve. He never asked me about Omar or Alba, he was just there, the only measure of goodness in my dark world.

Then one day, I got a phone call from Inspector Awang. I was at home and was washing dishes when my handphone rang. With my soapy hand, I picked up the phone nervously and my voice cackled into the speaker.

Hello, Inspector Awang...yes... you have some news?

He was curt and to the point.

We would like you and your husband to come to the station. We have a few leads we can discuss with you. We have not found your daughter, but we can tell you what we do know.

An hour later, I was in an office on Jalan Taman Pantai, the police headquarters for the Bangsar area. Inspector Awang was seated at a desk an open file in front of him, and Omar was facing the window. Omar was dressed in a grey suit, he looked polished, determined. He turned and nodded at me, his lips a firm line. There were more lines on his face and I spotted some grey streaks. I was flustered and in disarray. Strung out, still coked out. I sat on a chair opposite Inspector Awang. Alba's picture was there on the top corner, and I stifled a sob. Omar walked towards the table and stood next to it, refusing to sit. Inspector Awang was to the point.

We know that it has taken us a while to come back to you, but this is a very difficult case. Three more children have also gone missing under similar circumstances and there are still no leads. But last night, we did a raid in Serdang and we found nineteen women from China who had been held in a shophouse for six months. They were sex slaves. We managed to get some information from the person who was running that brothel... There are at least four human trafficking syndicates in the city right now, dealing mostly in women and children. Young children who are kidnapped are usually sold to adoption agencies or sold into the sex industry. We have ruled out that neither of you are suspects, we have also spoken to your friends, and we do not suspect them at all. Your daughter could be in one of many places.

Omar was silent, and I was starting to feel ill. Inspector Awang paused, then continued.

I know this is difficult but you need to understand that this is a reality now here in KL. We are a hub for traffickers in the region, because of the number of foreign workers and refugees... and because of the foreign gangs that are now running the drugs and prostitution rings. Your daughter could be in KL or she could be somewhere as far as Australia. Or Thailand. I am very sorry but it does not look good now, and if she was sold into adoption, she could be anywhere in the world. And because Alba is fair, she will be very popular and get the seller a lot of money. Exotic looking women and girls are very popular and…

I got up. I could not listen to another word. I ran out of the office and asked the nearest police officer outside for the bathroom. Startled, he said, "Go out, take right then left." I steadied myself on the wall outside and found the door to the female toilet. It stank of mothballs and urine. I locked myself in the nearest cubicle and threw up the bright yellow bile that was building in my stomach. My baby girl was in the hands of human traffickers. I threw up again and again until I felt weak. At the dirty sink, I stared at my reflection in the mirror and saw a woman haunted, impaled by the fact that her daughter could never be found. That she was in the clutches of monsters who were capable of unspeakable things. I splashed cold water on my face and decided that I needed to hear everything Inspector Awang had to say. I had to know everything that he knew.

I walked in and saw that Omar was looking out the window again. He turned when he saw me come in and I could see that his eyes were red. I burst into tears and he came towards me. He held me as the sobs racked my body, both of us standing there in grief. Inspector Awang handed us a box of tissues. I grabbed a clump of the fine white paper and thrust it under my nose. Omar sucked in his breath and swore quietly.

Inspector Awang put down the box of tissues on this desk, crossed his arms, looked at us squarely in the eyes and said:

I am sorry. I wish I had better news for you, but I don't. But this is new for us also. The fact that they are going after young children is very worrying. The fact also that she is very small in size means that it is easier to move her. So, these syndicates operate very differently, and they work in different areas of the city. The fact that she was taken in Bangsar tells us that this is a very sophisticated gang. To go into such an area is high-risk and they obviously know the territory and their clientele. We are not going to give up, this is part of an ongoing investigation, but we also don't want to tip them off, so we need to be careful… These are very dangerous people and they are very clever. Everything is planned, nothing is random. These people have been following you for a long time and they knew exactly when the time was right… Anything is possible, so it's difficult to come to any kind of conclusion right now.

They had been following us? Sex slaves? Kiddy porn? New parents? Sold? Taken by traffickers? My baby could be anywhere, more alive than dead?

This is all we have right now.

Omar and I kept silent. There was nothing to say, only a barrage of questions that would render us even more distraught.

Do you think she's in KL? I blurted.

We have no idea of knowing where she is at all. Like I said, she could be anywhere.

But she's alive? You think she's alive?

It's highly possible that she is, yes, she is worth more alive…

Omar stifled a gasp, raked his fingers through his hair and said, in a pained voice.

Thank you, Inspector, thank you for your time. Please keep us updated.

He then walked past me, stopped and attempted a weak smile.

Take care of yourself, Del.

And he walked out the door as I turned away and stifled a scream. I was breaking, breaking, breaking up into little pieces.

I counted all the pills again before I swallowed them. I had prescription Xanax for panic attacks and for sleeping and I lay them out in a row, all twenty of them. Like sweets. I had bought a bottle of vodka and I was ready. I re-read the note I had written.

I am sorry. I have no more reasons. I am beyond pain. I just want to sleep forever and dream of Alba. Please cremate me, I have no wish to be buried. Thank you.

How stupid. How banal. My mundane life, reduced to a pathetic note. The days after the police station were spent in complete catatonia. I had crawled into bed and stayed there for three whole days, weeping, screaming, sleeping. I did not eat, I drank bottle after bottle and took whatever pills I had. By the fourth day, I was less of a shell than I had ever been and I had decided that the only way to end the misery was to end my life. There was no strength left in me, apart from feeling completely and utterly alone, I was afraid for my mind. I could not stop it from going to the deepest reaches of my subconscious—the images that stayed with me for most of my walking hours were unrelenting. I had images of Alba splayed out in front of my eyes; Alba screaming from pain, Alba crying, Alba wandering around looking for me, *Mama Mama Mama, where are you?*

Alba with strange men doing unimaginable things to

her. With a camera, with objects, with knives. *No,* I told myself, *I cannot do this anymore. She will never be found and I will go crazy in the process. It is not worth it.* And really, apart from Alba there was nothing for me to live for. I might as well have been dead to Omar. And he to me. I was staring at the abyss and there was no way out. I took one pill then a swig of vodka. Then two, and another swig. Then three, and another swig, then four, then five and the final five. All twenty pills were in me. And soon I had drunk almost two thirds of the bottle. I staggered to the couch and managed to get comfortable enough, soon I felt a wave come over me. It felt like damp cotton wool coursing through my veins. Yes, sleep would claim me and there would be no more tomorrow. No more pain, no more nightmares. No more.

Then, a lightness came over me, as if I was being lifted toward an orange cloud. It was the richest sunset I'd ever seen. Streaks of aquamarine, blue, crimson, pinks of all hues. It was glorious. I closed my eyes and drifted towards some kind of tunnel. Yes, I was almost there, *take me angels, take me home.*

When my handphone rang, I had apparently managed to answer it, how I don't know. I must have found some strength to reach an arm out, press a button then speak. *Hello...* Then I went silent, thrust back into the orange universe. This prompted Marina to race over to the apartment with her lover, knock furiously on the door, break it down with the help of the security guard and then get me into an ambulance. When I woke up, she was there by my side. Her lover, he was there too. I looked at her then turned away.

I want to die, Marina. I can't...

No, you are not going to die. You can't, Del. You cannot give up.

But I had, I had. And I was not good anymore. Not to anyone, not to Omar, not to myself. I closed my eyes and saw Alba. Sitting on a swing in the playground, looking at her new yellow shoes with delight. I had just bought them after she picked them out from a store. Jelly shoes, see-through ones. We had doughnuts at a bakery in the same mall, laughing when we had identical sugary moustaches, we sang in the car as we drove to the playground, where I pushed her up on a swing, higher and higher until her laughter turned to tears, and then cradling her in my arms, her chubby hands tugging my ears and cheeks, her warm lips kissing me, saying *Mama, Mama* for the very first time.

OMAR NOTICED THAT the bottle was almost empty when he heard his handphone ring. It was an unlisted number and as he pressed it to his ear, he regretted picking it up and was going to end the call when he heard a familiar female voice.

"Omar, it's Nim."

His hand reached for the snifter of whisky and he took another gulp.

"Nim?"

"Imran's friend. Remember?" she spoke again.

Omar cleared his throat and spoke slowly, trying not to slur, "Ah…from the wedding…Alba's birthday… and Hanoi airport!" He heard silence.

"Am I intruding?," she asked quietly.

"Not intruding at all," Omar slurred back. He leaned back on the couch and took another swig of whisky. His head was throbbing and he thought to get up for some water, but he found himself to be unsteady and fell back onto the couch.

"Are you all right?" she asked, her voice probing gently.

"No," he replied, his voice breaking. "My baby is gone…"

"Yes, I know. Omar," she continued, "I am so sorry, I wish I could help…"

"Come over," he said gruffly. "Right now."

"Now?" Nim asked, her voice surprised.

"Yes, will SMS you my address. See you soon."

Omar hung up, drained the glass, tapped his address and pressed the send button. He got up, pulled his clothes off and strode through the living room, through the bedroom and into the shower. When he emerged ten minutes later, he heard a police siren from the street below. Momentarily confused, he thought himself to be in London, in his apartment in Shoreditch where police sirens were an everyday affair. He shook his head and remembered the time when he had arrived from London, and how he'd met Del, all those years ago. He ruffled his hair dry on a fluffy white towel and walked towards the window. He looked down and saw people going in and out of the building across. He wondered if Del would be there that night, getting high and off her head. He pressed his head against the glass pane and sighed.

He looked up and saw the KL Tower looming above him, its red eye pulsating at the top. He turned around, pulled some clothes from the open wardrobe, straightened the sheets on his bed, found two white pills from his bedside drawer and swallowed them with water from a bottle. He sat on the side of his bed and looked at his watch. He had no idea if Nim was going to show up and felt a pang of regret. It was impulsive, asking her to come over. He had no idea if she was even in town, and had assumed that she was.

Omar walked into the kitchen and opened another bottle of whisky. He had been drinking heavily for three days, and had thought to stock up for the weekend ahead. After the meeting with Inspector Awang, he had called the office, told his secretary to cancel all meetings and appointments, drove home and started drinking. He had called PT Raja to update him of the new findings, put the volume down on his handphone, closed the curtains, turned on the stereo and sat on the couch, unmoving, until he drank an entire bottle and had passed out on the couch.

When he woke up, he ran to the bathroom and retched violently. Only bile came up, and his stomach growled in pain. He stumbled into the shower and vomited again, his stomach heaving in waves. The cold water revived him and he glared at his reflection in the mirror. His face unshaven, his eyes bloodshot, his right fist shaking with anger. His mouth contorted in anger and he let us a scream, his mouth widening into an O and then a snarl and then as an image of Alba flashed into his mind, his body shook and heaved with tears, and on the bathroom floor, he wept.

AFTER THE SUICIDE attempt, I was inundated by calls from Sumi, Fairman, Imran and once by Omar, but I felt the distance in his voice, and responded appropriately with the same measure of coldness. My near-death-experience had informed me that there were beings of light—I was certain that I had been carried by a guardian angel of some sort—and that the promise of an afterlife was real. The road to heaven was not paved with roses, it was paved with the unending rays of a brilliant, undying sun.

Papa was beside himself and it pained me to see him like that, but I assured him that it would never happen again. I had resolved to see things differently. My father was at death's door, waiting, and I realised that he was only living for me, that if I ended my life, he would end his own. The cyclical nature of life and death was not profound, we had glimmers of love, and perhaps it was enough.

Marina decided to move in with me temporarily to make sure that I got out of my sex- and drug-fuelled frenzy. She made sure that I ate; cooked simple dishes with a variety of soups, noodles and rice and for the first time in months, I felt a sense of normality. She deleted Karin's number from my phone and said that I could see Shah but *you have to use a condom, god knows how many women he has slept with. And no more coke!* She dragged me to do an AIDS and STD test, which was humiliating, and she got rid of all the alcohol in the house. We sat in the evenings and sipped herbal tea and watched film after feel-good film. It was the most mundane week, but it worked. Marina had shown me that she was really and truly concerned and that she was going to make sure that I got back on track. In truth, she was the only one who cared.

Because I had punished my body so much in the previous weeks, I went through withdrawals and would wake up in cold sweats and panic attacks. I smoked copiously to keep my hands from shaking, and once begged her to let me drink some wine. The entire bottle was gone in ten minutes. She sat there at the dinner table, cigarette in right hand, her crimson nails perfectly manicured.

You can drink yourself to death too, you know. You want to go into rehab?

I knew that I needed help, but it wasn't the kind of help that you could get in rehab. I wasn't an addict, I was grieving and was temporarily lapsing into a dark place—I knew that I would get myself out of it, and perhaps Marina's presence was the kind of trigger I needed. I had pushed myself to the edge and I needed to find my way back. I knew then that Marina was family—she was the only real person I could trust implicitly. She cared for me, she loved me and she was going to make sure that I survived this.

Fuck Omar, what a loser. Some men don't know how to deal with anything.

I opened my mouth to defend Omar and then I stopped. We were both to blame, I had put up a wall since Alba's disappearance. I, too, did not know how to deal with it. My father's example wasn't model behaviour, and I had not been available to Omar in any way at all. I told Marina that I had shut myself down emotionally and physically, so it was no wonder that he had left.

That's not an excuse, Del. I saw the way he looked at you at the wedding. That man would never do this to you. He's changed, something has happened to him. You have to stop blaming yourself.

Blame. How could I not blame myself? It was easy to blame Omar. Marina did not know the brutality of marriage, the banality of motherhood. Alba was with me when she was taken, I was responsible, how could I spare myself from the residue of responsibility? All that I thought I knew about love, friends and family—everything I knew had been compromised. I had to redefine everything from scratch. And it had to start with myself.

But love, Marina was in the throes of love with Mr Ferrari.

He says he loves me. He is the kindest, gentlest, most generous person. And he wants to be with me! He says that I am his soul mate, that he has been searching for me his whole life. Can you imagine?

Yes, I could imagine her happiness. Marina, who had come from the backwaters of Sabah, who had to spread her legs every night for men who spat at her and called her filthy names would one day find love—and happiness. I too had it, for a few years only, but I did have it, once.

He's very well connected, he knows a lot of people in KL, you know. Gangsters, he knows them. In the construction business, it's all run by these people. Bloody gangsters, they control everything in KL. Even politicians are involved you know?

I recalled that moment in the club when Karin introduced the man with the long fingernail. *Your husband is not a good man, he makes bad deals.*

Your boyfriend. Can you ask him if he knows anything about trafficking in KL?

I told her what Inspector Awang had told Omar and me. Marina listened intently, smoked cigarette after cigarette and then said, very quietly.

I know of a woman who sells babies. I've heard of a girl who sold her baby once. This was a few months ago. This woman is very bad, she runs an adoption agency, but she sells the babies to couples who cannot have children.

A woman who sells babies? Like babies that are just born or toddlers? How old?

I don't know, I need to ask more.

I stood up and bent over, my stomach heaving with pain and relief. A realm of possibility had opened up. Perhaps Alba had been sold to a childless couple in KL. Perhaps she was in a happy home somewhere in the city. Perhaps she was really and truly all right. Then again, perhaps not. I had to find her. But how?

THE DOORBELL RANG and Omar knew that it was Nim. He drained the last of his whisky and glanced at his watch. It was almost 10pm. He opened the door. Nim stood outside, dressed in a knee-length grey dress with long sleeves. She smiled and held out her hand.

"Hi there, good to see you," she said.

Omar took her hand and shook it lightly, he thought it slightly formal, but perhaps it was the best option, under the circumstances.

"Come in," he gestured her inside, "Keep your shoes on, if you like."

"Oh no," she said, "I prefer to walk barefoot when indoors," and slipped her black heels off.

"Drink?" Omar asked.

"Sure, whatever you're having," Nim replied, as Omar walked towards the low table by the couch. He picked up the remote for the stereo and turned it down.

"You like jazz, I see," Nim commented quietly as she sat down on one end of the couch.

Omar nodded and asked, "How many fingers? I hope you like single malt…"

"Three is good," Nim replied quickly.

Omar handed her the thick, hand-cut crystal snifter with the golden liquid, picked up his own and clinked hers. They both took a sip and leaned back on the couch. Omar took another sip, "Thanks for coming over, I wasn't sure if you were even in KL, but… thanks." He looked at her, pained. "It's been a horrific time, these past weeks…"

"I am so sorry, I cannot imagine what you must be going through…"

"Have never felt so helpless in my life," he continued. "The police have nothing, absolutely fucking nothing…"

Nim shook her head and sighed. "Surely, they must have something…?"

"Well they told us that she could be anywhere really, that a child like her is worth more alive than dead, that she could be sold, she could be in Thailand, Australia, or even still in KL…!" He smiled bitterly. "These people are monsters… who would sell someone else's child?" Omar drank the rest of the whisky, slammed the glass on the table and poured himself another drink.

"Have you eaten anything today, Omar?" Nim asked firmly. "I think you've had more than enough to drink…"

Omar sat down resigned and shook his head. "I can't… can't stop thinking about her…" He held his head in his arms and sighed.

Nim got up. "Do you have eggs?" She walked towards the modern open-style kitchen, and opened the refrigerator. "Yup, you do…"

Omar looked up and her and smiled weakly. "Do what you must," he said.

Nim took out four eggs, some butter and milk and placed it on the kitchen island. She rummaged in the cupboards below and stove and found a saucepan. She beat the eggs in a bowl, added some milk, salt and pepper, melted some butter in a pan and lightly scrambled the eggs on the expensive cast iron stove until they were partially cooked.

The smell of food made Omar nauseous initially, but then the hunger pangs that he had subdued for days came back and he felt nauseous again, but now, from hunger.

Nim slipped the eggs expertly onto a slim white plate and found some cutlery in another drawer. She carried the plate to Omar, who was already sitting up.

"Here, eat," Nim demanded with a smile.

Omar took the plate gratefully and with his fork, pierced the soft mound of eggs and put it in his mouth. He nodded as he tasted the buttery, creamy goodness. Within seconds had eaten half the portion on the plate. Nim sat and watched him quietly, sipping her whisky.

Omar took one final mouthful, chewed thoughtfully and set the plate down on the table. He took a deep sigh and said, "That was delicious, thank you." He sat back in the couch and closed his eyes. His body felt more relaxed than it had in days, now nourished with something other than whisky. He suddenly felt exhausted. That all the nutrients in his belly demanded relief, and rest.

"Listen," he said, "I need to lie down," and stood up slowly.

"Sure, I'll leave you to rest, Omar. Try to keep your strength up." Nim walked towards the front door and slipped her heels back on.

"Thanks, really. I...will speak to you soon." Omar unlocked the heavy wooden door and a cool breeze blew in. He felt lightheaded but calm. Nim smiled and leaned over to peck him lightly on the cheek. Omar recoiled. Her touch unnerved him, but it did not feel like pity, it felt of genuine concern.

"Sure. I'm in KL for a few more days, so let me know..." she smiled and walked away, her shapely calves sashaying steadily away from him, her hair blowing to the right from the breeze. As she stood at the lift lobby, she turned and smiled again. He heard the lift doors ding, stepped inside, closed the door firmly and locked it.

YOU'RE WHAT? I exclaimed. The two well-dressed white women at the table next to ours turned and stared in annoyance.

Del, keep it down please, Sumi whispered.

Sumi and Fairman had been trying to have a baby, and after her first miscarriage, she had another one, which was equally devastating. She had become fat in her wealth, with the IVF treatments, and had become one of those "ladies-who-lunch", one of the many social butterflies that flitted in and around KL's many trendy cafés. I could see that boredom had set in. She was dressed in an all-black ensemble, matching shoes, a patent black leather handbag and large Jackie O-type sunglasses. She masked her extra weight well; she was taller than I and had sleeker limbs, so the extra padding around her waist was well camouflaged.

Sumi had only seen me once after the suicide attempt and by all accounts, I was already a different person. But I had been nervous when I sat down to wait. It was a humid afternoon after the hot rains which had left the roads steaming. Tendrils of warm vapour eased upwards, disappearing into the underbellies of cars, briefly entwining with the feet and calves of pedestrians before evaporating. We had arranged to meet in a new patisserie, which had a selection of French breads, cakes and pastries, and I was nursing my second café latte when she swung into the booth with a flourish.

Sorry I'm late. Terrible parking today, and it's so bloody humid! Whooh!

Kiss kiss, twice on the cheek. The glasses came off, and then a perfectly made-up face gleamed back at me. How she had changed. How she had changed from the sweaty, drenched, despairing person on the street, dodging tear gas and police batons, clad in cheap jeans and faded sneakers. How we had both changed.

So, how are you? Feeling better? You look better! Tell me all.

And where was I supposed to start? The pills, the vodka, the bags of cocaine, the club, Shah, the hospital, Inspector Awang? Omar?

I shrugged. *I don't know where to start, Sumi, it's been, just... hard. You know, just trying to live every day without going crazy...*

She patted my hand, waved to a waiter, pointed to my latte and said, *Okay... I know this might be hard for you... Oh well, I'll just come out and say it.* She took a breath and continued. *We have decided to try and adopt. I can't have a baby, that's clear and the IVF has made me so fat. Look at me! I'm not even menopausal yet, these bloody hormones, they just make you so fat! So, yes, we're going to adopt!*

I gulped my café latte and sputtered.

Adopt? My hands started shaking and I felt a cold shiver on my neck. *How?*

Sumi continued, unperturbed. *Well, there are ways, you know. I know a couple of people who've recently just adopted baby girls, it's all legit of course, paperwork and all, you pay for quick service but yes... we've been talking about it and so, what do you think?* Her café latte appeared and she took a cultured sip.

I said quietly, my eyes downcast. *Good luck, I hope you find a child who... deserves a home like yours.*

It was as if she didn't hear me. And then she told me about their recent holiday in Barcelona, where they ate non-stop *oh my god, Iberico ham, the tapas! So fresh, ahh the wine, the shopping, the leather shoes, the hand stitching! Fairman went crazy, this villa, oh my god the view of the vineyards, olive oil from the trees! The scent of lemons in the morning...* A run-down of what they saw and a slew of haphazardly-linked vignettes about her life since being Mrs Fairman. And such. Then it was onto the baby. The monologue continued. I wanted to leave, just run out the door, but I forced myself to stay, to listen to her drone on and on. I was feeling unhinged, the conversation drifting precariously into territory I really did not want to venture into.

You're not really a woman until you have a child and I feel so inadequate, but Fairman is okay with it, he just thinks that we can have more freedom without lugging a baby around whenever we feel like taking off, but then I ask myself, how long can I do this for? This kind of jet-setting will wear off after a while and then what? I don't need to work so what the hell was I supposed to do? Socialise? Find a charity? Orphans? Shop? If I am going to do all that then I might as well have a child, right? After all there are so many kids who need loving homes and I think it would do me good, what do you think? I'm sorry for rambling on and on but you know sometimes I am by myself for days and days and all I do is just ramble on and on...

What about the law? You wanted to get into law, remember? I broke my silence.

I'm lonely, Del, she replied.

And you think a child is going to make you feel less lonely? I snapped back.

If only she knew what loneliness meant. If only she knew how selfish it all sounded. I wanted to walk away there and then and let her stew in her imagined misery. I wanted to slap her and say, you have a husband who loves you, you have a life that some women would kill for and now you want a child to complete it, like another handbag. But I didn't.

Once Fairman and I find a baby, our lives will be perfect. I know it.

You know Fairman is married to the company, just like Omar. You know that right? You know that having a baby is the hardest, most difficult thing in the world, right? That you don't sleep for weeks and months, that you're tired all the time…and when they're sick…

She cut in. *Del, I know. And I will be prepared.* Her eyes suddenly looked hard. *I am not an idiot.* Her hand reaching out to grasp mine and as if to say… *I will not do it the way you did.* I pulled away.

Look, I'm sorry if I am being insensitive, but you're my friend and friends talk to each other. Sorry for saying this, but I really want a child…It's a simple as that. Surely you would understand…?

I do, I replied sharply. *It's just hard okay. My life is fucked, really…* I was trying to stay calm and not disintegrate into a sobbing mess. I took a large gulp to steady myself. *So tell me about the baby then, how is this going to happen?*

You know Kim Harrison? She already has one kid and has been trying to have another for years, but it just never happened. She heard of a woman called Mary who runs an adoption agency or something like that. Mary put the word out and apparently in a couple of weeks there was already a child…

How old? I asked.

I think she was a newborn, or maybe a week old? Very cute, curly hair, high nose, beautiful child. Her name is Natasha.

Natasha. I wondered if Natasha was someone else before she became Natasha.

This woman, do you think she has older kids as well?

I don't know, but I was planning to call her next week, once Fairman gets back and we have a serious conversation about this... He's been waffling, so I need to get a definite yes from him before I do this. But yes, it's entirely possible! She clapped her hands in glee.

Sounds like a plan. I said quietly.

And how are you?

As if she really wanted to know. As if she really cared.

I don't really know any more, you know. I need to find Alba.

Sumi took a look around the room, pursed her lips and snapped back.

You can't find Alba, Del. The cops will find her.

I was filled with a sense of violence, of wanting to smash the white ceramic cup which held the rest of my coffee, of wanting to punch Sumi and thrust her head onto the table again and again, of wanting to draw blood.

Fuck you. I said. *Fuck you, Sumi.*

I got up to leave and she pulled at my arm. *I'm sorry... I'm such a fucking idiot, I know.*

I looked at her straight in the eye and said, *Yes, you are.*

And walked right out of the café into the afternoon light.

SIX

YEAR OF THE MONKEY

ALL CITIES RUN on sex, on what is penetrable and what is not. KL is no different. At night the city breathes into a different kind of life, conflagrations of the possible and impossible, inhabited by beings of light and darkness, elegant and decaying, who scour the streets for temporary emancipation, whose needs are alleviated by wild fumblings, alcohol and opiates. Bukit Bintang, Star Hill, is at the heart of KL's vices and dens. This half-mile strip of shopping malls, hotels, brothels, restaurants and beggars where dreams are made and trampled upon.

Every day millions of ringgit exchange hands: from exhausted Bangladeshi construction workers who fuck thin Indonesian prostitutes, to millionaires who have cocaine-fuelled orgies with Russian and East European models, to drug pushers and transsexuals who loiter in dark alleys, to fat, rich housewives who buy endless handbags, clothes two sizes smaller and pearls with their platinum cards, to nubile teenagers who score everything from cocaine to E to marijuana, to bankers who sign blank cheques, to politicians who deposit those cheques. Everybody comes into some kind of slaughter, people leave bits of themselves on the streets, and try to pick up the pieces the next time they return.

But the city had not changed, the city had become bitter, bloated from greed, pestilence, rot. There was a poison, a vileness that had penetrated the skin of it. People no longer looked at each other on the streets, their eyes were sullen, jaded, there was unbridled anger, a hostility that was a contagion. There was cruelty, a disregard for manners, there was selfishness. People got into their cars and drove to work and back, single persons in luxury cars, clogging the roads. People honked to get past, flashed their lights to bully slower drivers, screamed and shouted at each other for parking spaces, dodged red lights, raced like madmen in the dead of night. Cut lines in queues, lied to their husbands and wives, all to get ahead, to feel happier, less lonely, less trapped, less afraid.

Money was the new god, friends who were already shallow became even more shallow, some became gods, some monsters, blinded by power, wealth, false security. Everything was black or white, there was no grey, there was an arrogance, and piteousness that assailed people.

"I don't owe you shit, man!" screamed a teenage boy on a motorbike when he accidentally rammed into Omar's car one night. "You're fucking rich, you can afford it! Fuck off!" He was high.

Perhaps it was better that Alba was gone. She could have turned out in terrible ways. She could have turned into a spoilt, rich brat, selfish and sullen, she could have become a burden to him and to Del. The city was already corrupt, and perhaps it was going to stay that way.

Marina looked up from her manager's table as her nine o'clock stumbled in through the heavy wooden doors. He was already drunk and was being held up by two giggling Chinese girls. Marina walked up to him, her long skirt swishing against her legs, "Good evening, Mr Chan, welcome back to Noble Inn. Always a pleasure to see you," she chimed.

"Gimme my regular room," he growled, "And my bottle."

"Of course, follow me, please," she replied. Marina led them through the long corridor to the private rooms. The two girls almost stumbled to the floor in their heels. The corridor was dark, lit only by low lamps on the walls, and all three almost tumbled to the floor until a pair of hands reached out to stop them, as if by magic.

Marina whispered softly, "Thank goodness you're here, Hassan. Mr Chan is drunker than usual tonight."

Hassan smiled back, "Yes, madam, all okay now," and strode off, Mr Chan in tow.

Hassan was a tall, strapping Bangladeshi, the club's resident bouncer who was more accustomed to hauling sacks of rice on his shoulders than slovenly, overweight men. But it was the eve of Chinese New Year, so he was more than prepared to have a sore back the following day. Tips were good this time of the year, so he was grateful. The two giggling girls tottered off into the dark corridor into the comfortable air-conditioned room where Mr Chan would snore to the singing of Cantonese pop songs. Hassan came out and straightened his black suit.

"All okay, madam, I give him water first, but you know he will drink again when he wakes up."

"Uh huh." Marina smiled, and checked her bookings for the night again. It was going to get packed later on, and she had to make sure that there were rooms for walk-ins. As if on cue, the phone rang.

"Hello, Noble Inn, Gong Xi Fa Cai! How can I help you?"

Hassan disappeared into the corridor, headed for the kitchen. He had to make sure that the chefs had enough food prepared for the buffet, that ice was aplenty, and that the rooms were ready.

"Yes, we are very full tonight, but we can accommodate five more people, no problem. What time can we expect you? In one hour? See you then, Mr. Ali."

She snapped her appointment book shut and decided to freshen up. She had been on her feet since seven o'clock and they were starting to hurt. There were three bookings at nine-thirty so she had enough time to have a cigarette, a lie down and a hot tea. She walked down the corridor, turned right, walked all the way down, past three rooms on the right and two on the left until she came to a small door. She unlocked it, walked in, peeled off her heels—a new pair of black leather Miu Mius—and heaved a swift sigh.

Marina took out a cigarette from a gold case that Mr Ferrari had given her for her birthday and lit it. Smoke curled around her face and she shook her hair out. She sat down at a small dressing table and smiled at the reflection. Her coloured hair was blown into soft waves and the bronze highlights glinted under the yellow light. Her eyebrows were teased and filled into perfect arches. Her light blue contact lenses made her look like a screen siren and her low-cut scarlet dress clearly accentuated her breasts. She looked and felt wonderful.

She was now the manager of the karaoke club, which also served as a high-class brothel. During the day, the club's office doubled as the headquarters of the Mak Nyah Association of Malaysia. She had five volunteers who staffed the office, processing cases of police abuse and harassment to high-powered human rights lawyers who did the work pro bono. She was becoming the voice of trans rights in Malaysia and she had a job she loved. Her sex change surgery had been a success and she was still getting used to the fact that she no longer had a penis. When she peed, she now sat on the toilet seat, and had already used more toilet paper than she ever imagined.

Her handphone beeped. It was him, right on time. The SMS read.

How are you, darling? See you soon, so we can yam seng later, okay?

Marina chuckled. Mr Ferrari would have to do the rounds later that night and she would have to accompany him, carrying a bottle of cognac while he drank to each and every one of his clients.

"Bottoms up! Yaaaaaaaaam seng! Yaaaaaaaaaam seng!"

It was 2004 and the Year of the Monkey, a time for beginnings and endings.

THE KLANG VALLEY is dotted by verdant areas where only the rich live. The first gentrified neighbourhood in KL was Kenny Hills, or now known as Bukit Tunku. This was where our first Prime Minister lived, in a beautiful colonial house with hardwood floors, high ceilings and majestic balustrades. Some of those houses still remain, but many had been torn down to make way for kitsch condominiums with million-dollar price tags. The ones that do remain are houses like the one Fairman's parents own, and a few more that are scattered all over the hill. At night, the entire area is transformed and the trees take on a life of its own. Snakes and wild boar creep out, along with prowling civet cats and monitor lizards. Monkeys whoop and whistle from treetops, frogs and cicadas provide a veritable orchestra. You can't take the rainforest out of the city—no matter how hard you try.

Mother had a friend who lived in a colonial bungalow on Jalan Syers. She was the wife of an ambassador from an undetermined European country. I was eight. Perhaps it was Belgium or Holland? Or was it Germany? Aunty Katherine, mother's schoolmate from Ipoh was a flamboyant character, who walked around the house as if she were a memsahib from the pages of Somerset Maugham. She wore loose-fitting flowery dresses, wide hats and talked with a poncy English accent, as she had been sent to boarding school when she was very young. Once we went there for tea and I was transported onto the set of an English summer, with tables on the lawn, white lace doilies, silverware, pink roses in vases, tea in delicate china cups with flowers, fresh scones made by the Indian housekeeper, clotted cream, homemade strawberry and rhubarb jam, and the thinnest cucumber sandwiches imaginable. Aunty Katherine never had any children but she owned at least twenty cats. *Keeps the snakes away!* she used to say.

Then, Mother and Aunty Katherine started drinking gin and tonics with slivers of lemon until it got late in the evening and when her husband, the Ambassador, came home after work, we all sat down and had dinner. He was a little bald man who spoke in a thick accent, he could have been German, but I wasn't sure. We ate from plates with gold trimmings and I drank orange juice from a crystal wine glass, while the adults drank white wine, then red, then cognac. Dinner was delicious—there was a meat pie with mashed potatoes, French beans with melted garlic butter and a trifle for dessert. It was the most sumptuous meal I had ever had in all my eight years, and as the conversation drifted later and later into the night, I was carried by the Ambassador to a couch in the study, where I was covered by a fluffy blanket and left to sleep.

Years later, I found out that Aunty Katherine had committed suicide in that house. She had apparently hanged herself from the rafters in the living room, and her ghost still roamed around the area. The house had since been abandoned and it lay in complete ruin. I remembered that afternoon and how happy Mother and Aunty Katherine had been. I never knew what happened to the Ambassador, but I often wondered what had driven Aunty Katherine to hang herself. Was it because he was having an affair? Or perhaps she was the one who had been unfaithful. I wondered what happened to all those beautiful things in the house. All the curtains, and plates and silverware, was it all left in the house? Or did the little bald man pack it all up and have it shipped to where he was going next?

One day I decided to go and look for that house, to see if it was still standing. I drove past the construction site on Jalan Bukit Tunku, found the street sign for Jalan Syers and drove along a gravel road until I came to the house. There were two other similar ones, all in a row. Then I saw a large, orange sign by the road.

Property of Keretapi Tanah Melayu (KTM). Scheduled for demolition. Property Developer –TMF Sdn Bhd.

My heart sank. Omar and Fairman's company was going to demolish those beautiful houses. The land was owned by the national railway company, so there was no way it could be bought. Or saved.

I parked my car and wandered up the road. The old angsana trees were still there. All three houses had long been abandoned. And I saw that scavengers had been around. Windows had been taken, old fixtures on the doors, hinges, old black bakelite switches missing. The Burmese teak floorboards had been ripped out. I walked into the hallway and heard a flutter of feathers. Pigeons had roosted in the roof. Light pierced from a gaping hole, shadows flitted in between the rafters and green mould charted out archipelagos on the walls. I walked in and felt a shiver.

I walked in and out of the dining room, into the vast kitchen which still had shelves intact, the old ceramic sink was still there, probably too heavy to cart off single-handedly. The servants quarters were more dilapidated, with wooden slats falling off, and holes in the concrete floors. That is where the Indian housekeeper used to live with her son. *What happened to them?*

As I walked along the side of the house, the creepers thick, the papaya trees overgrown with fruit, I saw a glint of something in the grass. It was a tiny silver spoon, like the one that I had used to stir sugar in my mother's teacup that day. Perhaps marauding robbers had dropped it in their haste? Perhaps one of the servants had taken the entire set deep in the night, and dropped one lone spoon? I picked it up, brushed it clean against my skirt, and as I walked away from the house, I heard a light hush and I forced myself to not look back.

I NEEDED TO do something. I had to look for Alba.

After a few more conversations with Inspector Awang, I somehow convinced myself that she was somewhere in KL, that she had perhaps been "adopted" by a wealthy couple. It was a thread of thought that was logical, that I kept to myself as there was nothing to prove any of my assumptions, and quietly went about my plan to map out certain areas in the Klang Valley where she was most likely to be. I also ascertained that she was probably in the most wealthy residential parts of KL, namely Bukit Tunku, Bangsar, Damansara Heights, Petaling Jaya—which was huge, so only the wealthier sections had to be considered—and Taman Tun Dr Ismail.

I got a map of the Klang Valley and pinned it on the wall of the dining room. Out came a stack of post-its, multi-coloured pins and marker pens. I traced the borders of those areas in black and then subdivided those in red. Each red section would translate to one day of searching.

My conclusions were this. Alba had probably been adopted by a family that was either half-expat and local, or all expat, or all local. The demographic of white-mixed couples in the Klang Valley had increased exponentially in the few years after the economic crisis, and especially since there was a renewed faith in the country. Expats loved living in Malaysia—the "expat package" was synonymous with top-notch housing, free international schooling for kids, a maid and or housekeeper, cars and a big, fat salary.

I stood back after marking out the map and I felt for the first time, a sense of purpose that I had not felt since I ran the streets of KL six years before. There was of course some measure of insanity and ludicrousness to this whole scheme, but I had to try, I had to try something. Not doing anything was more detrimental than anything else. No more drugs, no more alcohol. It was drastic but I had to get to a point where it all had to stop. I needed to have a clear head, I needed to be meticulous about it all. I knew in my heart that nothing would ever destroy my desire to find my daughter. It was the only thing I had left, the only thing that made sense, to keep living.

I don't know how parents with missing kids survived. In my hours perusing the Internet for statistics and research on missing children, I knew that the percentage of marriages that were destroyed after children died or had gone missing, was high. Few survived. It was the worst nightmare for any married couple, one that took the light out of days and made it an eternal night.

Then, one bright morning Marina called me.

You remember that woman I was telling you about... one of the girls said that she has been coming around again...

What? I choked on my coffee.

She wanted to know if anyone was pregnant or if anyone wanted to give up their babies.

Did she leave a number? I asked, my voice leaning into a panic.

No, but I can find out.

Oh my god, Marina, what if... What if... What if she knows about Alba, what if she was the one who kidnapped Alba? I lit a cigarette and inhaled deeply.

Del...relax. One step at a time...okay?

Can...you find out her name?

I have to be careful. The girls will get suspicious... You know they need the money.

Okay...okay. I said. *So she buys the babies?*

Marina went quiet. *Yes, she pays them cash.*

Oh my god, oh my god. I fell to the floor. *Please help me find her, please dear god help me, help me. Marina, I need you to find out her name, please. I need to know her name. Who is she? What kind of person does this...*

Marina whispered over the phone.

A monster. A devil. Syaitan.

If you're a well-to-do mother with a young child, chances are, you or your maid will push a pram around your affluent neighbourhood, to daycare or nursery, the playground, assuming that all of the above are within walking distance of your home. There are selected playgrounds in posh residential areas, so it's easy to stake them out. Most parents prefer to take their kids to indoor gyms where they can romp around in tunnelled mazes, enclosed pens with coloured plastic balls, and jump on mini trampolines, all under the supervision of vigilant care-givers who will only allow you to take your kids once you reveal a secret password. But still, the lowly playground is still an early morning and evening haunt for babies and their carers.

I took to jogging around Damansara Heights in the mornings. As early at 6.30am I would park my car opposite the secondary school and wait for the drivers, or mothers or fathers to drop their kids off. This was probably the top government school in KL and also the most difficult to get in. Sons and daughters of politicians were a priority, and I'd heard of parents who put their children's names down on a register the minute they were born. I looked like a parent in a running outfit and after the bell rang at 7.30 sharp and all the cars disappeared, I started jogging. I saw Filipino nannies with babies and toddlers in pushchairs, Indonesian twenty-somethings with babies in sarongs, wrapped tightly around their chests, walking up and down the leafy streets. These were bungalows, houses with multiple bedrooms and bathrooms, with pools, indoor gyms, European cars. I waved and said hi to them, cooed and chatted with the babies and toddlers.

I jogged up and down the Setiakasih streets, going up and down the numbers, looking into houses, cars, windows that were open. I was an eavesdropper, an intruder of sorts, entering the lives of these strangers, imagining their most intimate secrets, their deepest fears. I saw retired men in shorts and baseball caps walking their yappy dogs, I saw teenage girls with headphones stuck in their ears running in candy-coloured shoes, I saw executive types with portly stomachs and early jowls run up hilly slopes and walk with uneven breaths after. Mornings were cool until nine o'clock, when the sun came out in all its glory. Unless you wanted to sweat profusely and unnecessarily, it was time to get into air-conditioning or under a cold shower.

For one week I alternated between mornings and evenings. I saw a pattern that emerged with nannies, joggers and dog-walkers. I started recognising faces, and started saying hi to some. Then it was the Setiabudi streets,

Setiaraya—past even bigger houses, more opulent, more modern. I saw similarities in gate designs, plants and flower pots placed outside, water features and fake rocks—good for feng shui—older women in hats and gloves squatting over flower beds. It was mundane, normal, sedate. I saw lonely people wandering in and out of their cars. I saw mothers with shopping bags, babies, maids carrying all manner of things big and small. People going in and out of their houses. All this time I saw nothing suspicious, until one day I went into a cul-de-sac at the end of Setiakasih 7. I saw a neighbourhood guard post with two Nepali guards. One came up to me.

Morning, madam, where are you going?

I was breathless and said, *Oh, just going to jog up and down the road.*

Sorry, madam, I need to see your IC or drivers' licence.

I don't have it, sorry.

Then you cannot go in.

Oh, I see. Not even to jog?

Cannot, madam, last night got robbery here, so boss said cannot let anyone without IC first.

Okay, I understand, thank you.

As I turned to run in the opposite direction, he said, *Madam, where you staying? I walk with you, not safe here now.*

No, it's okay. I am not far.

I ran back to my car, and sat in silence as I drank an entire bottle of water in a slight panic. Then I hit my head on the steering wheel and screamed. I was not going to find anything there. It was stupid. A waste of time. How on earth was I going to find my child? By jogging the streets of the city? By staking out playgrounds? By peeking into stranger's houses? All I had seen were semblances of human lives, families, fragments of minutes spent on roads, insights into people's time. I felt like a criminal, stealing glances into babies faces, adoring their chubby hands and feet, their gurgles, the way the adult hands dug into young, soft flesh, the sweetness in the cheeks, necks, I just yearned for my baby, my darling baby girl. Where was she? I drove home, tears streaming down my face, I was screaming into the traffic, screaming for the loss of everything that I knew to be human.

The incident with the security guard at Damansara Heights had rattled me more than I imagined. I felt like an intruder, and the way I had skulked around nannies and their prams, peering into babies with dummies in their mouths was simply wrong. But I was a desperate mother, looking for desperate measures, what was I to do? After that day, I had a terrible sense of foreboding, which kept me anxious and awake at night. I had not had a drink and I was determined not to, but when I got home that evening, my hands were shaking.

I called Shah and asked if he wanted to hang out. In an hour I was at his apartment and bent over my second line of coke. He came up behind me and started caressing me, *I missed you. I really did.* After I did three lines, the panic had subsided but I still felt like there was a light bulb going off in my head, every ten minutes. I paced up and down his apartment and stared out the floor-to-ceiling glass panes.

The city spread out in front of me. I saw the gleaming Twin Towers to my immediate right, the KL Tower to my left yet, a chasm of humanity in between. What untold horrors lay beneath those buildings? What scale of human misery was there? Were there young girls who were being forced to have sex with twenty, thirty men in one night? Was Marina still spreading her legs for some filthy man with unwashed hands? How many beggars were being tortured for not bringing back enough money from the streets? How many Bangladeshi workers were lining up to fuck a Burmese woman at twenty ringgit a pop?

How many people were begging for their lives; for more leniency, more compassion, more mercy at the hands of gangsters, loan sharks, cruel traffickers, cops? The city stewed defiantly right back at me, right at the top of another building that was the folly of thousands of workers. Slave labour, that's what it was. We were a nation that was built on the sweat and tears of slaves. Just like so many developed countries, just like most of the bloody world.

You look tense, what's up? Why you keeping away from me? You know I like hanging out with you.

Sorry, been trying to stay clean…

Come here baby… just come here.

Shah was kind, he really was. He knew how to make me feel at ease, and it wasn't just when we were high, he just knew how to talk to me, that low-slung purring of his, so feline, so utterly sexy. *Come here, come here, my sweet, sweet Del.* Sometimes I just wanted him to talk to me, in that low sonorous timbre, it was so relaxing it could put me to sleep.

I walked towards him, and for a moment I wished that it was Omar I was walking to.

I pestered Marina for the name of the woman, but she kept telling me, *I will give it to you when I have it.*

Until the morning when Sumi called me and said: *Hey… the woman from the adoption agency is coming over today, do you still want to meet her?*

An hour before she was due to arrive, I was at Sumi's with a box of hot, flaky curry puffs, from the legendary stall in SS2. The Fairmans now lived in a guarded community in Mont Kiara and the pre-fabricated house was in a row along with other houses that all looked the same. Kids ran down the pebbled pathways on roller-blades and scooters, babies in push prams, some walking precariously hanging onto foreign hands. Trees were planted exactly ten feet away from each other. It was suburban heaven. Pre-fabricated homes. What KL's middle classes aspired to own. Sumi was at the gate in full make-up and an expensive silk shirt, looking as nervous as I was.

So, she's going to come over and brief us about the process, how long it takes, paperwork and so on and so forth.

I sucked on my cigarette, nodding. Then a quick, familiar hug. I was there to help Sumi, that was the plan, and that was what I was going to do. Appear non-fussed, helpful, supportive.

So the same one that Kim recommended?

Yeah, and apparently another friend just got a baby from her too.

I tried to keep my face unchanged, and managed a fixed smile.

Right, okay. Well let's wait and see.

I knew that Sumi was in a state as well; this was no Tupperware lady hedging in on us, this was a woman plying infants for sale, in the middle of Kuala Lumpur, in broad daylight, in one of the most exclusive neighbourhoods in town.

Thanks for being here, I hope you're okay with this.

Yes, of course. No worries. It's kinda exciting, no?

We sat around drinking cups of tea and eating curry puffs, trying to keep the conversation easy. I had two curry puffs in one go and suddenly felt the bits of spiced chicken, potato and fried flour churning in my stomach. My appetite wavered from day to day. Some days all I could eat was fruit and salad and other days vegetables and tofu. Meat turned my stomach.

Suddenly, the buzzer went. We both jumped and Sumi ran to the wall consul.

Hello, hello. Mrs Fairman? The voice crackled through.

A woman stood outside, in a dark blue skirt, carrying a large handbag. Her hair looked slightly disheveled from the breeze that was picking up, and in her arms was a bundle. In a rehearsed sing-song voice, she said.

Hello, Mrs Fairman, here's your baby!

A baby? You brought me a baby? I don't want a baby right now… I just wanted to talk to you first.

We were stunned. This woman, this complete and utter stranger had brought a baby to us. Standing at Sumi's front door, baby in hand, just like that.

Well, Mrs Fairman, sometimes you get a gift, and this baby girl… is a gift. I just picked her up from her mother, who wanted her to find the best home as soon as possible… so I said why not? And I came straight here. She smiled and beamed widely with the whitest set of teeth I had ever seen.

Sumi had turned pale underneath her make-up and gestured for her to come in. The baby was asleep, she made no sound and when I asked to carry her, I could see immediately that she was of mixed heritage. Approximately a month old, healthy, with pink rosebud lips. A full head of black hair.

So, who is this baby? Where is she from? How did this happen? Sumi asked, trying to be nonchalant.

Ah, Mrs Fairman, like I said, this baby was with her mother for a month and then… she called me today to say that she could no longer take care of her… her milk was running out, she said that she wanted the baby to go to a nice home, so… I brought her here.

The woman spoke in low tones, in her sing-song manner and waved her arms effectively, like a seasoned saleswoman.

So, you mean I can take this baby? If I want her? Sumi delivered a shrill retort.

Yes, why not? I can leave her here for one night, see how you feel…?

The woman was clearly insistent. Sumi protested. *One night? What? But…I have nothing here, no cot, no diapers… nothing, and my husband isn't even around!*

The baby started to cry and I could see that she had perfect fingers. She was warm in my hands. She felt lovely. A baby in my arms. My body softened. I wanted to melt into a sleep. My body swayed automatically, the way mothers do when they want to soothe their babies. I answered softly, not wanting to alarm the baby.

Sumi, I can get a few things from the supermarket, it's not a problem.

But...

Here, come, come... take the baby. I walked towards Sumi, trying to reassure her.

The woman said: *Mrs Fairman, by the way... the baby's name is Samiya... starts with an S, just like yours. What a coincidence.* Then, she chuckled.

Sumi, startled, turned to me, then back to the woman and asked: *Oh, how do you spell that?*

I interrupted. *Sorry, what's your name?* I asked the woman with the white teeth.

Madam, my name is Mary. People call me Mother Mary... So nice to meet you. She held her hand out. I shook it and felt that it was sticky, like slime. She realised it when I wiped my hand on my pants.

Sorry, madam, very hot day today.

Sumi looked up at me and grinned. *Oh my god, she's so cute!*

I could see that the baby had opened her eyes, they were wide and brown and clear. Mother Mary sat down on the couch and looked around, her toes digging into the fluffy carpet.

Wow, nice place here, Mrs Fairman... So perfect to raise a family...

I had no doubts that this woman knew exactly what to say. There were a slew of questions I wanted—needed—to ask, but I did not want to seem too obvious in my suspicions. So I began indiscreetly.

So, what is the baby's... heritage?

She took a big breath, let out a smile and spoke with a large measure of confidence.

This one is very interesting. Her mother is half Thai, half Malay, father is Nepali. That's why she is so pretty lah...Father is a security guard, mother works in a factory. Cannot afford to raise a child, plus the father already has a wife back home, so he won't pay. The poor girl has no choice...

Sumi was half listening as the baby had started to gurgle and smile, and immediately started cooing. *Del, look at her fingers, she's so lovely, look...ooh, ooh you're gorgeous, yes you are...So, how do we do this, Mary?* She looked up, questioning.

By this time Mother Mary had helped herself to a cup of tea with milk and sugar, and was munching loudly on a curry puff. She finished the last bits of it, swallowed a big sip of tea quickly then cleared her throat.

We will do all the paperwork, registration, everything. She coughed slightly. *Sorry, the curry puff is stuck in my throat...* She drank another large sip of tea.

I asked brusquely. *Wait, does she have a birth certificate?*

No madam, her parents cannot register her, they are not married and the mother is Muslim... so very difficult, as you know. But we can do everything... this is what my company does, don't worry we will take care of it.

Sumi interjected, saying. *We have to pay you, obviously...?*

Mother Mary smiled widely. *Yes, Mrs Fairman, you see the parents have to be compensated a little bit, and then of course the paperwork, you know...how it works here...*

Her teeth were so white they were almost blue, startling against her dark complexion and high cheekbones. She looked like she could have been a beauty queen twenty years ago. I wondered how much those veneers cost.

So, how much for everything?

Mother Mary was quick and to the point. *Only twenty thousand, Mrs Fairman, her skin is very fair, so you know lah,*

Malaysians, we still like to be fair, even though I am not, she tittered. *So she will be very pretty when she grows up...*

I wanted to gag, I wanted to shout and scream and say to Sumi, don't do this, don't do this, you're buying a fucking baby, Sumi, what are you thinking? Sumi looked at me and she saw my panic, then she looked down at the baby and asked:

Is this legal? What you're doing... is it... legal?

Mary looked at her, put a rehearsed hand to her mouth, cleared her throat again and spoke clearly, with resolution.

Mrs Fairman, I run a serious business here, I have helped many couples find babies, I help people... so of course it's legal. In Malaysia we can do anything here, as long as we can find a way. You know what I mean... Don't worry, she reassured. *We do this all the time...* She trailed off.

Sumi paced up and down, looking perplexed, the baby content in her arms. *But my husband, he's not here. What do I do?*

Well, Mrs Fairman, if you are not sure... no problem. If you don't want her, someone else will take her... No problem. She shook her head and smiled widely.

Something seized me, like an invisible hand, cold, tenacious. It rose from the soles of my feet and into my stomach, where it tightened and turned into a cold insidious knot. My teeth started to chatter. Goosebumps appeared on my hands, my neck prickly with sudden sweat. Had I found her? Was this the woman who had taken my daughter? I wanted to accuse her, I wanted to scream, *Did you take my baby? What did you do to her?*

But I didn't. Sumi wanted this baby, it was obvious, and I didn't want to ruin it. I was assuming a great deal, and that was dangerous. Who was this woman? What kind of woman did this? To sell babies? Where did they come from?

Sumi disappeared into the kitchen to call Fairman, while I walked around cradling the baby who was now fully awake and restless. She was hungry. I asked Mother Mary, *Do you have a bottle? Anything at all for the baby?*

Mother Mary stood up and grabbed her large handbag, which was stretched to the seams. I imagined large wads of cash inside, or diapers perhaps? *Yes, yes, of course. Sorry, sorry, baby is hungry yes. There is something in my car, let me get it.*

Mary rushed out the door, her skirt bunched up under her ample derriere. Her car was a brand new blue Perodua. License plate WHJ 8965. I repeated it until it was in my head. The situation was simply surreal. A baby. A woman with a baby. To leave overnight. Twenty thousand ringgit. What fuckery was this?

Sumi was talking to Fairman on the phone. *A baby, yes darling, a real one…she's a girl… just gorgeous… So what do we do? I don't know, that's why I'm calling you…her parents… yes, registration and all…I guess so…uh huh…so?*

The baby looked healthy enough, I didn't see vaccination scars so that was going to need paramount attention. I lifted her faded flowery cotton top and saw that she had good colour. Her tummy did not look bloated but she would also need a full check-up. And a blood test. Mother Mary came in the door flushed, fanning herself.

Aiyoh! So hot outside!

She handed me a plastic bag, which had some diapers, a Nuk milk bottle and several sachets of milk powder.

The kind that was given away for free at supermarkets and hospitals. There were also a couple of rompers, one blue, one pink.

I asked. *You say she's been on the breast? So you're not sure if she will take the bottle?*

Yes madam, we will have to try and see.

Right, well. Let's try and see...

Mother Mary followed me into the kitchen where Sumi had just hung up. She cleared her throat and said, *I need to wait till my husband gets back, which is in two days, can you wait?*

Mary nodded furiously. *Of course, of course, this is a husband and wife decision, I understand. Serious decision.* She looked at the baby and clucked softly.

After filling the bottle with a mixture of milk powder, hot and lukewarm water, I shook the bottle and tested the hole in the teat—it was very small—so I widened it with a knife. Sumi was observing me closely. I put the bottle to the baby's mouth and thrust it in gently. She wouldn't take it and she started crying. Ah, a baby's cry. It had been so long.

Sumi... here. You take the baby, and give her the bottle.

As if by instinct, Sumi embraced the baby the only way a mother knew how, pressed the baby's cheek into her own, whispered something into her ear, kissed her neck gently and then finally, eased the teat into the baby's mouth. She started sucking loudly.

Sumi looked up and smiled. *Look, she's drinking, she's drinking!*

Mother Mary beamed and clapped her hands. *Mrs Fairman...such a natural. Wonderful!*

Sumi looked at us, a warm glow suffused her face.

A wave of confusion came over me, a perplexing suffusion of anger and remorse.

I blurted out. *So you have other babies too? Big ones? Small ones?*

Mother Mary chuckled and replied, *Please lah, madam, this is not a baby factory, it takes time you know. Sometimes I don't have a baby for months, sometimes a few in one week. Depends.*

Depends, on what? What if I wanted a baby of a certain age, race… a certain look? Could you find me one?

Not so easy, madam. Not so easy. But I can ask around…if you like, might take some time.

Sumi looked startled and glared at me as if to say *not now Del, not now.*

No, it's fine. But, if I change my mind, could I give you a call? Sure!

With a big smile she rummaged in her big bag, fished out a name card and shoved it into my hand. It had an image of a stork carrying a baby in a bundle. "Bundles of Joy. Child Adoption Agency. Mary Margaret. 016 3339900." I shoved the card in my pants pocket.

Okay, ladies, I have to go. Mrs Fairman, good luck with the baby, I will call you in two days, okay? Look forward to hearing from you. I have another appointment now. She tucked her handbag tightly into her armpit, jiggled her car keys, took one final look at the baby sucking at the bottle.

So sweet, look she is happy! Okay then. Byeee…

And with that she flashed her white, white smile and swooshed out the living room and out the door. Sumi looked at me. The baby had finished the entire bottle of milk and was gurgling happily. Sumi looked completely startled.

Del, now what do I do?

THE HUMAN MIND is feeble, it can only take so much anguish. When I lost my mother, my father lost his mind. There is no slow deterioration of grey matter, it is a swift, brutish act. To lose possession of one's faculties is denigrating, almost shameful, it implies that you are not strong enough, it shows weakness of character, of self, that you are not close enough to your ancestors, that you are unable to reach back and claim the strength of memory, of collective suffering, of hope, that you don't know who you are. And how was I to? When my father was already lost in the shadows, it was only inevitable that I suffer the same fate. My mother met her maker whilst being compacted into a lamp pole and car parts. She had no time to consider anything, her soul struck by an insolent fate on a highway. And this is the realisation I had when I woke up in the psychiatric ward at University Hospital.

I tried to sit up in bed but I could not, my arms and legs were fastened and I could not move. Straps, with buckles, yes I had seen them somewhere before. Probably a TV drama series about doctors and nurses falling in and out of love with each other. I tried to open my mouth but the sound that came out of me was hoarse, a whimper. The screaming went on within my oesophagus, the force whirling itself deeper and deeper into an emotional hurricane, all the while not being able to move. There was a box on my chest, of human hearts, sliced and torn open from grief, sadness. Perpetual loneliness, condemned to a tiresome pit of vipers. My eyes darted left to right, then up and down, it was all white. I looked down and saw the shape of my feet. Socks, I don't remember wearing socks. They were thick and grey. I tried to wriggle my toes and within seconds I was exhausted.

What manner of drugs had they given me? Why wasn't I high in a land above the clouds, feeling euphoric, with hands and lips caressing me? Was there a worm slowly moving inside me? Why did I feel like I had been encased in concrete from my neck down? What did I do to get here?

A nurse came in, mask covering her nose and mouth. Her eyes looked stern.

Miss, you need to take your medicine.

I looked at her, certain that my eyes were glazed, dead like an upside down goldfish. She took my right arm and pressed in a syringe. I winced. The ceiling started contorting into a fevered swirl, I felt the bed move upwards, like I was being lifted, *but wait, the ceiling is above it, wait, I am going to smash into concrete,* but then there was light, a soft breeze, keen laughter, something jabbing into my thighs, teeth? Fangs? A scratching from inside my loins, under my skin. *What is that thing?* The bed swooping down back into the room, *swish swish swish,* then carousel music, a clown's red nose jabbed itself into my cheek, then the scene from *One Flew Over the Cuckoo's Nest,* where Jack Nicholson and the nurses are screaming, they are all screaming, then there's blood on the walls and on the floor. A cobra, one, two then there are three, they are bowing down in front of me, their hooded heads bowed to the ground, then they slither away in fright, *animals, you should be with the animals, not humans, you are like a bird, a black bird with bright red feathers with flecks of green, you don't belong with us, you don't belong to us, you are not one of us. I am on top of a mountain, then God cast me down below. Who said that? Do you know who said that? Why can't I remember? Where is she? Do you know where she* is?

My little girl is lost, I have to find her, can you help me?

Then I am falling, falling, falling, *it is so dark, the walls are moving in, the walls are moving in*, I have to find a way out of this chasm, it is wet and the water is coming up, I need to swim, but I can't. The ceiling is above me, I can barely move, I can see light, but it is so far away, *I cannot move, I am scared, please get me out of here, please please please. Alba, where are you? Alba! Alba! Alba! Where is my little girl? Please god, help me find her, I need to find her.*

Alba!

Alba!

Alba!

Apparently, I was found in a mall in Petaling Jaya wandering around with a headless doll in my hand. I had first gone to the basement where the weekend flea market was. In a pile of junk along with toys I recognised from my childhood, I found a rubber doll with pale blue eyes, long flappy lashes and cornflower hair. Just like the one I got for Christmas one year. The head was falling off, the old rivet was showing wear and tear and the vendor said that I could have it for *only five ringgit, miss.* I remember handing him a ten dollar note and then I started walking to other vendors, looking for a head or another doll—whichever I could find first. I went to the vendor who sold books and old lamps and I tried to fit a book onto the head of the doll. Then I went to a vendor who sold ceramics—Made in England plates, cups, soup tureens—and I tried to fit a cup onto the head. Then I saw the old lady who sold antique blue bowls and when I tried to fit a small bowl with flowers on the doll's head, she started shouting. *Oi, crazy woman lah, this one, orang gila!* By now, there was a commotion and an older gentleman who had followed me with interest was now quite concerned.

I had started talking to myself in a sing-song voice, talking gibberish—I had no recollection of this—and I apparently went to almost every vendor at the flea market—including the ones who sold vinyl and large antique furniture—and I was trying to fit things onto the doll's head.

I then went up the escalator, and into the shop that sold toys like the latest Lego sets, light-sabres, more dolls, costumes. I had brought Alba there once to get a fairy costume. It was here that the owner threatened to call security, as I was taking down boxes, trying to open them and then overturning bowls of miniature cars and plastic dolls. When security did come, I was in the middle of the shop, on the floor surrounded by half-opened boxes and toys. It was then that I started screaming. It was a knot that began in the pit of my stomach, it started as a whimper, and then my entire body resonated with this primal scream that emanated with brute strength from every fibre of my being.

Alba.

Alba.

Alba.

I fought and struggled with the security guards until the older gentleman said *be gentle*, that I was suffering from some kind of psychotic episode. He called an ambulance and within an hour I was strapped, sedated and on my way to the psych ward. I remember going down the escalator, all those faces staring at me, like I was a freak. I held on to that doll for dear life, thinking I *am not going crazy, I am not going crazy, I am not crazy.*

This is what the nurses told me, in between more medication, sips of water, Milo and sleep. I had screamed like I *was possessed, like the devil was in me.* The old man who had followed me had come to see me twice at the hospital, he was concerned, and when he was told about the truth of the matter, he wondered why I had no friends or family present. My father had come once, Sumi was busy with the baby and Marina was nowhere to be found.

That old man, the only one who seemed to care, was then struck down by a hit-and-run motorist one day outside the hospital, presumably on his way to see me. I never even knew his name, only the fact that he too seemed alone in the world, and when the nurses said that he had been killed instantly, I knew that he was no longer in any pain, and that death should have come earlier, but it did come when it did.

That night, in the delirium of a drug-addled sleep, I felt a soft hand on my chest and when I opened my eyes, I saw him, the one who had saved me. He smiled and before he vanished, I felt strangely complete.

AFTER A WEEK, I was discharged. Marina had finally resurfaced.

Sorry darls, I was in Hong Kong and someone stole my phone. Oh my god, what happened to you?

The psychological evaluation stated that I was suffering from "extreme stress, grief-related trauma, exhaustion, suicidal tendencies and severe depression." The doctor had wanted to put me on anti-depressants but I had refused. Pills were not going to help me, not the kind that numbed me, that would render me into a submission I did not want to be in.

I needed to see Sumi, I needed to find that woman who had the babies. I needed to find out if she had others, if she was part of a ring of baby traffickers. I needed to pull myself together, to figure it all out, to make sense of everything that I knew. Marina was the only person I could trust. That, by far, was the only certainty in my life. My world was becoming smaller and smaller. In contrast, my daughter was out in a world that had become more and more hostile. I was a fool to believe it, but in my mind I believed that I could find Alba.

Sumi and Fairman had become instant parents. Samiya stayed as Samiya. It just seemed fitting that the first two syllables of her name were so similar to Sumi's. It was meant to be. It made sense. The baby made sense. It all did.

That Sunday afternoon they celebrated her christening of sorts with a party. I avoided the prayers earlier as I knew Omar would be there. When I walked into the Fairman residence that sweaty, sticky afternoon, I knew that I would come face to face with people who would question me, look at me with pity combined with some form of trepidation.

I parked my car along the side of the road, which was already lined with BMWs, the latest Mercedes models, sleek black Range Rovers, brand-new European four-wheel drives, all of which indicated that babies were on board. I wore a simple white top with black pants, easy brown leather pumps and a smile. I walked into chatter, cries and salutations, and when I entered, everything stopped. All eyes were on me. At least ten couples, with multiple babies and toddlers in between them, Indonesian and Filipino maids—all in blue and white uniforms—all stopped and stood and stared at me.

And there I was. The most pitied woman in KL. The one who was unfortunate enough to lose her child in KL's most exclusive supermarket. The one who had to be checked into a psych ward. The one who was found screaming and delusional in a flea market. The one whose husband left her. The one who went crazy from grief. The one every woman in that room felt sorry for.

Sumi broke the deafening silence. *Darling, you made it. So happy you're here!*

She walked towards me, dressed elegantly in slacks and a flowery blouse. Fairman followed in a crisp white shirt and tailored slacks. They were the perfect couple. They took turns to hug and kiss me. She smelled of vanilla; he, of bergamot and sandalwood. And then as if by some unspoken admission, the chatter started, babies started wailing and the nannies rose in unison to cater to the slew of distressed cries.

You did something to your hair, it's gorgeous! Sumi said.

Yeah, I said. *Cut it myself!*

Well, it really suits you, Fairman said, beaming with sincerity.

I need a drink. I brushed past his shoulder and walked towards a waitress who was carrying a tray of champagne. I gulped it down, then took another and another. People incapable of guilt have a good time.

Del, look at her, hasn't she grown! Sumi was immediately at my side showing off the baby.

She had. Samiya's eyes glowed with the joys of wealth and privilege. Her white dress was frilled and cuffed, a hairband glistening with crystals around her small temple, shoes a soft white leather. She looked fat, contented. So did all the other babies in the room, most of whom resembled their parents. Some didn't. I was certain that all these babies came from Mother Mary the baby-dealer, the one who made sure that all these childless couples were endowed with babies. Babies who came from where? Was Alba in a room like this too? In a house like this, somewhere in KL?

I kissed Samiya. She smelled of possibility, of hope, of goodness. Yet another baby who went from rags to riches, whose mothers all looked the same. Pinched blood-shot eyes, thin arched brows, hair that fell in soft shoulder waves, nude expensive make-up, diamond encrusted fingers, jewelled watches, designer shoes, bags, clothes. Cookie-cutter women, high-class bitches married to husbands who had wallets so fat, they had no choice but to be slaves for life. Perhaps I was like that once, perhaps I was.

I kissed Sumi and Fairman and said, *I wish you all the happiness in the world,* kissed Samiya as I inhaled her scent one last time, drank another tube of champagne and walked out the door.

* * *

I called Omar and said that I wanted to speak in person.
I wasn't sure if he would agree to meet, but he did. I wanted
to tell him about Mother Mary and that Fairman and Sumi's
baby had been bought from her. We met in the café that we
used to go to on weekends, where we would have a typical
English breakfast with sausages, eggs sunny side up, hash
browns, tomatoes, mushrooms and toast, where Alba would
sit on her high-chair and have her own little plate of bits from
ours, where she would pick with her hands, put a sliver of
food in her mouth, grin and show her teeth and put more
food in her mouth until it was all gone. Sunday had been our
favourite day of the week, it was when Omar was most relaxed
and able to take Alba off me for hours at a time. They would
play with her wooden blocks, paint, mould play dough, watch
cartoons and swim. Sundays were easy on me, as it was all
father-daughter bonding time, and she would go to bed easily,
completely exhausted from the day with her father.

I was nervous about meeting him. I still felt fractured and
emotionally unhinged from the incident at the flea market.
But I also needed to tell him of what I knew. When I walked
in, he was already sitting there with a glass of wine. He stood
up when I was by the table and then sat down. Still the perfect
gentleman, I thought.

Hi, thanks for meeting me. I said.

He gestured to the waiter. It was a new guy, someone
neither of us knew. *Red or white?*

Whatever you're having is fine. I replied.

I looked at his face closely. His eyes were tight, his face had thinned out, there was stubble that was probably a few days old. There were more lines around his eyes and mouth, his hairline higher than I remembered it to be. His eyes caught mine and I looked away. The wine arrived and I took a big sip.

I just want to get straight to the point, I said quickly.

His eyebrows arched. *Sure. What is it?*

I took a deep breath and started.

You know Fairman and Sumi's baby? Well I think she was trafficked, you know, sold. This woman who apparently runs an adoption agency—I placed the card in front of him—*sold the baby to them for twenty thousand ringgit.*

Omar's face was unchanged, but a muscle twitched in his cheek.

I asked her if she had other babies, and she said that she could get more, but it would take time, so… what if, what if…Alba was taken, trafficked by the same woman? Sold? To someone in KL?

My voice had risen and the couple behind us turned to look. The woman looked horrified, probably reacting to the word "trafficked".

Omar leaned over, and said very quietly.

Del, firstly, babies are different. Alba was two. There is a difference.

I stammered. *What…what… do you mean?*

Omar continued.

My investigator has told me this too. Yes, there are traffickers operating in town, but there is a marked difference between babies and toddlers. Babies can be bought, but toddlers…they are for a whole different reason.

I knew what he was going to say and swallowed all my wine in a big gulp.

It's for sex isn't it? Or kiddy porn?

Omar leaned even closer, and I could see the flecks in his eyes, they were dark now and dangerous. *Yes and no. Girls can be used for all kinds of things. Organs, begging, child rearing, sex… and so on and so forth. It's endless.*

I gritted my teeth and tried to push away the images that were conjured in my head. My baby, my baby. It was grotesque.

And what about this woman then? Can she get away with this?

Omar gestured to the waiter and twirled his finger, which indicated one more round.

Apparently. According to the Malaysian Penal Code, which I have been reading, it's not illegal for parents to sell their children. It was customary in Asian families, as you know, to give away a child if you couldn't afford to raise it. I know that one of my cousins was actually my aunt. So the Penal Code protects that. I suppose if you were poor and were on your eighth child, you could very well give it up, no? And expect a little compensation…

Two more glasses of red wine appeared. This was a lot of information to process and I was beginning to feel a little lightheaded.

So, you're condoning what Fairman and Sumi did?

He sighed and said. *No, of course not. But we would have done the same. Give a poor child a better life? Sure. We would have done exactly the same thing.* He took a sip and tapped his fingers impatiently on the table.

I took a sip and kept quiet, contemplating all that had been said. He then raked his hand through his hair and spoke again. *So… basically. No. You can't arrest someone for selling their baby if they're poor. And this woman, she's basically facilitating the exchange.*

I shook my head. *This is insane, absolutely insane.*

Omar agreed. *Well, that's the law for you.*

I asked. *What else has the detective told you?*

These trafficking rings, drugs, prostitution, they're run by gangsters, who are basically protected by the police, because everyone is on the take. They're all complicit. So, unless you know someone personally, it's like finding a needle in a fucking haystack.

I suddenly remembered the man I'd met in the club a while ago and said: *I met this guy in a club, he knew who I was, and he said... "Your husband is a bad businessman," or something like that... do you know who he is?*

One eyebrow raised, he looked at me, almost with disdain. *Some company you keep, Del.* He smirked.

He knew Karin! I retorted. *So? Who is he? He looked really dubious. I should be asking you who you keep company with!* I responded angrily.

Big guy? Large head?

I nodded.

Right... Omar leaned in. *He runs the biggest brothel in town. Russians, Mongolians, Ukrainians, Albanians, you name it. High-class girls. Minimum three thousand an hour. He wants protection money but we're not going to give it to him.*

What for?

We're building a new road that's going to cut through KL. This guy is not happy about it, he'll lose clients. The brothels will have to go.

A chill ran down my back when I remembered what he had said.

He also said, that there would be more trouble…what did that mean?

Omar picked up his glass and drained it. *Fuck knows.*

I hesitated before I asked the next question. *Do you think he took Alba?*

Omar looked at me right in the eye. *No. Because there would have been a ransom, the whole thing would have been a message for me, for us, the company…they want to teach you a lesson, show you who's the boss…*

How can you be so sure? Omar? What if…?

My hand started shaking, I picked up my glass and took a large sip of wine.

There are no what-if's, Del. He is a glorified pimp, he just wants money.

Omar sat back in his chair. I stood up, then sat down again. I wanted to run out of the café. I was furious.

But how do you know? I hissed. *What if they took her?*

Omar stared at me and said. *If they did, they would have made it very clear. To me. Besides, the police and the investigator would have found out. There would have been a connection…of some kind. But there's nothing. Okay…there's nothing.* He leaned back and sighed.

I drank the last of the wine, wiped my mouth with my hand and stared at Omar in silence.

Del, I have looked at all possibilities, don't you think—

Okay! I interrupted him. *Okay.*

We sat in silence, my head was reeling and Omar looked away, his eyes pained.

Finally I said, *I don't know what to feel anymore… I don't know what to do.*

He replied softly, *We can't give up, yet. I won't give up.*

Him, sitting there reassured me in a way I had not felt in a long time. It was perhaps our first real conversation after Alba was taken. All those months of anguish had exhausted us, and there we were, bereft of anger, completely vulnerable, open. There was nothing left to do except listen to each other.

We sat and ordered another glass of wine each, we nibbled on olives and he asked how I was. He said he had come to the hospital but I was asleep, he needed to see that I was okay. *They only let me in when I said I was your husband, and then I saw that they had tied you to the bed. I couldn't take it. I left after three seconds. I felt so—bad. But I knew that you would be all right.*

I kept quiet. He continued.

All these months, all I could think of… was the fact that it could have happened to me too. I could have turned my back and she could have been taken. It's not your fault, Del, I have never blamed you. I blame these monsters. People who take other people's children to sell them… to do terrible, unspeakable things to them. For profit. Del… and it happens all the time. All the bloody time.

His head was in his hands. He looked up at me, and I saw dark pools of anguish penetrating through his eyes. *It has to be stopped. I need to stop it. I need to do something, Del. I need to.*

What are you going to do?

And he said. *There is only one solution for this. There is only one way to stop this… I have to go into politics.*

* * *

Omar and I got back together. It just made sense. I cleaned up, stopped drinking, stopped the drugs, stopped seeing Shah, started doing yoga, started to heal. I went into therapy. I saw a shrink twice a week, sat on the proverbial couch, smoked cigarettes, wept, I felt better. I started talking about my dead mother, my silent father, my missing child. And of the man who was still there. Of Omar. Omar who was there in the beginning and there in the end.

The elections in March came and went. The Barisan National under Pak Lah's leadership won 199 out of 219 seats. They still had the majority, Anwar was still in prison but there was an air of change in the country. There was hope, there was renewed confidence. People smiled more at each other, there was a lightness in the air. The city could breathe again.

Omar and I sat in front of the TV, toasting to the results. Pak Lah's speech was buoyant, he had claimed victory, but there was no gloating, no arrogance, no malice, no avarice, there was only humility. He pledged to do his best and to serve the people and the country. Malaysians all over the world celebrated. The era of Mahathir was well and truly over.

Marina had become a success. She ran the club and yes, she was good at it. I was happy for her. She had a man who loved her and whom she loved back. Sumi and Fairman were parents. Samiya thrived, they were happy. They were all happy, my friends were happy.

I was glad. But in truth, I was still hollowed out, grieving, there was no word about Alba. I struggled to live, one day at the time.

Omar said he was going into politics. He believed in the will of the new Prime Minister. He felt that he could help clean up the city, weed out the criminals, the triad bosses, the pimps, the drug dealers, the traffickers. I thought he was a fool, but I couldn't say no, this is foolhardy, no. I never told him that. I tried to live again, I tried to believe again, I tried to be happy. I tried to work on my marriage, I tried to love my husband again and I tried to love myself.

I knew I had to atone for saying all those terrible things when Alba was ill. Yes, I did say them when I was on the verge of complete and utter exhaustion, but I should have had the judgement to not say them, those words that could render any mother complicit in the disappearance of her child. Did I wish for it to happen? Did I will it to happen? Was it my fault that Alba was taken? Was it?

Of course I blamed myself, how could I not? I loved my child, but my inability to look after her, at times, meant that I was just human, or did it not mean that? Should I have employed an army of minders to look after her? To help stave all manner and possibility of casualty? Was having a maid some form of insurance? Was I a bad mother? Was it my fault? I could barely remember the litany of curses I cast that day. I was not myself, I was a mother exhausted beyond comprehension, I was just simply, tired. I did not mean what I said, but perhaps what I said had been heard by the dark gods, that they had set their evil plans into motion, that I was undeserving of my child, that I was at fault. That I was a terrible person, for willing my child to not have been born. There it was, I said it.

And with Omar, he had forgiven me again and all was good until we got that call, that call that would change everything.

I had just finished yoga and I was walking to my car when my handphone started flashing. It was Omar.

They've found something. We need to go to Bukit Aman, right now.

My hands started shaking on the steering wheel, the sweat that had dried on my forehead broke out again. Traffic was starting to swell. I drove as steadily as I could, past the slope on the Bangsar hill, past the traffic lights on Jalan Maarof onto Jalan Bangsar, past the National Museum and onto the roundabout, past the National Mosque, up the slope, past the Islamic Museum, the Butterfly Farm, the Bird Park and onto the slip road that led to the Police Headquarters at Bukit Aman. Bukit—Hill. Aman—Peace. Hill of Peace, ironic indeed.

Omar was already there. He walked quickly towards me as I got out of my car.

What's going on? What have they found? My teeth were already chattering from fear.

He shook his head. Then his phone rang. *Yes, yes, we're outside. We're walking in now.*

At the security, we gave them our ICs and they waved us through the side gate, curious eyes looking at me in my yoga pants, Omar in his blue suit. PT Raja stood outside the glass doors, looking grim. He nodded and led us inside, the cold air blasted my face. Omar was holding onto me, tight, his fingers later leaving a mark on my arm. I looked at him, his mouth was set in a grim line.

The conference room was full of police officers, standing on one side of the wall. I smiled weakly at Inspector Awang. How I used to harass him. How I used to pummel him with questions. We were asked to sit across three officers. A tall turbaned Sikh police officer stood up, held up some notes in his hand and started speaking.

Encik Malik and Puan Delonix, thank you for coming in on such short notice. I am OCPD Baljit Singh and I have been briefed about your case from Inspector Awang. Last night, or rather, this morning, we found something that may or may not be connected to your missing daughter.

He paused slightly.

There was a body of a child that was found in a suitcase by the side of the road in Jalan Ulu Kelang and we believe that there is reason that this could be the body of your child, Alba. The body is in very bad condition and we will need to run DNA tests, as it is highly decomposed and beyond recognition. As your child went missing more than six months ago, we know that it will be difficult to identify her, so we will need samples of your DNA.

He stopped suddenly, then continued. *I am very, very sorry but we had to contact you and tell you this. I am...*

I stood up, pulled away from Omar's firm grip, and ran. I pulled the heavy glass doors open, I ran past the blue-clad officers who stood stoically and silently, I ran down the stairs, I ran past the lady with the white tudung at the entrance who stood up saying something inaudible to me, I ran past the security guards who tried to stop me, I ran and ran and ran until I could run no more, and there on that road, by the side of tall trees and the sound of birds, I tried to scream, but nothing came out.

Omar found me sitting on a concrete slab by the side of the road, smoking a cigarette that one of the cops had given me. They pitied me, I could see it on their faces and they let me sit there, until they let Omar through the gates.

I looked up, and saw that his eyes looked haunted.

It's not over yet, Del. They have something to show us. Come on.

I finished the rest of the cigarette, stubbed it out with my right sandal and found Omar's hand. We walked slowly into the compound of the police headquarters. How strange that we were there being assisted by the cops, so hated by us once upon a time. How the tables had turned. We entered the room for the second time and sat down.

Please continue, sorry about that just now. Omar spoke with an air of resignation in his voice. I gripped his hand tightly, my breath short.

We know this is going to be difficult, but we have something we need to show you. Inspector Awang spoke, his voice echoing across the room. He continued.

In cases like this, where the body has deteriorated so badly, we will instead show photos taken by our forensics team. We will show you only one image, and if you recognise anything at all in this picture, please identify it and let us know.

I looked at Omar in a panic, our eyes locked for a second. He gripped my hand tightly. I turned and saw OCPD Baljit walk towards us holding a paper file. He stood next to me and I shut my eyes so tight, I wished for momentary blindness to prevent me from seeing the image that he had put on the

table. I heard Omar gasp as he wrenched his hand from mine.
I opened my eyes.

I saw a large photograph in colour and I could make out
the body of a small child curled in a foetal position inside a
blue fabric suitcase. Flesh had been eaten away in parts and fat
maggots were curled comfortably in both eyesockets, in the
open mouth and the gaping nasal cavity. The child's abdomen
was bloated. There was no evidence of any kind of clothing.
The child had hair, but it was short, and looked like it had
been cut, carelessly. The thighs and calves were discoloured,
a dark purple, blue, and the feet were tied by some kind of
string. Raffia, I thought. Pink perhaps? And on one disfigured
foot, there was a yellow jelly sandal. I screamed.

Omar hugged me with all his might and I felt his body
heave, I felt a deep gurgle come from deep within him and I
heard him say, *I need the bathroom.*

A strange calm came over me. I looked at Inspector Awang,
OCPD Baljit and all the other police officers in the room and
I said in a voice that I did not recognise as my own.

*Alba had shoes like that, yellow ones... She loved those shoes.
They were her favourite.*

I stood up, turned around to look for Omar and when I
saw him coming towards me, we found each other and I smelt
the vomit on him, I reached for his face and mouth and eyes
and there, we found each other.

We gave them the DNA samples that they needed and
like two broken stone statues, we walked out into the harsh
afternoon light.

* * *

THAT YELLOW JELLY sandal. That dirty, maggot-infested yellow plastic sandal. There, in that suitcase, with a dead body of a child.

It stuck to him. He tried to make sense of it, he tried to reason with the fact that there were other children who wore that very *same* sandal, that surely there were other children in KL whose parents had bought the *same* shoes. That surely there had to be another child who wore the *same coloured* shoes who was also perhaps kidnapped, surely...no matter how hard he tried, Omar could not find reason for the fact that the yellow jelly sandal had appeared six months later after Alba's disappearance.

OCPD Baljit had said, "The DNA testing will take anything from 24 hours to one week. Our forensics team at the Police College in Cheras will do their best to expedite this."

He'd continued: "DNA testing for parents and children is rather complicated, and we need to match all twenty-two markers to be sure." OCPD Baljit was apologetic but firm. "And let's just hope that the body has not decomposed beyond recognition. Fingers crossed." He smiled.

Another week of waiting, another hellish week. Omar needed to find a way of thinking, a way of getting through each day, of finding meaning in his life, his work. Del was falling apart again, she had completely distanced herself from him, she had stopped eating, stopped yoga, stopped everything that she had been doing to make herself well again. The only thing she did was stand in front of the fridge, take out yet another bottle of vodka, twist open the cap and take a large swig, and then stumbling to her spot at the couch for another day of mourning.

He did not know what to say to her. There was nothing left to say except, "We have to wait, we don't know if it's Alba, until we know for sure." But it fell on deaf ears. PT Raja had been dismissed, there was no new evidence and he had not managed to find anything at all. It was as if Alba had disappeared off the face of the earth and had now, possibly, been found. That she could have been in KL all that time drove Omar into a crazed frenzy. That they did nothing. Nothing! So Del was right, that Alba could have been kidnapped and held in KL. That she could have been saved, somehow. Omar had never felt so helpless in his life. He wanted to blame the cops, he wanted to blame PT Raja, he wanted to blame Del, but he couldn't. He blamed himself.

One day, he stopped by to get groceries from a mini-mart in Bangsar and as he walked to his car, his arms full of bags, he heard the sound of the evening azan, the Maghrib prayer coming out loud and clear over the speakers from the nearby mosque. He bowed his head and a calm came over him. He opened the car boot, placed all the bags neatly, locked the car and walked across the road to the mosque.

He washed his hands, face and feet, finished the wudhu' and entered the cool, silent mosque. He joined a line of men performing the prayers and remembered what his Tok had taught him all those years ago. There were three rakats for the Maghrib prayer and he remembered the familiar prostrations his grandmother performed with him over and over again. When he said the last Allahu Akhbar, he felt a peace come over him, a calm serenity, and he imagined

Alba's newborn face, and the awe he felt when she was born. And it was this thought that filled him when he walked back across the road.

It is God's will. It is God's will.

Alba has returned to God.

Omar did not think himself religious, nor spiritual. He had often wondered what his faith meant to him. That he was half Malay and half English meant that he had grown up in the most liberal household with parents who ate and drank everything, celebrated Christmas, Hari Raya and even the occasional Wiccan celebration. Once his mother took him and Lulu to a Beltane celebration, which happened on May Day, deep in the Norfolk countryside. He remembered women and men in long flowing cloaks, children wearing flower necklaces who ran freely on the large open field, a bonfire and a maypole which they all took turns dancing around. There was much feasting and chanting and some kind of ritual in a circle, which involved wands—*Real ones, Omar!* said his mother—and the invocation of the four archangels by a tall man with long black hair. His father had probably last set foot in a mosque when his Tok died, and was not a man who lived by any kind of religious code or creed.

But he felt closer to God than he ever had. It gave him a kind of strength he so desperately needed. No, he was not going to start praying five times a day, but he would at least once a day, put his head on the ground and prostate himself in the direction of the Kaabah. The Al Fatihah held more and more meaning for him, and became a prayer that he would utter several times a day, when he was in the car driving or waiting for a coffee at a café. This kind of horror was incomprehensible, he felt that the only way to understand what had possibly happened to Alba was because God had shown mercy, that Alba had been spared of a life of suffering. That God had taken her because she was good and pure.

Eight days after their DNA samples had been taken, Omar received a call from Inspector Awang. He had just come out of a meeting with Fairman and their accountants when his phone rang. He felt his stomach lurch, walked quickly into his office and shut the door.

Inspector Awang was quick and to the point, as if he'd read from a script, Omar later thought.

"The body has decomposed too badly, it has been in water and humidity and we cannot get a match. There are no dental records and there is no other way of identifying the body. Our forensics team did the test three times, but the DNA is unreliable and has been severely compromised. We are truly sorry but we cannot confirm that the body is that of your child, Alba. And finally, Encik Omar, as this case has been ongoing for several months now, and this was our last resort of finding any leads towards your daughter's disappearance, we have no choice but to close this case. This is a *dead case,* Encik Omar. We are very sorry, but we have done everything that is humanly possible by our police officers to find your daughter. We hope you will accept our sympathies and we are confident that you will try to find some way of moving on with your lives. Please convey our sincerest sympathies to your wife. We are very sorry but we have no choice but to classify this as a dead case.

This case is now closed. Thank you for your patience and have a good day."

Omar remained wordless until the end, when he managed a "Thank you for everything," which croaked out of his mouth. He hung up and stared at the skyline ahead of him. A sunset was starting to break and the clouds looked like a steam engine of sorts. The blue behind the clouds was startling, like cornflowers, or like the blue in one of Van Gogh's paintings. He tried to remember which one, but the painting eluded him.

He stood there for a very long time, until the cloud formation had transformed to resemble the head of a giant, and then he saw a turtle and then the sky was brilliant red, yellow and pink, and the glow of the sunset was reflected in Omar's face which gleamed with golden tears.

It DIDN'T MATTER anymore if it was Alba. It may not have been her at all. It didn't matter. I didn't want to know. I didn't want Omar to tell me. It was someone's child, it was once alive, and now it was dead.

I was already dead. And Alba was in a place that I could no longer imagine. She too, was dead. Her soul now hung in the balance, in between the guardians of light and darkness. I had given her life, and she had given me death. I was too weak to fight, there was nothing left. Nothing left to imagine, only torture. I went back to the only thing I knew, I went back to losing myself, to finding the shreds of life that I once had.

Life, before Alba.

I could not live for Omar, he deserved far more. He deserved a woman who was unbroken from life. I was no good. My body racked from drugs, from drink, numbed eternally. I was too far gone, too far away from anyone. From myself. I chose to live in the shadows, I chose to live in the dark. There was no more light, there was no more good sense, there was no more hope.

There was only darkness in the places I once loved.

Papa was in his study as usual that day. He had taken to listening to the radio, BBC World Service, and it droned on day and night. He looked up and said to me.

Did you hear? Anwar has been released. They overturned his conviction and he has been flown to Germany for medical treatment. Those German doctors, he chuckled, *if anyone can fix his back, it will be them.*

Imagine that, he is free. Anwar is free.

Papa's book was taking shape and he had managed to find an obscure university publisher who was interested in diasporic writings and the history of an uncertain Malaya. Then, I was certain that Papa was meant to be a writer, his silence, solitude and sullenness with the world were all befitting of a morose penman, someone who had more comfort in words than in humanity. I had learnt to forgive him, for being a father who was never present, a man who was ultimately the most selfish human being I had ever met, a man who only lived for the woman he loved, who shunned the only child he had. From the moment of my birth, I was all alone in the world. The only people who mattered flitted in and out of my days when I was still alive, people who left slight impressions on my memory, people who ceased to matter after a while, people whose lives were inextricably linked to ego, money, sex, loneliness. Addiction leads to lack of empathy. My parents were addicted to each other, it was as simple as that. They should not have brought me into their world.

The only time I ever felt peace was when the rains came, in the darkest of nights, the thunderous applause of raindrops on glass windowpanes and the roof would soothe me to sleep, and when the soft murmurings of raindrops arrived, I would find peace in the sanctuary of my blanket, oblivious to the world.

It rained that day when I arrived at my father's house. The tree that was named after me swayed and was buffeted by the wind, flowers scattered across the lawn like red bullets, landing like sodden scars in the swimming pool. That tree, that tree that sheltered me during hot, humid days, now reminded me that I too was of the earth, that I too was born, and I too was still alive. That tree had my heart. It was the only thing that knew my presence, and I it. And that it would one day die too, pained, in a pool of crimson.

I crawled into my bed and there I slept, soothed by the syncopated raindrops outside my window. The next morning I saw my father, huddled over his typewriter, the radio muted, the birds already chirping. When I said, *Goodbye Papa, see you soon,* he looked up and his eyes were bright with the morning.

A room. A large bed. A window. A syringe. Someone passed out on the floor. A life. Alive. *Is she still alive?*

A for Alba. B for Boss. C for Candy. D for Delonix. E for Esctasy. F for failure. G for… G for…

Was it "green"? Or was it "germ"? Or "Germany"? Did it matter?

Wake up, wake up!

Wakey wakey, morning glory.

A set of margins. Butterflies. Casualties. Machines. Ephemera. Dismemberment. Wreckage. Thanatos. Thanatonic. Was that even a word? Disjunctions. Disjuncture. Collision. Rendering. Taiping. Aunty Ping. Ping-a-ling. Ting. Tong.

How many days? There, on the wall. There is a tick every day. Thirty. Exactly. What month is it? Itch. Itch. Lickety split. Tick tock, tick tock. The mouse ran up the clock. There is no clock. Mouse. Mouse. Mice. A mouse. Mice. Rice. Nice.

What have they done to you?

No, no. No. No more, please.

She is dead.

No, she is not dead. She is alive. I can see her from here. Look, she is smiling and waving at me. Oh, my darling girl. Mama is coming for you soon. Look, here I am. Can you see me? Can you? Look how you've grown. My little princess. I have missed you so much. I will never leave you again, I promise. Never, ever. Ever. Till the end of the world. Till the end. Of. The. World. Pinky promise.

See. I told you I would find her.

Hey, stop pulling my hand. You need to help her. No, no. No more thanks, please, thank you very much. Oh God, can you be a bit more gentle? You really should learn to be a gentleman. Good lord. Goodness gracious me. My goodness. Jiminy Christmas. Hark the herald angels sing, glory to the newborn king…

Ouch, that hurt. Please, stop. You're hurting me. I don't want any more. I need to stand up.

Oh God, look at me. I peed my pants. Good lord, oh goodness. How terribly rude of me.

Could I have some tissue please? A car would be nice too. Champagne. Caviar. Child.

There. C for child. I got it! Candy got it! I'm clever! That's "c" too.

You monster. Monster.

Monster.

There are snakes crawling all over me. All over. Big ones, small ones. Thin ones, thick ones. There you are!

All long and slithery. The room smelled of rust and rot. It was dark but I still saw them, their eyes glowing in the dark.

All those eyes looking at me, waiting to strike. But they don't. I reached out my hand to them. *Please say something, don't leave me here. I know you. I know you.*

Then one came towards me. It slithered all the way up my thigh and it coiled itself around my waist, and up onto my shoulder, then my neck. I heard it whisper, *not yet, not yet.*

On the floor, wet, covered in water, rising higher. The walls closing in. *Get me out of here!*

I have turned into a snake, I am limbless. I can slide in and out wherever I want. Wait, I see a hole, light comes from outside, let me slide into it. I am out.

People. Cars. On the road. Traffic. Feet. Filth.

A man comes towards me with an axe. He brings it down on my head. He cuts it off. I see my body and tail, wriggling away, like a worried ferret, disappearing into the foray of feet. I look up, and all I can see is the sky.

OMAR FOUND HER after five days in a place they called Heroin Alley.

The shophouse, once a popular dance club, was now abandoned. All furniture and ornamentation had been stripped away, and the pockmarked concrete floor was a festering petri dish of human and animal matter. With each step, flies swarmed up and he brought out a handkerchief to cover his nose. The walls were painted dark but he saw glints of a gold motif of some sort. It looked like expensive wallpaper.

There were shadows moving in between the pillars like tall, thin aliens. Bits of glass crunched underneath his shoes and there were a few remaining fluorescent tubes glowing in the dark, casting a blue hue on the walls. The room was airless, dank, humid. He could barely breathe.

He saw a staircase and switched his torch on. The thin line of light from the torch shone against steps leading upwards. The ornate, gold railing was still intact, but it had a slimy sheen on it. He dared not imagine what the slime might be.

"Oi," someone shouted, "Tutup lampu! Off the light!"

He switched the torch off. He was a stranger here and he had to respect its dwellers. Something scuttled past his feet and touched his ankle. He let out a gasp, and almost dropped his torch. He saw the outline of an animal the size of a cat. But what cat would live in this kind of filth? The beast streaked up the stairs forelegs first. It must be a rat, he thought and a shiver coiled up his neck. He had to find her. He inched slowly up the stairs, his back to the wall, away from the slime-covered railing.

Upstairs, human figures lined the walls, lying down, their limbs splayed out in complete surrender. He walked past them, scrutinising them one by one, trying to make out her form. The last figure in the corner was a man sitting cross-legged by a window, sucking hard on a cigarette.

The glow from the cigarette illuminated his face. The man glared at him, sniggered and started clicking his mouth, as if trying to suck morsels of food stuck in his teeth. Next to him was a stack of cardboard sheets. On top of it, a towel, grotesque with vomit. Omar's stomach heaved. He noticed another staircase, probably leading to the roof. She had to be up there, she had to be.

A sudden breeze struck his cheek. As he reached the top—air! He filled his lungs. And there she was. Standing by a low wall, looking at the sky. His heart gave a lurch.

"Del," he called softly. "It's me."

"I know."

He moved towards her, close enough to reach out to touch her. His heart was breaking. She turned and her hair flicked across his face.

"I've been waiting for you."

"Took a while to find you. Let's go home."

She stepped back.

"I can't."

She looked at him, her eyes were clear, pleading.

"I just want to be with her. Help me."

A sudden breeze rose up, swirling the dried leaves around them.

Her eyes were suddenly clear, lucid, as if he could see right through them. The wind picked up speed, trees started swaying and leaves blew around the roof in small circles. She whispered above the wind, barely, but he heard her.

"We will meet again, when there is only light, no more darkness." She faced the wind, and stood closer to the edge. "I gave you the ground I stood on, I'm sorry. So sorry…"

She reached out her arms and he went to her, he kissed her cheek, her eyes, caressed her neck and breathed in her scent. The wind was dying, her pulse fading. He kissed her lips, they were cold.

"I love you Del. I *love* you."

"You've been so good to me. I did try, I *really* did."

"Let's try harder, shall we? I promise… just come home."

"I can't. No good anymore." Her eyes were nothing but pain.

"We need to fight this. We promised each other, remember? I can't do this alone." Omar pleaded. "I need you…." He took a deep breath. "I am *all* you have left, Del… it's just us now."

"You think she's dead?"

"I don't know, but *you* are alive. That's all that matters."

Del stiffened, she tried to push him away, but he held fast and strong. He held her like that for a while until they both felt the droplets on their skin.

She looked up and said, "It's starting to rain."

EPILOGUE

I CAN SEE the sky. Vermillion. Then a slow blue. A sparrow chirps. I turn my head to look for it. There. A little head bobbing up and down. Streaks of white against brown feathers. A darting mouth.

I stand up slowly. The rows of white buds are just starting to flower and I'm pleased.

The gardener has just left, and together we watered all the plants in the garden. He wanted to rake the leaves and red flower petals that were strewn all over after the heavy storm the night before, but I insisted that I would do it myself.

"Madam, you must be careful, in your condition," he said.

"It's okay. I'm fine. The doctor says exercise is good," I chuckled, reassuring him.

As I walk into the kitchen, I feel the baby kicking again. Papa is making dinner, since I'm craving something meaty and spicy. A pot of mutton curry is simmering on the stove and Omar will be home soon. It smells delicious. There is music coming from Papa's study, and the evening light casts shadows on the wall. I take a sip from the cup of tea left on the kitchen counter. My handphone rings; it's Marina.

"Hi darls, how are you?" She sounds cheery.

"I'm good. Just waiting for Omar so we can have dinner," I reply.

"Who cooked?"

"Papa."

"Lucky you!" she laughs.

"Yeah, can't wait. Smells amazing."

"Ready for court tomorrow?"

"Uh huh," I say. "Are you ready?"

"Of course! So excited!"

"We need to set a precedent. If you can change it, it will be such a…a triumph for us all."

"Yeah. Marina binti Rashid. Perempuan. Female. That's it," Marina says firmly.

"And Sumi is really pumped about this. She's worked so hard."

"I can finally be the daughter my mother always wanted," Marina says, getting choked up.

"Will you go home to see her?"

"With my new IC!"

I take another sip of tea and hear the sound of tires squeaking in the driveway. "Hey, Omar is home, he's been at the orphanage today… Have to go now."

"Okay, darls. Have a good dinner!"

"See you tomorrow." I hang up.

I hear the front door open, the sound of keys clattering onto the wooden dresser in the hallway, shoes kicked off and quick steps into the kitchen. Omar reaches out for me and I'm enveloped in his arms; then a kiss on the lips, a beaming smile.

"How are you, my darlings?" He leans down and kisses my belly.

"We're fine. Really fine," I say. He smells of sweat and wood shavings and I see flecks of sawdust in his hair.

"I showed the kids how to use chisels today; it got a little messy," he laughs.

"What did you make?"

"It's a work in progress, you'll see." He grins boyishly.

I take his hand and lead him out to the garden. The evening light is dipping and there is a hint of sunset in the sky.

"Look," I say, pointing to the row of thriving strelitzia. "Alba's flowers, they're blooming."

ACKNOWLEDGEMENTS

To Epigram Books—Edmund Wee, Jason Erik Lundberg, JY Yang, Allan Siew, Winston Tay, Kate Manning—for bringing this book to life; to my readers: Chuah Guat Eng, James Scudamore, Martin Axe, Umapagan Ampikaipakan, Tash Aw; the Anne Frank Huis in Merwedeplein and City of Refugees programme in Amsterdam, the writing residency at "het" Spui, Amsterdam and the Nederlands Letterenfonds; Mireille Berman, Judith Uyterlinde, Ton Van de Langkruis, Willemijn Lamp, Chris Keulemans, Helene Bergmans, Francis Broekhausen, Gerda Roest, Tineke van Manen, David van Reybrouck, Merel van Tilburg, Tatiana Bosteels, Ashraf Ibrahim, Syahrita Chairaty, Ton van Bragt, Ming; the International Writing Program (IWP) 2014, Christopher Merril and all staff of the IWP in Iowa City, my fellow writers Ali Cobby Eckermann, Yeow Kai Chai, Natasha Tiniacos, Cynthia Edul, Tang Sui Wa, Franca Treur, Daren Kamali, Lawrence Ypil, Andrea Wilson and our conversations at the Fox; Peter Bradley and Cathryn Klusmeier at the Sitka Island Institute, Alaska; the Stewards for their beautiful home in Sitka; WrICE 2014 in George Town; Francesca Rendel-Short, David Carlin, Maxine Beneba-Clarke, Melissa Lucashenko, Eddin Khoo, Laurel Fantauzzo, Alvin Pang, Robin Hemley

Amarlie Foster, Jennifer Down, and Harriet McKnight; Tim Tomlinson for publishing the fragment "The New Gods" in ducts.org; Scribe (Melbourne) for publishing the fragment "In the Eyes of the World"; Xu Xi and the City University Hong Kong Creative Writing MFA, Heidi Stalla at Yale-NUS Singapore, Valentine Willie and Karim Raslan, Jaime Thistleton and family, Tomasz Sajewicz, Sumitra Visvanathan and Sharaad Kuttan for access to the *Saksi* Archives, Sabri Zain and his Reformasi Diary; Omar Musa, Nisha Ayub, Sulastri Ariffin, Rozlan Mohd Noor, Tini Zainuddin, Alex Yoong, Gioia Guerzoni, Punita Visvanathan, Shirley Lim, Linda and Farouk Aljoffery, Yin Shao Loong, Hayati Mokhtar, Evelyn Hii, Alison Morgan, Lynda and Omar Merican. Thank you all.

PHOTO BY: DANIEL ADAMS

Bernice Chauly is the award-winning author of five books of poetry and prose; *going there and coming back* (1997), *The Book of Sins* (2008), *Lost in KL* (2008), *Growing Up With Ghosts* (2011) and *Onkalo* (2013, "Direct, honest and powerful" —JM Coetzee). Born in George Town, Penang to Chinese-Punjabi teachers, she read Education and English Literature in Canada as a government scholar. She was an Honorary Fellow at the University of Iowa's International Writing Program (IWP) in 2014, has served as Festival Director of the George Town Literary Festival since 2011, and currently lectures at the University of Nottingham Malaysia Campus (UNMC). She lives in Kuala Lumpur with her two daughters.

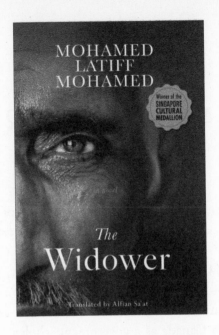

The Widower

MOHAMED LATIFF MOHAMED

Former political detainee and professor Pak Karman loses his wife in a car accident. The intensity of his mourning causes him to become untethered from his sanity. As reality, memory and fantasy become more and more blurred, he must come to terms with his past actions before his grief overwhelms him completely. Mohamed's novel, hailed as a landmark in modernist Malay fiction, is an unsettling tale of psychic disintegration and obsessive love.

The Tower

ISA KAMARI

A masterful tale of success and failure. A successful architect visits the new skyscraper he designed. As he climbs the tower with Ilham, his clerk of works, he reflects upon his life and spiritual journey in an increasingly materialistic world. As he struggles to reach the top, he is plagued by memories of a dark past. These memories are woven through the narrative as a series of fables and elliptical digressions, mirroring his own increasingly fractured state of mind.

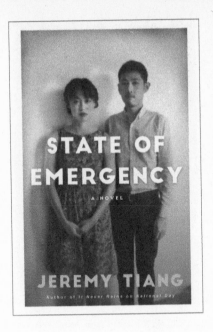

State of Emergency
JEREMY THIAM

A woman finds herself questioned for a conspiracy she did not take part in. A son flees to London to escape from a father, wracked by betrayal. A journalist seeks to uncover the truth of the place she once called home. A young wife leaves her husband and children behind to fight for freedom in the jungles of Malaya. *State of Emergency* traces the leftist movements of Singapore and Malaysia from the 1940s to the present day, centring on a family trying to navigate the choppy political currents of the region.

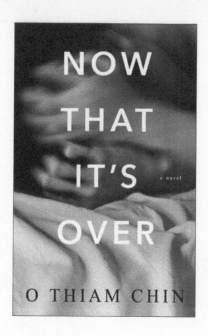

Now That It's Over
O THIAM CHIN

During the Christmas holidays in 2004, an earthquake in the Indian Ocean triggers a tsunami that devastates fourteen countries. Two couples from Singapore are vacationing in Phuket when the tsunami strikes. Alternating between the aftermath of the catastrophe and past events that led these characters to that fateful moment, *Now That It's Over* weaves a tapestry of causality and regret, and chronicles the physical and emotional wreckage wrought by natural and man-made disasters.

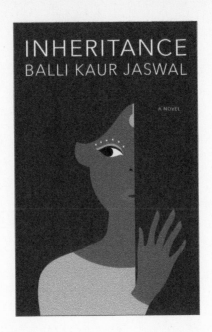

Inheritance

BALLI KAUR JASWAL

In 1971, a teenage girl briefly disappears from her house in the middle of the night, only to return a different person, causing fissures that threaten to fracture her Punjabi Sikh family. As Singapore's political and social landscapes evolve, the family must cope with shifting attitudes towards castes, youth culture, sex and gender roles, identity and belonging. Inheritance examines each family member's struggles to either preserve or buck tradition in the face of a changing nation.